lullaby

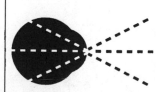

This Large Print Book carries the
Seal of Approval of N.A.V.H.

lullaby

Chuck Palahniuk

Thorndike Press • Waterville, Maine

Published in 2003 by arrangement with Doubleday, a division of the Doubleday Broadway Publishing Group, a division of Random House, Inc.

Thorndike Press Large Print Basic Series.

The tree indicium is a trademark of Thorndike Press.

The text of this Large Print edition is unabridged.
Other aspects of the book may vary from the original edition.

Set in 16 pt. Plantin.

Printed in the United States on permanent paper.

Library of Congress Cataloging-in-Publication Data

Palahniuk, Chuck.
    Lullaby : a novel / Chuck Palahniuk.
        p. cm.
    ISBN 0-7862-5098-4 (lg. print : hc : alk. paper)
    1. Sudden infant death syndrome — Fiction.
    2. Incantations — Fiction. 3. Journalists — Fiction.
    4. Large type books. I. Title.
    PS3566.A4554L86 2003
    813'.54—dc21   2002043014

I dedicate this book,
with special thanks, to . . .

Jason Cheung
Kyle McCormick
Dennis Widmyer
Amy Dalton
Kevin Kölsch

. . . who read my stuff when
nobody read my stuff.

Prologue

At first, the new owner pretends he never looked at the living room floor. Never really looked. Not the first time they toured the house. Not when the inspector showed them through it. They'd measured rooms and told the movers where to set the couch and piano, hauled in everything they owned, and never really stopped to look at the living room floor. They pretend.

Then on the first morning they come downstairs, there it is, scratched in the white-oak floor:

GET OUT

Some new owners pretend a friend has done it as a joke. Others are sure it's because they didn't tip the movers.

A couple of nights later, a baby starts to cry from inside the north wall of the master bedroom.

This is when they usually call.

And this new owner on the phone is not what our hero, Helen Hoover Boyle,

7

needs this morning.

This stammering and whining.

What she needs is a new cup of coffee and a seven-letter word for "poultry." She needs to hear what's happening on the police scanner. Helen Boyle snaps her fingers until her secretary looks in from the outer office. Our hero wraps both hands around the mouthpiece and points the telephone receiver at the scanner, saying, "It's a code nine-eleven."

And her secretary, Mona, shrugs and says, "So?"

So she needs to look it up in the codebook.

And Mona says, "Relax. It's a shoplifter."

Murders, suicides, serial killers, accidental overdoses, you can't wait until this stuff is on the front page of the newspaper. You can't let another agent beat you to the next rainmaker.

Helen needs the new owner at 325 Crestwood Terrace to shut up a minute.

Of course, the message appeared in the living room floor. What's odd is the baby doesn't usually start until the third night. First the phantom message, then the baby cries all night. If the owners last long enough, they'll be calling in another week about the face that appears, reflected in the water when you fill the bathtub. A wadded-up face of wrinkles, the eyes hollowed-out dark holes.

The third week brings the phantom shadows that circle around and around the dining room walls when everybody is seated at the table. There might be more events after that, but nobody's lasted a fourth week.

To the new owner, Helen Hoover Boyle says, "Unless you're ready to go to court and prove the house is unlivable, unless you can prove beyond a shadow of a doubt that the previous owners knew this was happening . . ." She says, "I have to tell you." She says, "You lose a case like this, after you generate all this bad publicity, and that house will be worthless."

It's not a bad house, 325 Crestwood Terrace, English Tudor, newer composition roof, four bedrooms, three and a half baths. An in-ground pool. Our hero doesn't even have to look at the fact sheet. She's sold this house six times in the past two years.

Another house, the New England saltbox on Eton Court, six bedrooms, four baths, pine-paneled entryway, and blood running down the kitchen walls, she's sold that house eight times in the past four years.

To the new owner, she says, "Got to put you on hold for a minute," and she hits the red button.

Helen, she's wearing a white suit and shoes, but not snow white. It's more the white of downhill skiing in Banff with a private car and driver on call, fourteen pieces of matched luggage, and a suite at the Hotel Lake Louise.

To the doorway, our hero says, "Mona? Moonbeam?" Louder, she says, "Spirit-Girl?"

She drums her pen against the folded newspaper page on her desk and says, "What's a three-letter word for 'rodent'?"

The police scanner gargles words, mumbles and barks, repeating "Copy?" after every line. Repeating "Copy?"

Helen Boyle shouts, "This coffee is not going to cut it."

In another hour, she needs to be showing a Queen Anne, five bedrooms, with a mother-in-law apartment, two gas fireplaces, and the face of a barbiturate suicide that appears late at night in the powder room mirror. After that, there's a split-level ranch with FAG heat, a sunken conversation pit, and the reoccurring phantom gunshots of a double homicide

10

that happened over a decade ago. This is all in her thick daily planner, thick and bound in what looks like red leather. This is her record of everything.

She takes another sip of coffee and says, "What do you call this? Swiss Army mocha? Coffee is supposed to taste like coffee."

Mona comes to the doorway with her arms folded across her front and says, "What?"

And Helen says, "I need you to swing by" — she shuffles some fact sheets on her blotter — "swing by 4673 Willmont Place. It's a Dutch Colonial with a sunroom, four bedrooms, two baths, and an aggravated homicide."

The police scanner says, "Copy?"

"Just do the usual," Helen says, and she writes the address on a note card and holds it out. "Don't resolve anything. Don't burn any sage. Don't exorcise shit."

Mona takes the note card and says, "Just check it for vibes?"

Helen slashes the air with her hand and says, "I don't want anybody going down any tunnels toward any bright light. I want these freaks staying right here, on this astral plane, thank you." She looks at her newspaper and says, "They have all eter-

11

nity to be dead. They can hang around in that house another fifty years and rattle some chains."

Helen Hoover Boyle looks at the blinking hold light and says, "What did you pick up at the six-bedroom Spanish yesterday?"

And Mona rolls her eyes at the ceiling. She pushes out her jaw and blows a big sigh, straight up to flop the hair on her forehead, and says, "There's a definite energy there. A subtle presence. But the floor plan is wonderful." A black silk cord loops around her neck and disappears into the corner of her mouth.

And our hero says, "Screw the floor plan."

Forget those dream houses you only sell once every fifty years. Forget those happy homes. And screw subtle: cold spots, strange vapors, irritable pets. What she needed was blood running down the walls. She needed ice-cold invisible hands that pull children out of bed at night. She needed blazing red eyes in the dark at the foot of the basement stairs. That and decent curb appeal.

The bungalow at 521 Elm Street, it has four bedrooms, original hardware, and screams in the attic.

12

The French Normandy at 7645 Weston Heights has arched windows, a butler's pantry, leaded-glass pocket doors, and a body that appears in the upstairs hallway with multiple stab wounds.

The ranch-style at 248 Levee Place — five bedrooms, four and a half baths with a brick patio — it has the reappearing blood coughed up on the master bathroom walls after a drain cleaner poisoning.

Distressed houses, Realtors call them. These houses that never sold because no one liked to show them. No Realtor wanted to host an open house there, risk spending any time there alone. Or these were the houses that sold and sold again every six months because no one could live there. A good string of these houses, twenty or thirty exclusives, and Helen could turn off the police scanner. She could quit searching the obituaries and the crime pages for suicides and homicides. She could stop sending Mona out to check on every possible lead. She could just kick back and find a five-letter word for "equine."

"Plus I need you to pick up my cleaning," she says. "And get some decent coffee." She points her pen at Mona and says, "And out of respect for professionalism, leave the little Rasta doohickeys at home."

Mona pulls the black silk cord until a quartz crystal pops out of her mouth, shining and wet. She blows on it, saying, "It's a crystal. My boyfriend, Oyster, gave it to me."

And Helen says, "You're dating a boy named Oyster?"

And Mona drops the crystal so it hangs against her chest and says, "He says it's for my own protection." The crystal soaks a darker wet spot on her orange blouse.

"Oh, and before you go," Helen says, "get me Bill or Emily Burrows on the phone."

Helen presses the hold button and says, "Sorry about that." She says there are a couple of clear options here. The new owner can move, just sign a quitclaim deed and the house becomes the bank's problem.

"Or," our hero says, "you give me a confidential exclusive to sell the house. What we call a vest-pocket listing."

And maybe the new owner says no this time. But after that hideous face appears between his legs in the bathwater, after the shadows start marching around the walls, well, everyone says yes eventually.

On the phone, the new owner says, "And you won't tell any buyers about the problem?"

And Helen says, "Don't even finish unpacking. We'll just tell people you're in the process of moving out."

If anybody asks, tell them you're being transferred out of town. Tell them you loved this house.

She says, "Everything else will just be our little secret."

From the outer office, Mona says, "I have Bill Burrows on line two."

And the police scanner says, "Copy?"

Our hero hits the next button and says, "Bill!"

She mouths the word *Coffee* at Mona. She jerks her head toward the window and mouths, *Go.*

The scanner says, "Do you copy?"

This *was* Helen Hoover Boyle. Our hero. Now dead but not dead. Here was just another day in her life. This was the life she lived before I came along. Maybe this is a love story, maybe not. It depends on how much I can believe myself.

This is about Helen Hoover Boyle. Her haunting me. The way a song stays in your head. The way you think life should be. How anything holds your attention. How your past goes with you into every day of your future.

That is. This is. It's all of it, Helen Hoover Boyle.

We're all of us haunted and haunting.

On this, the last ordinary day of her regular life, our hero says into the phone, "Bill Burrows?"

She says, "You need to get Emily on the extension because I've just found you two the perfect new home."

She writes the word "horse" and says, "It's my understanding that the sellers are very motivated."

Chapter 1

The problem with every story is you tell it after the fact. Even play-by-play description on the radio, the home runs and strikeouts, even that's delayed a few minutes. Even live television is postponed a couple seconds.

Even sound and light can only go so fast.

Another problem is the teller. The who, what, where, when, and why of the reporter. The media bias. How the messenger shapes the facts. What journalists call The Gatekeeper. *How the presentation is everything.*

The story behind the story.

Where I'm telling this from is one café after another. Where I'm writing this book, chapter by chapter, is never the same small town or city or truck stop in the middle of nowhere.

What these places all have in common are miracles. You read about this stuff in the pulp tabloids, the kind of healings and sightings, the miracles, that never get reported in the mainstream press.

This week, it's the Holy Virgin of Welburn, New Mexico. She came flying down Main Street last week. Her long red and black

17

dreadlocks whipping behind her, her bare feet dirty, she wore an Indian cotton skirt printed in two shades of brown and a denim halter top. It's all in this week's World Miracles Report, *next to the cashier in every supermarket in America.*

And here I am, a week late. Always one step behind. After the fact.

The Flying Virgin had fingernails painted bright pink with white tips. A French manicure, some witnesses call it. The Flying Virgin used a can of Bug-Off brand insect fogger, and across the blue New Mexican sky, she wrote:

STOP HAVING BABYS

(Sic)

The can of Bug-Off, she dropped. It's right now headed for the Vatican. For analysis. Right now, you can buy postcards of the event. Videos even.

Almost everything you can buy is after the fact. Caught. Dead. Cooked.

In the souvenir videos, the Flying Virgin shakes the can of fogger. Floating above one end of Main Street, she waves at the crowd. And there's a bush of brown hair under her arm. The moment before she starts writing, a gust of wind lifts her skirt and the Flying Virgin's not wearing any panties. Between her

18

legs, she's shaved.

This is where I'm writing this story from today. Here in a roadside diner, talking to witnesses in Welburn, New Mexico. Here with me is Sarge, a baked potato of an old Irish cop. On the table between us is the local newspaper, folded to show a three-column ad that says:

Attention Patrons of All Plush Interiors Furniture Stores

The ad says, "If poisonous spiders have hatched from your new upholstered furniture, you may be eligible to take part in a class-action lawsuit." And the ad gives a phone number you could call, but it's no use.

The Sarge has the kind of loose neck skin that if you pinch it, when you let go the skin stays pinched. He has to go find a mirror and rub the skin to make it go flat.

Outside the diner, people are still driving into town. People kneel and pray for another visitation. The Sarge puts his big mitts together and pretends to pray, his eyes rolled sideways to look out the window, his holster unsnapped, his pistol loaded and ready for skeet shooting.

After she was done skywriting, the Flying Virgin blew kisses to people. She flashed a two-finger peace sign. She hovered just above the trees, clutching her skirt closed with one fist, and she shook her red and black dreadlocks back and waved, and Amen. She was gone, behind the mountains, over the horizon. Gone.

Still, you can't trust everything you read in the newspaper.

The Flying Madonna, it wasn't a miracle.

It was magic.

These aren't saints. They're spells.

The Sarge and me, we're not here to witness anything. We're witch-hunters.

Still, this isn't a story about here and now. Me, the Sarge, the Flying Virgin. Helen Hoover Boyle. What I'm writing is the story of how we met. How we got here.

Chapter 2

They ask you just one question. Just before you graduate from journalism school, they tell you to imagine you're a reporter. Imagine you work at a daily big-city newspaper, and one Christmas Eve, your editor sends you out to investigate a death.

The police and paramedics are there. The neighbors, wearing bathrobes and slippers, crowd the hallway of the slummy tenement. Inside the apartment, a young couple is sobbing beside their Christmas tree. Their baby has choked to death on an ornament. You get what you need, the baby's name and age and all, and you get back to the newspaper around midnight and write the story on press deadline.

You submit it to your editor and he rejects it because you don't say the color of the ornament. Was it red or green? You couldn't look, and you didn't think to ask.

With the pressroom screaming for the front page, your choices are:

Call the parents and ask the color.

Or refuse to call and lose your job.

This was the fourth estate. Journalism. And where I went to school, just this one question is the entire final exam for the Ethics course. It's an either/or question. My answer was to call the paramedics. Items like this have to be catalogued. The ornament had to be bagged and photographed in some file of evidence. No way would I call the parents after midnight on Christmas Eve.

The school gave my ethics a D.

Instead of ethics, I learned only to tell people what they want to hear. I learned to write everything down. And I learned editors can be real assholes.

Since then, I still wonder what that test was really about. I'm a reporter now, on a big-city daily, and I don't have to imagine anything.

My first real baby was on a Monday morning in September. There was no Christmas ornament. No neighbors crowded around the trailer house in the suburbs. One paramedic sat with the parents in the kitchenette and asked them the standard questions. The second paramedic took me back to the nursery and showed me what they usually find in the crib.

The standard questions paramedics ask

include: Who found the child dead? When was the child found? Was the child moved? When was the child last seen alive? Was the child breast- or bottle-fed? The questions seem random, but all doctors can do is gather statistics and hope someday a pattern will emerge.

The nursery was yellow with blue, flowered curtains at the windows and a white wicker chest of drawers next to the crib. There was a white-painted rocking chair. Above the crib was a mobile of yellow plastic butterflies. On the wicker chest was a book open to page 27. On the floor was a blue braided-rag rug. On one wall was a framed needlepoint. It said: *Thursday's Child Has Far to Go.* The room smelled like baby powder.

And maybe I didn't learn ethics, but I learned to pay attention. No detail is too minor to note.

The open book was called *Poems and Rhymes from Around the World*, and it was checked out from the county library.

My editor's plan was to do a five-part series on sudden infant death syndrome. Every year seven thousand babies die without any apparent cause. Two out of every thousand babies will just go to sleep and never wake up. My editor, Duncan, he kept calling it crib death.

The details about Duncan are he's pocked with acne scars and his scalp is brown along the hairline every two weeks when he dyes his gray roots. His computer password is "password."

All we know about sudden infant death is there is no pattern. Most babies die alone between midnight and morning, but a baby will also die while sleeping beside its parents. It can die in a car seat or in a stroller. A baby can die in its mother's arms.

There are so many people with infants, my editor said. It's the type of story that every parent and grandparent is too afraid to read and too afraid not to read. There's really no new information, but the idea was to profile five families that had lost a child. Show how people cope. How people move forward with their lives. Here and there, we could salt in the standard facts about crib death. We could show the deep inner well of strength and compassion each of these people discovers. That angle. Because it ties to no specific event, it's what you'd call soft news. We'd run it on the front of the Lifestyles section.

For art, we could show smiling pictures of healthy babies that were now dead.

We'd show how this could happen to anyone.

That was his pitch. It's the kind of investigative piece you do for awards. It was late summer and the news was slow. This was the peak time of year for last-term pregnancies and newborns.

It was my editor's idea for me to tag along with paramedics.

The Christmas story, the sobbing couple, the ornament, by now I'd been working so long I'd forgotten all that junk.

That hypothetical ethics question, they have to ask that at the end of the journalism program because by then it's too late. You have big student loans to pay off. Years and years later, I think what they're really asking is: *Is this something you want to do for a living?*

Chapter 3

The muffled thunder of dialogue comes through the walls, then a chorus of laughter. Then more thunder. Most of the laugh tracks on television were recorded in the early 1950s. These days, most of the people you hear laughing are dead.

The stomp and stomp and stomp of a drum comes down through the ceiling. The rhythm changes. Maybe the beat crowds together, faster, or it spreads out, slower, but it doesn't stop.

Up through the floor, someone's barking the words to a song. These people who need their television or stereo or radio playing all the time. These people so scared of silence. These are my neighbors. These sound-oholics. These quiet-ophobics.

Laughter of the dead comes through every wall.

These days, this is what passes for home sweet home.

This siege of noise.

After work, I made one stop. The man

standing behind the cash register looked up when I limped into the store. Still looking at me, he reached under the counter and brought out something in brown paper, saying, "Double-bagged. I think you'll like this one." He set it on the counter and patted it with one hand.

The package is half the size of a shoe box. It weighs less than a can of tuna.

He pressed one, two, three buttons on the register, and the price window said a hundred and forty-nine dollars. He told me, "Just so you won't worry, I taped the bags shut tight."

In case it rains, he put the package in a plastic bag, and said, "You let me know if there's any of it not there." He said, "You don't walk like that foot is getting better."

All the way home, the package rattled. Under my arm, the brown paper slid and wrinkled. With my every limp, what's inside clattered from one end of the box to the other.

At my apartment, the ceiling is pounding with some fast music. The walls are murmuring with panicked voices. Either an ancient cursed Egyptian mummy has come back to life and is trying to kill the people next door, or they're watching a movie.

Under the floor, there's someone shouting, a dog barking, doors slamming, the auctioneer call of some song.

In the bathroom, I turn out the lights. So I can't see what's in the bag. So I won't know how it's supposed to turn out. In the cramped tight darkness, I stuff a towel in the crack under the door. With the package on my lap, I sit on the toilet and listen.

This is what passes for civilization.

People who would never throw litter from their car will drive past you with their radio blaring. People who'd never blow cigar smoke at you in a crowded restaurant will bellow into their cell phone. They'll shout at each other across the space of a dinner plate.

These people who would never spray herbicides or insecticides will fog the neighborhood with their stereo playing Scottish bagpipe music. Chinese opera. Country and western.

Outdoors, a bird singing is fine. Patsy Cline is not.

Outdoors, the din of traffic is bad enough. Adding Chopin's Piano Concerto in E Minor is not making the situation any better.

You turn up your music to hide the noise. Other people turn up their music to hide yours. You turn up yours again. Everyone buys a bigger stereo system. This is the arms race of sound. You don't win with a lot of treble.

This isn't about quality. It's about volume.

This isn't about music. This is about winning.

You stomp the competition with the bass line. You rattle windows. You drop the melody line and shout the lyrics. You put in foul language and come down hard on each cussword.

You dominate. This is really about power.

In the dark bathroom, sitting on the toilet, I fingernail the tape open at one end of the package, and what's inside is a square cardboard box, smooth, soft, and furred at the edges, each corner blunt and crushed in. The top lifts off, and what's inside feels like layers of sharp, hard complicated shapes, tiny angles, curves, corners, and points. These I set to one side on the bathroom floor, in the dark. The cardboard box, I put back inside the paper bags. Between the hard, tangled shapes are two sheets of slippery paper. These papers, I put in the bags, too. The bags, I crush and roll and twist into a ball.

All of this I do blind, touching the smooth paper, feeling the layers of hard, branching shapes.

The floor under my shoes, even the toilet seat, shakes a little from the music next door.

Each family with a crib death, you want to tell them to take up a hobby. You'd be surprised just how fast you can close the door on your past. No matter how bad things get, you can still walk away. Learn needlepoint. Make a stained-glass lamp.

I carry the shapes to the kitchen, and in the light they're blue and gray and white. They're brittle-hard plastic. Just tiny shards. Tiny shingles and shutters and bargeboards. Tiny steps and columns and window frames. If it's a house or a hospital, you can't tell. There are little brick walls and little doors. Spread out on the kitchen table, it could be the parts of a school or a church. Without seeing the picture on the box, without the instruction sheets, the tiny gutters and dormers might be for a train station or a lunatic asylum. A factory or a prison.

No matter how you put it together, you're never sure if it's right.

The little pieces, the cupolas and chimneys, they twitch with each beat of noise

30

coming through the floor.

These music-oholics. These calm-ophobics.

No one wants to admit we're addicted to music. That's just not possible. No one's addicted to music and television and radio. We just need more of it, more channels, a larger screen, more volume. We can't bear to be without it, but no, nobody's addicted.

We could turn it off anytime we wanted.

I fit a window frame into a brick wall. With a little brush, the size for fingernail polish, I glue it. The window is the size of a fingernail. The glue smells like hair spray. The smell tastes like oranges and gasoline.

The pattern of the bricks on the wall is as fine as your fingerprint.

Another window fits in place, and I brush on more glue.

The sound shivers through the walls, through the table, through the window frame, and into my finger.

These distraction-oholics. These focus-ophobics.

Old George Orwell got it backward.

Big Brother isn't watching. He's singing and dancing. He's pulling rabbits out of a hat. Big Brother's busy holding your attention every moment you're awake. He's making sure you're always distracted. He's making sure you're fully absorbed.

He's making sure your imagination withers. Until it's as useful as your appendix. He's making sure your attention is always filled.

And this being fed, it's worse than being watched. With the world always filling you, no one has to worry about what's in your mind. With everyone's imagination atrophied, no one will ever be a threat to the world.

I finger open a button on my white shirt and stuff my tie inside. With my chin tucked down tight against the knot of my tie, I tweezer a tiny pane of glass into each window. Using a razor blade, I cut plastic curtains smaller than a postage stamp, blue curtains for the upstairs, yellow for the downstairs. Some curtains left open, some drawn shut, I glue them down.

There are worse things than finding your wife and child dead.

You can watch the world do it. You can watch your wife get old and bored. You can watch your kids discover everything in the world you've tried to save them from. Drugs, divorce, conformity, disease. All the nice clean books, music, television. Distraction.

These people with a dead child, you want to tell them, go ahead. Blame yourself.

There are worse things you can do to the people you love than kill them. The regular way is just to watch the world do it. Just read the newspaper.

The music and laughter eat away at your thoughts. The noise blots them out. All the sound distracts. Your head aches from the glue.

Anymore, no one's mind is their own. You can't concentrate. You can't think. There's always some noise worming in. Singers shouting. Dead people laughing. Actors crying. All these little doses of emotion.

Someone's always spraying the air with their mood.

Their car stereo, broadcasting their grief or joy or anger all over the neighborhood.

One Dutch Colonial mansion, I installed fifty-six windows upside down and had to throw it out. One twelve-bedroom Tudor castle, I glued the downspouts on the wrong gable ends and melted everything by trying to fix it with a chemical solvent.

This isn't anything new.

Experts in ancient Greek culture say that people back then didn't see their thoughts as belonging to them. When ancient Greeks had a thought, it occurred to them as a god or goddess giving an order. Apollo was telling them to be brave. Athena was telling them to fall in love.

Now people hear a commercial for sour cream potato chips and rush out to buy, but now they call this free will.

At least the ancient Greeks were being honest.

The truth is, even if you read to your wife and child some night. You read them a lullaby. And the next morning, you wake up but your family doesn't. You lie in bed, still curled against your wife. She's still warm but not breathing. Your daughter's not crying. The house is already hectic with traffic and talk radio and steam pounding through the pipes inside the wall. The truth is, you can forget even that day for the moment it takes to make a perfect knot in your tie.

This I know. This is my life.

You might move away, but that's not enough. You'll take up a hobby. You'll bury yourself in work. Change your name. You'll cobble things together. Make order out of chaos. You'll do this each time your foot is healed enough, and you have the money. Organize every detail.

This isn't what a therapist will tell you to do, but it works.

You glue the doors into the walls next. You glue the walls into the foundation. You tweezer together the tiny bits of each chimney and let the glue dry while you build the roof. You hang the tiny gutters. Every detail exact. You set the tiny dormers. Hang the shutters. Frame the porch. Seed the lawn. Plant the trees.

Inhale the taste of oranges and gasoline. The smell of hair spray. Lose yourself in each complication. Glue a thread of ivy up one side of the chimney. Your fingers webbed with threads of glue, your fingertips crusted and sticking together.

You tell yourself that noise is what defines silence. Without noise, silence would not be golden. Noise is the exception. Think of deep outer space, the incredible cold and quiet where your wife and kid wait. Silence, not heaven, would be reward enough.

With tweezers, you plant flowers along the foundation.

Your back and neck curve forward over the table. With your ass clenched, your spine's hunched, arching up to a headache at the base of your skull.

You glue the tiny Welcome mat outside

the front door. You hook up the tiny lights inside. You glue the mailbox beside the front door. You glue the tiny, tiny milk bottles on the front porch. The tiny folded newspaper.

With everything perfect, exact, meticulous, it must be three or four in the morning, because by now it's quiet. The floor, the ceiling, the walls, are still. The compressor on the refrigerator shuts off, and you can hear the filament buzzing in each light bulb. You can hear my watch tick. A moth knocks against the kitchen window. You can see your breath, the room is that cold.

You put the batteries in place and flip a little switch, and the tiny windows glow. You set the house on the floor and turn out the kitchen light.

Stand over the house in the dark. From this far away it looks perfect. Perfect and safe and happy. A neat red-brick home. The tiny windows of light shine out on the lawn and trees. The curtains glow, yellow in the baby's room. Blue in your own bedroom.

The trick to forgetting the big picture is to look at everything close-up.

The shortcut to closing a door is to bury yourself in the details.

This is how we must look to God.

As if everything's just fine.

Now take off your shoe, and with your bare foot, stomp. Stomp and keep stomping. No matter how much it hurts, the brittle broken plastic and wood and glass, keep stomping until the downstairs neighbor pounds the ceiling with his fist.

Chapter 4

My second crib death assignment is in a concrete-block housing project on the edge of downtown, the deceased slumped in a high chair in the middle of the afternoon while the baby-sitter cried in the bedroom. The high chair was in the kitchen. Dirty dishes were piled in the sink.

Back in the City Room, Duncan, my editor, asks, "Single or double sink?"

Another detail about Duncan is, when he talks, he spits.

Double, I tell him. Stainless steel. Separate hot and cold knobs, pistol-grip-style with porcelain handles. No spray nozzle.

And Duncan says, "The model of refrigerator?" Little spits of his saliva flash in the office lights.

Amana, I say.

"They have a calendar?" Little touches of Duncan's spit spray my hand, my arm, the side of my face. The spit's cold from the air-conditioning.

The calendar had a painting of an old stone New England mill, I tell him, the waterwheel kind. Sent out by an insurance agent. Written on it was the baby's next appointment at the pediatrician. And the mother's upcoming GED exam. These dates and times and the pediatrician's name are all in my notes.

And Duncan says, "Damn, you're good."

His spit's drying on my skin and lips.

The kitchen floor was gray linoleum. The countertops were pink with black cigarette burns creeping in from the edge. On the counter next to the sink was a library book. *Poems and Rhymes from Around the World.*

The book was shut, and when I set it on its spine, when I let it fall open by itself, hoping it would show how far the reader had cracked the binding, the pages fluttered open to page 27. And I make a pencil mark in the margin.

My editor closes one eye and tilts his head at me. "What," he says, "kind of food dried on the dishes?"

Spaghetti, I say. Canned sauce. The kind with extra mushrooms and garlic. I inventoried the garbage in the bag under the sink.

Two hundred milligrams of salt per serving. One hundred fifty calories of fat. I don't know what I ever expect to find, but like everybody at the scene, it pays to look for a pattern.

Duncan says, "You see this?" and hands me a proof sheet from today's restaurant section. Above the fold, there's an advertisement. It's three columns wide by six inches deep. The top line says:

Attention Patrons of the Treeline Dining Club

The body copy says: "Have you contracted a treatment-resistant form of chronic fatigue syndrome after eating in this establishment? Has this food-borne virus left you unable to work and live a normal life? If so, please call the following number to be part of a class-action lawsuit."

Then there's a phone number with a weird prefix, maybe a cell phone.

Duncan says, "You think there's a story here?" and the page is dotted with his spit.

Here in the City Room, my pager starts to beep. It's the paramedics.

In journalism school, what they want you to be is a camera. A trained, objective, detached professional. Accurate, polished, and observant.

They want you to believe that the news

and you are always two separate things. Killers and reporters are mutually exclusive. Whatever the story, this isn't about *you.*

My third baby is in a farmhouse two hours downstate.

My fourth baby is in a condo near a shopping mall.

One paramedic leads me to a back bedroom, saying, "Sorry we called you out on this one." His name is John Nash, and he pulls the sheet off a child in bed, a little boy too perfect, too peaceful, too white to be asleep. Nash says, "This one's almost six years old."

The details about Nash are, he's a big guy in a white uniform. He wears high-top white track shoes and gathers his hair into a little palm tree at the crown of his head.

"We could be working in Hollywood," Nash says. With this kind of clean bloodless death, there's no death agonies, no reverse peristalsis — the death throes where your digestive system works backward and you vomit fecal matter. "You start puking shit," Nash says, "and that's a realistic-type death scene."

What he tells me about crib death is that it occurs most between two and four months after birth. Over 90 percent of deaths occur before six months. Most researchers say that beyond ten months, it's almost impossible. Beyond a year old, the medical examiner calls the cause of death "undetermined." A second death of this nature in a family is considered homicide until proven otherwise.

In the condo, the bedroom walls are painted green. The bed has flannel sheets printed with Scotch terriers. All you can smell is an aquarium full of lizards.

When someone presses a pillow over the face of a child, the medical examiner calls this a "gentle homicide."

My fifth dead child is in a hotel room out by the airport.

With the farmhouse and the condo, there's the book *Poems and Rhymes* . . . Open to page 27. The same book from the county library with my pencil mark in the margin. In the hotel room, there's no book. It's a double room with the baby curled up in a queen-size bed next to the bed where the parents slept. There's a color television in an armoire, a thirty-six-inch Zenith with fifty-six cable channels and four local. The carpet's brown, the curtains, brown and blue florals. On the bathroom floor is a wet towel spotted with blood and green shaving gel. Somebody didn't flush the toilet.

The bedspreads are dark blue and smell like cigarette smoke.

There's no books anywhere.

I ask if the family has removed anything from the scene, and the officer at the scene says no. But somebody from social services came by to pick up some clothes.

"Oh," he says, "and some library books that were past due."

Chapter 5

The front door swings open, and inside is a woman holding a cell phone to her ear, smiling at me and talking to somebody else.

"Mona," she says into the phone, "you'll have to make this quick. Mr. Streator's just arrived."

She shows me the back of her free hand, the tiny sparkling watch on her wrist, and says, "He's a few minutes early." Her other hand, her long pink fingernails with the tips painted white, with her little black cell phone, these are almost lost in the shining pink cloud of her hair.

Smiling, she says, "Relax, Mona," and her eyes go up and down me. "Brown sport coat," she says, "brown slacks, white shirt." She frowns and winces, "And a blue tie."

The woman tells the phone, "Middle-aged. Five-ten, maybe one hundred seventy pounds. Caucasian. Brown, green." She winks at me and says, "His hair's a little messy and he didn't shave today, but he looks harmless enough."

She leans forward a little and mouths, *My secretary.*

Into the phone, she says, "What?"

She steps aside and waves me in the door with her free hand. She rolls her eyes until they come around to meet mine and says, "Thank you for your concern, Mona, but I don't think Mr. Streator is here to rape me."

Where we're at is the Gartoller Estate on Walker Ridge Drive, a Georgian-style eight-bedroom house with seven bathrooms, four fireplaces, a breakfast room, a formal dining room, and a fifteen-hundred-square-foot ballroom on the fourth floor. It has a separate six-car garage and a guesthouse. It has an in-ground swimming pool and a fire and intruder alarm system.

Walker Ridge Drive is the kind of neighborhood where they pick up the garbage five days a week. These are the kind of people who appreciate the threat of a good lawsuit, and when you stop by to introduce yourself, they smile and agree.

The Gartoller Estate is beautiful.

These neighbors won't ask you to come inside. They'll stand in their half-open front doors and smile. They'll tell you they really don't know anything about the history of the Gartoller house. It's a house.

If you ask any more, people will glance over your shoulder at the empty street. Then they'll smile again and say, "I can't help you. You really need to call the Realtor."

The sign at 3465 Walker Ridge Drive says Boyle Realty. Shown by appointment only.

At another house, a woman in a maid's uniform answered the door with a little five- or six-year-old girl looking out from behind the maid's black skirt. The maid shook her head, saying she didn't know anything. "You'll have to call the listing agent," she said, "Helen Boyle. It's on the sign."

And the little girl said, "She's a witch."

And the maid closed the door.

Now inside the Gartoller house, Helen Hoover Boyle walks through the echoing, white empty rooms. She's still on her phone as she walks. Her cloud of pink hair, her fitted pink suit, her legs in white stockings, her feet in pink, medium heels. Her lips are gummy with pink lipstick. Her arms sparkle and rattle with gold and pink bracelets, gold chains, charms, and coins.

Enough ornaments for a Christmas tree. Pearls big enough to choke a horse.

Into the phone, she says, "Did you call

the people in the Exeter House? They should've run screaming out of there two weeks ago."

She walks through tall double doors, into the next room, then the next.

"Uh-huh," she says. "What do you mean, they're not living there?"

Tall arched windows look out onto a stone terrace. Beyond that is a lawn striped with lawn mower tracks, beyond that a swimming pool.

Into the phone, she says, "You don't spend a million-two on a house and then not live there." Her voice is loud and sharp in these rooms without furniture or carpets.

A small pink and white purse hangs from a long gold chain looped over her shoulder.

Five foot six. A hundred and eighteen pounds. It would be hard to peg her age. She's so thin she must be either dying or rich. Her suit's some kind of nubby sofa fabric, edged with white braid. It's pink, but not shrimp pink. It's more the color of shrimp pâté served on a water cracker with a sprig of parsley and a dollop of caviar. The jacket is tailored tight at her pinched waist and padded square at her shoulders. The skirt is short and snug. The gold buttons, huge.

She's wearing doll clothes.

"No," she says, "Mr. Streator is right here." She lifts her penciled eyebrows and looks at me. "Am I wasting his time?" she says. "I hope not."

Smiling, she tells the phone, "Good. He's shaking his head no."

I have to wonder what about me made her say *middle-aged.*

To tell the truth, I say, I'm not really in the market for a house. With two pink fingernails over the cell phone, she leans toward me and mouths, *Just one more minute.*

The truth is, I say, I got her name off some records at the county coroner's office. The truth is, I've pored over the forensic records for every local crib death within the past twenty-five years.

And still listening to the phone, without looking at me, she puts the pink fingernails of her free hand against my lapel and keeps them there, pushing just a little. Into the phone, she says, "So what's the problem? Why aren't they living there?"

Judging from her hand, this close-up, she must be in her late thirties or early forties. Still this taxidermied look that passes for beauty above a certain age and income, it's too old for her. Her skin already looks exfoliated, plucked, scruffed, moisturized, and made up until she could be a piece of refinished furniture. Reupholstered in pink. A restoration. Renovated.

Into her cell phone, she shouts, "You're joking! Yes, of course I know what a teardown is!" She says, "That's a historic house!"

Her shoulders draw up, tight against each side of her neck, and then drop. Turning her face away from the phone, she sighs with her eyes closed.

She listens, standing there with her pink shoes and white legs mirrored upside down in the dark wood floor. Reflected deep in the wood, you can see the shadows inside her skirt.

With her free hand cupped over her forehead, she says, "Mona." She says, "We cannot afford to lose that listing. If they replace that house, chances are it will be off the market for good."

Then she's quiet again, listening.

And I have to wonder, since when can't you wear a blue tie with a brown coat?

I duck my head to meet her eyes, saying, Mrs. Boyle? I needed to see her someplace private, outside her office. It's about a story I'm researching.

But she waves her fingers between us. In another second, she walks over to a fireplace and leans into it, bracing her free hand against the mantel, whispering, "When the wrecking ball swings, the neighbors will probably stand and cheer."

A wide doorway opens from this room into another white room with wood floors and a complicated carved ceiling painted white. In the other direction, a doorway opens on a room lined with empty white bookshelves.

"Maybe we could *start* a protest," she says. "We could write some letters to the newspaper."

And I say, I'm from the newspaper.

Her perfume is the smell of leather car seats and old wilted roses and cedar chest lining.

And Helen Hoover Boyle says, "Mona, hold on."

And walking back to me, she says, "What were you saying, Mr. Streator?" Her eyelashes blink once, twice, fast. Waiting. Her eyes are blue.

I'm a reporter from the newspaper.

"The Exeter House is a lovely, *historic* house some people want to tear down," she says, with one hand cupped over her phone. "Seven bedrooms, six thousand square feet. All cherry paneling throughout the first floor."

The empty room is so quiet you can hear a tiny voice on the telephone saying, "Helen?"

Closing her eyes, she says, "It was built in 1935," and she tilts her head back. "It has radiant steam heat, two point eight acres, a tile roof."

And the tiny voice says, "Helen?"

"— a game room," she says, "a wet bar, a home gym room —"

The problem is, I don't have this much time. All I need to know, I say, is did you ever have a child?

"— a butler's pantry," she says, "a walk-in refrigerator —"

I say, did her son die of crib death about twenty years ago?

Her eyelashes blink once, twice and she says, "Pardon me?"

I need to know if she read out loud to her son. His name was Patrick. I want to find all existing copies of a certain book.

Holding her phone between her ear and the padded shoulder of her jacket, Helen Boyle snaps open her pink and white purse and takes out a pair of white gloves. Flexing her fingers into each glove, she says, "Mona?"

I need to know if she might still have a copy of this particular book. I'm sorry, but I can't tell her why.

She says, "I'm afraid Mr. Streator will be of no use to us."

I need to know if they did an autopsy on her son.

To me, she smiles. Then she mouths the words *Get out*.

And I raise both my hands, spread open toward her, and start backing away.

I just need to make sure every copy of this book is destroyed. And she says, "Mona, please call the police."

Chapter 6

In crib deaths, it's standard procedure to assure the parents that they've done nothing wrong. Babies do not smother in their blankets. In the *Journal of Pediatrics*, in a study published in 1945 called "Mechanical Suffocation During Infancy," researchers proved that no baby could smother in bedding. Even the smallest baby, placed facedown on a pillow or mattress, could roll enough to breathe. Even if the child had a slight cold, there's no proof that it's related to the death. There's no proof to link DPT — diphtheria, pertussis, tetanus — inoculations and sudden death. Even if the child had been to the doctor hours before, it still may die.

A cat does not sit on the child and suck out its life. All we know is, we don't know.

Nash, the paramedic, shows me the purple and red bruises on every child, livor mortis, where the oxygenated hemoglobin settles to the lowest part of the body. The bloody froth leaking from the nose and mouth is what the medical examiner calls purge fluids, a natural part of decomposition. People desperate for an answer will look at livor mortis, at purge fluids, even at diaper rash, and assume child abuse.

The trick to forgetting the big picture is to look at everything close-up.

The shortcut to closing any door is to bury yourself in the little details. The facts. The best part of becoming a reporter is you can hide behind your notebook. Everything is always research.

At the county library, in the juvenile section, the book is back on the shelf, waiting. *Poems and Rhymes from Around the World.* And on page 27 there's a poem. A traditional African poem, the book says. It's eight lines long, and I don't need to copy it. I have it in my notes from the very first baby, the trailer house in the suburbs. I tear out the page and put the book back on the shelf.

In the City Room, Duncan says, "How's it going on the dead baby beat?" He says, "I need you to call this number and see what's what," and he hands me a proof sheet from the Lifestyles section, an ad circled in red pen.

Three columns by six inches deep, the copy says:

Attention Patrons of the
Meadow Downs
Fitness and Racquet Club

It says: "Have you contracted a flesh-eating fungal infection from the fitness equipment or personal-contact surfaces in their rest rooms? If so, please call the following number to be part of a class-action lawsuit."

At the phone number in question, a man's voice answers, "Deemer, Duke and Diller, Attorneys-at-Law."

The man says, "We'll need your name and address for the record." Over the phone, he says, "Can you describe your rash? Size. Location. Color. Tissue loss or damage. Be as specific as possible."

There's been a mistake, I say. There's no rash. I say, I'm not calling to be in the lawsuit.

For whatever reason, Helen Hoover Boyle comes to mind.

When I say I'm a reporter for the newspaper, the man says, "I'm sorry, but we're not allowed to discuss the matter until the lawsuit is filed."

I call the racquet club, but they won't talk either. I call the Treeline Dining Club from the earlier ad, but they won't talk.

The phone numbers in both ads are the same one. With the weird cell phone prefix. I call it again, and the man's voice says, "Diller, Doom and Duke, Attorneys-at-Law."

And I hang up.

In journalism school, they teach you to start with your most important fact. The inverted pyramid, they call it. Put the who, what, where, when, and why at the top of the article. Then list the lesser facts in descending order. That way, an editor can lop off any length of story without losing anything too important.

All the little details, the smell of the bedspread, the food on the plates, the color of the Christmas tree ornament, that stuff always gets left on the Composing Room floor.

The only pattern in crib death is it tends to increase as the weather cools in the fall. This is the fact my editor wants to lead with in our first installment. Something to panic people. Five babies, five installments. This way we can keep people reading the series for five consecutive Sundays. We can promise to explore the causes and patterns of sudden infant death. We can hold out hope.

Some people still think knowledge is power.

We can guarantee advertisers a highly invested readership. Outside, it's colder already.

Back at the City Room, I ask my editor to do me a little favor.

I think maybe I've found a pattern. It looks as if every parent might have read the same poem out loud to their child the night before it died.

"All five?" he says.

I say, let's try a little experiment.

This is late in the evening, and we're both tired from a long day. We're sitting in his office, and I tell him to listen.

It's an old song about animals going to sleep. It's wistful and sentimental, and my face feels livid and hot with oxygenated hemoglobin while I read the poem out loud under the fluorescent lights, across a desk from my editor with his tie undone and his collar open, leaning back in his chair with his eyes closed. His mouth is open a little, his teeth and his coffee mug are stained the same coffee brown.

What's good is we're alone, and it only takes a minute.

At the end, he opens his eyes and says, "What the fuck was that supposed to mean?"

Duncan, his eyes are green.

His spit lands in little cold specks on my arm, bringing germs, little wet buckshot, bringing viruses. Brown coffee saliva.

I say I don't know. The book calls it a culling song. In some ancient cultures, they sang it to children during famines or droughts, anytime the tribe had outgrown its land. You sing it to warriors crippled in battle and people stricken with disease, anyone you hope will die soon. To end their pain. It's a lullaby.

As far as ethics, what I've learned is a journalist's job isn't to judge the facts. Your job isn't to screen information. Your job is to collect the details. Just what's there. Be an impartial witness. What I know now is someday you won't think twice about calling those parents back on Christmas Eve.

Duncan looks at his watch, then at me, and says, "So what's your experiment?"

Tomorrow, I'll know if there's a causal relationship. A real pattern. It's just my job to tell the story. I put page 27 through his paper shredder.

Sticks and stones may break your bones, but words will never hurt you.

I don't want to explain until I know for sure. This is still a hypothetical situation, so I ask my editor to humor me. I say, "We both need some rest, Duncan." I say, "Maybe we can talk about it in the morning."

Chapter 7

During my first cup of coffee, Henderson walks over from the National desk. Some people grab their coats and head for the elevator. Some grab a magazine and head for the bathroom. Other people duck behind their computer screens and pretend to be on the phone while Henderson stands in the center of the newsroom with his tie loose around his open collar and shouts, "Where the hell is Duncan?"

He yells, "The street edition is going to press, and we need the rest of the damn front page."

Some people just shrug. I pick up my phone.

The details about Henderson are he's got blond hair combed across his forehead. He dropped out of law school. He's an editor on the National desk. He always knows the snow conditions and has a lift pass dangling from every coat he owns. His computer password is "password."

Standing next to my desk, he says, "Streator, is that nasty blue tie the only one you got?"

Holding the phone to my ear, I mouth the word *Interview*. I ask the dial tone, is that B as in "boy"?

Of course I'm not telling anybody about how I read Duncan the poem. I can't call the police. About my theory. I can't explain to Helen Hoover Boyle why I need to ask about her dead son.

My collar feels so tight I have to swallow hard to force any coffee down.

Even if people believed me, the first thing they'd want to know is: *What poem?*

Show it to us. Prove it.

The question isn't, *Would the poem leak out?*

The question is, *How soon would the human race be extinct?*

Here's the power of life and a cold clean bloodless easy death, available to anyone. To everyone. An instant, bloodless, Hollywood death.

Even if I don't tell, how long until *Poems and Rhymes from Around the World* gets into a classroom? How long until page 27, the culling song, gets read to fifty kids before nap time?

How long until it's read over the radio to thousands of people? Until it's set to music? Translated into other languages?

61

Hell, it doesn't have to be translated to work. Babies don't speak any language.

No one's seen Duncan for three days. Miller thinks Kleine called Duncan at home. Kleine thinks Fillmore called. Everybody's sure somebody else called, but nobody's talked to Duncan. He hasn't answered his e-mail. Carruthers says Duncan didn't bother to call in sick.

Another cup of coffee later, Henderson stops by my desk with a tear sheet from the Leisure section. It's folded to show an ad, three columns by six inches deep. Henderson looks at me tapping my watch and holding it to my ear, and he says, "You see this in the morning edition?"

The ad says:

**Attention First-Class Passengers
of Regent-Pacific Airlines**

The ad says: "Have you suffered hair loss and/or discomfort from crab lice after coming in contact with airline upholstery, pillows, or blankets? If so, please call the following number to be part of a class-action lawsuit."

Henderson says, "You called about this yet?"

I say, maybe he should just shut up and call.

And Henderson says, "You're Mr. Special Features." He says, "This isn't prison. I ain't your bitch."

This is killing me.

You don't become a reporter because you're good at keeping secrets.

Being a journalist is about telling. It's about bearing the bad news. Spreading the contagion. The biggest story in history. This could be the end of mass media.

The culling song would be a plague unique to the Information Age. Imagine a world where people shun the television, the radio, movies, the Internet, magazines and newspapers. People have to wear earplugs the way they wear condoms and rubber gloves. In the past, nobody worried too much about sex with strangers. Or before that, bites from fleas. Or untreated drinking water. Mosquitoes. Asbestos.

Imagine a plague you catch through your ears.

Sticks and stones will break your bones, but now words can kill, too.

The new death, this plague, can come from anywhere. A song. An overhead announcement. A news bulletin. A sermon. A street musician. You can catch death from a telemarketer. A teacher. An

Internet file. A birthday card. A fortune cookie.

A million people might watch a television show, then be dead the next morning because of an advertising jingle.

Imagine the panic.

Imagine a new Dark Age. Exploration and trade routes brought the first plagues from China to Europe. With mass media, we have so many new means of transmission.

Imagine the books burning. And tapes and films and files, radios and televisions, will all go into that same bonfire. All those libraries and bookstores blazing away in the night. People will attack microwave relay stations. People with axes will chop every fiber-optic cable.

Imagine people chanting prayers, singing hymns, to drown out any sound that might bring death. Their hands clamped over their ears, imagine people shunning any song or speech where death could be coded the way maniacs would poison a bottle of aspirin. Any new word. Anything they don't already understand will be suspect, dangerous. Avoided. A quarantine against communication.

And if this was a death spell, an incantation, there had to be others. If *I* know

64

about page 27, someone else must. I'm not the pioneer brain of anything.

How long until someone dissects the culling song and creates another variation, and another, and another? All of them new and improved. Until Oppenheimer invented the atom bomb, it was impossible. Now we have the atom bomb and the hydrogen bomb and the neutron bomb, and people are still expanding on that one idea. We're forced into a new scary paradigm.

If Duncan's dead, he was a necessary casualty. He was my atmospheric nuclear test. He was my Trinity. My Hiroshima.

Still, Palmer from the copy desk is sure Duncan's in Composing.

Jenkins from Composing says Duncan's probably in the art department.

Hawley from Art says he's in the clipping library.

Schott from the library says Duncan's at the copy desk.

Around here, this is what passes for reality.

The kind of security they now have at airports, imagine that kind of crackdown at all libraries, schools, theaters, bookstores, after the culling song leaks out. Anywhere information might be disseminated, you'll find armed guards.

The airwaves will be as empty as a public swimming pool during a polio scare. After that, only a few government broadcasts will air. Only well-scrubbed news and music. After that, any music, books, and movies will be tested on lab animals or volunteer convicts before release to the public.

Instead of surgical masks, people will wear earphones that will give them the soothing constant protection of safe music or birdsongs. People will pay for a supply of "pure" news, a source for "safe" information and entertainment. The way milk and meat and blood are inspected, imagine books and music and movies being filtered and homogenized. Certified. Approved for consumption.

People will be happy to give up most of their culture for the assurance that the tiny bit that comes through is safe and clean.

White noise.

Imagine a world of silence where any sound loud enough or long enough to harbor a deadly poem would be banned. No more motorcycles, lawn mowers, jet planes, electric blenders, hair dryers. A world where people are afraid to listen, afraid they'll hear something behind the din of traffic. Some toxic words buried in the loud music playing next door. Imagine a higher and higher resistance to language. No one talks because no one dares to listen.

The deaf shall inherit the earth.

And the illiterate. The isolated. Imagine a world of hermits.

Another cup of coffee, and I have to piss like a bastard. Henderson from National catches me washing my hands in the men's room and says something.

It could be anything.

Drying my hands under the blower, I yell I can't hear him.

"Duncan!" Henderson yells. Over the sound of water and the hand dryer, he yells, "We have two dead bodies in a hotel suite, and we don't know if it's news or not. We need Duncan to make the call."

I guess that's what he says. There's so much noise.

In the mirror, I check my tie and finger-comb my hair. In one breath, with Henderson reflected next to me, I could race through the culling song, and he'd be out of my life by tonight. Him and Duncan. Dead. It would be that easy.

Instead, I ask if it's okay to wear a blue tie with a brown jacket.

Chapter 8

When the first paramedic arrived on the scene, the first action he took was to call his stockbroker. This paramedic, my friend John Nash, sized up the situation in suite 17F of the Pressman Hotel and put in a sell order for all his shares of Stuart Western Technologies.

"They can fire me, okay," Nash says, "but in the three minutes I made that call, those two in the bed weren't getting any deader."

The next call he makes is to me, asking if I've got fifty bucks for him to find out a few extra facts. He says if I got shares of Stuart Western to dump them and then get my ass over to this bar on Third, near the hospital.

"Christ," Nash says over the phone, "this woman was beautiful. If Turner hadn't been there, Turner my partner, I don't know." And he hangs up.

According to the ticker, shares of Stuart Western Tech are already sliding into the toilet. Already the news must be out about

Baker Lewis Stuart, the company's founder, and his new wife, Penny Price Stuart.

Last night, the Stuarts had dinner at seven o'clock at Chez Chef. This is all easy enough to bribe out of the hotel concierge. According to their waiter, one had the salmon risotto, the other had Portabello mushrooms. Looking at the check, he said, you can't tell who had what. They drank a bottle of pinot noir. Somebody had cheesecake for dessert. Both of them had coffee.

At nine, they drove to an after-hours party at the Chambers Gallery, where witnesses told police the couple talked to several people including the gallery owner and the architect of their new house. They each had another glass of some jug wine.

At ten-thirty, they returned to the Pressman Hotel, where they'd been staying in suite 17F for almost a month since their wedding.

The hotel operator says they made several phone calls between ten-thirty and midnight. At twelve-fifteen, they called the front desk and asked for an eight o'clock wake-up call. A desk clerk confirms that they used the television remote control to order a pornographic movie.

At nine the next morning, the maid

found them dead.

"Embolism, if you ask me," Nash says. "You eat a girl out and you blow some air inside her, or if you fuck her too hard, either way you can force air into her bloodstream and the bubble goes right to her heart."

Nash is heavy. A big guy wearing a heavy coat over his white uniform, he's wearing his white track shoes and standing at the bar when I get there. Both elbows on the bar, he's eating a steak sandwich on a kaiser roll with mustard and mayo squeezing out of the far end. He's drinking a cup of black coffee. His greasy hair is pulled into a black palm tree on top of his head.

And I say, so?

I ask, was the place ransacked?

Nash is just chewing, his big jaw going around and around. He holds the sandwich in both hands but stares past it at the plate full of mess, dill pickles and potato chips.

I ask, did he smell anything in the hotel room?

He says, "Newlyweds like they were, I figure he fucks her to death, and then has himself a heart attack. Five bucks says they open her and find air in her heart."

I ask, did he at least star-69 their tele-

70

phone to find out who'd called last?

And Nash says, "No can do. Not on a hotel phone."

I say, I want more for my fifty bucks than just his drooling over a dead body.

"You'da been drooling, too," he says. "Damn, she was a looker."

I ask, were there valuables — watches, wallets, jewelry — left at the scene?

He says, "Still warm, too, under the covers. Warm enough. No death agonies. Nothing."

His big jaw goes around and around, slower now as he stares down at nothing in particular.

"If you could have any woman you wanted," he says, "if you could have her any way you wanted, wouldn't you do it?"

I say, what he's talking about is rape.

"Not," he says, "if she's dead." And he crunches down on a potato chip in his mouth. "If I'd been alone, alone and had a rubber . . . ," he says through the food. "No way would I let the medical examiner find my DNA at the scene."

Then he's talking about murder.

"Not if somebody else kills her," Nash says, and looks at me. "Or kills *him*. The husband had a fine-looking ass, if that's what floats your boat. No leakage. No livor mortis. No skin slippage. Nothing."

How he can talk this way and still eat, I don't know.

He says, "Both of them naked. A big wet spot on the mattress, right between them. Yeah, they did it. Did it and died." Nash chews his sandwich and says, "Seeing her there, she was better-looking than any piece of tail I've ever had."

If Nash knew the culling song, there wouldn't be a woman left alive. Alive or a virgin.

If Duncan is dead, I hope it's not Nash who responds to the call. Maybe this time with a rubber. Maybe they sell them in the bathroom here.

Since he had such a good look, I ask if he saw any bruises, bites, beestings, needle marks, anything.

"It's nothing like that," he says.

A suicide note?

"Nope. No apparent cause of death," he says.

Nash turns the sandwich around in his hands and licks the mustard and mayo leaked out the end. He says, "You remember Jeffrey Dahmer." Nash licks and says, "He didn't set out to kill so many people. He just thought you could drill a hole in somebody's skull, pour in some drain cleaner, and make them your sex zombie. Dahmer just wanted to be getting more."

So what do I get for my fifty bucks?

"A name's all I got," he says.

I give him two twenties and a ten.

With his teeth, he pulls a slice of steak out of the sandwich. The meat hangs against his chin before he tosses his head back to flip it into his mouth. Chewing, he says, "Yeah, I'm a pig," and his breath is nothing but mustard. He says, "The last person to talk to them, their call history on both their cell phones, it said her name is Helen Hoover Boyle."

He says, "You dump that stock like I told you?"

Chapter 9

It's the same William and Mary bureau cabinet. According to the note card taped to the front, it's black lacquered pine with Persian scenes in silver gilt, round bun feet, and the pediment done up in a pile of carved curls and shells. It has to be the same cabinet. We'd turned right here, walking down a tight corridor of armoires, then turned right again at a Regency press cupboard, then left at a Federal sofa, but here we are again.

Helen Hoover Boyle puts her finger against the silver gilt, the tarnished men and women of Persian court life, and says, "I have no idea what you're talking about."

She killed Baker and Penny Stuart. She called them on their cell phones sometime the day before they died. She read them each the culling song.

"You think I killed those unfortunate people by *singing* to them?" she says. Her suit is yellow today, but her hair's still big and pink. Her shoes are yellow, but her neck's still hung with gold chains and beads. Her cheeks look pink and soft with too much powder.

It didn't take much digging to find out the Stuarts were the people who'd bought a house on Exeter Drive. A lovely *historic* house with seven bedrooms and cherry paneling throughout the first floor. A house they planned to tear down and replace. A plan that infuriated Helen Hoover Boyle.

"Oh, Mr. Streator," she says. "If you could just hear yourself."

From where we're standing, a tight corridor of furniture stretches a few yards in every direction. Beyond that, each corridor turns or branches into more corridors, armoires squeezed side by side, sideboards wedged together. Anything short, armchairs or sofas or tables, only lets you see through to the next corridor of hutches, the next wall of grandfather clocks, enameled screens, Georgian secretaries.

This is where she suggested we meet, where we could talk in private, one of those warehouse antique stores. In this maze of furniture, we keep meeting the same William and Mary bureau cabinet, then the same Regency press cupboard. We're going in circles. We're lost.

And Helen Boyle says, "Have you told

anyone else about your killer song?"

Only my editor.

"And what did your editor say?"

I think he's dead.

And she says, "What a surprise." She says, "You must feel terrible."

Above us, crystal chandeliers hang at different heights, all of them cloudy and gray as powdered wigs. Frayed wires twist where their chains hook onto each roof beam. The severed wires, the dusty dead lightbulbs. Each chandelier is just another ancient aristocratic head cut off and hanging upside down. Above everything arches the warehouse roof, a lot of bow trusses supporting corrugated steel.

"Just follow me," Helen Boyle says. "Isn't moss supposed to grow only on the north side of an armoire?"

She wets two fingers in her mouth and holds them up.

The Rococo vitrines, the Jacobean bookcases, the Gothic Revival highboys, all carved and varnished, the French Provincial wardrobes, crowd around us. The Edwardian walnut curio cabinets, the Victorian pier mirrors, the Renaissance Revival chifforobes. The walnut and mahogany, ebony and oak. The melon bulb legs and cabriole legs and linenfold panels.

Past the point where any corridor turns, there's just more. Queen Anne chiffoniers. More bird's-eye maple. Mother-of-pearl inlay and gilded bronze ormolu.

Our footsteps echo against the concrete floor. The steel roof hums with rain.

And she says, "Don't you feel, somehow, buried in history?"

With her pink fingernails, from out of her yellow and white bag, she takes a ring of keys. She makes a fist around the keys so only the longest and sharpest juts out between her fingers.

"Do you realize that anything you can do in your lifetime will be meaningless a hundred years from now?" she says. "Do you think, a century from now, that anyone will even remember the Stuarts?"

She looks from one polished surface to the next, tabletops, dressers, doors, all with her reflection floating across them.

"People die," she says. "People tear down houses. But furniture, fine, beautiful furniture, it just goes on and on, surviving everything."

She says, "Armoires are the cockroaches of our culture."

And without breaking her stride, she drags the steel point of the key across the polished walnut face of a cabinet. The sound is as quiet as anything sharp slashing something soft. The scar is deep and shows the raw cheap pine under the veneer.

She stops in front of a wardrobe with beveled-glass doors.

"Think of all the generations of women who looked in that mirror," she says. "They took it home. They aged in that mirror. They died, all those beautiful young women, but here's the wardrobe, worth more now than ever. A parasite surviving the host. A big fat predator looking for its next meal."

In this maze of antiques, she says, are the ghosts of everyone who has ever owned this furniture. Everyone rich and successful enough to prove it. All of their talent and intelligence and beauty, outlived by decorative junk. All the success and accomplishment this furniture was supposed to represent, it's all vanished.

She says, "In the vast scheme of things, does it really matter how the Stuarts died?"

I ask, how did she find out about the culling spell? Was it because her son, Patrick, died?

And she just keeps walking, trailing her fingers along the carved edges, the polished surfaces, marring the knobs and smearing the mirrors.

It didn't take much digging to find out how her husband died. A year after Patrick, he was found in bed, dead without a mark, without a suicide note, without a cause.

And Helen Boyle says, "How was your editor found?"

Out of her yellow and white purse, she takes a gleaming silver little pair of pliers and a screwdriver, so clean and exact they could be used in surgery. She opens the door on a vast carved and polished armoire and says, "Hold this steady for me, please."

I hold the door and she's busy on the inside for a moment until the door's latch and handle fall free and hit the floor at my feet.

A minute later, and she has the door handles, and the gilded bronze ormolu, she's taken everything metal except the hinges and put them in her purse. Stripped, the armoire looks crippled, blind, castrated, mutilated.

And I ask, why is she doing this?

"Because I love this piece," she says. "But I'm not going to be another one of its victims."

She closes the doors and puts her tools away in her purse.

"I'll come back for it after they cut the price down to what it cost when it was new," she says. "I love it, but I'll only have it on my own terms."

We walk a few steps more, and the corridor breaks into a forest of hall trees and hat racks, umbrella stands and coat racks. In the distance beyond that is another wall of breakfronts and armoires.

"Elizabethan," she says, touching each piece. "Tudor . . . Eastlake . . . Stickley . . ."

When someone takes two old pieces, say a mirror and a dresser, and fastens them together, she explains that experts call the product a "married" piece. As an antique, it's considered worthless.

When someone takes two pieces apart, say a buffet and a hutch, and sells them separately, experts call the pieces "divorced."

"And again," she says, "they're worthless."

I say how I've been trying to find every copy of the poems book. I say how important it is that no one ever discovers the spell. After what happened to Duncan, I swear I'm going to burn all my notes and forget I ever knew the culling spell.

"And what if you can't forget it?" she says. "What if it stays in your head, repeating itself like one of those silly advertising songs? What if it's always there, like a loaded gun waiting for someone to annoy you?"

I won't use it.

"Hypothetically speaking, of course," she says, "what if I used to swear the same thing? Me. A woman you're saying accidentally killed her own child and husband, someone who's been tortured by the power of this curse. If someone like me eventually began using the song, what makes you think that you won't?"

I just won't.

"Of course you won't," she says, and then laughs without making a sound. She turns right, past a Biedermeier credenza, fast, then turns again past an Art Nouveau console, and for a minute she's out of sight.

I hurry to catch up, still lost, saying, if we're going to find our way out of this, I think we need to stay together.

Just ahead of us is a William and Mary bureau cabinet. Black lacquered pine with Persian scenes in silver gilt, round bun feet, and the pediment done up in a pile of

81

carved curls and shells. And leading me deeper into the thicket of cabinets and closets and breakfronts and highboys, the rocking chairs and hall trees and bookcases, Helen Hoover Boyle says she needs to tell me a little story.

Chapter 10

Back at the newsroom, everybody's quiet. People are whispering around the coffee-maker. People are listening with their mouths hanging open. Nobody's crying.

Henderson catches me hanging my jacket and says, "You call Regent-Pacific Airlines about their crab lice?"

And I say, nobody's saying anything until a suit is filed.

And Henderson says, "Just so you know, you report to me now." He says, "Duncan's not just irresponsible. It turns out he's dead."

Dead in bed without a mark. No suicide note, no cause of death. His landlord found him and called the paramedics.

And I ask, any sign he was sodomized?

And Henderson jerks his head back just a trace and says, "Say what?"

Did somebody fuck him?

"God, no," Henderson says. "Why would you ask such a thing?"

And I say, no reason.

At least Duncan wasn't somebody's

83

dead-body sex doll.

I say, if anybody needs me, I'll be in the clipping library. There's some facts I need to check. Just a few years of newspaper stories I need to read. A few spools of microfilm to run through.

And Henderson calls after me, "Don't go far. Just because Duncan's dead, that don't mean you're off the dead baby beat."

Sticks and stones may break your bones, but watch out for those damn words.

According to the microfilm, in 1983, in Vienna, Austria, a twenty-three-year-old nurse's aide gave an overdose of morphine to an old woman who was begging to die.

The seventy-seven-year-old woman died, and the aide, Waltraud Wagner, found she loved having the power of life and death.

It's all here in spool after spool of microfilm. Just the facts.

At first it was just to help dying patients. She worked in an enormous hospital for the elderly and chronically ill. People lingered there, wanting to die. Besides morphine, the young woman invented what she called her water cure. To relieve suffering, you just pinch the patient's nose shut. You depress the tongue, and you pour water down the throat. Death is slow torture, but old people are always found dead with water collected in their lungs.

The young woman called herself an angel.

It looked very natural.

It was a noble, heroic deed that Wagner was doing.

She was the ultimate end to suffering and misery. She was gentle and caring and sensitive, and she only took those who begged to die. She was the angel of death.

By 1987, there were three more angels. All four aides worked the night shift. By now the hospital was nicknamed the Death Pavilion.

Instead of ending suffering, the four women began to give their water cure to patients who snored or wet the bed or refused to take medication or buzzed the nurse's station late at night. Any petty annoyance, and the patient died the next night. Anytime a patient complained about anything, Waltraud Wagner would say, "This one gets a ticket to God," and glug, glug, glug.

"The ones who got on my nerves," she told authorities, "were dispatched directly to a free bed with the good Lord."

In 1989, an old woman called Wagner a common slut, and got the water cure. Afterward, the angels were drinking in a tavern, laughing and mimicking the old woman's convulsions and the look on her face. A doctor sitting nearby overheard.

By then, the Vienna health authorities estimate that almost three hundred people had been cured. Wagner got life in prison. The other angels got lesser sentences.

"We could decide whether these old fogies lived or died," Wagner said at her trial. "Their ticket to God was long overdue in any case."

The story Helen Hoover Boyle told me is true.

Power corrupts. And absolute power corrupts absolutely.

So just relax, Helen Boyle told me, and just enjoy the ride.

She said, "Even absolute corruption has its perks."

She said to think of all the people you'd like out of your life. Think of all the loose ends you could tie up. The revenge. Think how easy it would be.

And still echoing in my head was Nash. Nash was there, drooling over the idea of any woman, anywhere, cooperative and beautiful for at least a few hours before things start to cool down and fall apart.

"Tell me," he said, "how would that be different than most love relationships?"

Anyone and everyone could become your next sex zombie.

But just because this Austrian nurse and Helen Boyle and John Nash can't control themselves, that doesn't mean I'll become a reckless, impulsive killer.

Henderson comes to the library doorway and shouts, "Streator! Did you turn off your pager? We just got a call about another cold baby."

The editor is dead, long live the editor. Here's the new boss, same as the old boss.

And, sure, the world just might be a better place without certain people. Yeah, the world could be just perfect, with a little trimming here and there. A little house-cleaning. Some unnatural selection.

But, no, I'm never going to use the culling song again.

Never again.

But even if I did use it, I wouldn't use it for revenge.

I wouldn't use it for convenience.

I certainly wouldn't use it for sex.

No, I'd only ever use it for good.

And Henderson yells, "Streator! Did you ever call about the first-class crab lice? Did you call about the health club's butt-eating fungus? You need to pester those people at the Treeline or you'll never get anything."

And fast as a flinch, me flinching the other way down the hall, the culling song spools through my head while I grab my coat and head out the door.

But, no, I'm never going to use it. That's that. I'm just not. Ever.

Chapter 11

These noise-oholics. These quiet-ophobics.

There's the stomp and stomp and stomp of a drum coming down through the ceiling. Through the walls, you hear the laughter and applause of dead people.

Even in the bathroom, even taking a shower, you can hear talk radio over the hiss of the showerhead, the splash of water in the tub and blasting against the plastic curtain. It's not that you want everybody dead, but it would be nice to unleash the culling spell on the world. Just to enjoy the fear. After people outlawed loud sounds, any sounds that could harbor a spell, any music or noise that might mask a deadly poem, after that the world would be silent. Dangerous and frightened, but silent.

The tile beats a tiny rhythm under my fingertips. The bathtub vibrates with shouts coming through the floor. Either a prehistoric flying dinosaur awakened by a nuclear test is about to destroy the people downstairs or their television's too loud.

In a world where vows are worthless.

Where making a pledge means nothing. Where promises are made to be broken, it would be nice to see words come back into power.

In a world where the culling song was common knowledge, there would be sound blackouts. Like during wartime, wardens would patrol. But instead of hunting for light, they'd listen for noise and tell people to shut up. The way governments look for air and water pollution, these same governments would pinpoint anything above a whisper, then make an arrest. There would be helicopters, special muffled helicopters, of course, to search for noise the way they search for marijuana now. People would tiptoe around in rubber-soled shoes. Informers would listen at every keyhole.

It would be a dangerous, frightened world, but at least you could sleep with your windows open. It would be a world where each word was worth a thousand pictures.

It's hard to say if that world would be any worse than this, the pounding music, the roar of television, the squawk of radio.

Maybe without Big Brother filling us, people could think.

The upside is maybe our minds would become our own.

It's harmless so I say the first line of the culling poem. There's no one here to kill. No way could anyone hear it.

And Helen Hoover Boyle is right. I haven't forgot it. The first word generates the second. The first line generates the next. My voice booms as big as an opera. The words thunder with the deep rolling sound of a bowling alley. The thunder echoes against the tile and linoleum.

In my big opera voice, the culling song doesn't sound silly the way it did in Duncan's office. It sounds heavy and rich. It's the sound of doom. It's the doom of my upstairs neighbor. It's my end to his life, and I've said the whole poem.

Even wet, the hair's bristling on the back of my neck. My breathing's stopped.

And, nothing.

From upstairs, there's the stomp of music. From every direction, there's radio and television talk, tiny gunshots, laughter, bombs, sirens. A dog barks. This is what passes for prime time.

I turn off the water. I shake my hair. I pull back the shower curtain and reach for a towel. And then I see it.

The vent.

The air shaft, it connects every apartment. The vent, it's always open. It carries steam from the bathrooms, cooking smells from the kitchens. It carries every sound.

Dripping on the bathroom floor, I just stare at the vent. It could be I've just killed the whole building.

Chapter 12

Nash is at the bar on Third, eating onion dip with his fingers. He sticks two shiny fingers into his mouth, sucking so hard his cheeks cave in. He pulls the fingers out and pinches some more onion dip out of a plastic tub.

I ask if that's breakfast.

"You got a question," he says, "you need to show me the money first." And he puts the fingers in his mouth.

On the other side of Nash, down the bar is some young guy with sideburns, wearing a good pin-striped suit. Next to him is a gal, standing on the bar rail so she can kiss him. He tosses the cherry from his cocktail into his mouth. They kiss. Then she's chewing. The radio behind the bar is still announcing the school lunch menus.

Nash keeps turning his head to watch them.

This is what passes for love.

I put a ten-dollar bill on the bar.

His fingers still in his mouth, his eyes

look down at it. Then his eyebrows come up.

I ask, did anybody die in my building last night?

It's the apartments at Seventeenth and Loomis Place. The Loomis Place Apartments, eight stories, a kind of kidney-colored brick. Maybe somebody on the fifth floor? Near the back? A young guy. This morning, there's a weird stain on my ceiling.

The sideburns guy, his cell phone starts ringing.

And Nash pulls his fingers out, his lips dragged out around them in a tight pucker. Nash looks at his fingernails, close-up, cross-eyed.

The dead guy was into drugs, I tell him. A lot of people in that building are into drugs. I ask if there were any other dead people there. By any chance did a whole bunch of people die in the Loomis Place Apartments last night?

And the sideburns guy grabs the gal by a handful of hair and pulls her away from his mouth. With his other hand, he takes a phone from inside his coat and flips it open, saying, "Hello?"

I say, they'd all be found with no apparent cause of death.

Nash stirs a finger around in the onion dip and says, "That your building?"

Yeah, I already said that.

Still holding the gal by her hair, talking into the phone, the sideburns guy says, "No, honey." He says, "I'm at the doctor's office right now, and it doesn't look very good."

The gal closes her eyes. She arches her neck back and grinds her hair into his hand.

And the sideburns guy says, "No, it looks like it's metastasized." He says, "No, I'm okay."

The gal opens her eyes.

He winks at her.

She smiles.

And the sideburns guy says, "That means a lot right now. I love you, too."

He hangs up, and he pulls the gal's face into his.

And Nash takes the ten off the bar and stuffs it into his pocket. He says, "Nope. I didn't hear anything."

The gal, her feet slip off the bar rail, and she laughs. She steps back up and says, "Was that her?"

And the sideburns guy says, "No."

And without me trying, it happens. Me just looking at the sideburns guy, the song flits through my head. The song, my voice in the shower, the voice of doom, it echoes inside me. As fast as a reflex. As fast as a sneeze, it happens.

Nash, his breath is nothing but onions, he says, "It sounds kind of funny, you asking that." He puts his stirring finger into his mouth.

And the gal down the bar says, "Marty?"

And the sideburns guy leaning against the bar slides to the floor.

Nash turns to look.

The gal's kneeling next to the guy on the floor, her hands spread open just above, but not quite touching, his pin-striped lapels, and she says, "Marty?" Her finger-nails are painted sparkling purple. Her purple lipstick is smeared all around the guy's mouth.

And maybe the guy's really sick. Maybe he's choked on a cherry. Maybe I didn't just make another kill.

The gal looks up at Nash and me, her face glossy with tears, and says, "Does one of you know CPR?"

Nash puts his fingers back in the onion dip, and I step over the body, past the gal, pulling on my coat, headed for the door.

Chapter 13

Back in the newsroom, Wilson from the International desk wants to know if I've seen Henderson today. Baker from the Books desk says Henderson didn't call in sick, and he doesn't answer his phone at home. Oliphant from the Special Features desk says, "Streator, you seen this?"

He hands me a tear sheet, an ad that says:

Attention Patrons of the French Salon

It says: "Have you experienced severe bleeding and scarring as a result of recent facials?"

The phone number is one I haven't seen before, and when I dial, a woman answers: "Doogan, Diller and Dunne, Attorneys-at-Law," she says.

And I hang up.

Oliphant stands by my desk and says, "While you're here, say something nice about Duncan." They're putting together a feature, he says, a tribute to Duncan, a nice portrait and a summary of his career, and they need people to think up good quotes. Somebody in Art is using the photo from Duncan's employee badge to paint the portrait. "Only smiling," Oliphant says. "Smiling and more like a human being."

Before that, walking from the bar on Third, back to work, I counted my steps. To keep my mind busy, I counted 276 steps until a guy wearing a black leather trench coat shoves past me at a street corner, saying, "Wake up, asshole. The sign says, 'Walk'."

Hitting me as sudden as a yawn, me glaring at the guy's black leather back, the culling song loops through my head.

Still crossing the street, the guy in the trench coat lifts his foot to step over the far curb, but doesn't clear it. His toe kicks into the curb halfway up, and he pitches forward onto the sidewalk, flat on his forehead. It's the sound of dropping an egg on the kitchen floor, only a really big, big egg full of blood and brains. His arms lie straight down at his sides. The toes of his black wing tips hang off the curb a little, over the gutter.

I step past him, counting 277, counting 278, counting 279 . . .

A block from the newspaper, a sawhorse barricade blocks the sidewalk. A police officer in a blue uniform stands on the other side shaking his head. "You have to go back and cross the street. This sidewalk's closed." He says, "They're shooting a movie up the block."

Hitting me as fast as a cramp, me scowling at his badge, the eight lines of the song run through my mind.

The officer's eyes roll up until only the whites show. One gloved hand gets halfway to his chest, and his knees fold. His chin comes down on the top edge of the barricade so hard you can hear his teeth click together. Something pink flies out. It's the tip of his tongue.

Counting 345, counting 346, counting 347, I haul one leg then the other over the barricade and keep walking.

A woman with a walkie-talkie in one hand steps into my path, one arm straight out in front of her, her hand reaching to stop me. The moment before her hand should grab my arm, her eyes roll over and her lips drop open. A thread of drool slips out one corner of her slack mouth, and she falls through my path, her walkie-talkie saying, "Jeanie? Jean? Stand by."

The last words of the culling song trail

through my head.

Counting 359, counting 360, counting 361, I keep walking as people rush past me in the other direction. A woman with a light meter hanging on a cord around her neck says, "Did somebody call an ambulance?"

People dressed in rags, wearing thick makeup and drinking water out of little blue-glass bottles, they stand in front of shopping carts piled with trash under big lights and reflectors, stretching their necks to see where I've been. The curb is lined with big trailers and motor homes with the smell of diesel generators running in between them. Paper cups half full of coffee are sitting everywhere.

Counting 378, counting 379, counting 380, I step over the barricade on the far side and keep walking. It takes 412 steps to get to the newsroom. In the elevator, on the way up, there's already too many people crowded in. On the fifth floor, another man tries to shoulder his way into the car.

Sudden as breaking a sweat, me squeezed against the back of the elevator, my mind spits out the culling song so hard my lips move with each word.

The man looks at us all, and seems to

step back in slow motion. Before we see him hit the floor, the doors are closed and we're going up.

In the newsroom, Henderson is missing. Oliphant comes over while I'm dialing my phone. He tells me about the tribute to Duncan. Asks for quotes. He shows me the ad on the tear sheet. The ad about the French Salon, the bleeding facials. Oliphant asks where my next installment is on the crib death series.

The phone in my hand, I'm counting 435, counting 436, counting 437 . . .

To him, I say to just not piss me off.

A woman's voice on the phone says, "Helen Boyle Realty. May I help you?"

And Oliphant says, "Have you tried counting to 10?"

The details about Oliphant are he's fat, and his hands sweated brown handprints on the tear sheet he shows me. His computer password is "password."

And I say, I passed 10 a long time ago.

And the voice on the phone says, "Hello?"

With my hand over the phone, I tell Oliphant there must be a virus going around. That's probably why Henderson's gone. I'm going home, but I promise to file my story from there.

Oliphant mouths the words *Four o'clock deadline,* and he taps the face of his wristwatch.

And into the phone, I ask, is Helen Hoover Boyle in the office? I say, my name's Streator, and I need to see her right away.

I'm counting 489, counting 490, counting 491 . . .

The voice says, "Will she know what this is regarding?"

Yeah, I say, but she'll pretend she doesn't.

I say, she needs to stop me before I kill again.

And Oliphant backs away a couple steps before he breaks eye contact and heads toward Special Features. I'm counting 542, counting 543 . . .

On my way to the real estate office, I ask the cab to wait in front of my apartment building while I run upstairs.

The brown stain on my ceiling is bigger. It's maybe as big around as a tire, only now the stain has arms and legs.

Back in the cab, I try to buckle my seat belt, but it's adjusted too small. It cuts into me, my gut riding on top of it, and I hear Helen Hoover Boyle saying, "Middle-aged. Five-ten, maybe one hundred seventy pounds. Caucasian. Brown, green." I see her under her bubble of pink hair, winking at me.

I tell the driver the address for the real estate office, and I tell him that he can drive as fast as he wants, but just not to piss me off.

The details about the cab are it stinks. The seat is black and sticky. It's a cab.

I say, I have a little problem with anger.

The driver looks at me in his rearview mirror and says, "You should maybe get some anger management classes."

And I'm counting 578, counting 579, counting 580 . . .

Chapter 14

According to *Architectural Digest*, big mansions surrounded by vast estate gardens and thoroughbred horse farms are really good places to live. According to *Town & Country*, strands of fat pearls are lustrous. According to *Travel & Leisure*, a private yacht anchored in the sunny Mediterranean is relaxing.

In the waiting room of the Helen Boyle Real Estate Agency, this is what passes as a big news flash. A real scoop.

On the coffee table, there's copies of all these high-end magazines. There's a humpbacked Chesterfield couch upholstered in striped pink silk. The sofa table behind it has long lion legs, their claws gripping glass balls. You have to wonder how much of this furniture came here stripped of its hardware, its drawer pulls and metal details. Sold as junk, it came here and Helen Hoover Boyle put it back together.

A young woman, half my age, sits behind a carved Louis XIV desk, staring at a clock radio on the desk. Her desk plate says,

Mona Sabbat. Next to the clock radio is a police scanner crackling with static.

On the clock radio, an older woman is yelling at a younger woman. It seems the younger woman has gotten pregnant out of wedlock so the older woman is calling her a slut and a whore. A stupid whore, the older woman says, since the slut spread her legs without even getting paid.

The woman at the desk, this Mona person, turns off the police scanner and says, "I hope you don't mind. I love this show."

These media-holics. These quiet-ophobics.

On the clock radio, the older woman tells the slut to give her baby up for adoption unless she wants to ruin its future. She tells the slut to grow up and finish her degree in microbiology, then get married, but not have any more sex until then.

Mona Sabbat takes a brown paper bag from under the desk and takes out something wrapped in foil. She picks the foil open at one end and you can smell garlic and marigolds.

On the clock radio, the pregnant slut just cries and cries.

Sticks and stones may break your bones, but words can hurt like hell.

According to an article in *Town & Country*, beautifully handwritten personal correspondence on luxurious stationery is once again very in, in, in. In a copy of *Estate* magazine, there's an advertisement that says:

Attention Patrons of the
Bridle Mountain Riding and Polo Club

It says: "Have you contracted a parasitic skin infection from a mount?"

The phone number is one I haven't seen before.

The radio woman tells the slut to stop crying.

Here's Big Brother, singing and dancing, force-feeding you so your mind never gets hungry enough to think.

Mona Sabbat puts both elbows on her desk, and cradles her lunch in her hands, leaning close to the radio. The phone rings, and she answers it, saying, "Helen Boyle Realty. The Right Home Every Time." She says, "Sorry, Oyster, Dr. Sara's on." She says, "I'll see you at the ritual."

The radio woman calls the crying slut a bitch.

The cover of *First Class* magazine says: "Sable, the Justifiable Homicide."

And fast as a hiccup, me only half listening to the radio, me half reading, the culling song goes through my head.

From the clock radio, all you can hear is the slut sobbing and sobbing.

Instead of the older woman, there's silence. Sweet, golden silence. Too perfect to be anyone left alive.

The slut draws a long breath and asks, "Dr. Sara?" She says, "Dr. Sara, are you still there?"

And a deep voice comes on, saying the *Dr. Sara Lowenstein Show* is temporarily experiencing some technical difficulties. The deep voice apologizes. A moment later, dance music starts up.

The cover of *Manor-Born* magazine says: "Diamonds Go Casual!"

I put my face in my hands and groan.

The Mona person peels the foil back from her lunch and takes another bite. She turns off the radio and says, "Bummer."

On the backs of her hands, rusty brown henna designs trail down her fingers, her fingers and thumbs lumpy with silver rings. A lot of silver chains loop around her neck and disappear into her orange dress. On her chest, the crinkled orange fabric of her dress is bumpy from all the pendants hanging underneath. Her hair is a thousand coils and dreadlocks of red and black pinned up over silver filigree earrings. Her eyes look amber. Her fingernails, black.

I ask if she's worked here long.

"You mean," she says, "in earth time?" And she takes a paperback from a drawer in her desk. She uncaps a bright yellow highlighter and opens the book.

I ask if Mrs. Boyle ever talks about poetry.

And Mona says, "You mean Helen?"

Yeah, does she ever recite poetry? In her office, does she ever call people on the phone and read any poems to them?

"Don't get me wrong," Mona says, "but Mrs. Boyle's way too much into the money side of everything. You know?"

I have to start counting 1, counting 2 . . .

"It's like this," she says. "When traffic's bad, Mrs. Boyle makes me drive home with her — just so's she can use the carpool lane. Then I have to take three buses to get home myself. You know?"

I'm counting 4, counting 5 . . .

She says, "One time, we had this great sharing about the power of crystal. It's like we were finally connecting on some level, only it turns out we were talking about two totally different realities."

Then I'm on my feet. Unfolding a sheet

of paper from my back pocket, I show her the poem and ask if it looks familiar.

Highlighted in the book on her desk, it says: *Magic is the tuning of needed energy for natural change.*

Her amber eyes move back and forth in front of the poem. Just above the orange neckline of her dress, above her right collarbone, she has tattooed three tiny black stars. She's sitting cross-legged in her swivel chair. Her feet are bare and dirty, with silver rings around each big toe.

"I know what this is," she says, and her hand comes up.

Before her fingers close around it, I fold the paper and tuck it into my back pocket.

Her hand still in the air, she points an index finger at me and says, "I've heard of those. It's a culling spell, right?"

Highlighted in the book on her desk, it says: *The ultimate product of death is invoking rebirth.*

Across the polished cherry top of the desk is a long deep gouge.

I ask, what can she tell me about culling spells?

"All the literature mentions them," she says, and shrugs, "but they're supposed to be lost." She holds her hand out palm-up and says, "Let me see again."

And I say, how do they work?

And she wiggles her fingers.

And I shake my head no. I ask, how come it kills other people, but not the person who says it?

And tilting her head to one side a little, Mona says, "Why doesn't a gun kill the person who pulls the trigger? It's the same principle." She lifts both arms above her head and stretches, twisting her hands toward the ceiling. She says, "This doesn't work like a recipe in a cookbook. You can't dissect this with some electron microscope."

Her dress is sleeveless, and the hair under her arms is just regular mousy brown.

So, I say, how can it work on somebody who doesn't even hear the spell? I look at the radio. How can a spell work if you don't even say it out loud?

Mona Sabbat sighs. She turns her open book facedown on the desk and sticks the yellow highlighter behind one ear. She pulls open a desk drawer and takes out a pad and pencil, saying, "You don't have a clue, do you?"

Writing on the pad, she says, "When I was Catholic, this is years ago, I could say a seven-second Hail Mary. I could say a nine-second Our Father. When you get as much penance as I did, you get fast." She says, "When you get that fast, it's not even words anymore, but it's still a prayer."

She says, "All a spell does is focus an intention." She says this slow, word by word, and waits a beat. Her eyes on mine, she says, "If the practitioner's intention is strong enough, the object of the spell will fall asleep, no matter where."

The more emotion a person has bottled up, she says, the more powerful the spell. Mona Sabbat squints at me and says, "When was the last time you got laid?"

Almost two decades ago, but I do not tell her that.

"My guess," she says, "is you're a powder keg of something. Rage. Sorrow. Something." She stops writing, and flips through her highlighted book. Stopping at a page, she reads for a moment, then she flips to another page. "A well-balanced person," she says, "a functioning person, would have to read the song out loud to make someone fall asleep."

Still reading, she frowns and says, "Until you deal with your real personal issues, you'll never be able to control yourself."

I ask if her book says all that.

"Most of it's from Dr. Sara," she says.

And I say how the culling song does more than put people to sleep.

"How do you mean?" she says.

I mean they die. I say, are you sure you've never seen Helen Boyle with a book called *Poems and Rhymes from Around the World?*

Mona Sabbat's open hand drops to the desk and picks up her lunch wrapped in foil. She takes a bite, staring at the clock radio. She says, "Just now, on the radio," Mona says, "did you just do that?"

I nod.

"You just forced Dr. Sara to reincarnate?" she says.

I ask if she can just call Helen Hoover Boyle on her cell phone, and maybe I could talk to her.

My pager starts beeping.

And this Mona person says, "So you're saying Helen uses this same culling song?"

The message on my pager says to call Nash. The pager says it's important.

And I say, it's nothing I can prove, but Mrs. Boyle knows how. I say, I need her help so I can control it. So I can control myself.

And Mona Sabbat stops writing on the pad and tears off the page. She holds it halfway between us and says, "If you're serious about learning how to control this power, you need to come to a Wiccan practitioners' ritual." She shakes the paper at me and says, "We have over a thousand years of experience in one room." And she turns on the police scanner.

I take the paper. It's an address, date, and time.

The police scanner says, "Unit Bravo-nine, please respond to a code nine-fourteen at the Loomis Place Apartments, unit 5D."

"The mystical depth of this knowledge takes a lifetime to learn," she says. She picks up her lunch and peels back the foil. "Oh," she says, "and bring your favorite meat-free hot dish."

And the police scanner says, "Copy?"

Chapter 15

Helen Hoover Boyle takes her cell phone out of the green and white purse hanging from the crook of her elbow. She takes out a business card and looks from the card to the phone as she punches in a number, the little green buttons bright in the dim light. Bright green against the pink of her fingernail. The business card has a gold edge.

She presses the phone deep into the side of her pink hair. Into the phone, she says, "Yes, I'm somewhere in your lovely store, and I'm afraid I'll need some help finding my way out."

She leans into the note card taped to an armoire twice her height. Into the phone, she says, "I'm facing . . . ," and she reads, " 'an Adam-style neoclassical armoire with fire-gilded bronze arabesque cartouches'."

She looks at me and rolls her eyes. Into the phone, she says, "It's marked seventeen thousand dollars."

Her feet step out of green high heels, and she stands flatfooted on the concrete floor in sheer white stockings. It's not the white that makes you think of underwear. It's more the white of the skin underneath. The stockings make her toes look webbed.

The suit she's wearing, the skirt is fitted to her hips. It's green, but not the green of a lime, more the green of a key lime pie. It's not the green of an avocado, but more the green of avocado bisque topped with a paper-thin sliver of lemon, served ice cold in a yellow Sèvres soup plate.

It's green the way a pool table with green felt looks under the yellow 1 ball, not the way it looks under the red 3.

I ask Helen Hoover Boyle what a code nine-fourteen is.

And she says, "A dead body."

And I say, I thought so.

Into the phone, she says, "Now, was that a left or right turn at the rosewood Hepplewhite dresser carved with anthemion details and flocked with powdered silk?"

She puts her hand over the phone and leans closer to me, saying, "You don't know Mona." She says, "I doubt if her little witch party means anything more than a mob of hippies dancing naked around a flat rock."

This close, her hair isn't a solid color of pink. Each curl is lighter pink along the outside edge, with blush, peach, rose,

115

almost red, as you look deeper inside.

Into the phone, she says, "And if I pass the Cromwellian satinwood lolling chair with ivory escutcheons, then I've gone too far. Got it."

To me, she says, "Lord, I wish you'd never told Mona. Mona will tell her boyfriend, and now I'll never hear the end of it."

The labyrinth of furniture crowds around us, all browns, reds, and black. Gilt and mirrors here and there.

With one hand, she fingers the diamond solitaire on her other hand. The diamond chunky and sharp. She twists it around so the diamond rises over her palm, and she presses her open palm on the face of the armoire and gouges an arrow pointing left.

Blazing a trail through history.

Into the phone, she says, "Thank you so much." She flips it shut and snaps it inside her purse.

The beads around her neck are some green stone, alternating with beads made of gold. Under these are strands of pearls. None of this jewelry I've ever seen before.

She steps back into her shoes and says, "From now on, I can see my job is going to be keeping you and Mona apart."

She fluffs the pink hair over her ear and

says, "Follow me."

With her flat open hand, she gouges an arrow across the top of a table. A limned-oak Sheraton gateleg card table with a brass filigree railing, it says on the note card.

A cripple now.

Leading the way, Helen Hoover Boyle says, "I wish you'd let this whole issue drop." She says, "It really is no concern of yours."

Because I'm just a reporter, is what she means. Because I'm a reporter tracking down a story he can't ever risk telling the world. Because at best, this makes me a voyeur. At worst, a vulture.

She stops in front of a huge wardrobe with mirrored doors, and from behind her I can see myself reflected just over her shoulder. She snaps open her purse and takes out a small gold tube. "That's exactly what I mean," she says.

The note card says it's French Egyptian Revival with panels of papier-mâché palmette detailing and festooned with polychromed strapwork.

In the mirror, she twists the gold tube until a pink lipstick grows out.

And behind her, I say, what if I'm not just my job?

117

Maybe I'm not just some two-dimensional predator taking advantage of an interesting situation.

For whatever reason, Nash comes to mind.

I say, maybe I noticed the book in the first place because I used to have a copy. Maybe I used to have a wife and a daughter. What if I read the damn poem to my own family one night with the intention of putting them to sleep? Hypothetically speaking, of course, what if I killed them? I say. Is that the kind of credentials she's looking for?

She stretches her lips up and down and touches the lipstick to the pink lipstick already there.

I limp a step closer, asking, does that make me wounded enough in her book?

Her shoulders squared straight across, she rolls her lips together. They come apart slow, stuck together for the last moment.

God forbid anybody should ever suffer more than Helen Hoover Boyle.

And I say, maybe I've lost every bit as much as her.

And she twists her lipstick down. She snaps her lipstick in her purse and turns to face me.

Standing there, glittering and still, she says, "Hypothetically speaking?"

And I pull my face into a smile and say, of course.

With her open hand against the armoire, she gouges an arrow pointing right, and she starts walking, but slow, dragging her hand along the wall of cupboards and dressers, everything waxed and polished, ruining everything she touches.

Leading me on, she says, "Do you ever wonder where that poem originated?"

Africa, I say, staying right behind her.

"But the book it came from," she says. Walking, past gun cabinets and press cupboards and farthingale chairs, she says, "Witches call their collection of spells their Book of Shadows."

Poems and Rhymes from Around the World was published eleven years ago, I tell her. I did some calling around. The book had a pressrun of five hundred copies. The publisher, KinderHaus Press, has since gone bankrupt, and the press plates and reprint rights belong to someone who bought them from the original author's estate. The author died of no apparent cause about three years ago. If that makes the book public domain, I don't know. I couldn't find out who now owns the rights.

And Helen Hoover Boyle stops dragging her diamond, midway across the face of a wide, beveled mirror, and says, "I own the rights. And I know where you're going with this. I bought the rights three years ago. Book dealers have managed to find about three hundred of those original five hundred books, and I've burned every one."

She says, "But that's not what's important."

I agree. What's important is finding the last few books, and containing this disaster. Doing damage control. What's important is learning a way to forget it ourselves. Maybe that's what Mona Sabbat and her group can teach us.

"Please," Helen says, "you're not still planning to go to her witch party?" She says, "What did you find out about the original author of the book?"

His name was Basil Frankie, and there was nothing original about him. He found out-of-print, public domain stories and combined them to create anthologies. Old medieval sonnets, bawdy limericks, nursery rhymes. Some of it he ripped out of old books he found. Some of it he lifted off the Internet. He wasn't very choosy. Anything he could get for free he'd lump into a book.

"But the source of this particular poem?" she says.

I don't know. It's probably some old book still packed in a box in the basement of a house somewhere.

"Not Frankie's house," says Helen Hoover Boyle. "I bought the whole estate. The kitchen trash was still under his sink, his underwear still folded in his dresser drawers, everything. It wasn't there."

And I have to ask, did she also kill him?

"Hypothetically speaking," she says, "if I had just killed my husband, after killing my son, wouldn't I be a little angry that some plagiarizing, lazy, irresponsible, greedy fool had planted the bomb that would destroy everyone I loved?"

Just like she hypothetically killed the Stuarts.

She says, "My point is that original Book of Shadows is still out there somewhere."

I agree. And we need to find it and destroy it.

And Helen Hoover Boyle smiles her pink smile. She says, "You must be kidding." She says, "Having the power of life and death isn't enough. You must wonder what other poems are in that book."

Hitting me as fast as a hiccup, me resting my weight on my good foot, just staring at her, I say no.

She says, "Maybe you can live forever."

And I say no.

And she says, "Maybe you can make anyone love you."

No.

And she says, "Maybe you can turn straw into gold."

And I say no and turn on my heel.

"Maybe you could bring about world peace," she says.

And I say no and start off between the walls of armoires and bookcases. Between the barricades of curio cabinets and headboards, I head down another canyon of furniture.

Behind me, she calls, "Maybe you could turn sand into bread."

And I keep limping along.

And she calls, "Where are you going? This is the way out."

At an Irish pine vitrine with a broken pediment tympanum, I turn right. At a Chippendale bureau cabinet japanned in black lacquer, I turn left.

Her voice behind everything says, "Maybe you could cure the sick. Maybe you could heal the crippled."

At a Belgian sideboard with a cornice of egg and dart molding, I turn right then left at an Edwardian standing specimen case with a Bohemian art-glass mural.

And the voice coming after me says, "Maybe you could clean the environment and turn the world into a paradise."

An arrow gouged in a piecrust occasional table points one way so I go the other.

And the voice says, maybe you could generate unlimited clean energy.

Maybe you could travel through time to prevent tragedy. To learn. To meet people.

Maybe you could give people rich full happy lives.

Maybe limping around a noisy apartment for the rest of your life isn't enough.

On a folding screen of blackwork embroidery, an arrow points one way, and I turn the other.

My pager goes off again, and it's Nash.

And the voice says, if you can kill someone, maybe you can bring them back.

Maybe this is my second chance.

The voice says, maybe you don't go to hell for the things you do. Maybe you go to hell for the things you don't do. The things you don't finish.

My pager goes off again, and it says the message is important.

And I keep on limping along.

Chapter 16

Nash isn't standing at the bar. He's sitting alone at a little table in the back, in the dark except for a little candle on the table, and I tell him, hey, I got his ten thousand calls on my pager. I ask, what's so important?

On the table is a newspaper, folded, with the headline saying:

Seven Dead in Mystery Plague

The subhead says:

Esteemed Local Editor and Public Leader Believed to Be First Victim

Whom they mean, I have to read. It's Duncan, and it turns out his first name was Leslie. It's anybody's guess where they got the *esteemed* part. And the *leader* part.

So much for the journalist and the news being mutually exclusive.

Nash taps the newspaper with his finger and says, "You see this?"

And I tell him I've been out of the office

all afternoon. And damn it. I forgot to file my next installment on crib death. Reading the front page, I see myself quoted. Duncan was more than just my editor, I'm saying, more than just my mentor. Leslie Duncan was like a father to me. Damn Oliphant and his sweaty hands.

Hitting me as fast as a chill, chilling me all down my back, the culling song spins through my head, and the body count grows. Somewhere, Oliphant must be sliding to the floor or toppling out of his chair. All my powder keg rage issues, they strike again.

The more people die, the more things stay the same.

An empty paper plate sits in front of Nash with just some waxed paper and yellow smears of potato salad on it, and Nash is twisting a paper napkin between his hands, twisting it into a long, thick cord, and, looking at me across the candle from him, he says, "We picked up the guy in your apartment building this afternoon." He says, "Between the guy's cats and the cockroaches, there's not much to autopsy."

The guy we saw fall down in here this morning, the sideburns guy with the cell phone, Nash says the medical examiner's stumped. Plus after that, three people dropped dead between here and the news-paper building.

"Then they found another one in the newspaper building," he says. "Died waiting for an elevator."

He says the medical examiner thinks these folks could all be dead of the same cause. They're saying plague, Nash says.

"But the police are really thinking drugs," he says. "Probably succinylcholine, either self-administered or somebody gave them an injection. It's a neuromuscular blocking agent. It relaxes you so much you quit breathing and die of anoxia."

The woman, the one behind the barri-cade at the movie shoot who came running with her arm out to stop me, the one with the walkie-talkie, the details of her were long black hair, a tight T-shirt over right-up tits. She had a decent little pooper in tight jeans. It could be she and Nash took the scenic route back to the hospital.

Another conquest.

Whatever Nash is so hot to tell me, I don't want to know.

He says, "But I think the police are wrong."

Nash whips the rolled paper napkin through the candle flame, and the flame jumps, stuttering up a curl of black smoke.

The flame goes back to normal, and Nash says, "In case you want to take care of me the same's you took care of those other people," he says, "you have to know I wrote a letter explaining all this, and I left it with a friend, saying what I know at this point."

And I smile and ask what he means. What does he know?

And Nash holds the tip of his twisted paper a little over the candle flame and says, "I know you thought your neighbor was dead. I know I saw a guy drop dead in this bar with you looking at him, and four more died when you walked past them on your way back to work."

The tip of the paper's getting brown, and Nash says, "Granted, it's not much, but it's more than the police have right now."

The tip puffs into flame, just a tiny flame, and Nash says, "Maybe you can fill the police in on the rest of it."

The flame's getting bigger. There's people enough here that somebody's going to notice. Nash sitting here, setting fires in a bar, people are going to call the police.

And I say he's deluded.

The little torch is getting bigger.

The bartender looks over at us, at Nash's little fuse burning shorter and shorter.

Nash just watches the fire in his hand growing out of control.

The heat of it on my lips, the smoke in my eyes.

The bartender yells, "Hey! Quit screwing around!"

And Nash moves the burning napkin toward the waxed paper and paper plate on the table.

And I grab his wrist, his uniform cuff smeared yellow with mustard, and his skin underneath loose and soft, and I tell him, okay. I say, just stop, okay?

I say he has to promise never to tell.

And with the fuse still burning between us, Nash says, "Sure." He says, "I promise."

Chapter 17

Helen walks up with a wineglass in her hand, just a glimpse of red in the bottom, the glass almost empty.

And Mona says, "Where'd you get that?"

"My drink?" Helen says. She's wearing a thick coat made of some fur in different shades of brown with white on each tip. It's open in the front with a powder-blue suit underneath. She sips the last of the wine and says, "I got it off the bar. Over there, next to the bowl of oranges and that little brass statue."

And Mona digs both hands into her own red and black dreadlocks and squeezes the top of her head. She says, "That's the *altar.*" She points to the empty glass and says, "You just drank my sacrifice to *The Goddess.*"

Helen presses the empty glass into Mona's hand and says, "Well, how about you get *The Goddess* another sacrifice, but make it a double this time."

We're in Mona's apartment, where all the furniture is pushed out onto a little patio behind sliding glass doors and covered with a blue plastic tarp. All that's left is the empty living room with a little room branching off one side where the dinette set should be. The walls and shag carpet are beige. The bowl of oranges and the brass statue of somebody Hindu, dancing, they're on the fireplace mantel with yellow daisies and pink carnations scattered around them. The light switches are taped over with masking tape so you can't use them. Instead, Mona's got some flat rocks on the floor with candles set on them, purple and white candles, some lit, some not. In the fireplace, instead of a fire, more candles are burning. Strands of white smoke drift up from little cones of brown incense set on the flat rocks with the candles.

The only real light is when Mona opens the refrigerator or the microwave oven.

Through the walls come horses screaming and cannon fire. Either a brave, stubborn southern belle is trying to keep the Union army from burning the apartment next door, or somebody's television is too loud.

Down through the ceiling comes a fire siren and people screaming that we're supposed to ignore. Then gunshots and tires squealing, sounds we have to pretend are okay. They don't mean anything. It's just television. An explosion vibrates down from the upstairs. A woman begs someone not to rape her. It's not real. It's just a movie. We're the culture that cried wolf.

These drama-holics. These peace-ophobics.

With her black fingernails, Mona takes the empty wineglass, the lip smeared with Helen's pink lipstick, and she walks away barefoot, wearing a white terry-cloth bathrobe into the kitchen.

The doorbell rings.

Mona crosses back through the living room. Putting another glass of red wine on the mantel, she says, "Do not embarrass me in front of my coven," and she opens the door.

On the doorstep is a short woman wearing glasses with thick frames of black plastic. The woman's wearing oven mitts and holding a covered casserole dish in front of her.

I brought a deli take-out box of three-bean salad. Helen brought pasta from Chez Chef.

The glasses woman scrapes her clogs on the doormat. She looks at Helen and me and says, "Mulberry, you have guests."

And Mona conks herself in the temple with the heel of her hand and says, "That's me she means. That's my Wiccan name, I mean. Mulberry." She says, "Sparrow, this is Mr. Streator."

And Sparrow nods.

And Mona says, "And this is my boss —"

"Chinchilla," Helen says.

The microwave oven starts beeping, and Mona leads Sparrow into the kitchen. Helen goes to the mantel and takes a drink from the glass of wine.

The doorbell rings. And Mona calls from the kitchen for us to answer it.

This time, it's a kid with long blond hair and a red goatee, wearing gray sweatpants and a sweatshirt. He's carrying a Crock-Pot with a brown-glass lid. Something sticky and brown has boiled up around the lip, and the underside of the glass lid is fogged with condensation. He steps inside the door and hands the Crock-Pot to me. He kicks off tennis shoes and pulls the sweatshirt off over his head, his hair flying everywhere. He lays the shirt on top of the Crock-Pot in my hands and lifts his leg to pull first one leg then the other leg out of his sweatpants. He puts the pants in my arms, and he's standing here, hands on his hips, dick-and-balls naked.

Helen pulls the front of her coat shut and throws back the last of the wine.

The Crock-Pot is heavy and hot with the smell of brown sugar and either tofu or the dirty gray sweatpants.

And Mona says, "Oyster!" and she's standing beside us. She takes the clothes and the Crock-Pot from me, saying, "Oyster, this is Mr. Streator." She says, "Everybody, this is my boyfriend, Oyster."

And the kid shakes the hair off his eyes and looks at me. He says, "Mulberry thinks you have a culling poem." His dick tapers to a dribbling pink stalactite of wrinkled foreskin. A silver ring pierces the tip.

And Helen gives me a look, smiling but with her teeth clenched.

This kid, Oyster, grabs the terry-cloth lapels of Mona's bathrobe and says, "Jeez, you have a lot of clothes on." He leans into her and kisses her over the Crock-Pot.

"We do ritual nudity," Mona says, looking at the floor. She blushes and motions with the Crock-Pot, saying, "Oyster? This is Mrs. Boyle, who I work for."

The details about Oyster are his hair, it looks shattered, the way a pine tree looks struck by lightning, splintered blond and standing up in every direction. He's got one of those young bodies. The arms and legs look segmented, big with muscles, then narrow at the joints, the knees and elbows and waist.

Helen holds out her hand, and Oyster takes it, saying, "A peridot ring . . ."

Standing there naked and young, he lifts Helen's hand all the way to his face. Standing there all tan and muscled, he looks from her ring, down the length of her arm, to her eyes and says, "A stone this passionate would overpower most people." And he kisses it.

"We do ritual nudity," Mona says, "but you don't have to. I mean you *really* don't have to." She nods toward the kitchen and says, "Oyster, come help me for a little."

And going, Oyster looks at me and says, "Clothing is dishonesty in its purest form." He smiles with just half his mouth, winks, and says, "Nice tie, Dad."

And I'm counting 1, counting 2, counting 3 . . .

After Mona's gone into the kitchen, Helen turns to me and says, "I can't believe you told another person."

She means Nash.

It wasn't as if I had a choice. Besides, no copies of the poem are available. I told him I burned mine, and I've burned every copy

I found in print. He doesn't know about Helen Hoover Boyle or Mona Sabbat. There's no way he can use the information.

Okay, so there are still a few dozen copies in public libraries. Maybe we can track them down and eliminate page 27 while we hunt for the original source material.

"The Book of Shadows," Helen says.

The grimoire, as witches call it. The book of spells. All the power in the world.

The doorbell rings, and the next man drops his baggy shorts and peels off his T-shirt and tells us his name is Hedgehog. The details about Hedgehog include the empty skin shaking on his arms and chest and ass. His curly black pubic hair matches the couple of hairs stuck to my palm after we shake hands.

Helen's hands draw up inside the cuffs of her coat sleeves, and she goes to the mantel, takes an orange from the altar, and starts to peel it.

A man named Badger with a real parrot on one shoulder arrives. A woman named Clematis arrives. A Lobelia arrives. A Bluebird rings the doorbell. Then a Possum. Then someone named Lentils arrives, or someone brings lentils, it's not clear which.

Helen drinks another sacrifice. Mona comes out of the kitchen with Oyster, but without her bathrobe.

What's left is a pile of dirty clothes inside the front door, and Helen and I are the only ones still dressed. Deep in the pile a phone rings, and Sparrow digs it out. Wearing just her blackframed glasses, her breasts hanging as she leans over the pile, Sparrow answers the phone, "Dormer, Dingus and Diggs, Attorneys-at-Law . . ." She says, "Describe the rash, please."

It takes a minute to recognize Mona from just her head and the pile of chains around her neck. You don't want to get caught looking anywhere else, but her pubic hair is shaved. From straight on, her thighs are two perfect parentheses with her shaved V between them. From the side, her breasts seem to reach out, trying to touch people with her pink nipples. From behind, the small of her back splits into her two solid buttocks, and I'm counting 4, counting 5, counting 6 . . .

Oyster's carrying a white deli take-out carton.

A woman named Honeysuckle in just a calico head wrap talks about her past lives.

And Helen says, "Doesn't reincarnation

strike you as just another form of procrastination?"

I ask, when do we eat?

And Mona says, "Jeez, you sound just like my father."

I ask Helen how she keeps from killing everybody here.

And she takes another glass of wine off the mantel, saying, "Anybody in this room, and it would be a mercy killing." She drinks half and gives the rest to me.

The incense smells like jasmine, and everything in the room smells like the incense.

Oyster steps to the center of the room and holds the deli carton over his head and says, "Okay, who brought this abortion?"

It's my three-bean salad.

And Mona says, "Please, Oyster, don't."

And holding the deli carton by its little wire handle, the handle pinched between just two fingers, Oyster says, " 'Meat-free' means no meat. Now fess up. Who brought this?" The hair under his raised arm is bright orange. So is his other body hair, down below.

I say, it's just bean salad.

"With?" Oyster says, and jiggles the carton.

With nothing.

The room's so quiet you can hear the Battle of Gettysburg next door. You can hear the folk song guitar of somebody depressed in the apartment upstairs. An actor screams and a lion roars and bombs whistle down from the sky.

"With Worcestershire sauce in the dressing," Oyster says. "That means anchovies. That means meat. That means cruelty and death." He holds the carton in one hand and points at it with his other, saying, "This is going down the toilet where it belongs."

And I'm counting 7, counting 8 . . .

Sparrow is giving everyone small round stones out of a basket she carries in one hand. She gives one to me. It's gray and cold, and she says, "Hold on to this, and tune to the vibration of its energy. This will put us all on the same vibration for the ritual."

You hear the toilet flush.

The parrot on Badger's shoulder keeps twisting its head around and yanking out green feathers with its beak. Then the bird tilts its head back and gulps each feather in jerking, whiplash bites. Where the feathers are gone, plucked, the skin looks dimpled and raw. The man, Badger, has a folded towel thrown over his shoulder for the parrot to grip, and the towel is spotted down the back with yellowy bird shit. The bird yanks another feather and eats it.

Sparrow gives a stone to Helen, and she snaps it into her powder-blue handbag.

I take the wineglass from her and sip it. In the newspaper today, it says how the man at the elevator, the man I wished to death, he had three children, all under six years old. The cop I killed was supporting his elderly parents so they wouldn't be placed in a nursing home. He and his wife were foster parents. He coached Little League and soccer. The woman with the walkie-talkie, she was two weeks pregnant.

I drink more of the wine. It tastes like pink lipstick.

In the newspaper today is an ad that says:

Attention Owners of Dorsett Fine China

The ad copy says: "If you feel nauseated or lose bowel control after eating, please call the following number."

To me, Oyster says, "Mulberry thinks you killed Dr. Sara, but I don't think you know jack shit."

Mona reaches up to put another sacrifice

on the mantel and Helen lifts the glass out of her fingers.

To me, Oyster says, "The only power of life and death you have is every time you order a hamburger at McDonald's." His face stuck in my face, he says, "You just pay your filthy money, and somewhere else, the ax falls."

And I'm counting 9, counting 10 . . .

Sparrow shows me a thick manual open in her hands. Inside are pictures of wands and iron pots. There are pictures of bells and quartz crystals, different colors and sizes of everything. There are black-handled knives, called *athame*. Sparrow says this so it rhymes with "whammy." She shows me photos of herbs, bundled so you can use them to sprinkle purification water. She shows me amulets, polished to deflect negative energy. A white-handled ritual knife is called a *bolline*.

Her breasts rest on the open catalog, covering half of each page.

Standing next to me, the muscles jumping in his neck, making fists with both hands, Oyster says, "Do you know why most survivors of the Holocaust are vegan? It's because they know what it's like to be treated like an animal."

The body heat coming off him, he says,

"In egg production, did you know all the male chicks are ground up alive and spread as fertilizer?"

Sparrow flips through her catalog and points at something, saying, "If you check around, you'll find we offer the best deals for ritual tools in the medium price range."

The next sacrifice to *The Goddess*, I drink.

The one after that, Helen downs.

Oyster circles the room. He comes back to say, "Did you know that most pigs don't bleed to death in the few seconds before they're drowned in scalding, hundred-and-forty-degree water?"

The sacrifice after that, I get. The wine tastes like jasmine incense. The wine tastes like animal blood.

Helen takes the empty wineglass into the kitchen, and there's a flash of real light as she opens the refrigerator and takes out a jug of red wine.

And Oyster sticks his chin over my shoulder from behind and says, "Most cows don't die right away." He says, "They put a snare around the cow's neck and drag it screaming through the slaughterhouse, cutting off the front and back legs while it's still alive."

Behind him is a naked girl named Starfish, who flips open a cell phone and says, "Dooley, Donner and Dunne, Attorneys-at-Law." She says, "Tell me, what color is your fungus?"

Badger comes out of the bathroom, ducking to get his parrot through the doorway, a shred of paper stuck in his butt crack. Naked, his skin looks dimpled and raw. Plucked. If the bird sits on his shoulder while he sits on the toilet, I don't want to know.

And across the room is Mona.

Mulberry.

She's laughing with Honeysuckle. She's pinned her red and black dreadlocks up into a pile with just her little face sticking out the bottom. On her fingers are rings with heavy red-glass jewels. Around her neck, the carpet of silver chains comes down to a pile of amulets and pendants and charms on her breasts. Costume jewelry. A little girl playing dress-up. Barefoot.

She's the age my daughter would be, if I still had a daughter.

Helen stumbles back into the room. She pinches her tongue between two fingers and then goes around the room, using the two wet fingers to pinch out the cones of incense. She leans back against the fire-place mantel and lifts the glass of wine to her pink mouth. Over the glass, she watches the room. She watches Oyster circling me.

He's the age her son, Patrick, would be.

Helen's the age my wife would be, if I had a wife.

Oyster's the son she would have, if she had a son.

Hypothetically speaking, of course.

This might be the life I had, if I had a life. My wife distant and drunk. My daughter exploring some crackpot cult. Embarrassed by us, her parents. Her boyfriend would be this hippie asshole, trying to pick a fight with me, her dad.

And maybe you can go back in time.

Maybe you can raise the dead. All the dead, past and present.

Maybe this is my second chance. This is exactly the way my life might have turned out.

Helen in her chinchilla coat is watching the parrot eat itself. She's watching Oyster.

And Mona's shouting, "Everybody. Everybody." She's saying, "It's time to start the Invocation. So if we could just create the sacred space, we can get started."

Next door, the Civil War veterans are

limping home to sad music and Reconstruction.

With Oyster circling me, the rock in my fist is warm by now. And I'm counting 11, counting 12 . . .

Mona Sabbat has got to come with us. Someone without blood on her hands. Mona and Helen and me, and Oyster, the four of us will hit the road together. Just another dysfunctional family. A family vacation. The quest for an unholy grail.

With a hundred paper tigers to slay along the way. A hundred libraries to plunder. Books to disarm. The whole world to save from culling.

Lobelia says to Grenadine, "Did you read about those dead people in the paper? They say it's like Legionnaires' disease, but it looks like black magic, if you ask me."

And with her arms spread, the plain brown hair under her arms showing, Mona is herding people into the center of the room.

Sparrow points at something in her catalog and says, "This is the minimum you'll need to get started."

Oyster shakes the hair off his eyes and sticks his chin at me. He comes around to poke his index finger into my chest, poking it there, hard, pinned in the middle of my blue tie, and he says, "Listen, Dad." Poking me, he says, "The only culling song you know is 'Make mine medium-well done.' "

And I stop counting.

Fast as a muscle twitch, muscling Oyster back, I shove hard and slap the kid away, my hands loud against the kid's bare skin, everybody quiet and watching, and the culling song echoes through my head.

And I've killed again. Mona's boyfriend. Helen's son. Oyster stands there another moment, looking at me, the hair hanging over his eyes.

And the parrot falls off Badger's shoulder.

Oyster puts his hands up, fingers spread, and says, "Chill out, Dad," and goes with Sparrow and everybody to look at the parrot, dead, at Badger's feet. Dead and plucked half naked. And Badger prods the bird with his sandal and says, "Plucky?"

I look at Helen.

My wife. In this new creepy way. Till death do us part.

And maybe, if you can kill someone, maybe you can bring them back.

And Helen's already looking at me, the smeared-pink glass in her hand. She shakes

her face at me and says, "I didn't do it."
She holds up three fingers, her thumb and
pinkie touching in front, and says,
"Witch's honor. I swear."

Chapter 18

Here and now, me writing this, I'm near Biggs Junction, Oregon. Parked alongside Interstate 84, the Sarge and me have an old fur coat heaped on the shoulder of the road next to our car. The fur coat, spattered with ketchup, circled by flies, it's our bait.

This week, there's another miracle in the tabloids.

It's something folks call the Roadkill Jesus Christ. The tabloids call him "The I-84 Messiah." Some guy who stops along the highway, wherever there's a dead animal, he lays his hands on it, and Amen. The ragged cat or crushed dog, even a deer folded in half by a tractor-trailer, they gasp and sniff the air. They stand on their broken legs and blink their bird-pecked eyes.

Folks have this on video. They have snapshots posted on the Internet.

The cat or porcupine or coyote, it'll stand there another minute, the Roadkill Christ cradling its head in his arms, whispering to it.

Two minutes after it was shredded fur and bones, a meal for magpies and crows, the deer or dog or raccoon will run away complete, restored, perfect.

The Sarge and me, a ways down the highway from us, an old man pulls his pickup truck off the road. He gets out of the cab and lifts a plaid blanket out of the bed of the truck. He squats to lay the blanket on the side of the road, traffic blasting past him in the hot morning air.

The old man picks at the edges of the plaid blanket to uncover a dead dog. A wrinkled heap of brown fur, not too much different than my heap of fur coat.

The Sarge snaps the clip out of his pistol, and it's full of bullets. He snaps the clip back home.

The old man leans down, both his hands flat open on the hot asphalt, cars and trucks blasting past in both directions, and he rubs his cheek against the pile of brown fur.

He stands and looks up and down the highway. He gets back into the cab of his pickup and lights a cigarette. He waits.

The Sarge and I, we wait.

Here we are, a week late. Always one step behind. After the fact.

The first sighting of the Roadkill Christ, it was a crew of state workers shoveling up a dead dog a few miles from here. Before they could get it bagged, a rental car pulled over on the highway shoulder behind them. It was a man and a woman, the man driving. The woman stayed in the car, and the man jumped out and ran up to the road crew. He shouted for them to wait. He said he could help.

The dog was just maggots and bones inside a scrap of fur.

The man was young, blond, with his long blond hair whipping in the wind from cars blasting past them. He had a red goatee and scars cut sideways across both cheeks, just under his eyes. The scars were dark red, and the young man reached into the garbage bag with the dead dog and told the crew — it wasn't dead.

And the road crew laughed. They threw their shovel into their truck.

And something inside the garbage bag whimpered.

It barked.

Now, here and now, while I write this, while the old man waits down the road from us, smoking. The traffic blasting past. On the other side of Interstate 84, a family in a station wagon opens a quilt on the gravel shoulder of the road, and inside is a dead orange cat. A ways from them, a woman and a child sit in lawn chairs next to a hamster on a paper towel.

A ways from them, an older couple stands

holding an umbrella to shade a young woman, the young woman bony and twisted sideways in a wheelchair.

The old man, the mother and child, the family and older couple, their eyes scan every car as it goes past.

The Roadkill Christ appears in a different car every time, a two-door or a four-door or a pickup, sometimes on a motorcycle. Once in a motor home.

In the snapshots people take, in the videos, it's always the flying blond hair, the red goatee, the scars. It's always the same man. The outline of a woman waits in the distance in a car, truck, whatever.

While I'm writing this, the Sarge sights down the barrel of his pistol at our pile of fur coat. The ketchup and flies. Our bait. And like everyone else here, we're waiting for a miracle. For a messiah.

Chapter 19

Everywhere outside the car it was yellow. Yellow to the horizon. Not a lemon yellow, more a tennis-ball yellow. It was the way the ball looks on a bright green tennis court. The world on both sides of the highway, all this one color.

Yellow.

Billowing, foaming big waves of yellow move in the hot wind from the cars going past, spreading from the highway's gravel shoulder to the yellow hills. Yellow. Throwing yellow light into our car. Helen, Mona, Oyster, me, all of us. Our skin and eyes. The details of the whole world. Yellow.

"*Brassica tournefortii*," Oyster says, "Moroccan mustard in full bloom."

We're in the leather smell of Helen's big Realtor car with her driving. Helen and I sit up front, Oyster and Mona in the back. On the seat between Helen and me is her daily planner book, the red leather binding sticking to the brown leather seat. There's an atlas of the United States. There's a computer printout of cities with libraries that have the poems book. There's Helen's little blue purse, looking green in the yellow light.

"What I'd give to be a Native American," Mona says, and leans her forehead against the window, "to just be a free Blackfoot or Sioux two hundred years ago, you know, just living in harmony with all that natural beauty."

To see what Mona's feeling, I put my forehead against my window. Against the air-conditioning, the glass is blazing hot.

Creepy coincidence, but the atlas shows the entire state of California colored this same bright yellow.

And Oyster blows out his nose, one quick snort that rocks his head back. He shakes his face at Mona and says, "No Indian ever lived with *that*."

The cowboys didn't have tumbleweeds, he says. It wasn't until the late nineteenth century that tumbleweed seeds, Russian thistles, came over from Eurasia in the wool of sheep. Moroccan mustard came over in the dirt that sailing ships used for ballast. The silver trees out there, those are Russian olives, *Elaeagnus augustifolia*. The hundreds of white fuzzy rabbit ears growing along the highway shoulder are *Verbascum thapsus*, woolly mulleins. The twisted dark trees we just passed, *Robinia pseudoacacia,* black locust. The dark green brush flowering bright yellow is Scotch broom, *Cytisus scoparius.*

They're all part of a biological pandemic, he says.

"Those old Hollywood westerns," Oyster says, looking out the window at Nevada next to the highway, he says, "with the tumbleweeds and cheatgrass and shit?" He shakes his head and says, "None of this is native, but it's all we have left." He says, "Almost nothing in nature is natural anymore."

Oyster kicks the back of the front seat and says, "Hey, Dad. What's the big daily newspaper in Nevada?"

Reno or Vegas? I say.

And looking out the window, the reflected light making his eyes yellow, Oyster says, "Both. Carson City, too. All of them."

And I tell him.

The forests along the West Coast are choked with Scotch broom and French broom and English ivy and Himalayan blackberries, he says. The native trees are dying from the gypsy moths imported in 1860 by Leopold Trouvelot, who wanted to breed them for silk. The deserts and prairies are choked with mustard and

153

cheatgrass and European beach grass.

Oyster fingers open the buttons on his shirt, and inside, against the skin of his chest, is a beaded something. It's the size of a wallet, hanging around his neck from a beaded string. "Hopi medicine bag," he says. "Pretty spiritual, huh?"

Helen, looking at him in the rearview mirror, her hands on the steering wheel in skintight calfskin driving gloves, she says, "Nice abs."

Oyster shrugs his shirt off his shoulders and the beaded bag hangs between his nipples, his chest pumped up on each side of it. The skin's tanned and hairless down to his navel. The bag's covered solid with blue beads except for a cross of red beads in the center. His tan looks orange in the yellow light. His blond hair looks on fire.

"I made it," Mona says. "It took me since last February."

Mona with her dreadlocks and crystal necklaces. I ask if she's a Hopi Indian.

With his fingers, Oyster fishes around inside the bag.

And Helen says, "Mona, you're not a native *anything*. Your real last name is Steinner."

"You don't have to be Hopi," Mona says. "I made it from a pattern in a book."

"Then it's not really a Hopi anything," Helen says.

And Mona says, "It is. It looks just like the one in the book." She says, "I'll show you."

From out of his little beaded bag, Oyster takes a cell phone.

"The fun part about primitive crafts is they're so easy to make while you watch TV," Mona says. "And they put you in touch with all sorts of ancient energies and stuff."

Oyster flips the phone open and pulls out the antenna. He punches in a number. A curve of dirt shows under his fingernail.

Helen watches him in the rearview mirror.

Mona leans forward over her knees and drags a canvas knapsack off the floor of the backseat. She takes out a tangle of cords and feathers. They look like chicken feathers, dyed bright Easter shades of pink and blue. Brass coins and beads made of black glass hang on the cords. "This is a Navajo dream catcher I'm making," she says. She shakes it, and some of the cords come untangled and hang loose. Some beads fall into the knapsack in her lap. Pink feathers float loose in the air, and she says, "I thought to make it more powerful

155

by using some I Ching coins. To sort of superenergize it."

Somewhere under the knapsack, in her lap, the shaved V between her thighs. The glass beads roll there.

Into the phone, Oyster says, "Yeah, I need the number for the retail display advertising department at the *Carson City Telegraph-Star*." A pink feather drifts near his face, and he blows it away.

With her black-painted fingernails, Mona picks at some of the knots, saying, "It's harder than the book makes it look."

Oyster's one hand holds the phone to his ear. His other hand rubs the beaded bag around his chest.

Mona pulls a book out of her canvas knapsack and passes it to me in the front seat.

Oyster sees Helen, still watching him in the rearview mirror, and he winks at her and tweaks his nipple.

For whatever reason, Oedipus Rex comes to mind.

Somewhere below his belt, the pointed pink stalactite of his foreskin, pierced with its little steel ring. How could Helen want that?

"Old-time ranchers planted cheatgrass because it would green up fast in the spring and provide early forage for grazing cattle," Oyster says, nodding his head at the world outside.

This first patch of cheatgrass was in southern British Columbia, Canada, in 1889. But fire spreads it. Every year, it dries to gunpowder, and now land that used to burn every ten years, it burns every year. And the cheatgrass recovers fast. Cheatgrass loves fire. But the native plants, the sagebrush and desert phlox, they don't. And every year it burns, there's more cheatgrass and less anything else. And the deer and antelope that depended on those other plants are gone now. So are the rabbits. So are the hawks and owls that ate the rabbits. The mice starve, so the snakes that ate the mice starve.

Today, cheatgrass dominates the inland deserts from Canada to Nevada, covering an area over twice the size of the state of Nebraska and spreading by thousands of acres per year.

The big irony is, even cattle hate cheatgrass, Oyster says. So the cows, they eat the rare native bunch grasses. What's left of them.

Mona's book is called *Traditional Tribal Hobby-Krafts*. When I open it, more pink and blue feathers drift out.

"Now, my new life's dream is I want to find a really straight tree, you know," Mona says, a pink feather caught in her dreadlocks, "and make a totem pole or something."

"When you think about it from a native plant perspective," Oyster says, "Johnny Appleseed was a fucking biological terrorist."

Johnny Appleseed, he says, might as well be handing out smallpox.

Oyster's punching another number on his cell phone. He kicks the back of the front seat and says, "Mom, Dad? What's a really posh restaurant in Reno, Nevada?"

And Helen shrugs and looks at me. She says, "The Desert Sky Supper Club in Tahoe is very nice."

Into his cell phone, Oyster says, "I'd like to place a three-column display ad." Looking out the window, he says, "It should be three columns by six inches deep, and the top line of copy should read, 'Attention Patrons of the Desert Sky Supper Club'."

Oyster says, "The second line should say, 'Have you recently contracted a near-fatal case of campylobacter food poisoning? If so, please call the following number to be part of a class-action lawsuit.'"

Then Oyster gives a phone number. He fishes a credit card out of his medicine bag and reads the number and expiration date into the phone. He says for the account rep to call him after it's typeset and check the final ad copy over the phone. He says for the ad to run every day for the next week, in the restaurant section. He flips the phone shut and presses the antenna back inside.

"The way yellow fever and smallpox killed off your Native Americans," he says, "we brought Dutch elm disease to America in a shipment of logs for a veneer mill in 1930 and brought chestnut blight in 1904. Another pathogenic fungus is killing off the eastern beeches. The Asian long-horned beetle, introduced to New York in 1996, is expected to wipe out North American maples."

To control prairie dog populations, Oyster says, ranchers introduced bubonic plague to the prairie dog colonies, and by 1930, about 98 percent of the dogs were dead. The plague has spread to kill another thirty-four species of native rodents, and every year a few unlucky people.

For whatever reason, the culling song comes to mind.

"Me," Mona says as I pass her back the

book, "I like the ancient traditions. My hope is this trip will be, you know, like my own personal vision quest. And I'll come up with an Indian name and be," she says, "transformed."

Out of his Hopi bag, Oyster takes a cigarette and says, "You mind?"

And I tell him yes.

And Helen says, "Not at all." And it's her car.

And I'm counting 1, counting 2, counting 3 . . .

What we think of as nature, Oyster says, everything's just more of us killing the world. Every dandelion's a ticking atom bomb. Biological pollution. Pretty yellow devastation.

The way you can go to Paris or Beijing, Oyster says, and everywhere there's a McDonald's hamburger, this is the ecological equivalent of franchised life-forms. Every place is the same place. Kudzu. Zebra mussels. Water hyacinths. Starlings. Burger Kings.

The local natives, anything unique gets squeezed out.

"The only biodiversity we're going to have left," he says, "is Coke versus Pepsi."

He says, "We're landscaping the whole world one stupid mistake at a time."

Just staring out his window, Oyster takes a plastic cigarette lighter out of the beaded medicine bag. He shakes the lighter, smacking it against the palm of one hand.

A pink feather from the book, I sniff it and imagine Mona's hair has this same smell. Twirling the feather between two fingers, I ask Oyster, on the phone just now — his call to the newspaper — what he's up to.

Oyster lights his cigarette. He tucks the plastic lighter and the cell phone back in his medicine bag.

"It's how he makes money," Mona says. She's picking apart the tangles and knots in her dream catcher. Between her arms, inside her orange blouse, her breasts reach out with their little pink nipples.

And I'm counting 4, counting 5, counting 6 . . .

Both his hands buttoning his shirt, his mouth pinched around the cigarette, and his eyes squinting against the smoke, Oyster says, "Remember Johnny Apple-seed?"

Helen turns up the air-conditioning.

And buttoning his collar, Oyster says, "Don't worry, Dad. This is just me planting my seeds."

Looking out at all the yellow, with his yellow eyes, he says, "It's just my generation trying to destroy the existing culture by spreading our own contagion."

Chapter 20

The woman opens her front door, and here are Helen and I on her front porch, me carrying Helen's cosmetic case, standing a half-step behind her as Helen points the long pink nail of her index finger and says, "If you can give me fifteen minutes, I can give you a whole new you."

Helen's suit is red, but not a strawberry red. It's more the red of a strawberry mousse, topped with whipped crème fraîche and served in a stemmed crystal compote. Inside her pink cloud of hair, her earrings sparkle pink and red in the sunlight.

The woman's drying her hands in a kitchen towel. She's wearing men's brown moccasins with no socks. A bib apron patterned with little yellow chickens covers her whole front, and some kind of machine-washable dress underneath. With the back of one hand, she pushes some hair off her forehead. The yellow chickens are all holding kitchen tools, ladles and spoons, in their beaks. Looking at us through the rusted screen door, the woman says, "Yes?"

Helen looks back at me standing behind her. She looks back over her shoulder at Mona and Oyster ducked down, hiding in the car parked at the curb. Oyster whispering into his phone, "Is the itching constant or intermittent?"

Helen Hoover Boyle brings the fingertips of one hand together at her chest, the mess of pink gems and pearls hiding her silk blouse underneath. She says, "Mrs. Pelson? We're here from Miracle Makeover."

As she talks, Helen throws her closed hand open toward the woman, as if she's scattering the words.

Helen says, "My name is Mrs. Brenda Williams." With her pink fingertips, she scatters the words back over her shoulder, saying, "And this is my husband, Robert Williams." She says, "And we have a very special gift for you today."

The woman inside the screen door looks down at the cosmetic case in my hand.

And Helen says, "May we come in?"

It was supposed to be easier than this.

This whole traveling around, just dropping into libraries, taking a book off the shelf, sitting on a toilet in the library bathroom and cutting out the page. Then, flush. It was supposed to be that quick.

The first couple libraries, no problem. The next, the book isn't on the shelf. In library whispers, Mona and I go to the checkout desk and ask. Helen's waiting in the car with Oyster.

The librarian's a guy with his long straight hair pulled back in a ponytail. He's got earrings in both ears, pirate loop earrings, and he's wearing a plaid sweater vest and says the book is — he scrolls up and down his computer screen — the book is checked out.

"It's really important," Mona says. "I had it before that, and I left something between the pages."

Sorry, the guy says.

"Can you tell us who has it?" Mona says.

And the guy says, sorry. No can do.

And I'm counting 1, counting 2, counting 3 . . .

Sure, everybody wants to play God, but for me it's a full-time job.

I'm counting 4, counting 5 . . .

A beat later, Helen Hoover Boyle's standing at the checkout desk. She smiles until the librarian looks up from his computer, and she spreads her hands, her rings bright and crowded on each finger.

She smiles and says, "Young man? My daughter left an old family photograph between the pages of a certain book." She wiggles her fingers and says, "You can follow the rules, or you can do a good deed and take your pick."

The librarian watches her fingers, the prism colors and stars of broken light dancing across his face. He licks his lips. Then he shakes his head no and says it's just not worth it. The person with the book will complain and he'll get fired.

"We promise," Helen says, "we won't lose you your job."

In the car, I waiting with Mona, counting 27, counting 28, counting 29 . . . , trying the only way I know not to kill everybody in the library and look up the address on the computer myself.

Helen comes out to the car with a sheet of paper in her hand. She leans in the open driver's-side window and says, "Good news and bad news."

Mona and Oyster are lying across the backseat, and they sit up. I'm on the shotgun side of the front seat, counting.

And Mona says, "They have three copies, but they're all checked out."

And Helen gets in behind the steering

wheel and says, "I know a million ways to cold-call."

And Oyster shakes the hair off his eyes and says, "Good job, Mom."

The first house went easy enough. And the second.

In the car between house calls, Helen picks through the gold tubes and shiny boxes, her lipstick and makeup, her cosmetic case open in her lap. She twists a pink lipstick up and squints at it, saying, "I'm never using any of this again. If I'm not mistaken, that last woman had ringworm."

Mona leans forward from the backseat, looking over Helen's shoulder, and says, "You're really good at this."

Screwing open little round boxes of eye shadow, looking and sniffing at their tan or pink or peach insides, Helen says, "I've had a lot of practice."

She looks at herself in the rearview mirror and pulls around a few strands of pink hair. She looks at her watch, pinching the face between a thumb and index finger, and she says, "I shouldn't tell you this, but this was my first real job."

By now we're parked outside a rusted trailer house sitting in a square of dead grass scattered with children's plastic toys.

167

Helen snaps her case shut. She looks at me sitting beside her and says, "You ready to try it again?"

Inside the trailer, talking to the woman in the apron covered with little chickens, Helen's saying, "There's absolutely no cost or obligation on your part," and she backs the woman into the sofa.

Sitting across from the woman, the woman sitting so close their knees almost touch, Helen reaches toward her with a soft brush and says, "Suck in your cheeks, dear."

With one hand, she grabs a handful of the woman's hair and pulls it straight up into the air. The woman's hair is blond with an inch of brown at the roots. With her other hand, Helen runs a comb down the hair in fast strokes, holding the longer strands up, and crushing the shorter brown ones down against the scalp. She grabs another handful and rats, teases, back-combs until all but the longest hairs are crushed and tangled against the scalp. With the comb, she smooths the long blond strands over the ratted short hairs until the woman's head is a huge fluffed bubble of blond hair.

And I say, so *that's* how you do that.

It's identical to Helen's hairdo only blond.

On the coffee table in front of the sofa is a big arrangement of roses and lilies, but wilted and brown, the flowers standing in a green-glass vase from a florist, with only a little black water in the bottom. On the dinette table in the kitchen are more big flower arrangements, just dead stalks in thick, stinking water. Lined up on the floor, against the back wall of the living room are more vases, each holding a block of green foam pincushioned with curled, wasted roses or black, spindly carnations growing gray mold. Stuck in with each bouquet is a little card saying: *In Deepest Sympathy.*

And Helen says, "Now put your hands over your face," and she starts shaking a can of hair spray. She fogs the woman with hair spray.

The woman cowers blind, bent forward a little, with both hands pressed over her face.

And Helen jerks her head toward the rooms at the other end of the trailer.

And I go.

Pumping a mascara brush in its tube, she says, "You don't mind if my husband uses your bathroom, do you?" Helen says, "Now, look up at the ceiling, dear."

In the bathroom, there are dirty clothes

separated into different-colored piles on the floor. Whites. Darks. Somebody's jeans and shirts stained with oil. There's towels and sheets and bras. There's a red-checked tablecloth. I flush the toilet for the sound effect.

There's no diapers or children's clothes.

In the living room, the chicken woman is still looking at the ceiling, only now she's shaking with long, jerking breaths. Her chest, under the apron, shaking. Helen is touching the corner of a folded tissue to the watery makeup. The tissue is soaked and black with mascara, and Helen's saying, "It will be better someday, Rhonda. You can't see that, but it will." Folding another tissue and daubing, she says, "What you have to do is make yourself hard. Think of yourself as something hard and sharp."

She says, "You're still a young woman, Rhonda. You need to go back to school and turn this hurt into money."

The chicken woman, Rhonda, is still crying with her head tilted back, staring at the ceiling.

Behind the bathroom, there's two bedrooms. One has a water bed. In the other bedroom is a crib and a hanging mobile of plastic daisies. There's a chest of drawers painted white. The crib is empty. The little plastic mattress is tied in a roll at one end. Near the crib is a stack of books on a stool. *Poems and Rhymes* is on top.

When I put the book on the dresser, it falls open to page 27.

I run the point of a baby pin down the inside edge of the page, tight in next to the binding, and the page pulls out. With the page folded in my pocket, I put the book back on the stack.

In the living room, the cosmetics are dumped in a heap on the floor.

Helen's pulled a false bottom out of the inside of her cosmetic case. Inside are layered necklaces and bracelets, heavy brooches and pairs of earrings clipped together, all of them crusted and dazzling with shattered red and green, yellow and blue lights. Jewels. Draped between Helen's hands is a long necklace of yellow and red stones larger than her polished, pink fingernails.

"In brilliant-cut diamonds," she says, "look for no light leakage through the facets below the girdle of the stone." She lays the necklace in the woman's hands, saying, "In rubies — aluminum oxide — foreign bits inside, called rutile inclusions, can give the stone a soft pinkish look unless the jeweler bakes the stone under high heat."

The trick to forgetting the big picture is to look at everything close-up.

The two women sit so close, their knees dovetail together. Their heads almost touch. The chicken woman isn't crying.

The chicken woman is wearing a jeweler's loupe in one eye.

The dead flowers are shoved aside, and scattered on the coffee table are clusters of sparkling pink and smooth gold, cool white pearls and carved blue lapis lazuli. Other clusters glow orange and yellow. Other piles shine silver and white.

And Helen cups a blazing green egg in her hand, so bright both women look green in the reflected light, and she says, "Do you see the kind of uniform veil-like inclusions in a synthetic emerald?"

Her eye clenched around the loupe, the woman nods.

And Helen says, "Remember this, I don't want you to get burned the way I was." She reaches into the cosmetic case and lifts out a bright handful of yellow, saying, "This yellow sapphire brooch was owned by the movie star Natasha Wren." With both hands, she takes out a sparkling pink heart, trailing a long chain of smaller diamonds, saying, "This seven-hundred-carat beryl pendant was once owned by

Queen Marie of Romania."

In this heap of jewels, Helen Hoover Boyle would say, are the ghosts of everyone who has ever owned them. Everyone rich and successful enough to prove it. All of their talent and intelligence and beauty, outlived by decorative junk. All the success and accomplishment this jewelry was supposed to represent, it's all vanished.

With the same hairdo, the same makeup, leaning together so close, they could be sisters. They could be mother and daughter. Before and after. Past and future.

There's more, but that's when I go out to the car.

Sitting in the backseat, Mona says, "You find it?"

And I say yeah. Not that it does this woman any good.

The only thing we've given her is big hair and probably ringworm.

Oyster says, "Show us the song. Let's see what this trip is all about."

And I tell him, no fucking way. I tuck the folded page in my mouth and chew and chew. My foot aches, and I take off my shoe. I chew and chew. Mona falls asleep. I chew and chew. Oyster looks out the window at some weeds in a ditch.

I swallow the page, and I fall asleep.

173

Later, sitting in the car, driving to the next town, the next library, maybe the next makeover, I wake up and Helen has been driving for almost three hundred miles.

It's almost dark, and just looking out the windshield, she says, "I'm keeping track of expenses."

Mona sits up, scratching her scalp through her hair. She presses the finger next to her pinkie finger, she presses the pad of that finger into the inside corner of her eye and pulls it away, fast, with an eye goober stuck on it. She wipes the goober on her jeans and says, "Where are we going to eat?"

I tell Mona to buckle her seat belt.

Helen turns on the headlights. She opens one hand, wide, against the steering wheel and looks at the back of it, her rings, and says, "After we find the Book of Shadows, when we're the all-powerful leaders of the entire world, after we're immortal and we own everything on the planet and everyone loves us," she says, "you'll still owe me for two hundred dollars' worth of cosmetics."

She looks odd. Her hair looks wrong. It's her earrings, the heavy clumps of pink and red, pink sapphires and rubies. They're gone.

174

Chapter 21

This wasn't just one night. It just feels that way. This was every night, through Texas and Arizona, on into Nevada, cutting through California and up through Oregon, Washington, Idaho, Montana. Every night, driving in a car is the same. Wherever.

Every place is the same place in the dark.

"My son, Patrick, isn't dead," Helen Hoover Boyle says.

He's dead in the county medical records, but I don't say anything.

With Helen driving, Mona and Oyster are asleep in the backseat. Asleep or listening. I sit in the passenger side of the front seat. Leaning against my door, I'm as far from Helen as I can get. With my head pillowed on my arm, I'm where I can listen without looking at her.

And Helen talks to me without looking back. This is both of us looking straight ahead at the road in the headlights rushing under the hood of the car.

"Patrick's at the New Continuum Medical Center," she says. "And I fully believe that someday he'll make a complete recovery."

Her daily planner book, bound in red leather, is on the front seat between us.

Driving through North Dakota and Minnesota, I ask, how did she find the culling spell?

And with one pink fingernail, she pushes a button somewhere in the dark and puts the car in cruise control. With something else in the dark, she turns on the high-beam headlights.

"I used to be a client representative for Skin Tone Cosmetics," she says. "The trailer we lived in wasn't very nice." She says, "My husband and I."

His name is John Boyle in the county medical records.

"You know how it is with your first," she says. "People give you so many toys and books. I don't even know who actually brought the book. It was just a book in a pile of books."

According to the county, this must've been twenty years ago.

"You don't need me to tell you what happened," she says. "But John always thought it was my fault."

According to police records, there were

176

six domestic disturbance calls to the Boyle home, lot 176 at the Buena Noche Mobile Home Park, in the weeks following the death of Patrick Raymond Boyle, aged six months.

Driving through Wisconsin and Nebraska, Helen says, "I was going door-to-door, cold-calling for Skin Tone." She says, "I didn't go back to work right away. It must've been, God, a year and a half after Patrick's . . . after the morning we found Patrick."

She was walking around the trailer development where they lived, Helen tells me, and she met a young woman just like the woman wearing the apron patterned with little chickens. The same dead funeral flowers brought home from the mortuary. The same empty crib.

"I could make a lot of money just selling heavy foundation and cover-up," Helen says, smiling, "especially toward the end of the month, when money was tight."

Twenty years ago, this other woman was the same age as Helen, and while they talked, she showed Helen the nursery, the baby pictures. The woman's name was Cynthia Moore. She had a black eye.

"And I saw they had a copy of our same book," Helen says. *"Poems and Rhymes from*

Around the World."

These other people kept it open to the same page it was the night their child died. The book, the bedding in the crib, they were trying to keep everything the same.

"Of course it was the same page as our book," Helen says.

At home John Boyle was drinking a lot of beer every night. He said he didn't want to have another child because he didn't trust her. If she didn't know what she'd done wrong, it was too much of a risk.

With my hand on her heated leather seats, it feels as if I'm touching another person.

Driving through Colorado, Kansas, and Missouri, she says, "The other mother in the trailer park, one day there was a yard sale at their place. All their baby things, all folded in piles on the lawn, marked a quarter apiece. There was the book, and I bought it." Helen says, "I asked the man inside why Cindy was selling everything, and he just shrugged."

According to county medical records, Cynthia Moore drank liquid drain cleaner and died of esophageal hemorrhaging and asphyxiation three months after her child had died of no apparent cause.

"John was worried about germs so he'd

burned all of Patrick's things," she says. "I bought the book of poems for ten cents. I remember it was a beautiful day outside."

Police records show three more domestic disturbance calls to lot 175 at the Buena Noche Mobile Home Park. A week after Cynthia Moore's suicide, John Boyle was found dead of no apparent cause. According to the county, his high blood alcohol concentration might've caused sleep apnea. Another likely cause was positional asphyxiation. He may have been so drunk that he fell unconscious in a position that kept him from breathing. Either way, there were no marks on the body. There was no apparent cause of death on the death certificate.

Driving through Illinois, Indiana, and Ohio, Helen says, "Killing John wasn't anything I did on purpose." She says, "I was just curious."

The same as me and Duncan.

"I was just testing a theory," she says. "John kept saying that Patrick's ghost was with us. And I kept telling him that Patrick was still alive in the hospital."

Twenty years later, baby Patrick's still in the hospital, she says.

Crazy as this sounds, I don't say anything. How a baby must look after twenty years in a coma or on life support or whatever, I can't imagine.

Picture Oyster on a feeding tube and a catheter for most of his life.

There are worse things you can do to the people you love than kill them.

In the backseat, Mona sits up and stretches her arms. She says, "In ancient Greece, people wrote their strongest curses with the nails from shipwrecks." She says, "Sailors who died at sea weren't given a proper funeral. The Greeks knew that dead people who aren't buried are the most restless and destructive spirits."

And Helen says, "Shut up."

Driving through West Virginia, Pennsylvania, and New York, Helen says, "I hate people who claim they can see ghosts." She says, "There are no ghosts. When you die, you're dead. There's no afterlife. People who claim they can see ghosts are just looking for attention. People who believe in reincarnation are just postponing their lives."

She smiles. "Fortunately for me," she says, "I've found a way to punish those people and make a great deal of money."

Her cell phone rings.

She says, "If you don't believe me about Patrick, I can show you this month's hospital bill."

Her phone rings again.

We're driving across Vermont when she says this. She says part of it while we're crossing Louisiana in the dark, then Arkansas and Mississippi. All those little eastern states, some nights, we'd cross two or three.

Flipping her phone open, she says, "This is Helen." She rolls her eyes at me and says, "An invisible baby sealed inside your bedroom wall? And it cries all night? Really?"

Other parts of this story, I didn't know until we got home and I did some research.

Pressing the phone against her chest, Helen tells me, "Everything I'm telling you is strictly off the record." She says, "Until we find the Book of Shadows, we can't change what's happened. Using a spell from that book, I'll make sure Patrick makes a full recovery."

Chapter 22

We're driving through the Midwest with the radio on some AM station, and a man's voice says how Dr. Sara Lowenstein was a beacon of hope and morality in the wasteland of modern life. Dr. Sara was a noble, hard-line moralist who refused to accept anything but steadfast righteous conduct. She was a bastion of upright standards, a lamp that shone its light to reveal the evil of this world. Dr. Sara, the man says, will always be in our hearts and souls because her own soul was so strong and so un—

The voice stops.

And Mona hits the back of the front seat, hits right behind my kidneys, and says, "Not again." She says, "Quit venting your personal issues on innocent people."

And I say for her to stop accusing. Maybe it's just sunspots.

These talk-oholics. These listen-ophobics.

The culling song's spun through my head so fast I didn't even notice. I was half asleep. It's that far out of control. I can kill in my sleep.

After a few miles of silence, what radio journalists call dead air, another man's voice comes on the radio, saying how Dr. Sara Lowenstein was the moral yardstick against which millions of radio listeners measured their own lives. She was the flaming sword of God, sent down to rout the misdeeds and evildoers from the temple of —

And this new man's voice cuts off.

Mona hits the back of my seat, hard, saying, "That's not funny. Those radio preachers are real people!"

And I say, I didn't do anything.

And Helen and Oyster giggle.

Mona crosses her arms over her chest and throws herself back against the rear seat. She says, "You have no respect. None. This is a million years of power you're screwing around with."

Mona puts both hands against Oyster and shoves him away, hard, so he hits the door. She says, "You, too." She says, "A radio personality is just as important as a cow or a pig."

Now dance music comes on the radio. Helen's cell phone starts to ring, and she flips it open and presses it into her hair. She nods at the radio and mouths the words *Turn it down.*

Into the phone, she says, "Yes." She says, "Uh-huh, yes, I know who he is. Tell me where he's at right now, as close as you can pinpoint it."

I turn down the radio.

Helen listens and says, "No." She says, "I want a seventy-five-carat fancy-cut blue-white diamond. Call Mr. Drescher in Geneva, he knows the exact one I want."

Mona pulls her knapsack up from the floor of the backseat, and she takes out a pack of colored felt-tip pens and a thick book, bound in dark green brocade. She opens the book across her lap and starts scribbling in it with a blue pen. She caps the blue pen and starts with a yellow one.

And Helen says, "How much security doesn't matter. It'll be done inside the hour." She flips the phone shut and drops it on the seat beside her.

On the front seat, between us, is her daily planner, and she flips it open and writes a name and today's date inside.

The book in Mona's lap is her Mirror Book. All real witches, she says, keep Mirror Books. It's a kind of diary and cookbook where you collect what you learn about magic and rituals.

"For instance," she says, reading from

her Mirror Book, "Democritus says that burning the head of a chameleon on an oak fire will cause a thunderstorm."

She leans forward and says right into my ear, "You know, Democritus," she says, "like in the inventor of *democracy*."

And I'm counting 1, counting 2, counting 3 . . .

To shut someone up, Mona says, to make them stop talking, take a fish and sew its mouth shut.

To cure an earache, Mona says, you need to use the semen of a boar as it drips from a sow's vagina.

According to the Jewish *Sepher ha-Razim* collection of spells, you have to kill a black puppy before it sees the light of day. Then write your curse on a tablet and put the tablet inside the dog's head. Then seal the mouth with wax and hide the head behind someone's house, and that person will never fall asleep.

"According to Theophrastus," Mona reads, "you should only dig up a peony at night because if a woodpecker sees you doing it, you'll go blind. If the woodpecker sees you cutting the plant's roots, your anus will prolapse."

And Helen says, "I wish I had a fish . . ."

According to Mona, you shouldn't kill

185

people, because that drives you away from humanity. In order to justify killing, you have to make the victim your enemy. To justify any crime, you have to make the victim your enemy.

After long enough, everyone in the world will be your enemy.

With every crime, Mona says, you're more and more alienated from the world. More and more, you imagine the whole world is against you.

"Dr. Sara Lowenstein didn't start out by attacking and berating everybody who called her radio show," Mona says. "She used to have a little time slot and a little audience, and she seemed to really care about helping people."

And maybe it was after years and years of getting the same calls about unwanted pregnancies, about divorces, about family squabbles. Maybe it was because her audience grew and her show moved to prime time. Maybe it was the more money she earned. Maybe power corrupts, but she wasn't always a bitch.

The only way out, Mona says, will be to surrender and let the world kill Helen and me for our crimes. Or we can kill ourselves.

I ask if this is more Wiccan nonsense.

And Mona says, "No, actually, it's Karl Marx."

She says, "After killing someone, those are the only ways back to connect with humanity." Still drawing in her book, she says, "That's the only way you can get back to a place where the world isn't your nemesis. Where you're not totally alone."

"A fish," Helen says, "and a needle and thread."

And I'm not alone.

I have Helen.

Maybe this is why so many serial killers work in pairs. It's nice not to feel alone in a world full of victims or enemies. It's no wonder Waltraud Wagner, the Austrian Angel of Death, convinced her friends to kill with her.

It just seems natural.

You and me against the world . . .

Gary Lewingdon had his brother, Thaddeus. Kenneth Bianchi had Angelo Buono. Larry Bittaker had Roy Norris. Doug Clark had Carol Bundy. David Gore had Fred Waterfield. Gwen Graham had Cathy Wood. Doug Gretzler had Bill Steelman. Joe Kallinger had his son, Mike. Pat Kearney had Dave Hill. Andy Kokoraleis had his brother, Tom. Leo Lake had Charles Ng. Henry Lucas had Ottis

Toole. Albert Anselmi had John Scalise. Allen Michael had Cleamon Johnson. Clyde Barrow had Bonnie Parker. Doug Bemore had Keith Cosby. Ian Brady had Myra Hindley. Tom Braun had Leo Maine. Ben Brooks had Fred Treesh. John Brown had Sam Coetzee. Bill Burke had Bill Hare. Erskine Burrows had Larry Tacklyn. Jose Bux had Mariano Macu. Bruce Childs had Henry McKenny. Alton Coleman had Debbie Brown. Ann French had her son, Bill. Frank Gusenberg had his brother, Peter. Delfina Gonzalez had her sister, Maria. Dr. Teet Haerm had Dr. Tom Allgen. Amelia Sachs had Annie Walters.

Thirteen percent of all reported serial killers worked in teams.

On death row in San Quentin, Randy "the Scorecard Killer" Kraft played bridge with Doug "Sunset Slayer" Clark, Larry "Pliers" Bittaker, and Freeway Killer Bill Bonin. An estimated 126 victims between the four of them.

Helen Hoover Boyle has me.

"I couldn't stop killing," Bonin once told a reporter. "It got easier with each one . . ."

I have to agree. It does get to be a bad habit.

On the radio, it says how Dr. Sara

188

Lowenstein was an angel of unparalleled power and impact, a glorious hand of God, a conscience for the world around her, a world of sin and cruel intent, a world of hidd—

The more people die, the more things stay the same.

"Go ahead, prove yourself," Oyster says, and nods at the radio. He says, "Kill this fucker, too."

I'm counting 37, counting 38, counting 39 . . .

We've disarmed seven copies of the poems book since leaving home. The original press run was 500. That makes it 306 copies down, 194 copies to go.

In the newspaper, it says how the man in the black leather trench coat, the one who shoved past me at the crosswalk, he was a monthly blood donor. He spent three years overseas with the Peace Corps, digging wells for lepers. He gave up a chunk of his liver to a girl in Botswana who ate a poison mushroom. He answered phones during pledge drives against some crippling disease, I forget what.

Still, he deserved to die. *He called me an asshole.*

He pushed me!

In the newspaper, it shows the mother

189

and father crying over the coffin of my upstairs neighbor.

Still, *his stereo was too damn loud.*

In the newspaper, it says a cover girl fashion model named Denni D'Testro was found dead in her downtown loft apartment this morning.

And for whatever reason, I hope Nash didn't get the call to pick up the body.

Oyster points at the radio and says, "Kill him, Dad, or you're full of shit."

Really, this whole world is nothing but assholes.

Helen flips open her cell phone and calls ahead to libraries in Oklahoma and Florida. She finds another copy of the poems book in Orlando.

Mona reads to us how the ancient Greeks made curse tablets they called *defixiones.*

The Greeks used *kolossi,* dolls made of bronze or wax or clay, and they stabbed them with nails or twisted and mutilated them, cutting off the head or hands. They put hair from the victim inside the doll or sealed a curse, written on papyrus and rolled, inside the doll.

In the Louvre Museum is an Egyptian figure from the second century A.D. It's a naked woman, hog-tied, with nails stuck in her eyes, her ears, her mouth, breasts, hands, feet, vagina, and anus. Scribbling in her book with an orange felt-tip pen, Mona says, "Whoever made that doll, they'd probably love you and Helen."

The curse tablets were thin sheets of lead or copper, sometimes clay. You wrote your curse on them with the nail from a shipwreck, then you rolled the sheet and stuck the nail through it. When writing, you wrote the first line left to right, the next line right to left, the third left to right, and so on. If you could, you folded the curse around some of the victim's hair or a scrap of their clothing. You threw the curse into a lake or a well or the sea, anything that would convey it to the underworld where demons would read it and fill your order.

Still talking on her phone, Helen puts it against her chest for a moment and says, "That sounds like ordering stuff over the Internet."

I'm counting 346, counting 347, counting 348 . . .

In the Greco-Roman literary tradition, Mona says, there are night witches and day witches. Day witches are good and nurturing. Night witches are secretive and bent on destroying all civilization.

Mona says, "You two are definitely night witches."

These people who gave us democracy and architecture, Mona says magic was an everyday part of their lives. Businessmen put curses on each other. Neighbors cursed neighbors. Near the site of the original Olympic Games, archaeologists have found old wells full of curses placed by athletes on other athletes.

Mona says, "I'm not making this stuff up."

Spells to attract a lover were called *agogai* in ancient Greek.

Curses to ruin a relationship were called *diakopoi.*

Helen talks louder into her cell phone, saying, "Blood running down your kitchen walls? Well, of course you shouldn't have to live with that."

And into his phone, Oyster says, "I need the retail advertising number for the *Miami Telegraph-Observer.*"

And the radio interrupts everything with a chorus of French horns. A man's deep voice comes on with a Teletype clattering in the background.

"The suspected leader of South America's largest drug cartel has been found dead in his Miami penthouse," the voice says. "Gustave Brennan, aged thirty-nine, is believed to be the point man for almost three billion dollars in annual cocaine sales. Police do not have a cause of death, but plan to autopsy the body . . ."

And Helen looks at the radio and says, "Are you hearing this? This is ridiculous." She says, "Listen," and turns up the radio

". . . Brennan," the voice says, "who lived inside a fortress of armed bodyguards, has also been under constant FBI surveillance . . ."

And to me, Helen says, "Do they even use Teletypes anymore?"

The call she just got — the blue-white diamond — the name she wrote in her daily planner, it was Gustave Brennan.

Chapter 23

Centuries ago, sailors on long voyages used to leave a pair of pigs on every deserted island. Or they'd leave a pair of goats. Either way, on any future visit, the island would be a source of meat. These islands, they were pristine. These were home to breeds of birds with no natural predators. Breeds of birds that lived nowhere else on earth. The plants there, without enemies they evolved without thorns or poisons. Without predators and enemies, these islands, they were paradise.

The sailors, the next time they visited these islands, the only things still there would be herds of goats or pigs.

Oyster is telling this story.

The sailors called this "seeding meat."

Oyster says, "Does this remind you of anything? Maybe the ol' Adam and Eve story?"

Looking out the car window, he says, "You ever wonder when God's coming back with a lot of barbecue sauce?"

Outside is some Great Lake, water stretched to the horizon, nothing but zebra mussels and lamprey eels, Oyster says. The air stinks with rotting fish.

Mona has a pillow of barley and lavender pressed over her face with both hands. The red henna designs on the back of her hands spread down the length of each finger. Red snakes and vines twisted together.

His cell phone rings, and Oyster pulls out the antenna. He puts it to his head and says, "Deemer, Davis and Hope, Attorneys-at-Law."

He twists a finger in his nose, then takes it out and looks at the finger. Into his phone, Oyster says, "How long after eating there did the diarrhea manifest itself?" He sees me looking and flicks the finger at me.

Helen, with her own cell phone, says, "The people who lived there before were very happy. It's a beautiful house."

In the local newspaper, the *Erie Register-Sentinel*, an ad in the Entertainment section says:

Attention Patrons of the
Country House Golf Club

The ad says: "Have you contracted a medication-resistant staph infection from the swimming pool or locker room facilities? If so, please call the following number to be part of a class-action lawsuit."

You know the number is Oyster's cell phone.

In the 1870s, Oyster says, a man named Spencer Baird decided to play God. He decided the cheapest form of protein for Americans was the European carp. For twenty years, he shipped baby carp to every part of the country. He convinced a hundred different railroads to carry his baby carp and release them in every body of water their trains passed. He even outfitted special railroad tanker cars that carried nine-ton shipments of baby carp to every watershed in North America.

Helen's phone rings and she flips it open. Her daily planner open on the seat next to her, she says, "And where exactly is His Royal Highness at this time?" and she writes a name under today's date in the book. Into her phone, Helen says, "Ask Mr. Drescher to get me the pair of citron and emerald clips."

In another newspaper, the *Cleveland Herald-Monitor*, in the Lifestyles section is an ad that says:

Attention Patrons of the Apparel-Design Chain of Clothing Stores

The ad says: "If you've contracted genital herpes while trying on clothing, please call the following number to be part of a class-action lawsuit."

And, again, the same number. Oyster's number.

In 1890, Oyster says, another man decided to play God. Eugene Schieffelin released sixty *Sturnus vulgaris,* the European starling, in New York's Central Park. Fifty years later, the birds had spread to San Francisco. Today, there are more than 200 million starlings in America. All this because Schieffelin wanted the New World to include every bird mentioned by Shakespeare.

And into his cell phone, Oyster says, "No, sir, your name will be held in strictest confidence."

Helen flips her phone shut, and she cups a gloved hand over her nose and mouth, saying, "What is that awful smell?"

And Oyster puts his cell phone against his shirt and says, "Alewife die-off."

Ever since they reengineered the Welland Canal in 1921 to allow more shipping around Niagara Falls, he says, the sea lamprey has infested all the Great Lakes. These parasites suck the blood of the larger fish, the trout and salmon, killing them. Then the smaller fish are left with no predators and their population explodes. Then they run out of plankton to eat, and starve by the millions.

"Stupid greedy alewives," Oyster says. "Remind you of any other species?"

He says, "Either a species learns to control its own population, or something like disease, famine, war, will take care of the issue."

Mona's muffled voice through her pillow, she says, "Don't tell them. They won't understand."

And Helen opens her purse on the seat beside her. She opens it with one hand and takes out a polished cylinder. With the air-conditioning on high, she sprays breath freshener on a handkerchief and holds it over her nose. She sprays breath freshener into the air-conditioning vents, and says, "Is this about the culling poem?"

And without turning around, I say, "You'd use the poem for population control?"

And Oyster laughs and says, "Kind of."

Mona lowers the pillow to her lap and says, "This is about the grimoire."

And punching another number into his cell phone, Oyster says, "If we find it, we all have to share it."

And I say, we're destroying it.

"After we read it," Helen says.

And into his phone, Oyster says, "Yes, I'll hold." And to us, he says, "This is so typical. We have the entire power structure of Western society in this one car."

According to Oyster, the "dads" have all the power so they don't want anything to change.

He means me.

I'm counting 1, counting 2, counting 3 . . .

Oyster says all the "moms" have a little power, but they're hungry for more.

He means Helen.

I'm counting 4, counting 5, counting 6 . . .

And young people, he says, have little or no power so they're desperate for any.

Oyster and Mona.

I'm counting 7, counting 8 . . . , and Oyster's voice goes on and on.

This quiet-ophobic. This talk-oholic.

Smiling with just half his mouth, Oyster says, "Every generation wants to be the last." Into the phone, he says, "Yeah, I'd like to place a retail display ad." He says, "Yeah, I'll hold."

Mona puts the pillow back over her face. The red snakes and vines go down the length of each finger.

Cheatgrass, Oyster says. Mustard. Kudzu.

Carp. Starlings. Seeding meat.

Looking out the car window, Oyster says, "You ever wonder if Adam and Eve were just the puppies God dumped because they wouldn't house-train?"

He rolls down the window and the smell blows inside, the stinking warm wind of dead fish, and shouting against the wind, he says, "Maybe humans are just the pet alligators that God flushed down the toilet."

Chapter 24

At the next library, I ask to wait in the car while Helen and Mona go inside and find the book. With them gone, I flip through the pages of Helen's daily planner. Almost every day is a name, some of them names I know. The dictator of some banana republic or a figure from organized crime. Each name crossed out with a single red slash. The last dozen names I write on a scrap of paper. Between the names are Helen's notes for meetings, her handwriting scrolled and perfect as jewelry.

Watching me from the backseat, Oyster's kicked back with his arms folded behind his head. His bare feet are crossed and propped up on the back of the front seat so they hang next to my face. A silver ring around one of his big toes. Calluses on the soles, the gray calluses are cracked, dirty, and Oyster says, "Mom's not going to like that, you going through her personal secret shit."

Reading the book backward from today's date, I go through three years of names, assassinations, before Helen and Mona are walking back through the parking lot.

Oyster's phone rings, and he answers it, "Donner, Diller and Dunes, Attorneys-at-Law . . ."

There's still most of the book I don't get a chance to read. Years and years of pages. Toward the end of the book, there are years and years of blank pages for Helen still to fill.

Helen's talking on her phone when she gets to the car. She's saying, "No, I want the step-cut aquamarine that used to belong to the Emperor Zog."

Mona gets into the backseat, saying, "Did you miss us?" She says, "Another culling song down the toilet."

And Oyster folds his legs into the backseat, saying, "Does the rash bleed?" into his cell phone.

Helen snaps her fingers for me to hand her the daily planner. Into the phone, she says, "Yes, the two-hundred-carat aquamarine. Call Drescher in Geneva." She opens the planner and writes a name under today's date.

Mona says, "I was thinking." She says, "Do you think the original grimoire might have a flying spell? I'd love that. Or an invisibility spell?" She gets her Mirror

Book out of her knapsack and starts coloring in it. She says, "I want to be able to talk to animals, too. Oh, and do telekinesis, you know, move stuff with my mind . . ."

Helen starts the car and says, loud at the rearview mirror, "I'm sewing my fish."

She puts her cell phone and her pen in her purse. Still in her purse is the small gray stone from Mona's witch party, the stone the coven gave to her. When Oyster was naked. His wrinkled pink stalactite of skin pierced with its little silver ring.

Mona, that same night, Mulberry, and the two muscles of her back, the way they split into the two firm, creamy white halves of her ass, and I'm counting 1, counting 2, counting 3 . . .

In the next little town, in the next library, I ask Helen and Mona to wait in the car with Oyster while I go inside and hunt for the poems book.

This is some small-town library in the middle of the day. A librarian is behind the checkout desk. The most recent newspapers are mounted in big hardcover bindings you sit at a big table to read. In today's paper is Gustave Brennan. In yesterday's is some wacko religious leader in the Middle East. Two days ago, it was some death row inmate on his latest appeal.

Everyone in Helen's planner book died on the date their name is listed.

In between are newspaper articles about something worse. Denni D'Testro today. Three days ago, it's Samantha Evian. A week ago, it's Dot Leine. All of them young, all of them fashion models, all of them found dead without an apparent cause of death. Before that was Mimi Gonzalez, found dead by her boyfriend, dead in bed with no marks, nothing. No clues until the autopsy announced today shows signs of post-mortem sexual intercourse.

Nash.

Helen comes in, asking, "I'm hungry. What's taking you so long?"

My list of names is on the table beside me. Next to that is a newspaper article with a photo of Gustave Brennan. In front of me is another article showing the funeral of some convicted child molester I found listed in Helen's daily planner.

And Helen looks at everything in one glance and says, "So now you know."

She sits on the edge of the table, her thighs stretching her skirt tight across her lap, and she says, "You wanted to know how to control your power, well, this is what works for me."

The secret is to turn pro, she says. Do something only for money, and you're less likely to do it for free. "You don't think prostitutes want a lot of sex outside of their brothel?" she says.

She says, "Why do you think building contractors always live in unfinished houses?"

She says, "Why do you think doctors are in such poor health?"

She waves her hand at the library door and the parking lot outside and says, "The only reason why I haven't killed Mona a hundred times over is because I kill someone else every day. And I get paid a great deal of money for it."

And I ask, what about Mona's idea? Why can't you control the power by just loving people so much you don't want to kill them?

"This isn't about love and hate," Helen says. It's about control. People don't sit down and read a poem to kill their child. They just want the child to sleep. They just want to dominate. No matter how much you love someone, you still want to have your own way.

The masochist bullies the sadist into action. The most passive person is actually an aggressor. Every day, just you living means the misery and death of plants and animals and even some people. "Slaughterhouses, factory farms, sweatshops," she says, "like it or not, that's what your money buys."

And I tell her she's been listening to Oyster too much.

"The key is to kill people deliberately," Helen says, and picks up the picture of Gustave Brennan in the newspaper. Looking at it, up close, she says, "You kill strangers deliberately so you don't accidentally kill the people you love."

Constructive destruction.

She says, "I'm an independent contractor."

She's an international hired killer working for huge diamonds.

Helen says, "Governments do it every day."

But governments do it after years of deliberation and by due process, I tell her. It's only after weighty consideration that a criminal is deemed too dangerous to be released. Or to set an example. Or for revenge. Okay, so the process isn't perfect. At least it's not arbitrary.

And Helen puts a hand over her eyes to hide them for a moment, then moves her hand and looks at me, saying, "Who do you think calls me for these little jobs?"

The U.S. State Department calls her?

"Sometimes," she says. "Mostly it's other countries, any country in the world, but I don't do anything for free."

That's why the jewels?

"I *hate* haggling over the exchange rate, don't you?" she says. "Besides, an animal dies for every meal you eat."

Oyster again. I see my job will be keeping him and Helen apart.

And I say, that's different. Humans are above animals. Animals were put on this planet to feed and serve humanity. Human beings are precious and intelligent and unique, and God gave the animals to us. They're our property.

"Of course you'd say that," Helen says, "you're on the winning team."

I say, constructive destruction isn't the answer I was looking for.

And Helen says, "Sorry, it's the only one I have."

She says, "Let's get the book, fix it, and then go kill ourselves some lovely pheasant for lunch."

On the way out, I ask the librarian for their copy of the poems book. But it's checked out. The details about the librarian are he has frosted streaks of ash blond in his hair, and the hair's gelled into a solid awning over his face. Sort of an ash-blond visor. He's sitting on a stool behind a computer monitor and smells like cigarette smoke. He's wearing a turtleneck sweater with a plastic name tag that says, "Symon."

I tell him that a lot of lives depend on me finding that book.

And he says, too bad.

And I say, no, the fact is only *his* life depends on it.

And the librarian hits a button on his keyboard and says he's calling the police.

"Wait," Helen says, and spreads her hand on the counter, her fingers sparkling and loaded with step-cut emeralds and cabochon star sapphires and black, cushion-cut bort diamonds. She says, "Symon, take your pick."

And the librarian, his top lip sucks up to his nose so his upper teeth show. He blinks, once, twice, slow, and he says, "Honey, you can keep your tacky drag queen rhinestones."

And the smile on Helen's face doesn't even flicker.

The man's eyes roll up, and the muscles in his face and hands go smooth. His chin

208

drops to his chest, and he slumps forward against his keyboard, then twists and slides to the floor.

Constructive destruction.

Helen reaches a priceless hand to turn the monitor and says, "Damn."

Even dead on the floor, he looks asleep. His giant gelled hair broke his fall.

Reading the monitor, Helen says, "He changed the screen. I need to know his password."

No problem. Big Brother fills us all with the same crap. My guess is he was clever the same way everybody thinks they're clever. I tell her to type in "password."

Chapter 25

Mona rolls the sock off my foot. The stretchy sock insides, the fibers, they peel my scabs off. My crusted blood flakes off onto the floor. The foot is swollen until it's smooth with all its wrinkles stretched out. My foot, a balloon spotted red and yellow. With a folded towel under it, Mona pours the rubbing alcohol.

The pain's so instant you can't tell if the alcohol is boiling hot or ice cold. Sitting on the motel bed, my pant leg rolled up, with Mona kneeling on the carpet at my feet, I grab two handfuls of bedspread and grit my teeth. My back arched, my every muscle bunches tight for a few long seconds. The bedspread's cold and soaked with my sweat.

Pockets of something soft and yellow, these blisters almost cover the bottom of my foot. Under the layer of dead skin, you can see a dark, solid shape inside each blister.

Mona says, "What've you been walking on?"

She's heating a pair of tweezers over Oyster's plastic cigarette lighter.

I ask what the deal is with the advertisements Oyster's running in newspapers. Is he working for a law firm? The outbreaks of skin fungus and food poisoning, are they for real?

The alcohol drips off my foot, pink with dissolved blood, onto the folded motel towel. She sets the tweezers on the damp towel and heats a needle over Oyster's cigarette lighter. With a rubber band, she reaches back and bundles her hair into a thick ponytail.

"Oyster calls all that 'anti-advertising'," she says. "Sometimes businesses, the really rich ones, they pay him to cancel the ads. How much they pay, he says, reflects how true the ads probably are."

My foot won't fit inside my shoe anymore. In the car, earlier today, I asked if Mona could look at it. Helen and Oyster are out buying new makeup. They're stopping to defuse three copies of the poems book at a big used-book store down the street. The Book Barn.

I say what Oyster's doing is blackmail. It's casting aspersions.

Now it's almost midnight. Where Helen and Oyster really are I don't want to know.

"He's not saying he's a lawyer," Mona says. "He's not saying there's a lawsuit. He's just running an ad. Other people fill in the blanks. Oyster says he's just planting the seed of doubt in their minds."

She says, "Oyster says it's only fair since advertising promises something to make you happy."

With her kneeling, you can see the three black stars tattooed above Mona's collarbone. You can see down her blouse, past the carpet of chains and pendants, and she isn't wearing a bra, and I'm counting 1, counting 2, counting 3 . . .

Mona says, "Other members of the coven do it, too, but it's Oyster's idea. He says the plan is to undermine the illusion of safety and comfort in people's lives."

With the needle, she lances a yellow blister and something drops out. A little brown piece of plastic, it's covered in stinking ooze and blood and lands on the towel. Mona turns it over with the needle, and the yellow ooze soaks into the towel. She picks it up with the tweezers and says, "What the heck is this?"

It's a church steeple.

I say, I don't know.

Mona, her mouth gaps open with her tongue pushing out. Her throat slides up inside her neck skin, gagging. She waves a hand in front of her nose and blinks fast. The yellow ooze stinks that bad. She wipes the needle on the towel. With one hand she holds my toes, and with the other she lances another blister. The yellow sprays out in a little blast, and there on the towel is half of a factory smokestack.

She tweezers it and wipes it on the towel. Her face wrinkled tight around her nose, she looks at it close-up and says, "You want to tell me what's going on?"

She lances another blister, and out pops the onion dome from a mosque, covered in blood and slime. With her tweezers, Mona pulls a tiny dinner plate out of my foot. It's hand-painted with a border of red roses.

Outside our motel room, a fire siren screams by in the street.

Out of another blister oozes the pediment from a Georgian bank building.

The cupola from a grade school busts out of the next blister.

Sweating. Deep breathing. Gripping my soft, dripping handfuls of bedspread, I grit my teeth. Looking up at the ceiling, I say, someone is killing models.

Pulling out a bloody flying buttress, Mona says, "By stepping on them?"

And I tell her, *fashion* models.

The needle digs around in the sole of my foot. The needle fishes out a television antenna. The tweezers fish out a gargoyle. Then roof tiles, shingles, tiny slates and gutters.

Mona lifts one edge of the stinking towel and folds it so a clean side shows. She pours on more alcohol.

Another fire engine screams by the motel. Its red and blue lights flash across the curtains.

And I can't draw another full breath, my foot burns so bad.

We need, I say. I need . . . we need . . .

We need to go back home, I say, as soon as possible. If I'm right, I need to stop the man who's using the culling poem.

With the tweezers, Mona digs out a blue plastic shutter and lays it on the towel. She pulls out a shred of bedroom curtains, yellow curtains from the nursery. She pulls out a length of picket fence, and pours on more alcohol until it drips off my foot clear. She covers her nose with her hand.

Another fire engine screams by, and Mona says, "You mind if I just turn on the TV and see what's up?"

I stretch my jaws at the ceiling and say, we can't . . . we can't . . .

Alone with her now, I say, we can't trust

Helen. She only wants the grimoire so she can control the world. I say, the cure for having too much power is not to get more power. We can't let Helen get her hands on the original Book of Shadows.

And so slow I can't see her move, Mona draws a fluted Ionic column out of a bloody pit below my big toe. Slow as the hour hand on a clock. If the column's from a museum or a church or a college, I can't remember. All these broken homes and trashed institutions.

She's more of an archaeologist than a surgeon.

And Mona says, "That's funny."

She lines up the column with the other fragments on the towel. Frowning as she leans back into my sole with the tweezers, she says, "Helen told me the same thing about you. She says you only want to destroy the grimoire."

It should be destroyed. No one can handle that kind of power.

On television is an old brick building, three stories, with flames pouring up from every window. Firemen point hoses and feathery white arcs of water. A young man holding a microphone steps into the shot, and behind him Helen and Oyster are watching the fire, their heads leaned together. Oyster's holding a shopping bag. Helen holds his other hand.

Holding up the bottle of rubbing alcohol, Mona looks at how much is left. She says, "What I'd really like to be is an empath, where all I have to do is touch people and they're healed." Reading the label, she says, "Helen tells me we can make the world a paradise."

I sit up on the bed, halfway, propping myself on my elbows, and I say, Helen is killing people for diamond tiaras. That's the kind of savior Helen is.

Mona wipes the tweezers and the needle on the towel, making more smears of red and yellow. She smells the bottle of alcohol and says, "Helen thinks you only want to exploit the book for a newspaper story. She says once all the spells are destroyed — including the culling spell — then you can blab to everybody that you're the hero."

I say, nuclear weapons are bad enough. Chemical weapons. I say, certain people having magic is not going to make the world a better place.

I tell Mona, if it comes to it, I'll need her help.

I say, we may need to kill Helen.

And Mona shakes her head over the bloody ruins on the motel towel. She says,

"So your answer for too much killing is more killing?"

Just Helen, I say. And maybe Nash, if my theory about the dead fashion models is right. After we kill them, we can go back to normal.

On television, the young man with the microphone, he's saying how a three-alarm fire has most of the downtown area paralyzed. He says, the structure is fully involved. He says, it's one of the city's favorite institutions.

"Oyster," Mona says, "doesn't like your idea of normal."

The burning institution, it's the Book Barn. And behind him, Helen and Oyster are gone.

Mona says, "In a detective story, do you wonder why we root for the detective to win?" She says, maybe it's not just for revenge or to stop the killing. Maybe we really want to see the killer redeemed. The detective is the killer's savior. Imagine if Jesus chased you around, trying to catch you and save your soul. Not just a patient passive God, but a hardworking, aggressive bloodhound. We want the criminal to confess during the trial. We want him to be exposed in the drawing room scene, surrounded by his peers. The detective is a shepherd, and we want the criminal back in the fold, returned to us. We love him. We miss him. We want to hug him.

Mona says, "Maybe that's why so many women marry killers in prison. To help heal them."

I tell her, there's nobody who misses me.

Mona shakes her head and says, "You know, you and Helen are so much like my parents."

Mona. Mulberry. My daughter.

And flopping back on the bed, I ask, how's that?

And pulling a door frame out of my foot, Mona says, "Just this morning, Helen told me she might need to kill you."

My pager goes off. It's a number I don't know. The pager says it's very important.

And Mona digs a stained-glass window out of a bloody pit in my foot. She holds it up so the ceiling light comes through the colored bits, and looking at the tiny window, she says, "I'm more worried about Oyster. He doesn't always tell the truth."

And the motel room door, right then it blows open. The sirens outside. The sirens on the television. The flash of red and blue lights strobing across the window curtains. Right then Helen and Oyster fall into the room, laughing and panting. Oyster slinging a bag of cosmetics. Helen holding her high heels in one hand. They both smell like Scotch whisky and smoke.

Chapter 26

I imagine a plague you catch through your ears.

Oyster and his tree-hugging, eco-bullshit, his bio-invasive, apocryphal bullshit. The virus of his information. What used to be a beautiful deep green jungle to me, it's now a tragedy of English ivy choking everything else to death. The lovely shining black flocks of starlings, with their creepy whistling songs, they rob the nests of a hundred different native birds.

Imagine an idea that occupies your mind the way an army occupies a city.

Outside the car now is America.

> *Oh, beautiful starling-filled skies,*
> *Over amber waves of tansy ragwort.*
> *Oh, purple mountains of loosestrife,*
> *Above the bubonic-plagued plain.*

America.

A siege of ideas. The whole power grab of life.

After listening to Oyster, a glass of milk

isn't just a nice drink with chocolate chip cookies. It's cows forced to stay pregnant and pumped with hormones. It's the inevitable calves that live a few miserable months, squeezed in veal boxes. A pork chop means a pig, stabbed and bleeding, with a snare around one foot, being hung up to die screaming as it's sectioned into chops and roasts and lard. Even a hard-boiled egg is a hen with her feet crippled from living in a battery cage only four inches wide, so narrow she can't raise her wings, so maddening her beak is cut off so she won't attack the hens trapped on each side of her. With her feathers rubbed off by the cage and her beak cut, she lays egg after egg until her bones are so depleted of calcium that they shatter at the slaughterhouse.

This is the chicken in chicken noodle soup, the laying hens, the hens so bruised and scarred that they have to be shredded and cooked because nobody would ever buy them in a butcher's case. This is the chicken in corn dogs. Chicken nuggets.

This is all Oyster talks about. This is his plague of information. This is when I turn on the radio, to country and western music. To basketball. Anything, so long as it's loud and constant and lets me pretend my breakfast sandwich is just a breakfast sandwich. That an animal is just that. An egg is just an egg. Cheese isn't a tiny suffering veal. That eating this is my right as a human being.

Here's Big Brother singing and dancing so I don't start thinking too much for my own good.

In the local newspaper today, there's another dead fashion model. There's an ad that says:

Attention Patrons of Falling Star Puppy Farm

It says: "If your new dog spreads infectious rabies to any child in your household, you may be eligible to take part in a class-action lawsuit."

Driving through what used to be beautiful, natural country, while eating what used to be an egg sandwich, I ask why they couldn't just buy the three books they were shopping for at the Book Barn. Oyster and Helen. Or just steal the pages and leave the rest of the books. I say, the reason we're making this trip is so people *won't* be burning books.

"Relax," Helen says, driving. "The store had three copies of the book. The problem was they didn't know where."

222

And Oyster says, "They were all mis-shelved." Mona's head is asleep in his lap, and he's peeling apart the strands of her hair into skeins of red and black. "It's the only way she falls asleep," he says. "She'd sleep forever if I kept doing this."

For whatever reason, my wife comes to mind, my wife and daughter.

What with the sirens and fire engines, we were awake all night.

"That Book Barn place was like a rat's warren," Helen says.

Oyster is braiding the broken bits of civilization into Mona's hair. The artifacts from my foot, the broken columns and stairways and lightning rods. He's pulled apart her Navajo dream catcher and braids the I Ching coins and glass beads and cords into her hair. The Easter shades of blue and pink feathers.

"We spent the entire evening searching," Helen says. "We checked every book in the children's section. We looked through Science. We checked Religion. We checked Philosophy. Poetry. Folk Stories. We checked Ethnic Literature. We checked all through Fiction."

And Oyster says, "The books were on their computer inventory, but just lost in the store."

So they burned the whole place. For three books. They burned tens of thousands of books to make sure those three were destroyed.

"It seemed our only realistic option," Helen says. "You know what those books can do."

For whatever reason, Sodom and Gomorrah come to mind. How God would spare the city if there was even one good person still in it.

Here's just the opposite. Thousands killed in order to destroy a few.

Imagine a new Dark Age. Imagine the books burning. And the tapes and films and files, the radios and televisions, will all go into the same bonfire.

If we're preventing that world or creating it, I don't know.

It said on the television how two security guards were found dead after the fire.

"Actually," Helen says, "they were dead long before the fire. We needed some time to spread the gasoline."

We're killing people to save lives?

We're burning books to save books?

I ask, what is this trip turning into?

"What it's always been," Oyster says, threading some hair through an I Ching coin. "It's a big power grab."

He says, "You want to keep the world the way it is, Dad, with just you in charge."

Helen, he says, wants the same world, but with her in charge. Every generation wants to be the last. Every generation hates the next trend in music they can't understand. We hate to give up those reins of our culture. To find our own music playing in elevators. The ballad for our revolution, turned into background music for a television commercial. To find our generation's clothes and hair suddenly retro.

"Me," Oyster says, "I'm all for wiping the slate clean, of books and people, and starting over. I'm for nobody being in charge."

With him and Mona as the new Adam and Eve?

"Nope," he says, smoothing the hair back from Mona's sleeping face. "We'd have to go, too."

I ask, does he hate people so much that he'd kill the woman he loves? I ask, why doesn't he just kill himself?

"No," Oyster says, "I just love everything the same. Plants, animals, humans. I just don't believe the big lie about how we can continue to be fruitful and multiply without destroying ourselves."

I say, he's a traitor to his species.

"I'm a fucking patriot," Oyster says, and looks out his window. "This culling poem is a blessing. Why do you think it was created in the first place? It will save millions of people from the slow terrible death we're headed for from disease, from famine, drought, from solar radiation, from war, from all the places we're headed."

So he's willing to kill himself and Mona? I ask, so what about his parents? Will he just kill them, too? What about all the little children who've had little or no life? What about all the good, hardworking people who live green and recycle? The vegans? Aren't they innocent in his mind?

"This isn't about guilt or innocence," he says. "The dinosaurs weren't morally good or bad, but they're all dead."

That kind of thinking makes him an Adolf Hitler. A Joseph Stalin. A serial killer. A mass murderer.

And threading a stained-glass window into Mona's hair, Oyster says, "I want to be what killed the dinosaurs."

And I say, it was an act of God that killed the dinosaurs.

I say, I'm not going another mile with a wanna-be mass murderer.

And Oyster says, "What about Dr. Sara? Mom? Help me out. How many others has

Dad here already killed?"

And Helen says, "I'm sewing my fish."

At the sound of Oyster's cigarette lighter, I turn and ask, does he have to smoke? I say, I'm trying to eat.

But Oyster's got Mona's book about primitive crafts, *Traditional Tribal Hobby-Krafts*, and he's holding it open above the lighter, fanning the pages in the little flame. With his window open a crack, he slips the book out, letting the flames explode in the wind before he drops it.

Cheatgrass loves fire.

He says, "Books can be so evil. Mulberry needs to invent her own kind of spirituality."

Helen's phone rings. Oyster's phone rings.

Mona sighs and stretches her arms. With her eyes closed, Oyster's hands still picking through her hair, his phone still ringing, Mona grinds her head into Oyster's lap and says, "Maybe the grimoire will have a spell to stop overpopulation."

Helen opens the planner book to today's date and writes a name. Into her phone, she says, "Don't bother with an exorcism. We can put the house right back on the market."

Mona says, "You know, we need some

227

kind of universal 'gelding spell'."

And I ask, isn't anybody here worried about going to hell?

And Oyster takes his phone out of his medicine bag.

His phone ringing and ringing.

Helen puts her phone against her chest and says, "Don't think for a second that the government's not already working on some swell infectious ways to stop over-population."

And Oyster says, "In order to save the world, Jesus Christ suffered for about thirty-six hours on the cross." His phone ringing and ringing, he says, "I'm willing to suffer an eternity in hell for the same cause."

His phone ringing and ringing.

Into her phone, Helen says, "Really? Your bedroom smells like sulfur?"

"You figure out who's the better savior," Oyster says, and flips his cell phone open. Into the phone, he says, "Dunbar, Dunaway and Doogan, Attorneys-at-Law . . ."

Chapter 27

Imagine if the Chicago fire of 1871 had gone on for six months before anyone noticed. Imagine if the Johnstown flood in 1889 or the 1906 San Francisco earthquake had lasted six months, a year, two years, before anyone paid attention to it.

Building with wood, building on fault lines, building on floodplains, each era creates its own "natural" disasters.

Imagine a flood of dark green in the downtown of any major city, the office and condo towers submerged inch by inch.

Now, here and now, I'm writing from Seattle. A day, a week, a month late. Who knows how far after the fact. The Sarge and me, we're still witch-hunting.

Hedera helixseattle, *botanists are calling this new variety of English ivy. One week, maybe the planters around the Olympic Professional Plaza, they looked a little overgrown. The ivy was crowding the pansies. Some vines had rooted into the side of the brick facade and were inching up. No one noticed. It had been raining a lot.*

No one noticed until the morning the residents of the Park Senior Living Center found their lobby doors sealed with ivy. That same day, the south wall of the Fremont Theater, brick and concrete three feet thick, it buckled onto a sellout crowd. That same day, part of the underground bus mall caved in.

No one can really say when Hedera helixseattle *first took root, but you can make a good guess.*

Looking through back issues of the Seattle Times, *there's an ad in the May 5 Entertainment section. Three columns wide, it says:*

Attention Patrons of the Oracle Sushi Palace

The ad says, "If you experience severe rectal itching caused by intestinal parasites, you may be eligible to take part in a class-action lawsuit." Then it gives a phone number.

Me, here with the Sarge, I call the number.

A man's voice says, "Denton, Daimler and Dick, Attorneys-at-Law."

And I say, "Oyster?"

I say, "Where are you, you little fuck?"

And the line goes dead.

Here and now, writing this in Seattle, in a diner just outside of the Department of Public Works barricades, a waitress tells the Sarge and me, "They can't kill the ivy now," and she pours us more coffee. She looks out the window at the walls of green, veined with fat gray vines. She says, "It's the only thing holding that part of town together."

Inside the net of vines and leaves, the bricks are buckling and shifted. Cracks shatter the concrete. The windows are squeezed until the glass breaks. Door won't open because the frames are so warped. Birds fly in and out of the straight-up green cliffs, eating the ivy seeds, shitting them everywhere. A block away, the streets are canyons of green, the asphalt and sidewalks buried in green.

"The Green Menace," the newspapers call it. The ivy equivalent of killer bees. The Ivy Inferno.

Silent, unstoppable. The end of civilization in slow motion.

The waitress, she says every time city crews prune the vines, or burn them with flame-throwers, or spray them with poison — even the time they herded in pygmy goats to eat it — the ivy roots spread. The roots collapsed tunnels. They severed underground cables and pipes.

The Sarge dials the number from the sushi ad, again and again, but the line stays dead.

The waitress looks at the fingers of ivy already coming across the street. In another

231

week, she'll be out of a job.

"The National Guard promised us containment," she says.

She says, "I hear they've got the ivy in Portland now, too. And San Francisco." She sighs and says, "We're definitely losing this one."

Chapter 28

The man opens his front door, and here are Helen and I on his front porch, me carrying Helen's cosmetic case, standing a half-step behind her as Helen points the long pink nail of her index finger and says, "Oh God."

She has her daily planner tucked under one arm and says, "My husband," and she steps back. "My husband would like to witness to you about the promise of the Lord Jesus Christ."

Helen's suit is yellow, but not a buttercup yellow. It's more the yellow of a buttercup made of gold and pavé citrons by Carl Fabergé.

The man's holding a bottle of beer. He's wearing gray sweat socks with no shoes. His bathrobe hangs open in the front, and inside, he's wearing a white T-shirt and boxer shorts patterned with little race cars. With one hand, he sticks the beer in his mouth. His head tips back, and bubbles glub up inside the bottle. The little race cars have oval tires tilted forward. The man belches and says, "You guys for real?"

He has black hair hanging down a wrinkled Frankenstein forehead. He has sad baggy hound-dog eyes.

My hand out front to shake his, I say, Mr. Sierra? I say, we're here to share the joy of God's love.

And the race car guy frowns and says, "How is it you know my name?" He squints at me and says, "Did Bonnie send you to talk to me?"

And Helen leans around him, looking into the living room. She snaps open her purse and takes out a pair of white gloves and starts wiggling her fingers inside. She buttons a little button at the cuff of each glove and says, "May we come in?"

It was supposed to be easier than this.

Plan B, if we find a man at home, we bring out plan B.

The race car guy puts the beer bottle in his mouth, and his stubbly cheeks suck in around it. His head tilts back and the rest of the beer bubbles away. He steps to one side and says, "Well. Sit down." He looks at his empty bottle and says, "Can I get you a beer?"

We step in, and he goes in the kitchen. There's the hiss of him popping a bottle cap.

In the whole living room, there's just a

recliner chair. There's a little portable television sitting on a milk crate. Out through sliding glass doors, you can see a patio. Lined up along the far edge of the patio are green florist vases, brimful of rain, rotted black flowers bent and falling out of them. Rotted brown roses on black sticks fuzzy with gray mold. Tied around one arrangement is a wide black satin ribbon.

In the living room shag carpet, there's the ghost outlines left by a sofa. There's the outlines left by a china cabinet, the little dents left by the feet of chairs and tables. There's a big flat square where the carpet is all crushed the same. It looks so familiar.

The race car guy waves me at the recliner and says, "Sit down." He drinks some beer and says, "Sit, and we'll talk about what God's really like."

The big flat square in the carpet, it was left by a playpen.

I ask if my wife can use his bathroom.

And he tilts his head to one side, looking at Helen. With his free hand, he scratches the back of his neck, saying, "Sure. It's at the end of the hall," and he waves with his beer bottle.

Helen looks at the beer sloshed out on the carpet and says, "Thank you." She takes her daily planner from under her arm and hands it to me, saying, "In case you need it, here's a Bible."

Her book full of political targets and real estate closings. Great.

It's still warm from her armpit.

She disappears down the hallway. The sound of a bathroom fan comes on. A door shuts somewhere.

"Sit," the race car guy says.

And I sit.

He stands over me so close I'm afraid to open the daily planner, afraid he'll see it's not a real Bible. He smells like beer and sweat. The little race cars are eye level with me. The oval tires are tilted so they look like they're going fast. The guy takes another drink and says, "Tell me all about God."

The recliner chair smells like him. It's gold velvet, darker brown on the arms from dirt. It's warm. And I say God's a noble, hard-line moralist who refuses to accept anything but steadfast righteous conduct. He's a bastion of upright standards, a lamp that shines its light to reveal the evil of this world. God will always be in our hearts and souls because His own soul is so strong and so un—

"Bullshit," says the guy. He turns away

and goes to look out the patio doors. His face is reflected in the glass, just his eyes, with his dark stubbly jaw lost in shadow.

In my best radio preacher voice, I say how God is the moral yardstick against which millions of people must measure their own lives. He's the flaming sword, sent down to rout the misdeeds and evildoers from the temple of —

"Bullshit!" the guy shouts at his reflection in the glass door. Beer spray runs down his reflected face.

Helen is standing in the doorway to the hall, one hand at her mouth, chewing her knuckle. She looks at me and shrugs. She disappears back down the hallway.

From the gold velvet recliner, I say how God is an angel of unparalleled power and impact, a conscience for the world around Him, a world of sin and cruel intent, a world of hidd—

In almost a whisper, the guy says, "Bullshit." The fog of his breath has erased his reflection. He turns to look at me, pointing at me with his beer hand, saying, "Read to me where it says in your Bible something that will fix things."

Helen's daily organizer bound in red leather, I open it a crack and peek inside.

"Tell me how to prove to the police I

didn't kill anybody," the guy says.

In the organizer is the name Renny O'Toole and the date June 2. Whoever he is, he's dead. On September 10, Samara Umpirsi is entered. On August 17, Helen closed a deal for a house on Gardner Hill Road. That, and she killed the tyrant king of the Tongle Republic.

"Read!" the race car guy shouts. The beer in his hand foams over his fingers and drips on the carpet. He says, "Read to me where it says I can lose everything in one night and people are going to say it's my fault."

I peek in the book, and it's more names of dead people.

"Read," the guy says, and drinks his beer. "You read where it says a wife can accuse her husband of killing their kid and everybody is supposed to believe her."

Early in the book, the writing is faded and hard to read. The pages are stiff and flyspecked. Before that, someone's started tearing out the oldest pages.

"I asked God," the guy says. He shakes his beer at me and says, "I asked Him to give me a family. I went to church."

I say how maybe God didn't start out by attacking and berating everybody who prayed. I say, maybe it was after years and years of getting the same prayers about unwanted pregnancies, about divorces, about family squabbles. Maybe it was because God's audience grew and more people were making demands. Maybe it was the more praise He got. Maybe power corrupts, but He wasn't always a bastard.

And the race car guy says, "Listen." He says, "I go to court in two days to decide if I'm accused of murder." He says, "You tell me how God is going to save me."

His breath nothing but beer, he says, "You tell me."

Mona would have me tell the truth. To save this guy. To save myself and Helen. To reunite us with humanity. Maybe this guy and his wife would reunite, but then the poem would be out. Millions would die. The rest would live in that world of silence, hearing only what they think is safe. Plugging their ears and burning books, movies, music.

Somewhere a toilet flushes. A bathroom fan shuts off. A door opens.

The guy puts the beer in his mouth and bubbles glug up inside the bottle.

Helen appears in the doorway to the hall.

My foot aches, and I ask, has he considered taking up a hobby?

Maybe something he could do in prison.

Constructive destruction. I'm sure Helen would approve of the sacrifice. Condemning one innocent man so millions don't die.

Here's every lab animal who dies to save a dozen cancer patients.

And the race car guy says, "I think you'd better leave."

Walking out to the car, I hand Helen the daily planner and tell her, here's your Bible. My pager goes off, and it's some number I don't know.

Her white gloves are black with dust, and she says she tore up the culling song page and dropped it out the nursery window. It's raining. The paper will rot.

I say, that's not good enough. Some kid could find it. Just the fact that it's tore up will make someone want to put it back together. Some detective investigating the death of a child, maybe.

And Helen says, "That bathroom was a nightmare."

We drive around the block and park. Mona's scribbling in the backseat. Oyster's on his phone. Then Helen waits while I crouch down and walk back to the house. I duck around the back, the wet lawn sucking at my shoes, until I'm under the window Helen says is the nursery. The window's still open, the curtains hanging out a little at the bottom. Pink curtains.

The torn bits of page are scattered in the mud, and I start to pick them all up.

Behind the curtains, in the empty room, you can hear the door open. The outline of somebody comes in from the hallway, and I crouch in the mud under the window. A man's hand comes down on the windowsill so I pull back flat against the house. From somewhere above me where I can't see, a man starts crying.

It starts to rain harder.

The man stands in the window, leaning both hands on the open sill. He sobs louder. You can smell the beer inside him.

Me, I can't run. I can't stand up. With my hands clamped over my nose and mouth, I crouch inches away, squeezed tight against the foundation, hidden. And hitting me as fast as a chill, me breathing between my fingers, I start to cry, too. Sobs as hard as vomiting. My belly cramps. My teeth biting into my palm, the snot sprays into my hands.

The man sniffs, hard and bubbling. It's raining harder, and water seeps into my shoes through the laces.

The torn bits of the poem in my hand, I

241

hold the power of life and death. I just can't do anything. Not yet.

And maybe you don't go to hell for the things you do. Maybe you go to hell for the things you don't do.

My shoes full of cold water, my foot stops hurting. My hand slick with snot and tears, I reach down and turn off my pager.

When we find the grimoire, if there is some way to raise the dead, maybe we won't burn it. Not right away.

Chapter 29

The police report doesn't say how warm my wife, Gina, felt when I woke up that morning. How soft and warm she felt under the covers. How when I turned next to her, she rolled onto her back, her hair fanned out on her pillow. Her head was tipped a little toward one shoulder. Her morning skin smelled warm, the way sunlight looks bouncing up off a white tablecloth in a nice restaurant near the beach on your honeymoon.

Sun came through the blue curtains, making her skin blue. Her lips blue. Her eyelashes were lying across each cheek. Her mouth was a loose smile.

Still half asleep, I cupped my hand behind her neck and tilted her face back and kissed her.

Her neck and shoulder were so easy and relaxed.

Still kissing her warm, relaxed mouth, I pulled her nightgown up around her waist.

Her legs seemed to roll apart, and my hand found her loose and wet inside.

Under the covers, my eyes closed, I

worked my tongue inside. With my wet fingers, I peeled back the smooth pink edges of her and licked deeper. The tide of air going in and out of me. At the top of each breath, I drove my mouth up into her.

For once, Katrin had slept the whole night and wasn't crying.

My mouth climbed to Gina's belly button. It climbed to her breasts. With one wet finger in her mouth, my other fingers flick across her nipples. My mouth cups over her other breast and my tongue touches the nipple inside.

Gina's head rolled to one side, and I licked the back of her ear. My hips pressing her legs apart, I put myself inside.

The loose smile on her face, the way her mouth came open at the last moment and her head sunk deep into the pillow, she was so quiet. It was the best it had been since before Katrin was born.

A minute later, I slipped out of bed and took a shower. I tiptoed into my clothes and eased the bedroom door shut behind me. In the nursery, I kissed Katrin on the side of her head. I felt her diaper. The sun came through her yellow curtains. Her toys and books. She looked so perfect.

I felt so blessed.

No one in the world was as lucky as me that morning.

Here, driving Helen's car with her asleep in the front seat beside me. Tonight, we're in Ohio or Iowa or Idaho, with Mona asleep in the back. Helen's pink hair pillowed against my shoulder. Mona sprawled in the rearview mirror, sprawled in her colored pens and books. Oyster asleep. This is the life I have now. For better or for worse. For richer, for poorer.

That was my last really good day. It wasn't until I came home from work that I knew the truth.

Gina was still lying in the same position.

The police report would call it postmortem sexual intercourse.

Nash comes to mind.

Katrin was still quiet. The underside of her head had turned dark red.

Livor mortis. Oxygenated hemoglobin.

It wasn't until I came home that I knew what I'd done.

Here, parked in the leather smell of Helen's big Realtor car, the sun is just above the horizon. It's the same moment now as it was then. We're parked under a tree, on a treelined street in a neighborhood of little houses. It's some kind of flowering tree, and all night, pink flower

245

petals have fallen on the car, sticking to the dew. Helen's car is pink as a parade float, covered in flowers, and I'm spying out through just a hole where the petals don't cover the windshield.

The morning light shining in through the layer of petals is pink.

Rose-colored. On Helen and Mona and Oyster, asleep.

Down the block, an old couple is working in the flower beds along their foundation. The old man fills a watering can at a spigot. The old woman kneels, pulling weeds.

I turn my pager back on, and it starts beeping right away.

Helen jerks awake.

The phone number on my pager, I don't recognize it.

Helen sits up, blinking, looking at me. She looks at the tiny sparkling watch on her wrist. On one side of her face are deep red pockmarks where she slept on her dangling emerald earrings. She looks at the layer of pink covering all the windows. She plunges the pink fingernails of both hands into her hair and fluffs it, saying, "Where are we now?"

Some people still think knowledge is power.

I tell her, I have no idea.

Chapter 30

Mona stands at my elbow. She holds a glossy brochure open, pushing it in my face, saying, "Can we go here? Please? Just for a couple hours? Please?"

Photographs in the brochure show people screaming with their hands in the air, riding a roller coaster. Photos show people driving go-carts around a track outlined in old tires. More people are eating cotton candy and riding plastic horses on a merry-go-round. Other people are locked into seats on a Ferris wheel. Along the top of the brochure in big scrolling letters it says: *LaughLand, The Family Place.*

Except in place of the a's are four laughing clown faces. A mother, a father, a son, a daughter.

We have another eighty-four books to disarm. That's dozens more libraries in cities all over the country. Then there's the grimoire to find. There's people to bring back from the dead. Or just castrate. Or there's all of humanity to kill, depending on whom you ask.

There's so much we need to get fixed. To get back to God, as Mona would say. Just to break even.

Karl Marx would say we've made every plant and animal our enemy to justify killing it.

In the newspaper today, it says the husband of one of the fashion models is being held under suspicion of murder.

I'm standing at a public phone outside some small-town library while Helen's inside trashing another book with Oyster.

A man's voice on the phone says, "Homicide Division."

Into the phone, I ask, who is this?

And the voice says, "Detective Ben Danton, Homicide Division." He says, "Who is this?"

A police detective. Mona would call him my savior, sent to wrangle me back into the fold with the rest of humanity. This is the number that's been appearing on my pager for the past couple days.

Mona turns the brochure over and says, "Just look." Braided in her hair are broken windmills and train trestles and radio towers.

Photos show smiling children getting hugged by clowns. It shows parents strolling hand in hand and riding little skiffs through a Tunnel of Love.

She says, "This trip doesn't have to be all work."

Helen comes out of the library doors and starts down the front steps, and Mona turns and rushes at her, saying, "Helen, Mr. Streator said it was okay."

And I put the pay phone receiver to my chest and say, I did not.

Oyster is hanging back, a step behind Helen's elbow.

Mona holds the brochure in Helen's face, saying, "Look how much fun."

On the phone, Detective Danton says, "Who is this?"

It was okay to sacrifice the poor guy in his race car boxer shorts. It's okay to sacrifice the young woman in the apron printed with little chickens. To not tell them the truth, to let them suffer. And to sacrifice the widower of some fashion model. But sacrificing me to save the millions is another thing altogether.

Into the phone, I say my name, Streator, and that he paged me.

"Mr. Streator," he says, "we'd like you to come in for questioning."

I ask, about what?

"Why don't we talk about that in person?" he says.

I ask if this is about a death.

"When can you make it in?" he says.

I ask if this is about the series of deaths with no apparent cause.

"Sooner would be better than later," he says.

I ask if this is because one victim was my upstairs neighbor and three were my editors.

And Danton says, "You don't say?"

I ask if this is because I passed three more victims in the street the moment before they each died.

And Danton says, "That's news to me."

I ask if this is because I stood within spitting distance of the young sideburns guy who died in the bar on Third Avenue.

"Uh-huh," he says. "You'd mean Marty Latanzi."

I ask if this is because all the dead fashion models show signs of postmortem sex, the same way my wife did twenty years ago. And no doubt they have security camera film of me talking to a librarian named Symon at the moment he dropped dead.

You can hear a pencil somewhere scratching fast notes on paper.

Away from the phone, I hear someone else say, "Keep him on the line."

I ask if this is really a ploy to arrest me

250

for suspicion of murder.

And Detective Danton says, "Don't make us issue a bench warrant."

The more people die, the more things stay the same.

Officer Danton, I say. I ask, can he tell me where to find him at this exact moment?

Sticks and stones may break your bones, but here we go again. Fast as a scream, the culling song spins through my head, and the phone line goes dead.

I've killed my savior. Detective Ben Danton. I'm that much further from the rest of humanity.

Constructive destruction.

Oyster shakes his plastic cigarette lighter, slapping it against the palm of one hand. Then he gives it to Helen and watches while she takes a folded page out of her purse. She lights the page 27 and holds it over the gutter.

While Mona's reading the brochure, Helen holds the burning page near the edge of it. The photos of happy, smiling families puff into flame, and Mona shrieks and drops them. Still holding the burning page, Helen kicks the burning families into the gutter. The fire in her hand gets bigger and bigger, stuttering and smoking in the breeze.

And for whatever reason, I think of Nash and his burning fuse.

Helen says, "I don't do *fun*." With her other hand, Helen jingles her car keys at me.

Then it happens. Oyster has his arm locked around Helen's head from behind. That fast, he knocks her off her feet and as she throws her arms out for balance, he grabs the burning poem. The culling song.

Helen drops to her knees, drops out of his grip, she cries just one little scream when her knees hit the concrete sidewalk, and she tumbles into the gutter. Her keys still in her fist.

Oyster beats the burning page against his thigh. He holds it in both hands, his eyes twitching back and forth, reading down the page as the fire rolls up from the bottom.

Both his hands are on fire before he lets go, yelling, "No!" and sticks his fingers into his mouth.

Mona steps back, her hands pressed over her ears. Her eyes squeezed shut.

Helen on her hands and knees in the gutter, next to the burning families, she looks up at Oyster. Oyster as good as dead. Helen's hairdo is broken open and pink hair hangs in her eyes. Her nylons are torn. Her knees, bloody.

"Don't kill him!" Mona yells. "Don't kill him, please! Don't kill him!"

Oyster drops to his knees and grabs at the burned paper on the sidewalk.

And slow, slow as the hour hand on a clock, Helen rises to her feet. Her face is red. It's not the red of a Burmese ruby. It's more the red of the blood running down from her knees.

With Oyster kneeling. With Helen standing over him. With Mona holding both hands over her ears, squeezing her eyes shut. Oyster's sifting through his ashes. Helen's bleeding. Me, I'm still watching from the phone booth, and a flock of starlings flies up from the roof of the library.

Oyster, the evil, resentful, violent son Helen might have, if she still had a son.

Just the same old power grab.

"Go ahead," Oyster says, and he lifts his head to meet Helen's eyes. He smiles with just half his mouth and says, "You killed your real son. You can kill me."

And then it happens. Helen slaps him hard across the face, dragging her fistful of keys through each cheek. A moment later, more blood.

Another scarred parasite. Another mutilated cockroach armoire.

And Helen's eyes snap up from Oyster bleeding to the starlings circling above us, and bird by bird, they drop. Their black feathers flashing an oily blue. Their dead eyes just staring black beads. Oyster holds his face, both his hands full of blood. Helen glaring up into the sky, the shining black bodies hiss down and bounce, bird by bird, around us on the concrete.

Constructive destruction.

Chapter 31

A mile outside of town, Helen pulls over to the side of the highway. She puts on the car's emergency flashers. Looking at nothing but her hands, her skintight calfskin driving gloves on the steering wheel, she says, "Get out."

On the windshield, there are little contact lenses of water. It's starting to rain.

"Fine," Oyster says, and jerks his car door open. He says, "Isn't this what people do with dogs they can't house-train?"

His face and hands are smeared red with blood. The devil's face. His shattered blond hair sticks up from his forehead, stiff and red as devil's horns. His red goatee. In all this red, his eyes are white. It's not the white of white flags, surrender. It's the white of hard-boiled eggs, crippled chickens in battery cages, factory farm misery and suffering and death.

"Just like Adam and Eve getting evicted from the Garden of Eden," he says. Oyster stands on the gravel shoulder of the highway and leans down to look at Mona still in the backseat, and he says,

"You coming, Eve?"

It's not about love, it's about control.

Behind Oyster, the sun's going down. Behind him is Russian thistle and Scotch broom and kudzu. Behind him, the whole world's a mess.

And Mona with the ruins of Western civilization braided into her hair, the bits of dream catcher and I Ching, she looks at her black fingernails in her lap and says, "Oyster, what you did is wrong."

Oyster puts his hand into the car, reaching across the seat to her, his hand red and clotted, and he says, "Mulberry, despite all your herbal good intentions, this trip is not going to work." He says, "Come with me."

Mona sets her teeth together and snaps her face to look at him, saying, "You threw away my Indian crafts book." She says, "That book was very important to me."

Some people still think knowledge is power.

"Mulberry, honey," Oyster says, and strokes her hair, the hair sticking to his bloody hand. He tucks a skein of hair behind her ear and says, "That book was fucked."

"Fine," says Mona, and she pulls away and folds her arms.

And Oyster says, "Fine." And he slams the car door, his hand leaving a bloody print on the window.

His red hands raised at his sides, Oyster steps back from the car. Shaking his head, he says, "Forget about me. I'm just another one of God's alligators you can flush down the toilet."

Helen shifts the car into drive. She touches some switch, and Oyster's door locks.

And from outside the locked car, muffled and fuzzy, Oyster yells, "You can flush me, but I'll just keep eating shit." He shouts, "And I'll just keep growing."

Helen puts on her turn signal and starts out into traffic.

"You can forget me," Oyster yells. With his red yelling devil face, his teeth big and white, he yells, "But that doesn't mean I don't still exist."

For whatever reason, the first gypsy moth that flew out a window in Medford, Massachusetts, in 1860 comes to mind.

And driving, Helen touches her eye with one finger, and when she puts her hand back on the steering wheel, the glove finger is a darker brown. Wet. And for better or for worse. For richer or poorer. This is her life.

Mona puts her face in both hands and starts to sob.

And counting 1, counting 2, counting 3 . . . , I turn on the radio.

Chapter 32

The town's name is Stone River on the map. Stone River, Nebraska. But when the Sarge and I get there, the sign at the city limits is painted over with the name "Shivapuram."

Nebraska.

Population 17,000.

In the middle of the street, straddling the center line dashes is a brown and white cow we have to swerve around. Chewing its cud, the cow doesn't flinch.

The downtown is two blocks of red-brick buildings. A yellow signal light blinks above the main intersection. A black cow is scratching its side against the metal pole of a stop sign. A white cow eats zinnias out of a window box in front of the post office. Another cow lies, blocking the sidewalk in front of the police station.

You smell curry and patchouli. The deputy sheriff's wearing sandals. The deputy, the mailman, the waitress in the café, the bartender in the tavern, they're all wearing a black dot pasted between their eyes. A bindi.

"Crimony," the Sarge says. "The whole

town's gone Hindu."

According to this week's Psychic Wonders Bulletin, this is all because of the talking Judas Cow.

In any slaughterhouse operation, the trick is to fool cows into climbing the chute that leads to the killing floor. Cows trucked in from farms, they're confused, scared. After hours or days squeezed into trucks, dehydrated and awake the whole trip, the cows are thrown in with other cows in the feedlot outside the slaughterhouse.

How you get them to climb the chute is you send in the Judas Cow. This is really what this cow is called. It's a cow that lives at the slaughterhouse. It mingles with the doomed cows, then leads them up the chute to the killing floor. The scared, spooked cows would never go except for the Judas Cow leading the way.

The last step before the ax or the knife or the steel bolt through the skull, at that last moment, the Judas Cow steps aside. It survives to lead another herd to their death. It does this for its entire life.

Until, according to the Psychic Wonders Bulletin, the Judas Cow at the Stone River Meatpacking Plant, one day it stopped.

The Judas Cow stood blocking the doorway to the killing floor. It refused to step aside and let the herd behind it die. With the whole slaughterhouse crew watching, the Judas Cow sat on its hind legs, the way a dog sits, the cow sat there in the doorway and looked at everyone with its brown cow eyes and talked.

The Judas Cow talked.

It said, "Reject your meat-eating ways."

The cow's voice was the voice of a young woman. The cows in line behind it, they shifted their weight from foot to foot, waiting.

The slaughterhouse crew, their mouths fell open so fast their cigarettes dropped out on the bloody floor. One man swallowed his chewing tobacco. A woman screamed through her fingers.

The Judas Cow, sitting there, it raised one front leg to point its hoof at the crew and said, "The path to moksha is not through the pain and suffering of other creatures."

"Moksha," says the Psychic Wonders Bulletin, is a Sanskrit word for "redemption," the end of the karmic cycle of reincarnation.

The Judas Cow talked all afternoon. It said human beings had destroyed the natural world. It said mankind must stop exterminating other species. Man must limit his numbers, create a quota system which allows only a small percentage of the planet's beings to be human. Humans could live any way they liked so long as they were not the majority.

It taught them a Hindi song. The cow made the whole crew sing along while it swung its hoof back and forth to the beat of the song.

The cow answered all their questions about the nature of life and death.

The Judas Cow just droned on and on and on.

Now, here and now, the Sarge and I, we're here after the fact. Witch-hunting. We're looking at all the cows released from the meatpacking plant that day. The plant is empty and quiet on the far edge of town. Someone's painting the concrete building pink. Making it into an ashram. They've planted vegetables in the feedlot.

The Judas Cow hasn't said a word since. It eats the grass in people's front yards. It drinks from birdbaths. People hang daisy chains around its neck.

"They're using the occupation spell," the Sarge says. We're stopped in the street, waiting for a huge slow hog to cross in front of our car. Other pigs and chickens stand in the shade under the hardware store awning.

An occupation spell lets you project your consciousness into the physical body of another being.

I look at him, too long, and ask if he isn't the pot calling the kettle black.

"Animals, people," the Sarge says, "you can

261

put yourself into pretty much any living body."

And I say, yeah, tell me about it.

We drive past the man painting the pink ashram, and the Sarge says, "If you ask me, reincarnation is just another way to procrastinate."

And I say, yeah, yeah, yeah. He's already told me that one.

The Sarge reaches across the front seat to put his wrinkled spotted hand over mine. The back of his hand is carpeted with gray hairs. His fingers are cold from handling his pistol. The Sarge squeezes my hand and says, "Do you still love me?"

And I ask if I have a choice.

Chapter 33

The crowds of people shoulder around us, the women in halter tops and men in cowboy hats. People are eating caramel apples on sticks and shaved ice in paper cones. Dust is everywhere. Somebody steps on Helen's foot and she pulls it back, saying, "I find that no matter how many people I kill, it's never enough."

I say, let's not talk shop.

The ground is crisscrossed with thick black cables. In the darkness beyond the lights, engines burn diesel to make electricity. You can smell diesel and deep-fried food and vomit and powdered sugar.

These days, this is what passes for fun.

A scream sails past us. And a glimpse of Mona. It's a carnival ride with a bright neon sign that says: *The Octopus*. Black metal arms, like twisted spokes, turn around a hub. At the same time, they dip up and down. At the end of each arm is a seat, and each seat spins on its own hub. The scream sails by again, and a banner of red and black hair. Her silver chains and charms are flung straight out from the side of Mona's neck. Both her hands are clamped on the guard bar fastened across her lap.

The ruins of Western civilization, the turrets and towers and chimneys, fly out of Mona's hair. An I Ching coin bullets past us.

Helen watches her, saying, "I guess Mona got her flying spell."

My pager goes off again. It's the same number as the police detective. A new savior is already hot on my tail.

The more people die, the more things stay the same.

I turn the pager off.

And watching Mona scream by, Helen says, "Bad news?"

I say, nothing important.

In her pink high heels, Helen picks through the mud and sawdust, stepping over the black power cables.

Holding out my hand, I say, "Here."

And she takes it. And I don't let go. And she doesn't seem to mind. And we're walking hand in hand. And it's nice.

She's only got a few big rings left so it doesn't hurt as much as you'd think.

The carnival rides thrash the air around us, diamond-white, emerald-green, ruby-red lights, turquoise and sapphire-blue lights, the yellow of citrons, the orange of honey amber. Rock music blares out of speakers mounted on poles everywhere.

These rock-oholics. These quiet-ophobics.

I ask Helen, when was the last time she rode a Ferris wheel?

Everywhere, there are men and women, hand in hand, kissing. They're feeding each other shreds of pink cotton candy. They walk side by side, each with one hand stuck in the butt pocket of the other's tight jeans.

Watching the crowd, Helen says, "Don't take this the wrong way, but when was your last time?"

My last time for what?

"You know."

I'm not sure if my last time counts, but it must be about eighteen years ago.

And Helen smiles and says, "It's no wonder you walk funny." She says, "I have twenty years and counting since John."

On the ground, with the sawdust and cables, there's a crumpled newspaper page. A three-column advertisement says:

Attention Patrons of the Helen Boyle Real Estate Agency

The ad says, "Have you been sold a haunted house? If so, please call the following number to be part of a class-action lawsuit."

Then Oyster's cell phone number. Then I say, please, Helen, why did you tell him that stuff?

Helen looks down at the newspaper ad. With her pink shoe, she grinds it into the mud, saying, "For the same reason I didn't kill him. He could be very lovable at times."

Next to the ad, covered in mud is the photo of another dead fashion model.

Looking up at the Ferris wheel, a ring of red and white fluorescent tubes holding seats that sway full of people, Helen says, "That looks doable."

A man stops the wheel and all the carts swing in place while Helen and I sit on the red plastic cushion and the man snaps a guard bar shut across our laps. He steps back and pulls a lever, and the big diesel engine catches. The Ferris wheel jerks as if it's rolling backward, and Helen and I rise into the darkness.

Halfway up into the night, the wheel jerks to a stop. Our seat swings, and Helen makes a fast grab for the guard bar. A diamond solitaire slips off one finger and flashes straight through the struts and lights, through the colors and faces, down into the gears of the machine.

Helen looks after it, saying, "Well, that was roughly thirty-five thousand dollars."

I say, maybe it's okay. It's a diamond.

And Helen says that's the problem. Gemstones are the hardest things on earth, but they still break. They can take constant stress and pressure, but a sudden, sharp impact can shatter them into dust.

Across the midway floor, Mona comes running over the sawdust to stand below us, waving both hands. She jumps in place and yells, "Whooooo! Go, Helen!"

The wheel jerks, starting again. The seat tilts, and Helen's purse starts to fall but she grabs it. The gray rock's still inside it. The gift from Oyster's coven. Instead of her purse, her planner book slides off the seat, flapping open in the air, tumbling down to land in the sawdust, and Mona runs over and picks it up.

Mona slaps the book on her thigh to knock off the sawdust, then shakes it in the air to show it's okay.

Helen says, "Thank God for Mona."

I say, Mona said you planned to kill me.

And Helen says, "She told me that you wanted to kill me."

We both look at each other.

I say, thank God for Mona.

And Helen says, "Buy me some caramel corn?"

On the ground, farther and farther away, Mona's looking through the pages of the planner. Every day, the name of Helen's political target.

Looking up, out of the colored lights and into the night sky, we're getting closer to the stars. Mona once said that stars are the best part of being alive. On the other side, where people go after they die, they can't see the stars.

Think of deep outer space, the incredible cold and quiet. The heaven where silence is reward enough.

I tell Helen that I need to go home and clean something up. It has to be pretty soon, before things get worse.

The dead fashion models. Nash. The police detectives. All of it. How he got the culling spell, I don't know.

We rise higher, farther away from the smells, away from the diesel engine noise. We rise up into the quiet and cold. Mona, reading the planner book, gets smaller. All the crowds of people, their money and elbows and cowboy boots, get smaller. The food booths and the portable toilets get smaller. The screams and rock music, smaller.

At the top, we jerk to a stop. Our seat sways less and less until we're sitting still. This high up, the breeze teases, rats, back-combs Helen's pink bubble of hair. The neon and grease and mud, from this far away it all looks perfect. Perfect, safe, and happy. The music's just a dull thud, thud, thud.

This is how we must look to God.

Looking down at the rides, the spinning colors and screams, Helen says, "I'm glad you found me out. I think I always hoped someone would." She says, "I'm glad it was you."

Her life isn't so bad, I say. She has her jewels. She has Patrick.

"Still," she says, "it's nice to have one person who knows all your secrets."

Her suit is light blue, but it's not a reg-ular robin's-egg blue. It's the blue of a robin's egg you might find and then worry that it won't hatch because it's dead inside. And then it *does hatch,* and you worry about what to do next.

On the guard bar locked across us, Helen puts her hand on mine and says, "Mr. Streator, do you even *have* a first name?"

Carl.

I say, Carl. It's Carl Streator.

I ask, why did she call me middle-aged?

And Helen laughs and says, "Because you are. We both are."

The wheel jerks again, and we're coming back down.

And I say, her eyes. I say, they're blue.

And this is my life.

At the bottom, the carnival man snaps open the guard bar and I give Helen my hand as she steps out of the seat. The sawdust is loose and soft, and we limp and stumble through the crowds, holding each other around the waist. We get to Mona, and she's still reading the planner book.

"Time for some caramel corn," Helen says. "Carl, here, is going to buy."

And the book still open in her hands, Mona looks up. Her mouth open a little, her eyes blink once, twice, three times, fast. She sighs and says, "You know the grimoire we're looking for?" She says, "I think we just found it."

Chapter 34

Some witches write their spells in runes, secret coded symbols. According to Mona, some witches write backward so the spell can only be read in a mirror. They write spells in spirals, starting in the center of the page and curving outward. Some write like the ancient Greek curse tablets with one line running from left to right, then the next running right to left and the next, left to right. This, they call the *boustrophedon* form because it mimics the back-and-forth pacing of an ox tied to a tether. To mimic a snake, Mona says, some write each line so it branches in a different direction.

The only rule was, a spell has to be twisted. The more hidden, the more twisted, the more powerful the spell. To witches, the twists themselves are magical. They draw or sculpt the magician-god Hephaestus with his legs twisted.

The more twisted the spell, the more it will twist and hobble the victim. It'll confuse them. Occupy their attention. They'll stumble. Get dizzy. Not concentrate.

The same as Big Brother with all his singing and dancing.

In the gravel parking lot, halfway between the carnival and Helen's car, Mona holds the daily planner book so the lights of the carnival shine through just one page. At first, the only things there are the notes Helen's written for that day. The name "Captain Antonio Cappelle," and a list of real estate appointments. Then you can see a faint pattern in the paper, red words, yellow sentences, blue paragraphs, as each colored light passes behind the page.

"Invisible ink," Mona says, still holding the page out.

It's faint as a watermark, ghostwriting.

"What tipped me off is the binding," Mona says.

The cover and binding are dark red leather, polished almost black with handling.

"It's human skin," Mona says.

It was in Basil Frankie's house, Helen says. It looked like a lovely old book, an empty book. She bought it with Frankie's estate. On the cover is a black five-pointed star.

"A pentagram," Mona says. "And before it was a book, this was somebody's tattoo.

This little bump," she says, touching a spot on the book's spine, "this is a nipple."

Mona closes the book and holds it out to Helen and says, "Feel." She says, "This is beyond ancient."

And Helen snaps her purse open and gets out her pair of little white gloves with a button at the cuff. She says, "No, you hold it."

Looking at the book, open in her hands, Mona leafs back and forth. She says, "If I just knew what they used as ink, I'd know how to read it."

If it's ammonia or vinegar, she says, you'd boil a red cabbage and daub on some of the broth to turn the ink purple.

If it's semen, you could read it under fluorescent light.

I say, people wrote spells in peter tracks?

And Mona says, "Only the most powerful type of spells."

If it's written in a clear solution of cornstarch, she could daub on iodine to make the letters stand out.

If it was lemon juice, she says, you'd heat the pages to make the ink turn brown.

"Try tasting it," Helen says, "to see if it's sour."

And Mona slams the book shut. "It's a thousand-year-old witch book bound in mummified skin and probably written in ancient cum." She says to Helen, *"You lick it."*

And Helen says, "Okay, I get your point. Try at least to hurry and translate it."

And Mona says, "I'm not the one who's been carrying it around for ten years. I'm not the one who's been ruining it, writing over the top of everything." She holds the book in both hands and shoves it at Helen. "This is an ancient book. It's written in archaic forms of Greek and Latin, plus some forgotten kinds of runes." She says, "I'm going to need some time."

"Here," Helen says, and snaps open her purse. She takes out a folded square of paper and hands it to Mona, saying, "Here's a copy of the culling song. A man named Basil Frankie translated this much. If you can match it to one of the spells in that book, you can use that as a key to translate all the spells in that language." She says, "Like in the Rosetta stone."

And Mona reaches to take the folded paper.

And I snatch it from Helen's hand and ask, why are we even having this discussion? I say, my idea was we'd burn the book. I open the paper, and it's a page 27 stolen from some library, and I say, we

274

need to think about this.

To Helen, I say, are you sure you want to do this to Mona? This spell has pretty much ruined our lives. I say, besides, what Mona knows, Oyster is going to know.

Helen is flexing her fingers into the white gloves. She buttons each cuff and reaches out to Mona, saying, "Give me the book."

"I can do it," Mona says.

Helen shakes her hand at Mona and says, "No, this is best. Mr. Streator's right. It will change things for you."

The night air is full of faint faraway screams and glowing colors.

And Mona says, "No," and wraps both arms around the book, holding it to her chest.

"You see," Helen says. "It's already started. When there's the possibility of a little power, you already want more."

I tell her to give the book to Helen.

And Mona turns her back to us, saying, "I'm the one who found it. I'm the only one who can read it." She turns to look over one shoulder at me and says, "You, you just want to destroy it so you can sell the story. You want everything resolved so it's safe to talk about."

And Helen says, "Mona, honey, don't."

275

And Mona turns to look over her other shoulder at Helen and says, "You just want it so you can rule the world. You're just into the money side of everything." Her shoulders roll forward until she seems to wrap her whole body around the book, and she looks down on it, saying, "I'm the only one who appreciates it for what it is."

And I tell her, listen to Helen.

"It's a Book of Shadows," Mona says, "a *real* Book of Shadows. It belongs with a real witch. Just let me translate it. I'll tell you what I find. I promise."

Me, I fold the culling spell from Helen and tuck it in my back pocket. I take a step closer to Mona. I look at Helen, and she nods.

Still with her back to us, Mona says, "I'll bring Patrick back." She says, "I'll bring back all the little children."

And I grab her around the waist from behind and lift. Mona's screaming, kicking her heels into my shins and twisting from side to side, still holding the book, and I work my hands up under her arms until I'm touching it, touching dead human skin. The dead nipple. Mona's nipples. Mona's screaming, and her fingernails dig into my hands, the soft skin between my fingers. She digs into the skin on the back of my hands until I get her around the wrists and twist her arms up and away from her sides. The book falls, and her kicking legs knock it away, and in the dark parking lot, with the distant screams, nobody notices.

This is the life I got. This is the daughter I knew I'd lose someday. Over a boyfriend. Over bad grades. Drugs. Somehow this break always happens. This power struggle. No matter how great a father you think you'll make, at some time you'll find yourself here.

There are worse things you can do to the people you love than kill them.

The book lands in a spray of dust and gravel.

And I yell for Helen to get it.

The moment Mona is free, Helen and I step back. Helen holding the book, I'm looking to see if anybody's around.

Her hands in fists, Mona leans toward us, her red and black hair hanging in her face. Her silver chains and charms are tangled in her hair. Her orange dress is twisted tight around her body, the neckline torn on one side so her shoulder shows, bare. She's kicked off her sandals so she's barefoot. Her eyes behind the dark snarls of her hair, her eyes reflecting the carnival lights, the screams in the distance could be the echo of her screams going on and on, forever.

How she looks is wicked. A wicked witch. A sorceress. Twisted. She's no longer my daughter. Now she's someone I may never understand. A stranger.

And through her teeth, she says, "I could kill you. I could."

And I finger-comb my hair. I straighten my tie and tuck the front of my shirt smooth. I'm counting 1, counting 2, counting 3, and I tell her, no, but we could kill her. I tell her she owes Mrs. Boyle an apology.

This is what passes as tough love.

Helen stands, holding the book in her white-gloved hands, looking at Mona.

Mona says nothing.

The smoke from the diesel generators, the screams and rock music and colored lights, do their best to fill the silence. The stars in the night sky don't say a word.

Helen turns to me and says, "I'm okay. Let's just get going." She gets out her car keys and gives them to me. Helen and I, we turn away and start walking. But looking back, I see Mona laughing into her hands.

She's laughing.

Mona stops laughing when I see, but her smile is still there.

And I tell her to wipe the smirk off her face. I ask, what the hell does she have to smirk about?

Chapter 35

With me driving, Mona sits in the backseat with her arms folded. Helen sits in the front seat next to me, the grimoire open in her lap, lifting each page against her window so she can see sunlight through it. On the front seat between us, her cell phone rings.

At home, Helen says, she still has all the reference books from Basil Frankie's estate. These include translation dictionaries for Greek, Latin, Sanskrit. There are books on ancient cuneiform writing. All the dead languages. Something in one of these books will let her translate the grimoire. Using the culling spell as a sort of code key, a Rosetta stone, she might be able to translate them all.

And Helen's cell phone rings.

In the rearview mirror, Mona picks her nose and rolls the booger against the leg of her jeans until it's a hard dark lump. She looks up from her lap, her eyes rolling up, slow, until she's looking at the back of Helen's head.

Helen's cell phone rings.

And Mona flicks her booger into the back of Helen's pink hair.

And Helen's cell phone rings. Her eyes still in the grimoire, Helen pushes the phone across the seat until it presses my thigh, saying, "Tell them I'm busy."

It could be the State Department with her next hit assignment. It could be some other government, some cloak-and-dagger business to conduct. A drug kingpin to rub out. Or a career criminal to retire.

Mona opens her green brocade Mirror Book, her witch's diary, in her lap and starts scribbling in it with colored pens.

On the phone is a woman.

It's a client of hers, I tell Helen. Holding the phone against my chest, I say, the woman says a severed head bounced down her front stairway last night.

Still reading the grimoire, Helen says, "That would be the five-bedroom Dutch Colonial on Feeney Drive." She says, "Did it disappear before it landed in the foyer?"

I ask.

To Helen, I say, yes, it disappeared about halfway down the stairway. A hideous bloody head with a leering smile.

The woman on the phone says something.

And broken teeth, I say. She sounds very upset.

Mona's scribbling so hard the colored pens squeak against the paper.

And still reading the grimoire, Helen says, "It disappeared. End of problem."

The woman on the phone says, it happens every night.

"So call an exterminator," Helen says. She holds another page against the sunlight and says, "Tell her I'm not here."

The picture that Mona's drawing in her Mirror Book, it's a man and woman being struck by lightning, then being run over by a tank, then bleeding to death through their eyes. Their brains spray out their ears. The woman wears a tailored suit and a lot of jewelry. The man, a blue tie.

I'm counting 1, counting 2, counting 3 . . .

Mona takes the man and woman and tears them into thin strips.

The phone rings again, and I answer it.

I hold the phone against my chest and tell Helen, it's some guy. He says his shower sprays blood.

Still holding the grimoire against the window, Helen says, "The six-bedroom on Pender Court."

And Mona says, "Pender *Place*. Pender

Court has the severed hand that crawls out of the garbage disposal." She opens the car window a little and starts feeding the shredded man and woman out through the crack.

"You're thinking of the severed hand at Palm Corners," Helen says. "Pender Place has the biting phantom Doberman."

The man on the phone, I ask him to please hold. I press the red HOLD button.

Mona rolls her eyes and says, "The biting ghost is in the Spanish house just off Millstone Boulevard." She starts writing something with a red felt-tip pen, writing so the words spiral out from the center of the page.

I'm counting 9, counting 10, counting 11 . . .

Squinting at the lines of faint writing on the page she has spread against the window, Helen says, "Tell them I'm out of the real estate business." Trailing her finger along under each faint word, she says, "The people at Pender Court, they have teenagers, right?"

I ask, and the man on the phone says yes.

And Helen turns to look at Mona in the backseat, Mona flicking another rolled booger, and Helen says, "Then tell him a bathtub full of human blood is the least of his problems."

I say, how about we just keep driving? We could hit a few more libraries. See some sights. Another carnival, maybe. A national monument. We could have some laughs, loosen up a little. We were a family once, we could be one again. We still love each other, hypothetically speaking. I say, how about it?

Mona leans forward and yanks a few strands of hair out of my head. She leans and yanks a few pink strands from Helen.

And Helen ducks forward over the grimoire, saying, "Mona, that hurt."

In my family, I say, my parents and I, we could settle almost any squabble over a rousing game of Parcheesi.

The strands of pink and brown hair, Mona folds them inside the page of spiral writing.

And I tell Mona, I just don't want her to make the same mistakes I made. Looking at her in the rearview mirror, I say, when I was about her age, I stopped talking to my parents. I haven't talked to them in almost twenty years.

And Mona sticks a baby pin through the page folded with our hair inside.

Helen's phone rings again, and this time

it's a man. A young man.

It's Oyster. And before I can hang up, he says, "Hey, Dad, you'll want to make sure and read tomorrow's newspaper." He says, "I put a little surprise in it for you."

He says, "Now, let me talk to Mulberry."

I say her name's Mona. Mona Sabbat.

"It's Mona Steinner," Helen says, still holding a page of the grimoire to the window, trying to read the secret writing.

And Mona says, "Is that Oyster?" From the backseat, she reaches around both sides of my head, grabbing for the phone and saying, "Let me talk." She shouts, "Oyster! Oyster, they have the grimoire!"

And me trying to steer the car, the car veering all over the highway, I flip the phone shut.

Chapter 36

Instead of the stain on my apartment ceiling, there's a big patch of white. Pushpinned to my front door, there's a note from the landlord. Instead of noise, there's total quiet. The carpet is crunchy with little bits of plastic, broken-down doors and flying buttresses. You can hear the filament buzzing in each lightbulb. You can hear my watch tick.

In my refrigerator, the milk's gone sour. All that pain and suffering wasted. The cheese is huge and blue with mold. A package of hamburger has gone gray inside its plastic wrap. The eggs look okay, but they're not, they can't be, not after this long. All the effort and misery that went into this food, and it's all going in the garbage. The contributions of all those miserable cows and veals, it gets thrown out.

The note from my landlord says the white patch on the ceiling is a primer coat. It says when the stain stops bleeding through, they'll paint the whole ceiling. The heat's on high to dry the primer faster.

Half the water in the toilet's evaporated. The plants are dry as paper. The trap under the kitchen sink's half empty and sewer gas is leaking back up. My old way of life, everything I call home, smells of shit.

The primer coat is to keep what was left of my upstairs neighbor from bleeding through.

Out in the world, there's still thirty-nine copies of the poems book unaccounted for. In libraries, in bookstores, in homes. Give or take, I don't know, a few dozen.

Helen's in her office today. That's where I left her, sitting at her desk with dictionaries open around her, Greek, Latin, and Sanskrit dictionaries, translation dictionaries. She's got a little bottle of iodine and she's using a cotton swab to daub it on the writing, turning the invisible words red.

Using cotton swabs, Helen's daubing the juice from a purple cabbage on other invisible words, turning them purple.

Next to the little bottles and cotton swabs and dictionaries sits a light with a handle. A cord trails from it to an outlet in the wall.

"A fluoroscope," Helen says. "It's rented." She flicks a switch on the side and holds the light over the open grimoire, turning the pages until one page is filled with glowing pink words. "This one's written in semen."

On all the spells, the handwriting's different.

Mona, at her desk in the outer office, hasn't said a nice word since the carnival. The police scanner is saying one emergency code after another.

Helen calls to Mona, "What's a good word for 'demon'?"

And Mona says, "Helen Hoover Boyle."

Helen looks at me and says, "Have you seen today's paper?" She shoves some books to one side, and under them is a newspaper. She flips through it, and there on the back page of the first section is a full-page ad. The first line says:

Attention, Have You Seen This Man?

Most of the page is an old picture, my wedding picture, me and Gina smiling twenty years ago. This has to be from our wedding announcement in some ancient Saturday edition. Our public declaration of commitment and love for each other. Our pledge. Our vows. The old power of words. Till death do us part.

Below that, the ad copy says, "Police are currently looking for this man for questioning in connection with several recent deaths. He is forty years old, five feet ten inches tall, weighs one hundred and eighty pounds, and has brown hair and green eyes. He's unarmed, but should be considered highly dangerous."

The man in the photo is so young and innocent. He's not me. The woman is dead. Both of these people, ghosts.

Below the photo, it says, "He now goes by the alias 'Carl Streator.' He often wears a blue tie."

Below that, it says, "If you know his whereabouts, please call 911 and ask for the police." If Oyster ran this ad or the police did, I don't know.

Helen and me standing here, looking down at the picture, Helen says, "Your wife was very pretty."

And I say, yeah, she was.

Helen's fingers, her yellow suit, her carved and varnished antique desk, they're all stained and smudged red and purple with iodine and cabbage juice. The stains smell of ammonia and vinegar. She holds the fluoroscope over the book and reads the ancient peter tracks.

"I've got a flying spell here," she says.

"And one of these might be a love spell." She flips back and forth, each page smelling like cabbage farts or ammonia piss. "The culling spell," she says, "it's this one here. Ancient Zulu."

In the outer office, Mona's talking on the phone.

Helen puts her hand on my arm and pushes me back, a step away from her desk, she says, "Watch this," and stands there, both hands pressed to her temples, her eyes closed.

I ask, what's supposed to happen?

Mona hangs up her telephone in the outer office.

The grimoire open on Helen's desk, it shifts. One corner lifts, then the opposite corner. It starts to close by itself, then opens, closes and opens, faster and faster until it rises off the desk. Her eyes still closed, Helen's lips move around silent words. Rocking and flapping, the book's a shining dark starling, hovering near the ceiling.

And the police scanner crackles and says, "Unit seventeen." It says, "Please proceed to 5680 Weeden Avenue, Northeast, the Helen Boyle real estate office, and apprehend an adult male for questioning . . ."

The grimoire hits the desk with a crash. Iodine, ammonia, vinegar and cabbage juice splashing everywhere. Papers and books sliding to the floor.

Helen yells, "Mona!"

And I say, don't kill her, please. Don't kill her.

And Helen grabs my hand in her stained hand and says, "I think you'd better get out of here." She says, "Do you remember where we first met?" Whispering, she says, "Meet me there tonight."

In my apartment, all the tape in my answering machine is used up. In my mailbox, the bills are packed so tight I have to dig them out with a butter knife.

On the kitchen table is a shopping mall, half built. Even without the picture on the box, you can tell what it is because the parking lots are laid out. The walls are in place. The windows and doors sit off to one side, the glass installed already. The roof panels and big heating-cooling units are still in the box. The landscaping is sealed in a plastic bag.

Coming through the apartment walls, there's nothing. No one. After weeks on the road with Helen and Mona, I've forgotten how silence was so golden.

I turn on the television. It's some black-

291

and-white comedy about a man come back from the dead as a mule. He's supposed to teach somebody something. To save his own soul. A man's spirit occupying a mule's body.

My pager goes off again, the police, my saviors, needling me toward salvation.

The police or the manager, this place has got to be under some kind of surveillance.

On the floor, scattered all over the floors, there's the stomped fragments of a lumber mill. There's the busted ruins of a train station flecked with dried blood. Around that, a medical-dental office building lies in a billion pieces. And an airplane hangar, crushed. A ferryboat terminal, kicked apart. All the bloody ruins and artifacts of what I worked so hard to put together, all of them scattered and crackling under my shoes. What's left of my normal life.

I turn on the clock radio next to the bed. Sitting cross-legged on the floor, I reach out and scrape together the remains of gas stations and mortuaries and hamburger stands and Spanish monasteries. I pile up the bits covered with blood and dust, and the radio plays big band swing music. The radio plays Celtic folk music and ghetto rap and Indian sitar music. Piled in front of me are the parts for sanatoriums and movie studios, grain elevators and oil refineries. On the radio is electronic trance music, reggae, and waltz music. Heaped together are the parts of cathedrals and prisons and army barracks.

With the little brush and glue, I put together smokestacks and skylights and geodesic domes and minarets. Romanesque aqueducts run into Art Deco penthouses run into opium dens run into Wild West saloons run into roller coasters run into small-town Carnegie libraries run into tract houses run into college lecture halls.

After weeks on the road with Helen and Mona, I've forgotten how perfection was so important.

On my computer, there's a draft of the crib death story. The last chapter. It's the type of story that every parent and grandparent is too afraid to read and too afraid not to read. There's really no new information. The idea was to show how people cope. People move forward with their lives. We could show the deep inner well of strength and compassion each of these people discovers. That angle.

All we know about infant sudden death is there is no pattern. A baby can die in its mother's arms.

The story's still unfinished.

The best way to waste your life is by taking notes. The easiest way to avoid living is to just watch. Look for the details. Report. Don't participate. Let Big Brother do the singing and dancing for you. Be a reporter. Be a good witness. A grateful member of the audience.

On the radio, waltz music runs into punk runs into rock runs into rap runs into Gregorian chanting runs into chamber music. On television, someone is showing how to poach a salmon. Someone is showing why the *Bismarck* sank.

I glue together bay windows and groin vaults and barrel vaults and jack arches and stairways and clerestory windows and mosaic floors and steel curtain walls and half-timbered gables and Ionic pilasters.

On the radio is African drum music and French torch songs, all mixed together. On the floor in front of me are Chinese pagodas and Mexican haciendas and Cape Cod colonial houses, all combined. On television, a golfer putts. A woman wins ten thousand dollars for knowing the first line of the Gettysburg Address.

My first house I ever put together was four stories with a mansard roof and two staircases, a front one for family and a rear servant's staircase. It had metal and glass chandeliers you wired with tiny lightbulbs. It had a parquet floor in the dining room that took six weeks of cutting and gluing to piece together. It had a ceiling in the music room that my wife, Gina, stayed up late, night after night, painting with clouds and angels. It had a fireplace in the dining room with a fire I made out of cut glass with a flickering light behind it. We set the table with tiny dinner plates, and Gina stayed up at night, painting roses around the border of each plate. The two of us, those nights, with no television or radio, Katrin asleep, it seemed so important at the time. Those were the two people in that wedding photo. The house was for Katrin's second birthday. Everything had to be perfect. To be something that would prove our talent and intelligence. A masterpiece to outlive us.

Oranges and gasoline, the glue smell, mixes with the smell of shit. On my fingers, on the glue slopped there, my hands are crusted with picture windows and porches and air conditioners. Stuck to my shirt are turnstiles and escalators and trees, and I turn the radio up.

All that work and love and effort and time, my life, wasted. Everything I hoped would outlive me I've ruined.

That afternoon I came home from work and found them, I left the food in the fridge. I left the clothes in the closets. The afternoon I came home and knew what I'd done, that was the first house I stomped. An heirloom without an heir. The tiny chandeliers and glass fire and dinner plates. Stuck in my shoes, I left a trail of tiny doors and shelves and chairs and windows and blood all the way to the airport.

Beyond that, my trail ended.

And sitting here, I've run out of parts. All the walls and roofs and handrails. And what's glued to the floor in front of me is a bloody mess. It's nothing perfect or complete, but this is what I've made of my life. Right or wrong, it follows no great master plan.

All you can do is hope for a pattern to emerge, and sometimes it never does.

Still, with a plan, you only get the best you can imagine. I'd always hoped for something better than that.

A blast of French horns comes on the radio, the clatter of a Teletype, and a man's voice says how police have found yet another dead fashion model. The television shows her smiling picture. They've arrested another suspect boyfriend. Another autopsy shows signs of postmortem sexual intercourse.

My pager goes off again. The number on my page is my new savior.

My hands lumpy with shutters and doors, I pick up the phone. My fingers rough with plumbing and gutters, I dial a number I can't forget.

A man answers.

And I say, Dad. I say, Dad, it's me.

I tell him where I'm living. I tell him the name I use now. I tell him where I work. I tell him that I know how it looks, with Gina and Katrin dead, but I didn't do it. I just ran.

He says, he knows. He saw the wedding picture in today's newspaper. He knows who I am now.

A couple weeks ago, I drove by their house. I say how I saw him and Mom working in the yard. I was parked down the street, under a flowering cherry tree. My car, Helen's car, covered in pink petals. Both he and Mom, I say, they both look good.

I tell him, I've missed him, too. I love him, too. I tell him, I'm okay.

I say, I don't know what to do. I say, but it's all going to be okay.

After that, I just listen. I wait for him to stop crying so I can say I'm sorry.

Chapter 37

The Gartoller Estate in the moonlight, an eight-bedroom Georgian-style house with seven bathrooms, four fireplaces, all of it's empty and white. All of it's echoing with each step across the polished floors. The house is dark without lights. It's cold without furniture or rugs.

"Here," Helen says. "We can do it here, where no one will see us." She flicks a light switch inside a doorway.

The ceiling goes up so high it could be the sky. Light from a looming chandelier, the size of a crystal weather balloon, the light turns the tall windows into mirrors. The light throws our shadows out behind us on the wood floor. This is the fifteen-hundred-square-foot ballroom.

Me, I'm out of a job. The police are after me. My apartment stinks. My picture's full-page in the paper. I spent my day hiding in the shrubs around the front door, waiting for dark. For Helen Hoover Boyle to tell me what she has in mind.

She has the grimoire under one arm.

The pages stained pink and purple. She opens it in her hands, and shows me a spell, the English words written in black pen below the foreign gibberish of the original.

"Say it," she says.

The spell?

"Read it out loud," she says.

And I ask, what's this do?

And Helen says, "Just watch out for the chandelier."

She starts reading, the words dull and even, as if she were counting, as if they were numbers. She starts reading, and her purse starts to float up from where it hangs near her waist. Her purse floats higher until it's tethered to her by the shoulder strap, floating above her head as if it were a yellow balloon.

Helen keeps reading, and my tie floats out in front of me. Rising like a blue snake out of a basket, it brushes my nose. Helen's skirt, the hem starts to rise, and she grabs it and holds it down, between her legs with one hand. She keeps reading, and my shoelaces dance in the air. Her dangle earrings, pearls and emeralds, float up alongside her ears. Her pearl necklace, it floats up around her face. It floats over her head, a hovering pearl halo.

Helen looks up at me and keeps reading.

My sport coat floats up under my arms. Helen's getting taller. She's eye level with me. Then I'm looking up at her. Her feet hang, toes pointed down, they're hanging above the floor. One yellow shoe then the other drops off and clatters on the wood.

Her voice still flat and even, Helen looks down at me and smiles.

And then one of my feet isn't touching the ground. My other foot goes limp, and I kick the way you do in deep water, trying to find the bottom of the swimming pool. I throw my hands out for purchase. I kick, and my feet pitch up behind me until I'm looking facedown at the ballroom floor four, six, eight feet below me. Me and my shadow getting farther and farther apart. My shadow getting smaller and smaller.

Helen says, "Carl, watch out."

And something cold and brittle wraps around me. Sharp bits of something loose drape around my neck and snag in my hair.

"It's the chandelier, Carl," Helen says. "Be careful."

My ass buried in the middle of the crystal beads and shards, I'm wrapped in a shivering, tinkling octopus. The cold glass arms and fake candles. My arms and legs tangle in the hanging strands of crystal

300

chains. The dusty crystal bobs. The cob-
webs and dead spiders. A hot lightbulb
burns through my sleeve. This high above
the floor, I panic and grab hold of a
swooping glass arm, and the whole sparkling mess rocks and shakes, ringing wind
chimes. Flashing bits clatter on the floor
below. All of it with me inside pitches back
and forth.

And Helen says, "Stop. You're going to
ruin it."

Then she's next to me, floating just
behind a shimmering beaded curtain of
crystal. Her lips move with quiet words.
Helen's pink fingernails part the beads,
and she smiles in at me, saying, "Let's get
you right side up, first."

The book's gone, and she holds the crystals to one side and swims closer.

I'm gripping a glass chandelier arm in
both hands. The million flickering bits of it
shake with my every heartbeat.

"Pretend you're underwater," she says,
and unties my shoe. She slips the shoe off
my foot and drops it. With her stained
hands, she unties my other shoe, and the
first shoe clatters on the floor. "Here," she
says, and slips her arms under mine. "Take
off your jacket."

She drops my jacket out of the chandelier. Then my tie. She slips out of her own jacket and lets it fall. Around us, the chandelier is a shimmering million rainbows of lead crystal. Warm with a hundred tiny lightbulbs. The burning smell of dust on all those hot lightbulbs. All of it dazzling and shivering, we're floating here in the hollow center.

We're floating in nothing but light and heat.

Helen mouths her silent words, and my heart feels full of warm water.

Helen's earrings, all her jewelry is blazing bright. All you can hear is the tinkling chimes around us. We sway less and less, and I start to let go. A million tinkling bright stars around us, this is how it must feel to be God.

And this, too, is my life.

I say, I need a place to stay. From the police. I don't know what to do next.

Holding out her hand, Helen says, "Here."

And I take it. And she doesn't let go. And we kiss. And it's nice.

And Helen says, "For now, you can stay here." She flicks a pink fingernail against a gleaming glass ball, cut and faceted to throw light in a thousand directions. She says, "From now on, we can do anything."

She says, "Anything."

We kiss, and her toes peel off my socks. We kiss, and I open the buttons down the back of her blouse. My socks, her blouse, my shirt, her panty hose. Some things drop to the floor far below, some things snag and hang from the bottom of the chandelier.

My swollen infected foot, Helen's crusted, scabby knees from Oyster's attack, there's no way to hide these from each other.

It's been twenty years, but here I am, somewhere I never dreamed I'd ever be again, and I say, I'm falling in love.

And Helen, blazing smooth and hot in this center of light, she smiles and rolls her head back, saying, "That's the idea."

I'm in love with her. In love. With Helen Hoover Boyle.

My pants and her skirt flutter down into the heap, the fallen crystals, our shoes, all on the floor with the grimoire.

Chapter 38

At the offices of Helen Boyle Realty, the doors are locked, and when I knock, Mona shouts through the glass, "We're not open."

And I shout, I'm not a customer.

Inside, she's sitting at her computer, keyboarding something. Every couple keystrokes, Mona looks back and forth between the keys and the screen. On the screen, at the top in big letters, it says, "Resume."

The police scanner says a code nine-twelve.

Still keyboarding, Mona says, "I don't know why I shouldn't charge you with assault."

Maybe because she cares about me and Helen, I say.

And Mona says, "No, that's not it."

Maybe she won't blow the whistle because she still wants the grimoire.

And Mona doesn't say anything. She turns in her chair and pulls up the side of her peasant blouse. The skin on her ribs under her arms, is white with purple blotches.

Tough love.

Through the door into Helen's office, Helen yells, "What's another word for 'tormented'?" Her desk is covered with open books. Under her desk, she's wearing one pink shoe and one yellow shoe.

The pink silk sofa, Mona's carved Louis XIV desk, the lion-legged sofa table, it's all frosted with dust. The flower arrangements are withered and brown, standing in black, stinking water.

The police scanner says a code three-eleven.

I say, I'm sorry. Grabbing her wasn't right. I pinch the crease in my pant legs and pull them up to show her the purple bruises on my shins.

"That's different," Mona says. "I was defending myself."

I stamp my foot a couple times and say my infection's a lot better. I say, thank you.

And Helen yells, "Mona? What's another way of saying 'butchered'?"

Mona says, "On your way out, we need to have a little talk."

In the inner office, Helen's facedown in an open book. It's a Hebrew dictionary. Next to it is a guide to classical Latin.

Under that is a book about Aramaic. Next to that is an unfolded copy of the culling spell. The trash can next to the desk is filled with paper coffee cups.

I say, hey.

And Helen looks up. There's a coffee stain on her green lapel. The grimoire is open next to the Hebrew dictionary. And Helen blinks once, twice, three times and says, "Mr. Streator."

I ask if she'd like to get some lunch. I still need to go up against John Nash, to confront him. I was hoping she might give me something for an edge. An invisibility spell, maybe. Or a mind-control spell. Maybe something so I won't have to kill him. I come around to see what she's translating.

And Helen slides a sheet of paper on top of the grimoire, saying, "I'm a little occupied today." With a pen in one hand, she waits. With the other hand, she shuts the dictionary. She says, "Shouldn't you be hiding from the police?"

And I say, how about a movie?

And she says, "Not this weekend."

I say, how about I get us tickets to the symphony?

And Helen waves a hand between us and says, "Do what you want."

And I say, great. Then it's a date.

Helen puts her pen in the pink hair behind her ear. She opens another book and lays it on top of the Hebrew book. With one finger holding her place in a dictionary, Helen looks up and says, "It's not that I don't like you. It's just that I'm very, very busy right now."

In the open grimoire, sticking out from one edge of it is a name. Written in the margin of a page is today's name, today's assassination target. It says, Carl Streator.

Helen closes the grimoire and says, "You understand."

The police scanner says a code seven-two.

I ask if she's coming to see me, tonight, in the Gartoller house. Standing in the doorway to her office, I say I can't wait to be with her again. I need her.

And Helen smiles and says, "That's the idea."

In the outer office, Mona catches me around the wrist. She picks up her purse and loops the strap over her shoulder, yelling, "Helen, I'm going out for lunch." To me, she says, "We need to talk, but outside." She unlocks the door to let us out.

In the parking lot, standing next to my car, Mona shakes her head, saying, "You have no idea what's happening, do you?"

I'm in love. So kill me.

"With Helen?" she says. She snaps her fingers in my face and says, "You're not in love." She sighs and says, "You ever hear of a love spell?"

For whatever reason, Nash screwing dead women comes to mind.

"Helen's found a spell to trap you," Mona says. "You're in her power. You don't really love her."

I don't?

Mona stares into my eyes and says, "When was the last time you thought about burning the grimoire?" She points at the ground and says, "This? What you call love? It's just her way of dominating you."

A car drives up and parks, and inside is Oyster. He just shakes the hair back off his eyes, and sits behind the steering wheel, watching us. The shattered blond hair exploded in every direction. Two deep parallel lines, slash scars, run across each cheek. Dark red war paint.

His cell phone rings, and Oyster answers it, "Doland, Dimms and Dorn, Attorneys-at-Law."

The big power grab.

But I love Helen.

"No," Mona says. She glances at Oyster.

"You just think you do. She's tricked you."

But it's love.

"I've known Helen a lot longer than you have," Mona says. She folds her arms and looks at her wristwatch. "It's not love. It's a beautiful, sweet spell, but she's making you into her slave."

Chapter 39

Experts in ancient Greek culture say that people back then didn't see their thoughts as belonging to them. When they had a thought, it occurred to them as a god or goddess giving them an order. Apollo was telling them to be brave.

Athena was telling them to fall in love.

Now people hear a commercial for sour cream potato chips and rush out to buy.

Between television and radio and Helen Hoover Boyle's magic spells, I don't know what I really want anymore. If I even believe myself, I don't know.

That night, Helen drives us to the antique store, the big warehouse where she's mutilated so much furniture. It's dark and closed, but she presses her hand over a lock and says a quick poem, and the door swings open. No burglar alarms sound. Nothing. We're wandering deep into the maze of furniture, the dark disconnected chandeliers hanging above us. Moonlight glows in through the skylights.

"See how easy," Helen says. "We can do *anything.*"

No, I say, *she* can do anything.

Helen says, "You still love me?"

If she wants me to. I don't know. If she says so.

Helen looks up at the looming chandeliers, the hanging cages of gilt and crystal, and she says, "Got time for a quickie?"

And I say, it's not like I have a choice.

I don't know the difference between what I want and what I'm trained to want.

I can't tell what I really want and what I've been tricked into wanting.

What I'm talking about is free will. Do we have it, or does God dictate and script everything we do and say and want? Do we have free will, or do the mass media and our culture control us, our desires and actions, from the moment we're born? Do I have it, or is my mind under the control of Helen's spell?

Standing in front of a Regency armoire of burled walnut with a huge mirror of beveled glass in the door, Helen strokes the carved scrolls and garlands and says, "Become immortal with me."

Like this furniture, traveling through life after life, watching everyone who loves us die. Parasites. These armoires. Helen and

I, the cockroaches of our culture.

Scarred across the mirrored door is an old gouged slash from her diamond ring. From back when she hated this immortal junk.

Imagine immortality, where even a marriage of fifty years would feel like a one-night stand. Imagine seeing trends and fashions blur past you. Imagine the world more crowded and desperate every century. Imagine changing religions, homes, diets, careers, until none of them have any real value. Imagine traveling the world until you're bored with every square inch. Imagine your emotions, your loves and hates and rivalries and victories, played out again and again until life is nothing more than a melodramatic soap opera. Until you regard the birth and death of other people with no more emotion than the wilted cut flowers you throw away.

I tell Helen, I think we're immortal already.

She says, "I have the power." She snaps open her purse and fishes out a sheet of folded paper, she shakes the paper open and says, "Do you know about 'scrying'?"

I don't know what I know. I don't know what's true. I doubt I really know anything. I say, tell me.

Helen slips a silk scarf from around her neck and wipes the dust off the huge mirrored door of the armoire. The Regency armoire with inlaid olive-wood carvings and Second Empire fire-gilded hardware, according to the index card taped to it. She says, "Witches spread oil on a mirror, then they say a spell, and they can read the future in the mirror."

The future, I say, great. Cheatgrass. Kudzu. The Nile perch.

Right now, I'm not even sure I can read the present.

Helen holds up the paper and reads. In the dull, counting voice she used for the flying spell, she reads a few quick lines. She lowers the paper and says, "Mirror, mirror, tell us what our future will be if we love each other and use our new power."

Her new power.

"I made up the 'mirror, mirror' part," Helen says. She slips her hand around mine and squeezes, but I don't squeeze back. She says, "I tried this at the office with the mirror in my compact, and it was like watching television through a microscope."

In the mirror, our reflections blur, the shapes swim together, the reflection mixes into an even gray.

"Tell us," Helen says, "show us our future together."

And shapes appear in the gray. Light and shadows swim together.

"See," she says. "There we are. We're young again. I can do that. You look like you did in the newspaper. The wedding photo."

Everything's so unfocused. I don't know what I see.

"And look," Helen says. She tosses her chin toward the mirror. "We're ruling the world. We're founding a dynasty."

But what's enough? I can hear Oyster say, him and his overpopulation talk.

Power, money, food, sex, love. Can we ever get enough, or will getting some make us crave even more?

Inside the shifting mess of the future, I can't recognize anything. I can't see anything except just more of the past. More problems, more people. Less biodiversity. More suffering.

"I see us together forever," she says.

I say, if that's what she wants.

And Helen says, "What's that supposed to mean?"

Just whatever she wants it to mean, I say. She's the one pulling the strings here. She's the one planting her little seeds.

Colonizing me. Occupying me. The mass media, the culture, everything laying its eggs under my skin. Big Brother filling me with need.

Do I really want a big house, a fast car, a thousand beautiful sex partners? Do I really want these things? Or am I trained to want them?

Are these things really better than the things I already have? Or am I just trained to be dissatisfied with what I have now? Am I just under a spell that says nothing is ever good enough?

The gray in the mirror is mixing, swirling, it could be anything. No matter what the future holds, ultimately it will be a disappointment.

And Helen takes my other hand. Holding both my hands in hers, she pulls me around, saying, "Look at me." She says, "Did Mona say something to you?"

I say, you love you. I just don't want to be used anymore.

Above us are the chandeliers, glowing silver in the moonlight.

"What did Mona say?" Helen says.

And I'm counting 1, counting 2, counting 3 . . .

"Don't do this," Helen says. "I love you." Squeezing my hands, she says, "Do

315

not shut me out."

I'm counting 4, counting 5, counting 6 . . .

"You're being just like my husband," she says. "I just want you to be happy."

That's easy, I say, just put a "happy" spell on me.

And Helen says, "There's no such spell." She says, "They have drugs for that."

I don't want to keep making the world worse. I want to try and clean up this mess we've made. The population. The environment. The culling spell. The same magic that ruins my life is supposed to fix it.

"But we can do that," Helen says. "With more spells."

Spells to fix spells to fix spells to fix spells, and life just gets more miserable in ways we never imagined. That's the future I see in the mirror.

Mr. Eugene Schieffelin and his starlings, Spencer Baird and his carp, history is filled with brilliant people who wanted to fix things and just made them worse.

I want to burn the grimoire.

I tell her about what Mona told me. About how she's put a spell on me to make me her immortal love slave for all of eternity.

"Mona's lying," Helen says.

316

But how do I know that? Whom do I believe?

The gray in the mirror, the future, maybe it's not clear to me because now nothing's clear to me.

And Helen drops my hands. She waves her hands at the Regency armoires, the Federalist desks and Italian Renaissance coat racks, and says, "So if reality is all a spell, and you don't really want what you think you want . . ." She pushes her face in my face and says, "If you have no free will. You don't really *know* what you *know*. You don't really *love* who you *only think* you love. What do you have left to live for?"

Nothing.

This is just us standing here with all the furniture watching.

Think of deep outer space, the incredible cold and quiet where your wife and kid wait.

And I say, please. I tell her to give me her cell phone.

The gray still shifting and liquid in the mirror, Helen snaps open her purse and hands me the phone.

I flip it open and dial 911.

And a woman's voice says, "Police, fire, or medical?"

And I say, medical.

"Your location?" the voice says.

And I tell her the address of the bar on Third where Nash and I meet, the bar near the hospital.

"And the nature of your medical emergency?"

Forty professional cheerleaders overcome with heat exhaustion. A women's volleyball team needing mouth-to-mouth. A crew of fashion models wanting breast examinations. I tell her, if they've got an emergency med tech named John Nash, he's the one to send. I tell her, if they can't find Nash, not to bother.

Helen takes the phone back. She looks at me, blinking once, twice, three times, slow, and says, "What are you up to?"

What I have left, maybe the only way to find freedom, is by doing the things I don't want to. Stop Nash. Confess to the police. Accept my punishment.

I need to rebel against myself.

It's the opposite of following your bliss. I need to do what I most fear.

Chapter 40

Nash is eating a bowl of chili. He's at a back table in the bar on Third Avenue. The bartender is slumped forward on the bar, his arms still swinging above the barstools. Two men and two women are facedown at a booth table. Their cigarettes still burn in an ashtray, only half burned down. Another man is laid out in the doorway to the bathrooms. Another man is dead, stretched out on the pool table, the cue still clutched in his hands. Behind the bar, there's a radio blaring static in the kitchen. Somebody in a greasy apron is facedown on the grill among the hamburgers, the grill popping and smoking and the sweet, greasy smoke from the guy's face rolling out along the ceiling.

The candle on Nash's table is the only light in the place.

And Nash looks up, chili red around his mouth, and says, "I thought you'd like a little privacy for this."

He's wearing his white uniform. A dead body nearby is wearing the same uniform. "My partner," Nash says, nodding at the body. As he nods, his ponytail, the little black palm tree, flops around on top of his head. Red chili stains run down the front of his uniform. Nash says, "Me culling him was long overdue."

Behind me, the street door opens and a man steps in. He stands there, looking around. He waves a hand through the smoke and looks around, saying, "What the fuck?" The street door shuts behind him.

And Nash tucks his chin and fishes two fingers inside his chest pocket. He brings out a white index card smeared with red and yellow food and he reads the culling song, his words flat and steady as someone counting out loud. As Helen.

The man in the doorway, his eyes roll up white. His knees buckle and he slumps to one side.

I just stand here.

Nash tucks the index card back in his pocket and says, "Now, where were we?"

So, I say, where did he find the poem?

And Nash says, "Guess." He says, "I got it the only place where you can't destroy it."

He picks up a bottle of beer and points the long neck at me, saying, "Think." He says, "Think hard."

The book, *Poems and Rhymes from Around the World*, will always be out there for people to find. Hiding in plain sight. Just in this one place, he says. No way can it ever be rooted out.

For whatever reason, cheatgrass comes to mind. And zebra mussels. And Oyster.

Nash drinks some beer and sets it down and says, "Think hard."

I say, the fashion models, the killings. I say, what he's doing is wrong.

And Nash says, "You give up?"

He has to see that having sex with dead women is wrong.

Nash picks up his spoon and says, "The good old Library of Congress. Your tax dollars at work."

Damn.

He digs the spoon into the bowl of chili. He puts the spoon in his mouth and says, "And don't lecture me about the evils of necrophilia." He says, "You're about the last person who can give that lecture." His mouth full of chili. Nash says, "I know who you are."

He swallows and says, "You're still wanted for questioning."

He licks the chili smeared around his lips and says, "I saw your wife's death certificate." He smiles and says, "Signs of postmortem sexual intercourse?"

Nash points at an empty chair, and I sit.

"Don't tell me," he leans across the table and says. "Don't tell me it wasn't just about the best sex you've ever had."

And I say, shut up.

"You can't kill me," Nash says. He crumbles a handful of crackers into his bowl and says, "You and me, we're exactly alike."

And I say, it was different. She was my wife.

"Your wife or not," Nash says, "dead means dead. It's still necrophilia."

Nash jabs his spoon around in the crackers and red and says, "You killing me would be the same as you killing yourself."

I say, shut up.

"Relax," he says. "I didn't give nobody a letter about this." Nash crunches a mouthful of crackers and red. "That would've been stupid," he says. "I mean, think." And he shovels in more chili. "All's they'd have to do is read it, and I don't need the competition."

Imperfect and messy, this is the world I live in. This far from God, these are the people I'm left with. Everybody grabbing for power. Mona and Helen and Nash and Oyster. The only people who know me

322

hate me. We all hate each other. We all fear each other. The whole world is my enemy.

"You and me," Nash says, "we can't trust nobody."

Welcome to hell.

If Mona is right, Karl Marx's words coming out of her mouth, then killing Nash would be saving him. Returning him to God. Connecting him to humanity by resolving his sins.

My eyes meet his eyes, and Nash's lips start to move. His breath is nothing but chili.

He's saying the culling song. As hard as a dog barking, he says each word so hard that chili bubbles out around his mouth. Drops of red fly out. He stops and looks into his chest pocket. His hand digs to find his index card. With two fingers, he holds it and starts to read. The card is so smeared he rubs it on the tablecloth and starts to read again.

It sounds heavy and rich. It's the sound of doom.

My eyes relax and the world blurs into unfocused gray. All my muscles go smooth and long. My eyes roll up and my knees start to fold.

This is how it feels to die. To be saved.

But by now, killing is a reflex. It's the way I solve everything.

My knees fold, and I hit the floor in three stages, my ass, my back, my head.

As fast as a belch, a sneeze, a yawn from deep inside me, the culling song whips through my mind. The powder keg of all my unresolved shit, it never fails me.

The gray comes back into focus. Flat on my back on the bar floor, I see the greasy, gray smoke roll along the ceiling. You can hear the guy's face still frying.

Nash, his two fingers let the card drop onto the table. His eyes roll up. His shoulders heave, and his face lands in the bowl of chili. Red flies everywhere. The bulk of his body in his white uniform, it heaves over and Nash hits the floor next to me. His eyes look into my eyes. His face smeared with chili. His ponytail, the little black palm tree on the top of his head, it's come loose and the stringy black hair hangs limp across his cheeks and forehead.

He's saved, but I'm not.

The greasy smoke settling over me, the grill popping and sizzling, I pick up Nash's index card off the floor. I hold it over the candle on the table, adding smoke to the smoke, and I just watch it burn.

A siren goes off, the smoke alarm, so

loud I can't hear myself think. As if I ever think. As if I ever could think. The siren fills me. Big Brother. It occupies my mind, the way an army does a city. While I sit and wait for the police to save me. To deliver me to God and reunite me with humanity, the siren wails, drowning out everything. And I'm glad.

Chapter 41

This is after the police read me my rights. After they cuff my hands behind my back and drive me to the precinct. This is after the first patrolman arrived at the scene, looked at the dead bodies, and said, "Sweet, suffering Christ." After the paramedics rolled the dead cook off the grill, took one look at his fried face, and puked in their own cupped hands. This is after the police gave me my one phone call, and I called Helen and said I was sorry, but this was it. I was arrested. And Helen said, "Don't worry. I'll save you." After they fingerprinted me and took a mug shot. After they confiscated my wallet and keys and watch. They put my clothes, my brown sport coat and blue tie, in a plastic bag tagged with my new criminal number. After the police walked me down a cold, cinder-block hallway, naked into a cold concrete room. After they leave me alone with a beefy, buzz-cut old officer with hands the size of a catcher's mitt. Alone in a room with nothing but a desk, my bag of clothes, and a jar of petroleum jelly.

After I'm alone with this grizzled old ox,

he pulls on a latex glove and says, "Please turn to the wall, bend over, and use your hands to spread your ass cheeks."

And I say, what?

And this big frowning giant wipes two gloved fingers around in the jar of petroleum jelly and says, "Body cavity search." He says, "Now turn around."

And I'm counting 1, counting 2, counting 3 . . .

And I turn around. I bend over. One hand gripping each half of my ass, I pull them apart.

Counting 4, counting 5, counting 6 . . .

Me and my failed Ethics. The same as Waltraud Wagner and Jeffrey Dahmer and Ted Bundy, I'm a serial killer and this is how my punishment starts. Proof of my free will. This is my path to salvation.

And the cop's voice, all rough with the smell of cigarettes, he says, "Standard procedure for all detainees considered dangerous."

I'm counting 7, counting 8, counting 9 . . .

And the cop growls, "You're going to feel a slight pressure so just relax."

And I'm counting 10, counting 11, counting . . .

And damn.

Damn!

"Relax," the cop says.

Damn. Damn. Damn. Damn. Damn. Damn!

The pain, it's worse than Mona poking me with her red-hot tweezers. It's worse than the rubbing alcohol washing away my blood. I grip the two handfuls of my ass and grit my teeth, the sweat running down my legs. Sweat from my forehead drips off my nose. My breathing stops. The drips fall straight down and splash between my bare feet, my feet planted wide apart.

Something huge and hard twists deeper into me, and the cop's horrible voice says, "Yeah, relax, buddy."

And I'm counting 12, counting 13 . . .

The twisting stops. The huge, hard thing backs off, slow, almost all the way. Then it twists in deep again. Slow as the hour hand on a clock, then faster, the cop's greased fingers prod into me, retreat, prod in, retreat.

And close to my ear, the cop's gravel and ashtray old voice says, "Hey, buddy, you got time for a quickie?"

And my whole body does a spasm.

And the cop says, "Boy howdy, somebody just got tight."

I say, Officer. Please. You have no idea. I could kill you. Please don't do this.

And the cop says, "Let go of me so I can unlock your handcuffs. It's me, Helen."

Helen?

"Helen Hoover Boyle? Remember?" the cop says. "Two nights ago, you were doing almost this exact same thing to me inside a chandelier?"

Helen?

The huge hard something still twisted deep inside me. The cop says, "This is called an *occupation spell*. I translated it just a couple hours ago. I've got Officer whoever here crammed down into his subconscious right now. I'm running his show."

The hard cold sole of the officer's shoe shoves against my ass, and the huge hard fingers yank themselves out. Between my feet is a puddle of sweat. Still gritting my teeth, I stand up, fast.

The officer looks at his fingers and says, "I thought I was going to lose these." He smells the fingers and makes a nasty face.

Great, I say, breathing deep, eyes closed. First she's controlling me, now I have to worry about Helen controlling everyone around me.

And the cop says, "I had control of Mona for the last couple of hours this afternoon. Just to give the spell a test run, and to get even with her for scaring you, I gave her a little makeover."

The cop grabs his crotch. "This is amazing. Being with you like this, you're giving me an erection." He says, "This sounds sexist, but I've always wanted a penis."

I say, I don't want to hear this.

And Helen says, through the cop's mouth, she says, "I think as soon as I put you into a taxi, maybe I'll hang around in this guy and beat off. Just for the experience."

And I say, if you think this will make me love you, think again.

A tear runs down the cop's cheek.

Standing here naked, I say, I don't want you. I can't trust you.

"You can't love me," the cop says, Helen says in the cop's grizzled voice, "because I'm a woman and I have more power than you."

And I say, just go, Helen. Get the fuck out of here. I don't need you. I want to pay for my crimes. I'm tired of making the world wrong to justify my own bad behavior.

And the cop's crying hard now, and another cop walks in. It's a young cop, and he looks from the old cop, crying, to me, naked. The young cop says, "Everything

A-okay in here, Sarge?"

"It's just delightful," the old cop says, wiping his eyes. "We're having a wonderful time." He sees he's wiped his eyes with his gloved hand, the fingers out my ass, and he tears off the glove with a little scream. His whole body does a big shudder, and he throws the greasy glove across the room.

I tell the young cop, we were just having a little talk.

And the young cop puts a fist in my face and says, "You just shut the fuck up."

The old cop, Sarge, sits down on the edge of the desk and crosses his legs at the knee. He sniffs back tears and tosses his head as if tossing back hair and says, "Now, if you don't mind, we'd very much like to be alone."

I just look at the ceiling.

The young cop says, "Sure thing, Sarge."

And Sarge grabs a tissue and dabs his eyes.

Then the young cop turns fast, grabbing me under the jaw and jamming me up against the wall. My back and legs against the cold concrete. With my head pushed up and back, the young cop's hand squeezing my throat, the cop says, "You don't give the Sarge a hard time!" He shouts, "Got that?"

And the Sarge looks up with a weak smile and says, "Yeah. You heard him." And sniffs.

And the young cop lets loose of my throat. He steps back toward the door, saying, "I'll be out front if you need . . . well, anything."

"Thank you," the Sarge says. He clutches the young cop's hand, squeezing it, saying, "You're too sweet."

And the young cop jerks his hand away and leaves the room.

Helen's inside this man, the way a television plants its seed in you. The way cheatgrass takes over a landscape. The way a song stays in your head. The way ghosts haunt houses. The way a germ infects you. The way Big Brother occupies your attention.

The Sarge, Helen, gets to his feet. He fiddles with his holster and pulls out his gun. Holding the pistol in both hands, he points it at me and says, "Now get your clothes out of the bag and put them on." The Sarge sniffs back tears and kicks the garbage bag full of clothes at me and says, "Get dressed, damn it." He says, "I came here to save you."

The pistol trembling, the Sarge says, "I want you out of here so I can beat off."

Chapter 42

Everywhere, words are mixing. Words and lyrics and dialogue are mixing in a soup that could trigger a chain reaction. Maybe acts of God are just the right combination of media junk thrown out into the air. The wrong words collide and call up an earthquake. The way rain dances called storms, the right combination of words might call down tornadoes. Too many advertising jingles commingling could be behind global warming. Too many television reruns bouncing around might cause hurricanes. Cancer. AIDS.

In the taxi, on my way to the Helen Boyle real estate offices, I see newspaper headlines mixing with hand-lettered signs. Leaflets stapled to telephone poles mix with third-class mail. The songs of street buskers mix with Muzak mix with street hawkers mix with talk radio.

We're living in a teetering tower of babble. A shaky reality of words. A DNA soup for disaster. The natural world destroyed, we're left with this cluttered world of language.

Big Brother is singing and dancing, and we're left to watch. Sticks and stones may break our bones, but our role is just to be a good audience. To just pay our attention and wait for the next disaster.

Against the taxi's seat, my ass still feels greasy and stretched out.

There are thirty-three copies of the poems book left to find. We need to visit the Library of Congress. We need to mop up the mess and make sure it will never happen.

We need to warn people. My life is over. This is my new life.

The taxi pulls into the parking lot, and Mona's outside the front doors, locking them with a huge ring of keys. For a minute, she could be Helen. Mona, her hair's ratted, back-combed, teased into a red and black bubble. She's wearing a brown suit, but not chocolate brown. It's more the brown of a chocolate hazelnut truffle served on a satin pillow in a luxury hotel.

A box sits on the ground at Mona's feet. On top of the box is something red, a book. The grimoire.

I'm walking across the parking lot, and she calls, "Helen's not here."

There was something on the police scanner about everybody in a bar on Third Avenue being dead, Mona says, and me being arrested. Putting the box in the trunk of her car, she says, "You just missed Mrs. Boyle. She ran out of here sobbing just a second ago."

The Sarge.

Helen's big, leather-smelling Realtor's car is nowhere in sight.

Looking down at her own brown high heels, her tailored suit, padded and tucked, doll clothes with huge topaz buttons, her short skirt, Mona says, "Don't ask me how *this* happened." She holds up her hands, her black fingernails painted pink with white tips. Mona says, "Please tell Mrs. Boyle I don't appreciate having my body kidnapped and shit done to me." She points at her own stiff bubble of hair, her blusher cheeks and pink lipstick, and says, "*This* is the equivalent of a fashion rape."

With her new pink fingernails, Mona slams the trunk lid.

Pointing at my shirt, she says, "Did things with your friend get a little bloody?"

The red stains are chili, I tell her.

The grimoire, I say. I saw it. The red human skin. The pentagram tattoo.

"She gave it to me," Mona says. She

snaps open her little brown purse and reaches inside, saying, "She said she wouldn't need it anymore. Like I said, she was upset. She was crying."

With two pink fingernails, Mona plucks a folded paper out of her purse. It's a page from the grimoire, the page with my name written on it, and she holds it out to me, saying, "Take care of yourself. I guess somebody in some government must want you dead."

Mona says, "I guess Helen's little love spell must've backfired." She stumbles in her brown high heels, and leaning on the car, she says, "Believe it or not, we're doing this to save you."

Oyster's slumped in her backseat, too still, too perfect, to be alive. His shattered blond hair spreads across the seat. The Hopi medicine bag still hangs around his neck, cigarettes falling out of it. The red scars across his cheeks from Helen's car keys.

I ask, is he dead?

And Mona says, "You wish." She says, "No, he'll be okay." She gets into the driver's seat and starts the car, saying, "You'd better hurry and go find Helen. I think she might do something desperate."

She slams her car door and starts to

back out of her parking space.

Through her car window, Mona yells, "Check at the New Continuum Medical Center." She drives off, yelling, "I just hope you're not too late."

Chapter 43

In room 131 at the New Continuum Medical Center, the floor sparkles. The linoleum tile snaps and pops as I walk across it, across the shards and slivers of red and green, yellow and blue.

The drops of red. The diamonds and rubies, emeralds and sapphires. Both Helen's shoes, the pink and the yellow, the heels are hammered down to mush. The ruined shoes left in the middle of the room.

Helen stands on the far side of the room, in a little lamplight, just the edge of some light from a table lamp. She's leaning on a cabinet made of stainless steel. Her hands are spread against the steel. She presses her cheek there.

My shoes snap and crush the colors on the floor, and Helen turns.

There's a smear of blood across her pink lipstick. On the cabinet is a kiss of pink and red. Where she was lying is a blurry gray window, and inside is something too perfect and white to be alive.

Patrick.

The frost around the edges of the window has started to melt, and water drips down the cabinet.

And Helen says, "You're here," and her voice is blurry and thick. Blood spills out of her mouth.

Just looking at her my foot aches.

I'm okay, I say.

And Helen says, "I'm glad."

Her cosmetic case is dumped out on the floor. Among the shards of color are twisted chains and settings, gold and platinum. Helen says, "I tried to break the biggest ones," and she coughs into her hand. "The rest I tried to chew," she says, and coughs until her palm is filled with blood and slivers of white.

Next to the cosmetic case is a spilled bottle of liquid drain cleaner, the spill a green puddle around it.

Her teeth are shattered, bloody gaps, and pits show inside her mouth. She puts her face against the gray window. Her breath fogging the glass, her bloody hand goes to the side of her skirt.

"I don't want to go back to how it was before," she says, "the way my life was before I met you." She wipes her bloody hand and keeps wiping it on her skirt. "Even with all the power in the world."

I say, we need to get her to a hospital.

And Helen smiles a bloody smile and says, "This is a hospital."

It's nothing personal, she says. She just needed someone. Even if she could bring Patrick back, she'd never want to ruin his life by sharing the culling spell. Even if it meant living alone again, she'd never want Patrick to have that power.

"Look at him," she says, and touches the gray glass with her pink fingernails. "He's so perfect."

She swallows, blood and shattered diamonds and teeth, and makes a terrible wrinkled face. Her hands clutch her stomach, and she leans on the steel cabinet, the gray window. Blood and condensation run down from the little window.

With one shaking hand, Helen snaps open her purse and takes out a lipstick. She touches it around her lips and the pink lipstick comes away smeared with blood.

She says she's unplugged the cryogenic unit. Disconnected the alarm and backup batteries. She wants to die with Patrick.

She wants it to end here. The culling spell. The power. The loneliness. She wants to destroy all the jewels that people think will save them. All the residue that outlasts the talent and intelligence and beauty. All the decorative junk left behind by real accomplishment and success. She wants to destroy all the lovely parasites that outlive their human hosts.

The purse drops out of her hands. On the floor, the gray rock rolls out of the purse. For whatever reason, Oyster comes to mind.

Helen belches. She takes a tissue from her purse and cups it under her mouth and spits out blood and bile and broken emeralds. Flashing inside her mouth, stuck in the shredded meat of her gums are jagged pink sapphires and shattered orange beryls. Lodged in the roof of her mouth are fragments of purple spinels. Sunk in her tongue are shards of black bort diamond.

And Helen smiles and says, "I want to be with my family." She wraps the bloody tissue into a ball and tucks it inside the cuff of her suit. Her earrings, her necklaces, her rings, it's all gone.

The details of her suit are, it's some color. It's a suit. It's ruined.

She says, "Please. Just hold me."

Inside the gray window, the perfect infant is curled on its side in a pillow of white plastic. One thumb is in its mouth. Perfect and pale as blue ice.

I put my arms around Helen and she winces.

Her knees start to fold, and I lower her to the floor. Helen Hoover Boyle closes her eyes. She says, "Thank you, Mr. Streator."

With the gray rock in my fist, I punch through the cold gray window. My hands bleeding, I lift out Patrick, cold and pale. My blood on Patrick, I put him in Helen's arms. I put my arms around Helen.

My blood and hers, mixed now.

Lying in my arms, Helen closes her eyes and grinds her head into my lap. She smiles and says, "Didn't it feel too coincidental when Mona found the grimoire?"

Leering at me, she opens her eyes and says, "Wasn't it just a little too neat and tidy, the fact that we'd been traveling along with the grimoire the whole time?"

Helen lying in my arms, she cradles Patrick. Then it happens. She reaches up and pinches my cheek. Helen looks up at me and smiles with just half her mouth, a leer with blood and green bile between her lips. She winks and says, "Gotcha, Dad!"

My whole body, one muscle spasm wet with sweat.

Helen says, "Did you really think Mom would off herself over *you?* And trash her precious fucking jewels? And thaw this frozen piece of meat?" She laughs, blood and drain cleaner bubbling in her throat, and says, "Did you really think Mom would *chew* her fucking diamonds because you didn't love her?"

I say, Oyster?

"In the flesh," Helen says, Oyster says with Helen's mouth, Helen's voice. "Well, I'm in Mrs. Boyle's flesh, but I bet you've been inside her yourself."

Helen raises Patrick in her hands. Her child, cold and blue as porcelain. Frozen fragile as glass.

And she tosses the dead child across the room where it clatters against the steel cabinet and falls to the floor, spinning on the linoleum. Patrick. A frozen arm breaks off. Patrick. The spinning body hits a steel cabinet corner and the legs snap off. Patrick. The armless, legless body, a broken doll, it spins against the wall and the head breaks off.

And Helen winks and says, "Come on, Dad. Don't flatter yourself."

And I say, damn you.

Oyster occupies Helen, the way an army occupies a city. The way Helen occupied Sarge. The way the past, the media, the world, occupy you.

Helen says, Oyster says through Helen's

mouth, "Mona's known about the grimoire for weeks now. The first time she saw Mom's planner, she knew." He says, "She just couldn't translate it."

Oyster says, "My thing is music, and Mona's thing is . . . well, stupidity is Mona's thing."

With Helen's voice, he says, "This afternoon, Mona woke up in some beauty salon, getting her nails painted pink." He says, "She stormed back to the office, she found Mrs. Boyle facedown on her desk in some kind of a coma."

Helen shudders and grabs her stomach. She says, "Open in front of Mrs. Boyle was a translated spell, called an occupation spell. In fact all the spells were translated."

She says, Oyster says, "God bless Mom and her crossword puzzles. She's in here somewhere, mad as hell."

Oyster says, through Helen's mouth says, "Say hi to Mom for me."

The brittle blue statue, the frozen baby, is shattered, broken among the broken jewels, a busted-off finger here, the broken-off legs there, the shattered head.

I say, so now he and Mona are going to kill everybody and become Adam and Eve?

Every generation wants to be the last.

"Not everybody," Helen says. "We're

going to need some slaves."

With Helen's bloody hands, he reaches down and pulls her skirt up. Grabbing her crotch, he says, "Maybe you and Mom will have time for a quickie before she's toast."

And I heave Helen's body off my lap.

My whole body aching more than my foot ever ached.

Helen cries out, a little scream as she slides to the floor. And curled there on the cold linoleum with the shattered gems and fragments of Patrick, she says, "Carl?"

She puts a hand to her mouth, feels the jewels embedded there. She twists to look at me and says, "Carl? Carl, where am I?"

She sees the stainless-steel cabinet, the broken gray window. She sees the little blue arms first. Then the legs. The head. And she says, "No."

Spraying blood, Helen says, "No! No! No!" and crawling through the sharp slivers of broken color, her voice thick and blurred from her ruined teeth, she grabs all the pieces. Sobbing, covered in bile and blood, the room stinking, she clutches the broken blue pieces. The hands and tiny feet, the crushed torso and dented head, she hugs them to her chest and screams, "Oh, Patrick! Patty!"

She screams, "Oh, my Patty-Pat-Pat! No!"

Kissing the dented blue head, squeezing it to her breast, she asks, "What's happening? Carl, help me." She stares at me until a cramp bends her in half and she sees the empty bottle of liquid drain cleaner.

"God, Carl, help me," she says, clutching her child and rocking. "God, please tell me how I got here!"

And I go to her. I take her in my arms and say, at first, the new owner pretends he never looked at the living room floor. Never really looked. Not the first time they toured the house. Not when the inspector showed them through it. They'd measured rooms and told the movers where to set the couch and piano, hauled in everything they owned, and never really stopped to look at the living room floor. They pretend.

Helen's head is nodding forward over Patrick. The blood's drooling from her mouth. Her arms are looser, spilling little fingers and toes onto the floor.

In another moment, I'll be alone. This is my life. And I swear, no matter where or when, I'll track down Oyster and Mona.

What's good is this only takes a minute.

It's an old song about animals going to sleep. It's wistful and sentimental, and my face feels livid and hot with oxygenated hemoglobin while I say the poem out loud under the fluorescent lights, with the loose bundle of Helen in my arms, leaning back against the steel cabinet. Patrick's covered in my blood, covered in her blood. Her mouth is open a little, her glittering teeth are real diamonds.

Her name was Helen Hoover Boyle. Her eyes were blue.

My job is to notice the details. To be an impartial witness. Everything is always research. My job isn't to feel anything.

It's called a culling song. In some ancient cultures, they sang it to children during famines or droughts, anytime the tribe had outgrown its land. It was sung to warriors injured in accidents or the very old or anyone dying. It was used to end misery and pain.

It's a lullaby.

I say, everything will be all right. I hold Helen, rocking her, telling her, rest now. Telling her, everything is going to be just fine.

Chapter 44

When I was twenty years old, I married a woman named Gina Dinji, and that was supposed to be the rest of my life. A year later, we had a daughter named Katrin, and she was supposed to be the rest of my life. Then Gina and Katrin died. And I ran and became Carl Streator. And I became a journalist. And for twenty more years, that was my life.

After that, well, you already know what happened.

How long I held on to Helen Hoover Boyle I don't know. After long enough, it was just her body. It was so long she'd stopped bleeding. By then, the broken parts of Patrick Boyle, still cradled in her arms, they'd thawed enough to start bleeding.

By then, footsteps arrived outside the door to room 131. The door opened.

Me still sitting on the floor, Helen and Patrick dead in my arms, the door opens, and it's the grizzled old Irish cop.

Sarge.

And I say, please. Please, put me in jail. I'll plead guilty to anything. I killed my wife. I killed my kid. I'm Waltraud Wagner, the Angel of Death. Kill me so I can be with Helen again.

And the Sarge says, "We need to get a move on." He steps from the doorway to the steel cabinet. On a pad of paper, he writes something in pen. He tears off the note and hands it to me.

His wrinkled hand is spotted with moles, carpeted with gray hairs. His fingernails, thick and yellow.

"Please forgive me for taking my own life," the note says. "I'm with my son now."

It's Helen's handwriting, the same as in her planner book, the grimoire.

It's signed, "Helen Hoover Boyle," in her exact handwriting.

And I look from the body in my arms, the blood and green drain-cleaner vomit to the Sarge standing there, and I say, Helen?

"In the flesh," the Sarge says, Helen says. "Well, not my own flesh," he says, and looks at Helen's body dead in my lap. He looks at his own wrinkled hands and says, "I hate ready-to-wear, but any port in a storm."

So this is how we're on the road again.

Sometimes I worry that Sarge here is really Oyster pretending to be Helen occupying the Sarge. When I sleep with whoever this is, I *pretend it's Mona. Or Gina. So it all comes out even.*

According to Mona Sabbat, people who eat or drink too much, people addicted to drugs or sex or stealing, they're really controlled by spirits that loved those things too much to quit after death. Drunks and kleptos, they're possessed by evil spirits.

You are the culture medium. The host.

Some people still think they run their own lives.

You are the possessed.

We're all of us haunting and haunted.

Something foreign is always living itself through you. Your whole life is the vehicle for something to come to earth.

An evil spirit. A theory. A marketing campaign. A political strategy. A religious doctrine.

Driving me away from the New Continuum Medical Center in a squad car, the Sarge says, "They have the occupation spell and the flying spell." He ticks off each spell by holding up another finger. "They'll have a resurrection spell — but it only works on animals. Don't ask me why," he says. She says, "They have a rain spell and a sun spell . . . a fertility spell to make crops grow . . . a spell to communicate with animals . . ."

Not looking at me, looking at his fingers

spread on the steering wheel, the Sarge says, "They do not have a love spell."

So I am really in love with Helen. A woman in a man's body. We don't have hot sex anymore, but as Nash would say, how is that different than most love relationships after long enough?

Mona and Oyster have the grimoire, but they don't have the culling song. The grimoire page that Mona gave me, the one with my name written in the margin, it's the song. Along the bottom of the page is written, "I want to save the world too — but not Oyster's way." It's signed, "Mona."

"They don't have the culling song," the Sarge says, Helen says, "but they have a shield spell."

A shield spell?

To protect them from the culling song, the Sarge says.

"But not to worry," he says. "I have a badge and a gun and a penis."

To find Mona and Oyster, you only have to look for the fantastic, for miracles. The amazing tabloid headlines. The young couple seen crossing Lake Michigan on foot in July. The girl who made grass grow up, green and tall, through the snow for buffalo starving in Canada. The boy who talks to lost dogs at the animal shelter and helps them get home.

Look for magic. Look for saints.

The Flying Madonna. The Roadkill Jesus Christ. The Ivy Inferno. The Talking Judas Cow.

Keep going after the facts. Witch-hunting. This isn't what a therapist will tell you to do, but it works.

Mona and Oyster, this will be their world soon enough. The power has shifted. Helen and I will be forever playing catch-up. Imagine if Jesus chased you around, trying to catch you and save your soul. Not just a patient passive God, but a hardworking, aggressive bloodhound.

The Sarge snaps open his holster, the way Helen used to snap open her little purse, and he takes out a pistol.

He says, Helen says, whoever says, "How about we just kill them the old-fashioned way?"

Now this is my life.

WHO'S WHO
IN FASHION

WHO'S WHO
IN FASHION

SECOND EDITION

ANNE STEGEMEYER

Fairchild Publications   New York

contents

PREFACE

Who's Who in Fashion first came into being as an information source for students. Its purpose was to provide some knowledge of the many gifted and productive people in all parts of the world who have worked and contributed in the field of fashion.

Rewarding as fashion can be, it is also difficult—a demanding and volatile business with a constantly changing cast of stars and supporting actors. Some talents produce successfully and consistently year after year, others emerge in a blaze of critical acclaim, shine for a season or two and drop from sight. Many build durable, satisfying careers working quietly out of the spotlight.

My emphasis here is on designers with an established track record. In addition, you'll find greats and near-greats of the past, a brief survey of influential individuals in related fields, and a selection of the many newcomers who promise to become the establishment of the future.

With *Who's Who in Fashion*, I've tried to give some sense of the excitement of the world of fashion, the diversity of the people who've made their careers in it, the different ways they go about the business of clothing people, and the different paths they've followed to success. I hope the book will be useful to students and professionals, and to people everywhere who love clothes and share my fascination with this extraordinary business.

1988   Anne Stegemeyer

ACKNOWLEDGMENTS

Information for *Who's Who in Fashion* came from many sources: questionnaires, press clippings and other published material, personal interviews. In cases where repeated inquiries failed to produce a response and outside documentation was lacking or inadequate, the biography was omitted.

My thanks, then, to all those designers and their staffs who returned questionnaires and phone calls and supplied missing biographical details. To Merle Thomason of the *Women's Wear Daily* Library, my particular gratitude for her thorough and untiring searches for the missing date, the pertinent fact. And, not least, very special thanks for their considerable patience to my editor, Olga Kontzias, and publisher, Ed Gold.

WHO'S WHO
IN FASHION

a

ADOLFO

ADRI

GILBERT ADRIAN

AGNÈS B.

AZZEDINE ALAÏA

HARDY AMIES

JOHN ANTHONY

MARIA ANTONELLI

GIORGIO ARMANI

1984

ADOLFO

BORN: Havana, Cuba, 13 February 1933

AWARDS:
1955, 1969—Coty American Fashion
Critics' Special Award (millinery)

Adolfo

1975

Adolfo's early interest in fashion was fostered by his aunt, Maria Lopez, a perennial on international "best-dressed" lists. She took him to Paris to see designer showings, introduced him to BALENCIAGA and CHANEL. He began his career as an apprentice to Balenciaga, came to New York in 1948 as millinery designer for Bragaard. He went to Emme in 1953, received recognition as Adolfo of Emme in 1956.

In 1962, with a $10,000 loan from BILL BLASS, Adolfo opened his own millinery firm, gradually adding clothing—wrap skirts, capes, sleeveless shifts—finally switched entirely into apparel. He has gained and held a loyal clientele for the way he understands and meets their fashion needs and through his ability to turn current trends into flattering, wearable clothes, among the top status symbols of the 1970s and 1980s. His semi-annual showings bring out a large coterie of faithful fans. He is one of the favorite designers of Nancy Reagan.

Among his successes: the Panama planter's hat, 1966; shaggy Cossack hat, 1967; huge fur berets; such non-hats as fur hoods, kidskin bandannas, and long braids entwined with flowers to be attached to one's own hair. His "romantic look" appeared in 1968 with gingham dirndl skirts, lacy white cotton blouses, ribbons, sashes, big, floppy straw hats. In homage to Chanel he introduced a series of knits inspired by her famous tweed suits. These proved so popular he has continued to show variations in every collection. He is also known for beautifully tailored coats and suits, extravagant evening clothes in magnificent fabrics and subtle color combinations.

Adolfo has chosen to keep his company small, selling to private customers from his 57th Street salon and wholesale to a handful of top specialty stores. *Adolfo* perfume appeared in September 1978. His interests also extend to men's wear, active sportswear, accessories.

ADRI

BORN: St. Joseph, Missouri, c. 1935.

AWARDS:
  1982—Coty American Fashion Critics'
     Award, "Winnie"

1974

Adri studied design at Washington University, St. Louis, during her sophomore year was a guest editor for the August 1955 college issue of *Mademoiselle* magazine. She continued her studies at Parsons School of Design in New York, where CLAIRE MCCARDELL was her critic. McCardell, with her belief in functional, comfortable clothes that move with the body, was, and continues to be, an important influence.

After Parsons, Adri went to work at B. H. Wragge, where she stayed for eight years. She then opened her own small business and quickly made a name for herself, but little money. She continued to have her name on collections, leisure wear as well as ready-to-wear, until 1983 when she established her own business, Adri Clotheslab, Inc., of which she is owner-president. She is also president and part owner of Adri International, which manufactures clothes under the Adri label.

In October 1971, she was invited to show her clothes at the Smithsonian Institution, Washington, D.C., in a two-designer showing with the theme, Innovative Contemporary Fashion. The other designer honored was Claire McCardell.

Adri has always made soft clothes in the McCardell manner, preferring to work with pliant materials such as jersey, knit, challis, crepe de Chine, leather. She believes this softness is needed to mitigate the frequent harshness and angularity of modern life. She feels that styles should evolve naturally from one collection to the next so that a customer can collect them, add to them, mix them freely from season to season.

ADRIAN, GILBERT

BORN: Naugatuck, Connecticut,
  3 March 1903.

DIED: Los Angeles, California,
  13 September 1959.

A top Hollywood studio designer of the 1920s and 1930s, Adrian also made a success of made-to-order and ready-to-wear. He attended the School of Fine and Applied Arts in New York in 1921, went to Paris to study in 1922. There he met Irving Berlin and soon was designing for the *Music Box Revues*, Greenwich Village *Follies*, and George White's *Scandals*.

In 1923, he went to Hollywood at the behest of Rudolph Valentino's wife, Natacha Rombova, to design costumes for her husband. In 1925 he began an association with Metro-

AWARDS:
  1943 — Neiman-Marcus Award
  1945 — Coty American Fashion Critics'
    Award, "Winnie"
  1956 — Parsons Medal for
    Distinguished Achievement

The Letty Lynton Dress

1946

Goldwyn-Mayer which lasted until 1939. As MGM's chief designer, Adrian created costumes for many leading stars, including Joan Crawford, Greta Garbo, Katharine Hepburn, Rosalind Russell, Norma Shearer.

In 1941, he opened Adrian Ltd. in Beverly Hills, for both couture and top-ticket ready-to-wear. He closed the retail salon in 1948, continued in wholesale until 1953. Meanwhile, in addition to clothes for women, he designed stage costumes, produced several men's wear collections and two perfumes, *Saint* and *Sinner*.

Adrian's style was marked by exaggeratedly wide, padded shoulders, tapering dramatically to a small waist. Signature details were diagonal closings, dolman sleeves, floating tabs. He was a master of intricate cut, worked stripes in opposing directions, mixed gingham checks in different sizes, sometimes adding quilting and sequins. He used set-in patches of color, applied bold animal prints to sinuous black crepe evening gowns, influences traceable to his interest in modern art and to his African travels.

In general, the Adrian look was sleek and modern but he also did draped, swathed late-day dresses and romantic organdy evening gowns. One of these, the "Letty Lynton" gown designed for Joan Crawford, was widely copied. Reputedly, more than 500,000 were sold at Macy's alone.

After closing his business, Adrian retired to Brazil with his wife, actress Janet Gaynor, where he concentrated on landscape painting, a longtime avocation. He returned to Hollywood in 1958 and in 1959, at the time of his death, was working on costumes for the 1960 stage production of *Camelot*.

AGNÈS B.

BORN: Paris, France, 1942.

After an editorial stint at *Elle* magazine, Agnès B. worked as an assistant to a clothing designer, in the early 1970s went into business for herself. She felt that the clothes available at the time in Paris were too dressy, and so she evolved her own style of unforced, airy, low-key sportswear: cotton blazers, T-shirts, tank tops, and leather pants, skirts, jackets, big, casual cardigans, and hats.

The clothes, for men, women, and children, are sold primarily in her own stores around the world, including the United States and Japan. She lives in Paris with her husband, Jean-René, who manages the business side of the company.

ALAÏA, AZZEDINE

BORN: Tunis, Tunisia.

Until 1980, when he presented his first ready-to-wear collection, Alaïa worked in obscurity, a cult designer making clothes for a clientele that also patronized the great couture houses. His first international notice came from black leather gauntlets studded with silver rivets. His are said to be the sexiest clothes in Paris, seamed, molded and draped to define and reveal every curve of a woman's body. The heart of his style is his unique draping, inspired by his fashion idol, MADELEINE VIONNET. Alaïa's greatest achievement in ready-to-wear is in translating all his techniques of draping, molding, and seaming, from woven cloth into knits.

Raised in Tunis by his grandmother, Alaïa was sent to the École des Beaux-Arts of Tunis to study sculpture. While in art school, he worked for several dressmakers, in 1957 went to Paris, where he had been promised a job with Dior. He arrived a few months before Dior's death, did indeed get a job in the Dior cutting room but lasted only five days.

To support himself he worked as an *au pair* for several members of the fashionable younger set, at the same time making dresses for his employers and their friends. In 1960 he was able to have his own apartment, where for eighteen years, he lived, worked, and showed his clothes to a select group of adventurous and knowledgeable clients, ranging from Paloma Picasso to Dyan Cannon and Raquel Welch. By 1984 he had become so commercially successful that he bought his own townhouse in the Marais section of Paris.

Alaïa

1987

AMIES, HARDY

BORN: Maida Vale, London, England,
17 July 1909.

AWARDS:
1977—C.V.O.

Educated at Brentwood School, Amies spent the years 1927 to 1930 in France where he taught English, and Germany where he represented W. & T. Avery, Ltd., a maker of scales. In 1934 he went to Lachasse, a London couture house, as designer, and within a year became managing director. He left Lachasse in 1939 to serve in the British Army Intelligence Corps, gaining the rank of lieutenant colonel. In 1944 he was head of the Special Forces Commission to Belgium. While in the service, he designed on a limited basis for the house of WORTH, joined other designers to create a government-sponsored collection intended for South America. He also designed clothes for the government Utility Scheme, according to wartime restrictions. He was mustered out of the service in 1945.

In 1946 he founded his dressmaking business, added a boutique line in 1950. He began designing men's wear in 1959 and this quickly became a major interest.

From the beginning, Amies specialized in tailored suits and coats, cocktail and evening dresses. While one of the favorite designers of Queen Elizabeth II, he has also made breezy, contemporary clothes for women, such as pantsuits and wide yachting pants, and also casual classics.

In 1984, at 75, Amies announced plans to leave his multi-million dollar women's and men's fashion business to the 50 members of his staff. At the same time he denied any intention of an early departure. "I have managed to get tickets for center court at Wimbledon up to 1990 and I plan to be there. Plus I'm working now on an outline of how I believe men will be dressing up to the year 2000."

The ready-to-wear and couture business continues at 14 Savile Row, with licensing agreements in 46 countries, including one for men's wear with Greif & Co.

ANTHONY, JOHN

BORN: New York City, 1938

AWARDS:
Coty American Fashion Critics' Award:
1972—"Winnie"
1976—Return Award

Anthony attended the High School of Industrial Arts (now High School of Art and Design) where he won three European scholarships. After one year at the Academia d'Arte in Rome, he returned to New York City and two more years at the Fashion Institute of Technology.

His first job was with Devonbrook, where he stayed for nine years, followed by three years with Adolph Zelinka. John Anthony, Inc. was established in January 1971. The firm closed in 1979. After a number of years spent winning back the use of his own name, Anthony reopened for fall 1986, showing a small collection of ready-to-wear out of his couture salon.

The first Anthony design successes under his own label were coats and suits noted for masterly tailoring and refined elegance. He has preferred to confine himself in each collection to a few lean, simple shapes, a limited color palette, a few key textures and luxurious fabrics. His strength is in sophisticated, feminine clothes, marked by a feeling for asymmetry, expert tailoring, a sensuous suppleness.

The Anthony name has also been applied to men's clothing, shirts, neckwear, sweaters, and rainwear, furs for men and women.

John Anthony

1987

ANTONELLI, MARIA

BORN: Tuscany, Italy, 1903.

DIED: Rome, Italy, 1969.

Antonelli began as a dressmaker in 1924, soon became known and respected for the exceptional tailoring of her coats and suits. As one of the pioneers of Italian fashion when it came into international prominence in the 1950s, she participated in the first Florence showings of 1951. In 1958 she was made a Cavalier of the Republic by the Italian government in recognition of her contributions to Italian fashion. She started Antonelli Sport ready-to-wear in 1961 assisted by her daughter Luciana.

Both ANDRÉ LAUG and Guy Douvier, who became successful designers on their own, trained with Antonelli. Her list of clients included an international roster of film and stage personalities.

ARMANI, GIORGIO

BORN: Emilia-Romagna, Italy, July 1934.

AWARDS:
1979—Neiman-Marcus Award
1983—Council of Fashion Designers of America (CFDA) International Award

Giorgio Armani

Armani studied medicine for a while, tried photography briefly, then became an assistant buyer of men's clothing for La Rinascente, a large Italian department store. During seven years there he developed his ideas on men's dress, and a dislike for what he considered a stiff, formal look that disguised individuality. He spent the next ten years as a designer with a men's wear manufacturer of the Cerutti group, learning the practical and commercial aspects of the clothing business. He then free-lanced for a number of Italian manufacturers.

In 1974 Armani produced his first men's wear collection under his own label, incorporating the ideas he had developed while working for others. He first attracted notice with his unconstructed blazer. In 1975 he moved into the area of women's wear, bringing to it the same perfectionist tailoring and fashion attitude he applies to men's clothes.

From day into evening, the emphasis is on easy, uncontrived shapes cut from exquisite Italian fabrics, tailored with absolute mastery. With Armani, color and fabric are primary considerations. His preference is for neutrals such as taupe, beige, black, and infinite tones of gray. He claims to have taught women to dress with the ease of a man, but always with a feminine turn to even the most masculine cut. The word he uses most often is "modern."

Armani pursues his work singlemindedly, supervising every aspect of collections shown in his own theater in the two adjoining buildings where he both lives and works. He insists on complete control, down to such details as the models' hairstyles, even putting final touches to their makeup.

The Armani empire now includes free-standing shops in Italy and around the world, perfumes and accessories for men and women. The Emporio label and chain of Italian shops was developed to bring Armani styles to young men and women who could not afford the regular line. He has also done film work.

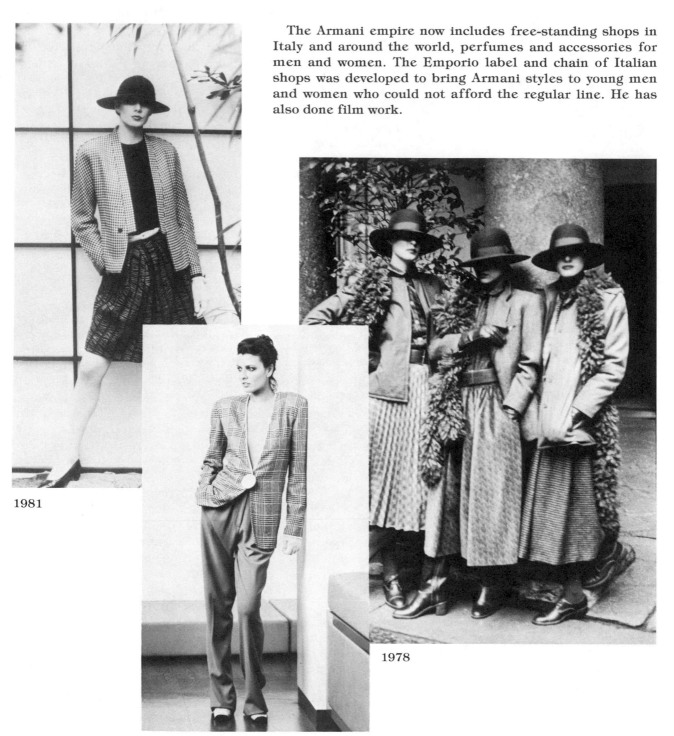

1981

1987

1978

b

CRISTOBAL BALENCIAGA

PIERRE BALMAIN

TRAVIS BANTON

JHANE BARNES

GEOFFREY BEENE

ANNE-MARIE BERETTA

ROSE BERTIN

LAURA BIAGIOTTI

BILL BLASS

MARC BOHAN

TOM BRIGANCE

DONALD BROOKS

STEPHEN BURROWS

BYBLOS

BALENCIAGA, CRISTOBAL

BORN: Guetaria, Spain,
21 January 1895.

DIED: Valencia, Spain, 24 March 1972.

Balenciaga, 1967

Master tailor, master dressmaker, Balenciaga was a great originator, possibly the greatest couturier of all time. Of them all, only he could do everything—design, cut, fit, and sew an entire garment. He worked alone, using only his own ideas, putting together with his own hands every model that later appeared in his collections. His clothes, so beautiful and elegant, were also so skillfully designed that a woman did not have to have a perfect figure to wear them. They moved with the body and were comfortable as well as chic.

Balenciaga's origins and early life are obscure, obscured still more by legends. His father has been said variously to have been captain of the Spanish royal yacht and a fishing boat captain. Upon his father's death, the boy and his mother moved to San Sebastián, where she became a seamstress and he followed in her footsteps to become a skilled tailor. According to legend, his career began at thirteen when the Marquesa de Casa Torres, impressed by his admiration for a Drécoll suit she was wearing, allowed him to copy it, later sending him to Paris to meet the designer. The Marquesa encouraged him to study design and in 1916 helped him set up his own shop in San Sebastián. This was the first of three houses called *Eisa*, the others were in Madrid and Barcelona.

Balenciaga moved to Paris in 1937, returned to Spain at the beginning of World War II, at its close reopened in Paris. There, in his salon on the avenue George V, he established himself as the preeminent designer of his time, one of the most imaginative and creative artists of the Paris couture.

Revered by his staff and known to them as "the master", Balenciaga was a perfectionist who tolerated nothing less than his ideal. He was also an influence on other designers: GIVENCHY, COURRÈGES, and UNGARO were among his disciples.

A great student of art, he understood how to interpret his sources rather than copy them. The somber blacks and browns of the old Spanish masters were among his favorite colors, and the influence of such early moderns as Monet and Manet can also be found in his work. His interest in the post cubists and abstract expressionists is apparent in his late designs.

His innovations, especially during the 1950s and 1960s, are still influential. The revolutionary semi-fitted suit jacket of 1951, the 1955 middy dress which evolved into the chemise, the cocoon coat, the balloon skirt, the flamenco evening gown cut short in front, long in back. To achieve his sculptural effects, he worked with the Swiss fabric house, Abraham, to develop a heavily-sized silk called gazar, very light but capable of holding a shape and floating away from the body. His sense of proportion and balance, his mastery of cut, his touches of wit, the architectural quality and essential "rightness" of his designs, still strike the onlooker.

1939

1938

1941

1942

1944

1945

1946

1947

1947

1950

1952

1954

1955

1956

Balenciaga, 1959 (The Brooklyn
Museum, Gift of Mrs. William Rand)

In 1968, Balenciaga abruptly closed his house and retired
to Spain. One theory is that he had taken his ideas as far as
the technical limitations of dressmaking would allow and
realized that he could go no farther. He came out of retirement to design the wedding dress of Generalissimo Franco's
granddaughter, whose marriage took place in 1972, just two
weeks before Balenciaga died.

A shy and private man who loathed publicity, Balenciaga
was seldom photographed. He never appeared in his own
salon and, except for his perfumes, refused to have anything
to do with commercial exploitation. Since his death he has
been honored by a number of exhibitions: in New York in
1973 at the Metropolitan Museum of Art and again in 1986
at the Fashion Institute of Technology; in France in 1985 at
the Museum of Historic Textiles in Lyons, the center of the
French silk industry.

He is rightly considered one of the giants of 20th-century
couture.

BALMAIN, PIERRE

BORN: St.-Jean-de-Maurienne, France,
18 May 1914.

DIED: Paris, France, 29 June 1982.

AWARDS:
1955—Neiman-Marcus Award

Pierre Balmain

An only child, Balmain was only seven when his father, a wholesale merchant, died. He was raised by his mother, who later worked with him in his couture salon. In 1934 he began sketching dresses while studying architecture at the École des Beaux Arts in Paris. He took his sketches to CAPTAIN MOLYNEUX, who allowed him to work for him in the afternoons, continuing his architectural studies in the mornings. Molyneux finally advised him to devote himself to dress design and gave him a job, in which he remained until called into the army in 1939.

After the fall of France in 1940, Balmain returned to Paris to work for LUCIEN LELONG. He left Lelong in 1945 to establish his own house on rue François Ier. He visited the United States in 1946, opened a New York ready-to-wear operation in 1951, designing special collections for the U.S. He also designed for theater and films.

Balmain took credit for beginning the New Look, others divide it between him, DIOR, FATH, and BALENCIAGA. His first collections accentuated the femininity of the figure with a small waist, high bust, rounded hips, long, full skirts. He continued making clothes of quiet elegance and at his death had just completed the sketches for his fall collection.

He had boutiques for women and men, over sixty licenses including men's fashions, luggage, jewelry, glasses, belts. He opened his perfume business with *Vent Vert*, introduced *Jolie Madame*, his best-known scent, in 1953. Revlon bought the perfume business in 1960, launched *Ivoire* in 1981.

1954

BANTON, TRAVIS

BORN: Waco, Texas, 1894.

DIED: Los Angeles, California,
2 February 1958.

Raised in New York, Banton attended Columbia University, the Art Student's League, the School of Fine and Applied Arts. He got into fashion after his return from naval service in World War I, received his training as a designer in the couture houses of Lucile and Madame Francis. In 1924, at the instigation of Walter Wanger, he went to Hollywood to design for Leatrice Joy in Paramount Pictures' *The Dressmaker from Paris**. He stayed on at Paramount and in the 1930s became head designer. While there he designed all of Marlene Dietrich's costumes.

At the expiration of his Paramount contract in 1938, he went to 20th Century Fox, then worked off and on for Universal Studios, meanwhile conducting his own dressmaking business. In the 1950s he turned to ready-to-wear. In addition, he designed Rosalind Russell's wardrobe for the stage production of *Auntie Mame*, dressed Dinah Shore for both her private life and television appearances.

Banton had an extraordinarily long career, is remembered particularly for what became known as "the Paramount look." He produced clothes of the highest quality, superb in fabric, workmanship, and fit. They were often cut on the bias, the effect was dreamy, elegant, understated.

*Title also given as *A Dressmaker of Paris* and *A Dressmaker in Paris*.

BARNES, JHANE

BORN: 1954.

AWARDS:
  Coty American Fashion Critics' Award:
    1980—Men's Wear
    1981—Men's Apparel
    1984—Men's Wear Return Award
    1981—Council of Fashion Designers
      of America (CFDA)

Barnes established her own company in 1977 when she was twenty-three. While mainly known for men's sportswear, she has also made sportswear for women. Her designs are unconstructed, beautifully tailored in luxurious and original fabrics, many of which she designs herself. They are marked by innovative details, carefully thought out and carried through. She is considered original and creative with architectural insight into clothing.

BEENE, GEOFFREY

BORN: Haynesville, Louisiana,
30 August 1927.

AWARDS:
Coty American Fashion Critics' Award
1964—"Winnie"
1966—Return Award
1974—Hall of Fame
1975—Hall of Fame Citation
1977—Special Award (jewelry)
1979—Special Award (contribution
to international status of
American fashion)
1981—Special Award (women's
fashions)
1982—Hall of Fame Citation
1964-65—Neiman-Marcus Award
1986—Council of Fashion Designers
of America (CFDA)

Beene spent three years at Tulane University, New Orleans, in pre-med and medicine before deciding he was not cut out to be a doctor. He went to Southern California, worked in display at I. Magnin, Los Angeles, where his talent was recognized by an executive who suggested he make a career of fashion. He attended Traphagen School of Fashion in New York, studied sketching and designing at L'Académie Julian in Paris. While in Paris he worked for MOLYNEUX, a master of tailoring and the bias cut. Beene returned to New York in 1949. Between 1949 and 1957 he designed for Samuel Winston and Harmay, in 1958 joined Teal Traina, who put Beene's name on the label. In 1962 he left Traina to go into business under his own name.

His first collection, shown in spring 1963, had elements characteristic of his work throughout the 1960s: looser fit, eased waistlines, bloused tops, flared skirts. He continued to work toward greater simplicity, increasing emphasis on cut and line animated with dressmaking details and unusual fabrics. Each showing included at least one tongue-in-cheek style to stir things up—a black coat made of wood buttons, a "tutu" evening dress with sequined bodice and feather skirt.

Geoffrey Beene

1964

In the late 1960s he branched out into furs, swimwear, jewelry, and scarves, designed Lynda Bird Johnson's wedding dress, went into men's wear. *Beene Bag*, his boutique collection, appeared in 1970. Beene licenses include shoes, gloves, hosiery, eyeglasses, loungewear, bedding, furniture. He has one fragrance, *Grey Flannel*, for men.

Some memorable Beene designs: long, sequined evening gowns cut like oversize football jerseys complete with numerals, tweed evening pants paired with jeweled or lamé jackets, gray "sweatshirt" bathing suit, soft evening coats made of striped Indian blankets from the Hudson's Bay Company.

He is noted for his subtle and imaginative use of color, accenting neutrals with pure intensities, and for the luxury of his fabrics. His designs stem from the qualities of the fabric and he enjoys mixing "poor" and "rich" materials to achieve a modern look. He believes that clothes must not only look attractive but must also move well, be comfortable to wear, and easy to pack. He has shown his clothes in Europe with great success—in Milan in 1975, in Vienna in 1985.

1963

1981

1982

BERETTA, ANNE-MARIE

BORN: Beziers, France, 1937.

Beretta began her career at eighteen, joined Jacques Esterel as a designer after taking a fashion course. In 1965 she left him to design ready-to-wear for Pierre d'Alby, opened her own boutique in 1975.

Considered strongest in coats, Beretta works with sculptural shapes, in the late 1970s was one of the first to pick up the exaggerated shoulder. She believes in the constant evolution of fashion, and that the first attraction in clothes is color, then fabric. Rubberized and ciré raincoats are a signature. She designs for the Italian Maxmara organization, does sports clothes for Ramosport, leathers for Mac-Douglas. In 1984 signed to do a coat collection for Abe Schrader.

BERTIN, ROSE

BORN: near Abbeville, France, 2 July 1747.

DIED: Epinay, France, 22 September 1813.

Marie Antoinette, patroness of Rose Bertin

Bertin began her career at sixteen as an apprentice in a Paris millinery shop run by a Mlle. Pagelle. When sent to deliver hats to royal princesses at the Conti palace, she was noticed by the Princesse de Conti, who became her sponsor. Taken on as a partner in the shop, Bertin was appointed court milliner in 1772, was introduced to Marie Antoinette and became her confidante.

Her establishment, *Au Grand-Mogol*, became extremely successful, not only with the French court but with the diplomatic corps. She executed commissions for dresses and hats to be sent to foreign courts, thus becoming one of the early exporters of French fashion. She also produced fantastic headdresses reflecting current events, enormously costly and symbolic of the excesses that led to the French Revolution.

Bertin could be considered the first "name" designer, celebrated in contemporary memoirs and encyclopedias. She was proud, arrogant, ambitious, and so influential she was dubbed "The Minister of Fashion." She remained loyal to the Queen, fled to England to escape the Revolution, returning to France in 1800. She eked out her last years selling trinkets and died in poverty.

At her death, an obituary recognized her accomplishments: "Mlle. Bertin is justly famous for the supremacy to which she has raised French fashions and for her services to the industries that made the material she used in her own creations and those that she inspired others to make."

BIAGIOTTI, LAURA

BORN: Rome, Italy, 1943.

After graduating in archaeology from Rome University, Biagiotti went to work at her mother's clothing company, then began producing clothes for other designers. Her first collection under her own label appeared in 1972 in Florence. Soon thereafter she bought a cashmere firm, thus discovering her true metier. She became known in Italy as "the Queen of Cashmere," producing beautiful sweaters in that precious fiber for both men and women, exceptional in their colorings and quality, sold under the Macpherson label. She also produces women's clothes in her own name, not on the leading edge of fashion, but wearable, interestingly detailed, and of excellent workmanship.

BLASS, BILL

BORN: Fort Wayne, Indiana,
22 June 1922.

AWARDS:
Coty American Fashion Critics' Award:
1961 — "Winnie"
1963 — Return Award
1968 — First Coty Award for Men's Wear
1970 — Hall of Fame
1971 — Hall of Fame Citation
1975 — Special Award (for Revillon America)
1982, 1983 — Hall of Fame Citations
1969 — Neiman-Marcus Award
1986 — Council of Fashion Designers of America (CFDA)

A 1939 graduate of Fort Wayne High School, Blass studied fashion in New York for six months, got his first fashion job in 1940 as sketch artist for David Crystal. He resigned to enlist in the Army in World War II, returned to work in 1946 as designer for Anna Miller & Co., which merged with Maurice Rentner in 1958. Blass stayed on as head designer, eventually becoming vice president, then owner. In 1970 the company was established as Bill Blass Ltd.

Blass is a leading member of the New York fashion establishment, producing high-priced, high-quality investment clothes, beautifully made from exquisite materials. He designs for a customer with an active social life and is admired for his glamorous, feminine evening clothes. His daytime fashions are elegant and simple, notable for refined cut, excellent tailoring, and for interesting mixtures of patterns and textures expertly coordinated for a polished, worldly look.

In addition to his designer clothes for women, the Blass design projects have included Blassport women's sportswear, rainwear, Vogue patterns, loungewear, scarves, men's clothing. He has also designed automobiles, uniforms for American Airlines flight attendants, even chocolates. *Bill Blass* perfume for women was introduced in 1978.

Blass has given time and support to his industry, was an early vice president of the Council of Fashion Designers of America. He has also been a perceptive and generous supporter of design talent in others.

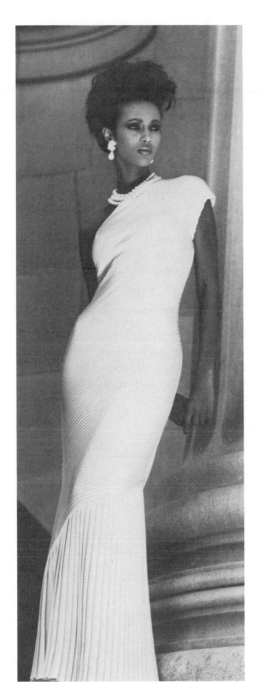

Bill Blass and model, 1987

1986

1986

BOHAN, MARC

BORN: Paris, France, 22 August 1926.

Marc Bohan

The son of a milliner who encouraged his early interest in sketching and fashion, Bohan had a sound background when he took over design direction at DIOR in 1960. From 1945 to 1953 he was assistant to ROBERT PIGUET and worked with CAPTAIN MOLYNEUX and MADELEINE DE RAUCH. He then opened his own couture salon which closed after one season due to undercapitalization. He became head designer at JEAN PATOU in 1954, stayed four years then left to free lance, worked in New York briefly designing for Originala.

In August 1958 Bohan went to work for CHRISTIAN DIOR, designing the collections for London, New York, South America. In September 1960, when SAINT LAURENT was drafted into the army, Bohan was chosen to design the January collection. Since then he has been chief designer and artistic director of Christian Dior, responsible for the couture and ready-to-wear collections, as well as accessories, men's wear, and bed linens. He has also designed costumes for theater and film.

Bohan's refined and romantic clothes are very wearable, very much in the Dior tradition of beautiful fabrics and exquisite workmanship. They have made Dior among the most commercially successful houses of the couture. He feels that elegance consists of adapting dress for the place, the atmosphere, and the circumstances.

1978

1987

BRIGANCE, TOM

BORN: Waco, Texas, 4 February 1913.

AWARDS:
  1953 — Coty American Fashion Critics'
    "Winnie" (for "revolutionizing the
    look of American women at the
    beach")
  1954 — International Silk Citation
  1955 — National Cotton Award
  1956 — Italian Internazionale delle Arti
    (for foreign sportswear)

The son of an English mother and French father, Brigance studied at the Parsons School of Design and the National Academy of Art in New York, at the Sorbonne in Paris. On his return to New York, his talent was recognized by Dorothy Shaver, president of Lord & Taylor, and in 1939 he became the store's designer. He spent the war years in Air Corps Intelligence, returned to Lord & Taylor in 1944. In 1949 he opened his own firm on Seventh Avenue. Since retiring, he has lectured extensively on fashion in major cities of the United States.

Brigance designed everything from coats and suits to day and evening dresses, beachwear, blouses, playclothes. He specialized in beachwear for many years and is well known for the swimsuits he designed for Sinclair. These were treasured by women for their flattering cut and excellent fit. He was among the first to use over-sized patterns, geometrics, florals, and to mix patterns.

1941

1946

BROOKS, DONALD

BORN: New York City, 10 January 1928.

AWARDS:
    1962—National Cotton Award
    Coty American Fashion Critics' Award:
        1958—Special Award (influence on
          evening wear)
        1962—"Winnie"
        1967—Return Award
        1974—Special Award (lingerie
          design)
    1963—New York Drama Critics' Award
      for costumes (for *No Strings*)
    1974—Parsons Medal for
      Distinguished Achievement

Brooks studied at the School of Fine Arts of Syracuse University and at Parsons School of Design in New York City. He had his own company from 1964 to 1973, has freelanced, specializing in better dresses, with collections for Albert Nipon, exclusive designs for Lord & Taylor. After an absence of several years, he presented a well-received evening collection for fall 1986.

Brooks has also designed extensively for theater and film. He received an award for his costumes for Diahann Carroll in the Broadway musical, *No Strings*. His movie credits include wardrobes for Liza Minelli in *Flora the Red Menace*, and for Julie Andrews in *Star* and *Darling Lili*. He has also designed furs, bathing suits, men's wear, shoes, costume jewelry, wigs, bed linens.

He is noted for romantic evening designs and uncluttered day clothes. Trademarks are his use of clear, unexpected colors, careful detailing, dramatic prints of his own design.

BURROWS, STEPHEN

BORN: Newark, New Jersey,
    15 September 1943.

AWARDS:
    Coty American Fashion Critics' Award:
        1974—Special Award (lingerie)
        1977—"Winnie"

Stephen Burrows and models, 1979

Burrows always loved clothes, started making them as a young boy under the tutelage of his grandmother. He studied at the Philadelphia Museum College of Art and the Fashion Institute of Technology in New York.

In 1968 he and Roz Rubenstein, an F.I.T. classmate, joined forces to open a boutique. The next year both went to work for Henri Bendel—Rubenstein as accessories buyer, Burrows as designer in residence. In 1973 they formed a partnership and opened a firm on Seventh Avenue, returned to Bendel's in 1977.

Always in the vanguard, Burrows is known for his young, flirty cut and unique color combinations. He used patches of color for a mosaic effect in the early 1960s, top-stitched seams in contrasting thread, stitched the edges of hems instead of hemming them, resulting in a fluted effect known as "lettuce hems," widely copied. He favors soft, clinging fabrics such as chiffon and matte jersey, and is partial to the asymmetrical—". . . . there's something nice about something wrong," is the way he puts it.

In November 1973, he was one of five American designers to show in France at a benefit for the Versailles Palace.

BYBLOS
ESTABLISHED: 1973.

Part of the Girombelli Group, Byblos has developed a strong sportswear orientation under the direction of Donatella Girombelli and her team of two English designers, Alan Cleaver and Keith Varty. Until 1975, when GIANNI VERSACE became designer, Byblos was designed by an international group of stylists. Guy Paulin took over in 1977, Varty and Cleaver in 1981. It is now noted for whimsical patterns, a young and affluent sportiness. Its designers have brought a touch of British wit, a bit of paradox to Italian sportswear and have become rising stars of the Italian fashion firmament.

1985

C

CALLOT SOEURS

GIULIANA CAMERINO

DAVID CAMERON

ROBERTO CAPUCCI

PIERRE CARDIN

HATTIE CARNEGIE

ZACK CARR

CARVEN

BONNIE CASHIN

JEAN-CHARLES DE CASTELBAJAC

SAL CESARANI

GABRIELLE CHANEL

ALDO CIPULLO

LIZ CLAIBORNE

SYBIL CONNOLLY

ANDRÉ COURRÈGES

JULES-FRANÇOIS CRAHAY

CHARLES CREED

ANGELA CUMMINGS

CALLOT SOEURS

Callot Soeurs was founded in 1895 by three sisters, daughters of an antique dealer who specialized in fabrics and lace. (He was also said to be a painter.) All were talented but it was Mme. Gerber, the eldest, who was the genius. Tall, gaunt, her hair dyed a brilliant red, she was usually dressed in a baglike costume covered with oriental jewelry and ropes of freshwater pearls. Her two sisters eventually retired and she became the sole proprietor of the house, which at one time had branches in London and New York.

Mme. Gerber possessed great technical skill—she was also an artist of impeccable taste, an originator. The second sister, Mme. Vertran, is given credit for the first draped evening dress fastened at the belt with an artificial rose. It was, however, the high standard of excellence maintained in collection after collection over many years which built the Callot reputation.

The house was noted for color richness, intricate cut, and particularly for formal evening wear. It was famous for delicate lace blouses, the use of gold and silver lamé, chiffon, georgette, organdy, flower embroidery, and embroidery in Chinese colors. The noted Spanish-American beauty, Mrs. Rita de Acosta Lydig, was a client and was rumored to have provided financial backing.

Henri Bendel was a great admirer of Mme. Gerber, referring to her as the backbone of the fashion world of Europe. She was an early influence on MADELEINE VIONNET, who worked for some time at Callot.

During the 1920s Callot produced every up-to-the-minute look, always with such taste, subtlety, and superb workmanship that the clothes had the timelessness and elegance of classics. The world's most fashionable women went there to dress. The house closed in 1937.

1931

CAMERINO, GIULIANA

BORN: Venice, Italy, 8 December 1920.

AWARDS:
1956—Neiman-Marcus Award

The Roberta name was established with beautiful and original handbags, especially striped and carved velvet satchels and pouches, and exceptional leathers. Giuliana Camerino began making handbags as a World War II refugee in Switzerland, established her firm when she, her husband, and young son returned to Venice in 1945. She named the company and a daughter after her favorite movie.

Begun with a single employee, the business now employs hundreds, plus several thousand free-lance artisans. Everything, from the velvets and leathers to the frames, handles, and locks, is produced in Camerino's own factories. She operates a tannery, a fabric-printing plant, factories for clothes and umbrellas. She has extended her range to include ready-to-wear, knits, raincoats, luggage, furs, umbrellas, men's ties and leathers, scarves, fragrances for men and women, all in the luxury classification. Her designs are carried in her own shops and by fine specialty stores.

Camerino, who took over direction of the business after the death of her husband, is assisted by her daughter and by her architect son. She has been praised by Stanley Marcus for her creativity and constant flow of new ideas. Her ready-to-wear, while not in the advance of fashion, is elegant and luxurious, featuring simplified, wearable shapes in fine fabrics, bold prints of her own design.

CAMERON, DAVID

BORN: Santa Barbara, California, 1961.

AWARDS:
1986—Council of Fashion Designers of America (CFDA) "Perry" (for "the greatest impact of an emerging new talent")

Cameron grew up in Santa Barbara, was coasting along as a beach boy and surfer when a high school guidance counselor suggested design training. He studied two years at the Fashion Institute of Design and Merchandising in Los Angeles, upon graduation moved to New York, worked for Michaele Vollbracht as a design assistant until the company folded. After three months with a major designer of women's sportswear, he managed to assemble financial backing and in the fall of 1985 presented his first collection, described as "fun and tongue in cheek." It was well received by retailers and the press. His second collection for fall 1986 retained a young, iconoclastic viewpoint yet was surprisingly classic in feeling, both fabrics and workmanship of superior quality. Cameron is keenly aware of the business aspect of fashion, works within strict budgetary limits.

CAPUCCI, ROBERTO

BORN: Rome, Italy, 1929.

Capucci comes from a wealthy Roman family, studied at the Accademia delle Belle Arti in Rome. In 1950, when he was twenty-one, he opened a small fashion house in Rome, showed successfully in Florence the same year. He opened in Paris in 1962, moved back to Rome seven years later.

Considered by some a genius ranking with BALENCIAGA and CHARLES JAMES, Capucci experiments daringly with cut and fabric, raises dressmaking to the level of an art. His clothes are sculptured and architectural, shown without histrionics in total silence. He does not use design assistants.

1985

1985

CARDIN, PIERRE

BORN: Venice, Italy, 2 July 1922.

The son of Italian immigrants, Cardin grew up in St. Étienne, France, moved to Vichy at the age of seventeen. He worked as a tailor, left Vichy for Paris at the end of World War II, went to work at PAQUIN. At Paquin he executed costume designs based on sketches of Christian Bérard for Jean Cocteau's film, *La Belle et la Bête,* and was introduced by Cocteau to Christian Dior. He worked briefly for SCHIAPARELLI, then as assistant to DIOR, in 1947 heading the coat and suit workroom, left to form his own business.

The first showing in his own house came in 1950. Boutiques followed for men and women, men's ready-to-wear in 1958, children's apparel ten years later. From there he has gone on to label the world with the Cardin name, with more than 600 licenses extending from wines to bicycles, jewelry to bed sheets to food to toiletries. In 1970 he established his own theater, L'Espace Pierre Cardin, now owns the famous Paris restaurant, Maxim's. In 1979 he entered into a trade agreement with the Peoples Republic of China where factories produce Cardin clothes. A Maxim's has been established in Beijing.

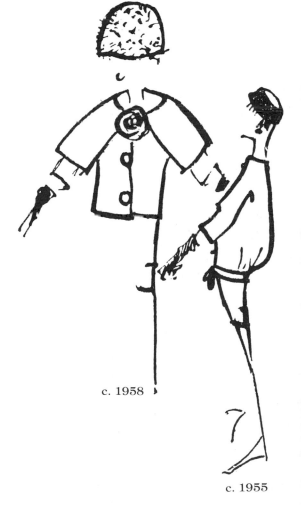

c. 1958

c. 1955

Pierre Cardin and model, 1987

Considered one of the most creative, intellectual, avant-garde couturiers of the 1950s and 1960s, Cardin showed the first nude look in 1966, followed by metal body jewelry, unisex astronaut suits, helmets, batwing jumpsuits and other clothing suitable for space travel. His fascination with the futuristic continues, coexisting with well-cut suits and coats showing the authority of his tailoring background, evening dresses in brilliant colors, often with uneven hemlines.

In July 1987, he named his longtime collaborator, ANDRÉ OLIVER, artistic director of the couture house. Cardin continued to share the design duties.

CARNEGIE, HATTIE

BORN: Vienna, Austria, 1889.

DIED: New York City, 22 February 1956.

AWARDS:
  1939—Neiman-Marcus Award
  1948—Coty American Fashion Critics' Award (for "consistent contribution to American elegance")

1950

Carnegie arrived in America with her parents when she was eleven. She started working in her early teens: in a millinery workroom, as a messenger at Macy's, as a millinery model—in her spare time she designed hats for neighborhood women. She changed her name from Henrietta Kanengeiser to Carnegie in emulation of Andrew Carnegie, "the richest man in the world." In 1909 she opened her own hat shop, and in 1915, with Rose Roth, a seamstress, opened a custom dressmaking salon on West 86th Street near fashionable Riverside Drive. Roth made dresses, Carnegie made hats and waited on customers; two years later she bought out her partner. She did not know how to cut or sketch, and never learned. What she did have was great fashion flair and an acute business intelligence.

She made her first buying trip to Europe in 1919, from then on went four times a year, bringing back quantities of Paris models which she would adapt. Over the years she expanded into a multi-million dollar business, including two resort shops, made-to-order workrooms, ready-to-wear factories, millinery, jewelry, perfumes. She is said to have been the first American custom designer with a ready-to-wear label.

She dressed society beauties, movie and stage stars such as Constance Bennett, Tallulah Bankhead, Joan Crawford. In the early 1930s, recognizing the hard facts of the depression, she opened a ready-to-wear department in her shop where a good Vionnet copy could be had for as little as $50.

Carnegie was tiny, less than five feet tall, and very feminine. Above all she loved clothes. She employed three assistant designers and two sketchers; her knack for discovering design talent was legendary. JAMES GALANOS, NORMAN NORELL, PAULINE TRIGÈRE, and CLAIRE MCCARDELL all worked for her.

Her designs were youthful and sophisticated, never faddy, never extreme, eternally Carnegie no matter what the trends might be. She was noted for suits with nipped waists and rounded hips, especially becoming to smaller women, embroidered, beaded evening suits, at-home pajamas, long wool dinner dresses and theater suits. Beautiful fabrics and excellent workmanship were hallmarks, anything but the best was abhorrent to her.

Carnegie was married briefly in 1918, again in 1922. In 1928 she married Major John Zanft, who survived her. Her clothing business continued for some years after her death.

CARR, ZACK

BORN: Kerrville, Texas, c. 1946.

Carr studied interior design and architecture at the University of Texas, worked in interior design planning fashion boutiques then went on to study fashion at New York's Parsons School of Design. He developed his skills in sportswear during nine years with CALVIN KLEIN.

After leaving Klein, he was asked by an Italian manufacturer to collaborate on a collection for the American market. His first collection for fall 1986, was extremely well received by both press and retailers. Showing a well-defined point of view, the clothes are spare and sleek, casual yet elegant, produced with Italian finesse in fabrics ranging from wool jersey to leather to mohair to denim. Although he rejects the term as too restricting, Carr is often pegged as a fashion minimalist.

CARVEN

The daughter of an Italian father and a French mother, Carven had planned to study achitecture and archaeology but was diverted into dressmaking by her tiny size, which made it difficult to find clothes. In 1945, with the backing of her decorator husband, she opened her Paris couture house.

She has made a success based on attractive, wearable clothes for petite women like herself, specializing in imaginative sports, beach, and dress-up clothes. Accessories, too, are kept in proportion to the small figure. An ardent traveller, she has been inspired by other countries in such silhouettes as the Greek-amphora look and in the use of Egyptian pleats.

There are Carven lines for children and teenagers. Among her perfumes, *Ma Griffe* and *Monsieur Carven* have been especially successful.

CASHIN, BONNIE

BORN: Oakland, California, 1915.

AWARDS:
- 1950—Neiman-Marcus Award
- Coty American Fashion Critics' Award:
  - 1950—"Winnie"
  - 1961—Special Award (for leather and fabric design)
  - 1968—Return Award
  - 1972—Hall of Fame

A third generation Californian, Cashin was raised in San Francisco where her father was an artist, photographer, and inventor, her mother a custom dressmaker. She played with fabrics from an early age, was taught to sew, and her ideas were encouraged. She studied at the Art Students League of New York, returned to California, where she designed costumes for the theater, ballet, and motion pictures. *Anna and the King of Siam* and *Laura* are among her sixty picture credits. She moved to New York in 1949.

Since 1953, Cashin has free lanced, designing collections for sportswear houses Adler and Adler and Philip Sills, bags for Coach Leatherware. In 1967 she started The Knittery, limited edition collections of hand knits, in recent years has largely concentrated on coats and raincoats.

Cashin has always been an innovator, working in her own idiom, uninfluenced by Paris. She believes in functional layers of clothing and showed this way of dressing long before it became an international fashion. From the beginning, she specialized in comfortable clothes for country and travel, using wool jersey, knits, canvas, leather, tweeds, in subtle, misty colors.

Signature details include leather bindings, the use of toggles and similar hardware for closings. She has always coordinated her clothes with hoods, bags, boots, belts of her own design. Some dominant Cashin themes are the toga cape, the kimono coat, the shell coat, a sleeveless leather jerkin, the poncho, the bubble top, the hooded jersey dress, the long, fringed, mohair plaid at-home skirt. Her clothes are included in the costume collections of museums, colleges, and schools around the country.

Early in the 1980s she established The Innovative Design Fund, of which she is president and treasurer. This is a public foundation with the purpose of nurturing uncommon, directional ideas in design, clothing, textiles, home furnishings, or other utilitarian objects. Awards are solely for use in producing prototypes.

Example of Cashin's layering

1973

CASTELBAJAC, JEAN-CHARLES DE

BORN: Casablanca, Morocco, 1950.

Castelbajac moved to France with his parents when he was five. His mother started her own small clothes factory and when he was eighteen, he went to work for her. He designed for Pierre d'Alby, joined a group of young designers in 1974, then opened his first retail shop. He designs for a number of manufacturers, including some in Italy, has done theatrical costumes.

Part of the ready-to-wear movement which burgeoned in France in the 1960s and came into full flower in 1970s, Castelbajac is best known for the fashion flair he gives to survival looks—blanket plaids, canvas, quilting, rugged coats—and sportswear for both men and women. He has been called "the space-age BONNIE CASHIN."

CESARANI, SAL

BORN: New York City, 25 September 1939.

AWARDS:
Coty American Fashion Critics' Award:
1974—Special Award (men's wear)
1976—Special Award (men's wear/ neckwear)
1982—Men's Wear Return Award

The son of Italian immigrants who worked in the garment industry, Cesarani attended the High School of Fashion Industries, graduated from the Fashion Institute of Technology.

From 1964 to 1969 he worked as fashion coordinator at Paul Stuart, the prestigious men's store, where he developed his sense of merchandising and color. He was merchandise director at Polo for two years, designer for Country Britches from 1973 to 1975, and for Stanley Blacker until he left to form Cesarani Ltd. in 1976. The Cesarani label is licensed both in the U.S. and internationally for men's clothing, ties, and accessories, and for men's and women's sportswear.

Essentially a traditionalist, Cesarani handles modern trends in a classic way. Cut and tailoring are impeccable: pants break at precisely the right point, jackets fit exactly without being hard edged. He prefers natural fibers, especially British woolens and Harris tweeds for fall-winter, linens and cottons for spring and summer.

He has served as a critic at Parson's School of Design, taught men's wear at the Fashion Institute of Technology.

CHANEL, GABRIELLE "COCO"

BORN: Saumur, France, 1883.

DIED: Paris, France, 10 January 1971.

AWARDS:
1957 — Neiman-Marcus Award

Chanel and Sam Goldwyn, 1931

Very little is known of Chanel's early life. When she was six, her mother died and she was sent to live with her paternal grandmother in Moulins. She started in fashion making hats—in a Paris apartment in 1910, later in a shop in Deauville. In 1914 she opened a shop in Paris, making her first dresses of wool jersey, a material not at that time considered suitable for fashionable clothes.

Her business was interrupted by the first World War but she reopened in 1919, by which time she was famous. Slender and vital, with a low, warm voice, she was a superb saleswoman, her personality and private life contributed to her success. Through Misia Sert, the wife of the Spanish painter José Maria Sert, she met and associated with the leading figures of the 1920s art world: Diaghilev, Picasso, Cocteau, dancer Serge Lifar, decorator-designer Léon Bakst. While she never married, there were many love affairs. Grand Duke Dmitri, grandson of Czar Alexander II, was a frequent escort and she maintained a three-year liaison with the Duke of Westminster.

Chanel closed her couture house in September 1939 at the outset of World War II. At the age of seventy she decided to go back into business, presenting her first postwar collection in 1954, six months before her seventy-first birthday. A continuation of her original themes of simplicity and wearability, it was not well received by the Paris press but was bought heavily by American stores and found instant acceptance among American women. Success followed in France, continuing into the 1960s, when her refusal to change her basic style or raise hemlines led to a decline in her influence. Within a few years, the pendulum swung back. In 1969 her life was the basis for *Coco*, a Broadway musical starring Katharine Hepburn.

In addition to couture, Chanel's empire encompassed perfumes, a costume jewelry workshop and for a time, a textile house. *Chanel No. 5* was created in 1922, and in 1924 Parfums Chanel was established to market the perfumes, which have continued to proliferate. A line of cosmetics was introduced after her death.

Chanel, "La Grande Mademoiselle," died on a Sunday night in January 1971, working to the last on a new collection. The House of Chanel has continued, directed by a succession of designers. Ready-to-wear was added in 1977 with PHILIPPE GUIBOURGÉ as designer. KARL LAGERFELD has since taken over design duties for both the couture and ready-to-wear.

In evaluating Chanel, some place her alongside such giants as VIONNET and BALENCIAGA, others see her as more personality than creator, with an innate knack for knowing what women would want a few seconds before they knew it themselves. Certainly her early designs exerted a liberating influence and even the evening clothes had a youthful qual-

1929

1957

1958

1960

ity that was all her own. Her daytime palette was neutral—black, white, beige, red—with pastels introduced at night. Trademark looks included the little-boy look, wool jersey dresses with white collars and cuffs, pea jackets, bell-bottom trousers, and her personal touches of suntanned skin, bobbed hair, and magnificent jewelry worn with sportswear.

In her second period she is best remembered for her suits, made of jersey or the finest, softest Scottish tweeds. Jackets were usually collarless and trimmed with braid, blouses soft and tied at the neckline, skirts at or just below the knee. Suits were shown with multiple strands of pearls and gold chains set with enormous fake stones, in her own case mixed with real jewels. Other signatures were quilted handbags with shoulder chains, beige sling-back pumps with black tips, flat black hairbows, a single gardenia.

Chanel remains a legend for her taste and wit and personal style, for her unfaltering dedication to perfection, and for a luxury based on the most refined simplicity of cut, superb materials, and workmanship of the highest order.

Karl Lagerfeld for Chanel, 1985

CIPULLO, ALDO

BORN: Rome, Italy, 18 November 1936.

DIED: New York City, 31 January 1984.

AWARDS:
  1974—Coty American Fashion Critics'
    Special Award (men's wear/jewelry)
  1977—Diamonds Today Competition

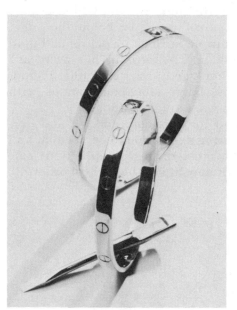

1969

Cipullo's family owned a large costume jewelry firm in Italy. He studied at the University of Rome, came to New York in 1959 and attended the School of Visual Arts. He worked as a designer at David Webb, Tiffany, and Cartier, opened his own design studio in 1974.

At Cartier, Cipullo designed the gold "love bracelet" for men and women that fastened on the wrist with a screw, came with its own small vermeil screwdriver. He enlarged the scope of men's jewelry with bracelets such as the wraparound gold nail, lapel pins to replace the boutonniere for evening, and pendants, as well as more conventional adornments: rings, cuff links, studs, buttons.

Cipullo's design projects extended from jewelry to silverware to textiles, included placemats, china, stationery, leather goods, and desk accessories. His design objectives were simplicity, elegance, function, and style.

CLAIBORNE, LIZ

BORN: Brussels, Belgium, 1929.

AWARDS:
  1985—Council of Fashion Designers
    of America (CFDA)

The daughter of a banker, Claiborne spent her early childhood in New Orleans, studied painting in Belgium and France. Her career in fashion began in 1949 when she won a trip to Europe in a *Harper's Bazaar* design contest.

On her return to the United States, she worked as a model sketcher, as assistant to TINA LESER, Omar Khayam, and others. She was top designer at Youth Guild for sixteen years, and in February 1976, formed Liz Claiborne, Inc., with her husband, Arthur Ortenberg, as business manager.

Claiborne made her name in sportswear. As her company has expanded into other areas, such as dresses and children's clothes, it has grown to the point that she has come to function largely as editor of the work of other designers.

Her strength lies in translating new trends into understandable and salable clothes. She is known for sensitive use of color and for excellent technical knowledge of fabric. Her designs are simple and uncomplicated with an easy, natural look. They are in the moderate price range.

She has served as critic at the Fashion Institute of Technology, is the recipient of numerous awards from retailers and industry associations.

CONNOLLY, SYBIL

BORN: Swansea, Wales,
24 January 1921.

When she was fifteen years old, Sybil Connolly's father died and her mother moved the family to Waterford in southern Ireland. In 1938 she went to work for Bradley's, a London dressmaker, returned to Ireland at the outset of World War II as buyer for Richard Alan, a Dublin specialty shop. By the time she was twenty-two, she was a company director. She built the store's couture department into a thriving business and when their designer left in 1950, herself designed a small collection, the start of her designing career.

America discovered Connolly in the early 1950s, thanks to CARMEL SNOW of *Harper's Bazaar* and to the Fashion Group of Philadelphia who were visiting Dublin. In 1953 she took a collection to the United States where her one-of-a-kind designs and beautiful Irish fabrics made a strong impression. In 1957 she set up her own firm, with a special boutique for ready-to-wear. Her clothes have been carried by fine specialty stores across the United States.

She is known for her use of iridescent Donegal tweeds and other Irish fabrics, and especially for evening dresses made of gossamer Irish linen worked in fine horizontal pleats. Her clothes are simple in cut, extremely wearable, notable for fabric and workmanship.

1957

COURRÈGES, ANDRÉ

BORN: Pau, France, 9 March 1923.

Courrèges studied civil engineering, then switched to textiles and fashion design. His first job was with Jeanne Lafaurie. From 1952 to 1960, he worked as a cutter for BALENCIAGA, whose influence showed clearly in his early designs.

He opened his own house in August 1961 with the help of his wife, Coqueline, who had spent three years with Balenciaga. Together they designed, cut, sewed and presented their first collection in a small apartment in the avenue Kleber.

Courrèges emerged as a brilliant tailor. Using woolens with considerable body, he cut his coats and suits with a triangular flare which disguised many figure defects, the balanced silhouettes defined by crisp welt seaming. His aim was to make functional, modern clothes. Among his suc-

1965

cesses, many of them widely copied, were all-white collections, tunics over narrow pants, with flared bottoms slanted from front to back. There were squared-off dresses ending above the knee, short, white baby boots, industrial zippers, zany accessories such as sunglasses with slit "tennis ball" lenses. He was called the couturier of the space age.

Courrèges was so widely plagiarized that he sold his business in 1965 and did only custom work for private clients. He returned in 1967 with see-through dresses, cosmonaut suits, knitted "cat" suits, flowers appliquéd on the body, knee socks.

There are Courrèges accessories, luggage, perfumes, men's wear. Boutiques in the United States and other countries carry everything from sports separates to accessories to his Couture Future deluxe ready-to-wear.

André Courrèges

1965

CRAHAY, JULES-FRANÇOIS

BORN: Liège, Belgium, 21 May 1917.

DIED: Monte Carlo, Monaco, 5 January 1988.

AWARDS: 1962—Neiman-Marcus Award

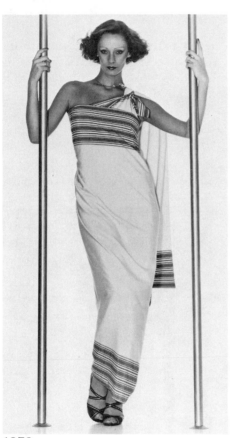

1976

Crahay's mother was a dressmaker who encouraged her son's interest in fashion. He literally grew up in the business, starting to work as a sketcher in her couture house when he was 13. After studying couture and painting in Paris in 1934 and 1935, he returned to Liege to work for his mother from 1936 to 1938. His service during World War II ended in capture by the Germans and imprisonment in Germany from 1940 to 1944.

In 1951 he returned to Paris and opened his own fashion house, closed within a year, then went as chief designer to NINA RICCI, receiving his first credit as sole designer in 1959. He stayed at Ricci until 1964 when he became head designer for the House of LANVIN, succeeding Antonio del Castillo. According to published reports, he was the highest-paid couturier of his time. For twenty years he created and maintained a recognizable Lanvin look, civilized and wearable, with his own flair for original details.

Recognized for his thoughtful, interesting cuts, Crahay was deeply influenced in his designs by fabrics and liked to design his own. He was probably best known for his use of folkloric themes, admiring their rich mixture of color, materials, and embroidery. Hard working, never satisfied, he is quoted as saying "I like ready-to-wear. I want to have fun making dresses. It is my love, it is my life." He retired from Lanvin in 1984 and the following year started a ready-to-wear collection under his own name in Japan. Shy and solitary, he had just a few close friends who served him as a surrogate family.

CREED, CHARLES

BORN: Paris, France, 1909.

DIED: London, England, July 1966.

Charles Creed's family were established in London as men's tailors in 1710. His grandfather, Henry, opened a Paris establishment in 1850, earning a reputation for the finest tailored riding habits for women in Europe. The client list included the actress Réjane, Empress Eugénie of France, England's Queen Victoria, opera singer Mary Garden, the spy Mata Hari. Under the direction of Henry's son, the house expanded into tailored suits, sports clothes, even evening dresses.

Charles entered the family business in Paris in 1930 after studies in France, Berlin, Vienna, Scotland, and the United States. He opened his own London house in 1932, closed the Paris business a few years later with the advent of World War II. In the 1950s he designed wholesale lines for firms in

London and the United States, closed his couture house in March 1966 to concentrate on ready-to-wear.

Creed was distinguished for sound traditonal tailoring and excellent fabrics, elegant suits for town, country, and evening, for bright printed blouses of sheer Rodier wool.

He was married in 1948 to Patricia Cunningham, fashion editor of British *Vogue*, who later went to work for him. The house closed with his death.

CUMMINGS, ANGELA

Angela Cummings

The daughter of a German diplomat, Cummings graduated from art school in Hanau, West Germany, studied at the Art Academy of Perugia, Italy. In 1967 she joined Tiffany & Co., remained until 1984 when she left to open her own business. The first Angela Cummings jewelry boutique was at Bergdorf Goodman, others following at stores such as Macy's San Francisco and Bloomingdale's in New York. Her design projects include flatware and tabletop accessories.

Thoroughly versed in gemology and goldsmithing as well as in jewelry design, Cummings works in the classic tradition. Yet her work is far from conventional, often combining materials such as wood, gold, and diamonds. She has revived old techniques including damascene, the ancient art of inlaying iron with precious metal. Much of her inspiration comes from nature and organic forms: silver jewelry derived from the leaf of a gingko tree, pieces influenced by the exotic orchids which she raises. She works in 18 karat gold, platinum or sterling silver, finds rings the most difficult to design because they must be entirely three dimensional, yet balanced, and must look good on the finger.

d

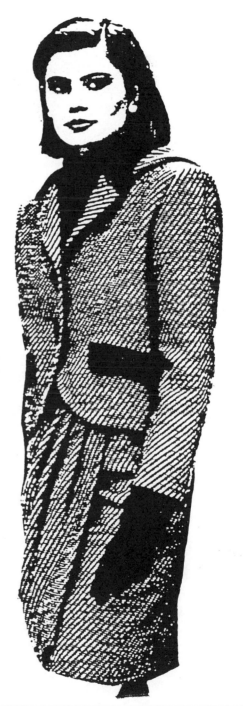

LILLY DACHÉ

WENDY DAGWORTHY

OSCAR DE LA RENTA

LOUIS DELL'OLIO

MADELEINE DE RAUCH

JACQUELINE DE RIBES

JEAN DESSÈS

CHRISTIAN DIOR

DOROTHÉE BIS

DACHÉ, LILLY

BORN: Bèigles, France, c. 1904.

AWARDS:
  1940—Neiman-Marcus Award
  1943—Coty American Fashion Critics'
    Special Award (millinery)

1940

Born and raised in France, Daché left school at fourteen to apprentice with a milliner aunt, at fifteen was apprentice in the workrooms of the famous Paris milliner Reboux, later worked at Maison Talbot. She came to the United States in 1924, spent one week behind the millinery counter at Macy's then, with a partner, opened a millinery shop in the West Eighties. When her partner left, Daché moved to Broadway and 86th Street in the same neighborhood as HATTIE CARNEGIE. Her next move was to Madison Avenue and, finally, to her own nine-story building on East 57th Street. This contained showrooms, workrooms, and a duplex apartment on the roof where she lived with her husband Jean Desprès, executive vice president of Coty. By 1949 Daché was designing dresses to go with her hats. She undertook lingerie, loungewear, gloves, hosiery, men's shirts and ties, even did a wired strapless bra.

Her major design contributions were draped turbans, brimmed hats molded to the head, half hats, colored snoods, romantic massed flower shapes. Also visored caps for war workers. She is still thought of as America's foremost milliner and has influenced many others in this country, including HALSTON. The hairdresser Kenneth worked in her beauty salon before going into business for himself.

She closed her business in 1969 upon her husband's retirement.

DAGWORTHY, WENDY

BORN: Gravesend, Kent, England, 1950.

One of the members of the lively younger London fashion establishment, Dagworthy studied at Medway College of Art from 1966 to 1968, studied fashion for three years at Hornsey College of Art. After graduating with honors, she designed for a wholesale firm for one year, opened her own company in 1972. Her clothes are extremely wearable and finely detailed, successful both in the United Kingdom and abroad.

In 1975 she joined the London Designer Collections, a cooperative of London designers. She feels a responsibility for the continuation of her craft and takes an active interest in fashion education.

DE LA RENTA, OSCAR

BORN: Santo Domingo, Dominican Republic, 22 July 1932.

AWARDS:
Coty American Fashion Critics' Award:
1967—"Winnie"
1968—Return Award
1973—Hall of Fame
1968—Neiman-Marcus Award
Numerous awards from the Dominican Republic

Educated in Santo Domingo and Madrid, de la Renta remained in Madrid after graduation to study art, intending to become a painter. His fashion career began when sketches he made for his own amusement were seen by the wife of the American ambassador to Spain, who asked him to design a gown for her daughter's debut.

His first professional job was with BALENCIAGA's Madrid couture house, *Eisa*. In 1961 he went to Paris as assistant to Antonio de Castillo at Lanvin-Castillo. In 1963 went with Castillo to New York to design at Elizabeth Arden. Joined Jane Derby in 1965, soon was operating as Oscar de la Renta, Ltd., producing luxury ready-to-wear.

De la Renta is known for sexy, extravagantly romantic evening clothes in opulent materials. His daytime clothes, sometimes overshadowed by the more spectacular evening designs, have a European flavor, sophisticated, feminine, and eminently wearable.

A signature perfume introduced in 1977 has been enormously successful; a second fragrance, *Ruffles*, appeared in 1983. He has also done boutique lines, bathing suits, wedding dresses, furs, jewelry, bed linens, and loungewear.

1979

Oscar de la Renta and models, 1987

DELL'OLIO, LOUIS

BORN: New York City, 23 July 1948.

AWARDS:
  Coty American Fashion Critics' Award:
    1977 – "Winnie" (with Donna Karan)
    1982 – Hall of Fame (with Donna Karan)
    1984 – Special Award (women's wear) (with Donna Karan)

Louis Dell'Olio

In 1967 Dell'Olio received the Norman Norell Scholarship to Parsons School of Design, graduated in 1969 winning the Gold Thimble Award for coats and suits. From 1969 to 1971 he assisted Dominic Rompollo at Teal Traina, was designer at the Giorgini and Ginori divisions of Originala, 1971 to 1974. In 1974, he joined DONNA KARAN, a friend from Parsons, as co-designer at Anne Klein & Co. Spring 1985 was their last joint collection. At that time, Karan was given her own company, leaving Dell'Olio sole designer for Anne Klein.

Dell'Olio has continued the direction begun with Karan, a modern, sophisticated interpretation of the classic Anne Klein sportswear. Marked by clean, sharp shapes in beautiful fabrics, the clothes are in the deluxe investment category. His other design projects include furs for Michael Forrest.

1987

DE RAUCH, MADELEINE

An accomplished sportswoman, de Rauch began in fashion in the 1920s designing her own clothes for active sports. When friends persuaded her to make clothes for them, she opened a business called the House of Friendship, employing a single worker. With the help of her two sisters, the business grew and in the 1930s evolved into the House of de Rauch overlooking the Cours de Reine.

De Rauch was known for beautiful, wearable, functional clothes. Soft fabrics were handled with great fluidity, draped close at the top of the figure. Wide necklines were often framed with folds or tucks. Plaids, checks and stripes were treated with simplicity and precision, so perfectly done they seemed to have been assembled on a drawing board. The house closed in 1973.

DE RIBES, JACQUELINE

BORN: France, c. 1930.

1987

An international society figure and clothes horse, the Vicomtesse de Ribes for years dressed at the Paris couture, presented her first fashion collection in 1982 with Saint Laurent in the audience.

From the initial group of just thirty pieces her line has expanded to over twice that number. Her evening wear is especially successful in the United States. Her day clothes have become stronger, especially the suits, and her jewelry designs are dazzling, lavish and luxurious. It is ready-to-wear with a decided couture feeling, showing a unified viewpoint from day to evening.

Originally dismissed as a dilettante, de Ribes has worked hard, is a meticulous businesswoman and a dedicated professional.

DESSÈS, JEAN

BORN: Alexandria, Egypt,
6 August 1904.

DIED: Athens, Greece,
2 August 1970.

1949

Dessès was of Greek ancestry, interested from childhood in beautiful clothes. He designed a dress for his mother when he was only nine. He attended school in Alexandria, studied law in Paris, and in 1925 switched to fashion design. For twelve years he worked for Mme. Jane on the rue de la Paix, opened his own establishment in 1937.

Dessès visited the United States in 1949, making agreements with two American manufacturers. He admired American women and in 1950 designed a lower-priced line for them called *Jean Dessès Diffusion*. This is seen as the beginning of the ready-to-wear trend in French couture.

A gentle man of refined and luxurious tastes, Dessès was inspired in his work by native costumes he saw in museums on his travels, especially in Greece and Egypt. He designed by draping fabrics directly on the dummy, is remembered primarily for draped evening gowns of chiffon and mousseline in beautiful colors, and for the subtlety with which he handled fur. Customers included Princess Margaret, the Duchess of Kent, and the Queen of Greece.

He gave up his couture business in 1965 because of ill health and retired to Greece, continuing to design on a freelance basis until his death.

DIOR, CHRISTIAN

BORN: Granville, France,
31 January 1905.

DIED: Montecatini, Italy,
24 October 1957.

AWARDS:
1947—Neiman-Marcus Award
1956—Parsons Medal for
Distinguished Achievement

Dior was the son of a well-to-do Norman manufacturer of fertilizer and chemicals. He wished to become an architect, his family wanted him to enter the diplomatic service. At their insistence, he studied political science at L'Ecole des Sciences Politiques, but in 1928, after obligatory military service, he opened a small art gallery with a friend. This was wiped out by the Depression which also ruined Dior's family. In 1931 he traveled to Russia, returned disillusioned by the reality of Soviet life and for the next few years lived from hand to mouth, eating little and sleeping on the floor of friends' apartments.

In 1934 he became seriously ill and had to leave Paris for an enforced rest in Spain and the south of France. There he learned tapestry weaving and discovered a desire to create something himself. He returned to Paris in 1935, thirty years old and without means of support. Unable to find any kind of job he started making design sketches and also did fashion illustrations for *Le Figaro*. That year he sold his first sketches — for twenty francs each.

His early hat designs were successful, his dresses less so. In 1937, after a two-year struggle to improve his dresses, he sold several sketches to ROBERT PIGUET and was asked to make a number of dresses for an upcoming collection. He was hired by Piguet in 1938, in 1939 went into the army. The fall of Paris in June 1940 found him stationed in the south

Christian Dior, 1978

1957

The New Look, 1947

Dior, 1955. Photograph by Louise Dahl-Wolfe/courtesy of Staley-Wise, New York

of France. Asked by Piguet to come back to work, Dior delayed his return until the end of 1941, by which time another designer had been hired. He then went to work for LUCIEN LELONG, a much larger establishment. At the end of 1946 he left Lelong to open his own house.

Dior was backed in his new project by Marcel Boussac, French financier, racehorse owner, and textile manufacturer, who originally was looking for someone to take over an ailing couture house he owned. Instead, Dior persuaded Boussac to back him, and in the spring of 1947, presented his wildly successful first collection, featuring what became known as the *New Look*.

This silhouette was, in essence, a polished continuation of the rounded line seen in the first postwar collections, appearing at the same time at a number of design houses. Dior's was a dream of flower-like women with rounded shoulders, feminine busts, tiny waists, enormous spreading skirts. Everything was exquisitely made of the best materials available.

He continued to produce collection after collection of beautiful clothes, each evolving from the one before, continually refining and expanding his talent. In 1952, with the sensuous line, he began to loosen the waist, freed it even more with the H-line in 1954, the A- and Y-lines in 1955.

Meanwhile, Christian Dior, Inc. had become a vast international merchandising operation with the Dior label on jewelry, scarves, men's ties, furs, stockings, gloves, and ready-to-wear. Dior-Delman shoes were designed by Roger Vivier.

Dior described himself as a silent, slow Norman, shy and reticent by nature, strongly attached to his friends. He loved good food, for relaxation and pleasure read history and archaeology and played cards. His chief passion was for architecture. Like many designers he was superstitious and believed in the importance of luck, consulted fortune tellers on the major decisions of his life.

Since his death, the House of Dior has continued under the direction of other designers: YVES SAINT LAURENT until 1960, and since then with MARC BOHAN.

Marc Bohan for Dior, 1987

DOROTHÉE BIS

Begun in the 1960s as a chain of trend-setting Paris boutiques, Dorothée Bis was established by Jacqueline Jacobson as designer and her husband, Elie, as manufacturer. Among the pioneers of French ready-to-wear, the Jacobsons began in the fur business, branched out into manufacturing skirts, then into knits.

Dorothée Bis clothes are sporty and casual, the firm is known for intarsia knits in imaginative patterns and for brilliant use of color, with collections totally color-keyed: knitted cap to knitted gloves to ribbed wool tights matched to shoes or boots. They were among the first in French ready-to-wear to sell a totally coordinated look.

FLORENCE EISEMAN

PERRY ELLIS

ELIZABETH & DAVID EMANUEL

EISEMAN, FLORENCE

BORN: Minneapolis, Minnesota, 27 September 1899.

DIED: Milwaukee, Wisconsin, 8 January 1988

AWARDS:
  1955—Neiman-Marcus Award (the first children's designer recipient)
  1956—Swiss Fabrics Award

Florence Eiseman took up sewing as a hobby following the birth of her second son, Robert. As her children grew she turned out quilts and clothing for them and for her neighbors' children. In 1945, when family finances were pinched, her husband, Laurence, took samples of her organdy pinafores to Chicago to Marshall Field & Co. The $3,000 order he came away with put them in business with her as designer, him as business manager-salesman.

Mrs. Eiseman first worked out of her home, enlisting other women to sew for her in theirs. Next, with two sewing machines, she took over a corner of her husband's toy factory. Within a few years, Laurie Eiseman gave up his toy

jumper and T-shirt, 1976-1979

"hello" dress, early 1950s

sailor top and culottes, 1982

stretch swimsuit,
1973

Renoir-inspired dress
and pinafore, 1964

business to devote himself to the clothing firm, which in a short time grew into a large concern, the clothes sold across the United States and abroad. Mrs. Eiseman functioned successively as vice president, president, chairman.

Two Florence Eiseman sayings are: "Children have bellies, not waists" and "You should see the child, and not the dress, first." Ruled by these precepts and by her belief that children should not be dressed in small versions of adult clothing, Eiseman has always produced simple styles distinguished by fine fabrics and excellent workmanship, with prices to match. The clothes are so classic and so well made they are frequently handed down from one generation to another. She became known as the "Norman Norell of children's clothes", making dresses and separates, swimsuits, playclothes, sleepwear, and boys' suits. In 1969 she added less expensive knits, brother-sister outfits, and, for a short time, a limited group of women's clothes.

In 1984, the company was asked by Neiman-Marcus to do a luxury collection of dress-up clothes at prices beginning where the regular collection left off. The result was Florence Eiseman Couture, not custom made but using rich fabrics and many hand touches. Its introduction in September 1984 coincided with Mrs. Eiseman's eighty-fifth birthday, finding her still actively involved in the company she founded. The same year, the Denver Art Museum presented a retrospective of her work. On her death she was praised for her role in raising the standards of fashion and quality in better children's wear and for encouraging manufacturers to think of trading up.

ELLIS, PERRY

BORN: Portsmouth, Virginia, 1940.

DIED: New York City, 30 May 1986.

Ellis grew up in Portsmouth, took his B.A. at William and Mary College, his M.A. in retailing from New York University. He was sportswear buyer for Miller & Rhoads in Richmond, in 1967 went as merchandiser to John Meyer of Norwich, a conservative sportswear firm. There he acquired three important design tools—sketching, patternmaking, and fabric selection. After seven years he joined the Vera Companies in the same capacity.

In 1975 Ellis became designer for the Portfolio division of Vera, and in 1978 Manhattan Industries, which owns Vera, established Perry Ellis Sportswear, Inc., with him as designer and president. Perry Ellis Menswear followed in 1980.

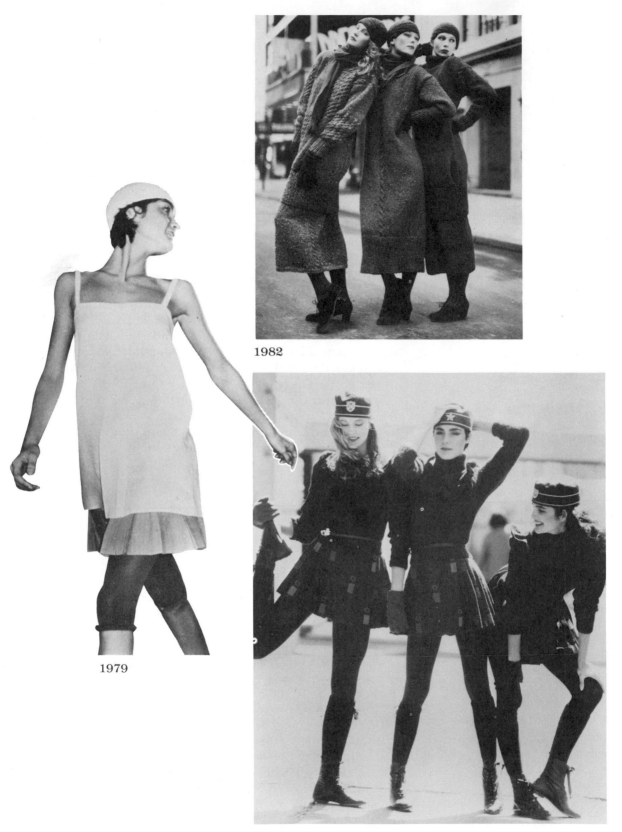

1982

1979

1981

AWARDS:
1979 — Neiman-Marcus Award
Coty American Fashion Critics' Award
   1979 — "Winnie"
   1980 — Return Award
   1981 — Hall of Fame
   1981 — Special Award (men's wear)
   1983 — Hall of Fame Citation
     (women's wear)
   1983 — Men's Wear Return Award
   1984 — Hall of Fame (men's wear)
   1984 — Hall of Fame Citation
     (women's wear)
Council of Fashion Designers of
  America (CFDA)
   1981 — Outstanding Designer in
     Women's Fashion
   1982, 1983 — Outstanding Designer
     in Men's Fashion
  1983, 1984 — Cutty Sark Award
    (outstanding men's wear designer)

Perry Ellis

Ellis designed furs, shearling coats for men and women, cloth coats, and for Japan, a complete sportswear line. Plus shoes, leg wear, scarves, Vogue patterns, and sheets, towels, blankets for Martex. A fragrance collection was launched in 1985.

From the beginning, the clothes were distinguished by a young, adventurous spirit and the use of natural fibers: cottons, silks, linens, pure wools. Hand-knitted sweaters in cotton, silk, cashmere became a trademark. This use of fine fabrics and hand work soon drove the collection up into a higher price bracket. Hence, in 1984, the revival of the Portfolio name for a moderately-priced collection with much the same relaxed classic look as the original. It was made without linings in less expensive fabrics, and with machine-made sweaters rather than hand-made.

Ellis believed that people should not take fashion too seriously or be overly concerned with what they wear, and following his own dictates, usually dressed informally for his rare public appearances. He disliked big parties, liked to read, cook, exercise, and dance, and loved film. He was active in the Council of Fashion Designers of America, served two terms as president and was elected to a third the week before his death. In his honor, the organization established the Perry Award, to be given annually "for the greatest impact on an emerging new talent." DAVID CAMERON was the first recipient in 1986.

The company continued in business under the direction of his two main design assistants, Patricia Pastor and Jed Krascella. Krascella, noted for bringing his wit and sense of humor to the collection, left in May 1987 to pursue an acting career and Pastor, vice president of design at the company, took over sole responsiblity for the designer collection.

EMANUEL, ELIZABETH & DAVID

BORN:
  Elizabeth—London, England, 1953.
  David—Bridgend, Wales, 1952.

The only married couple to be accepted at the Royal College of Art, where they took a postgraduate course in fashion, the Emanuels attended Harrow School of Art, married in 1975. Her father is American, her mother English, his parents are Welsh.

They opened their own firm in September 1977 with two wholesale collections a year. In 1979 they took the unusual step of closing their ready-to-wear business and concentrating on made-to-order. Their wedding dress for the Princess of Wales made them known worldwide. Licenses include bed linens, sunglasses, perfume. Their fantasy ball gowns and wedding dresses, afloat in lace, taffeta, organza, and tulle, evoke a romantic, bygone, never-never time.

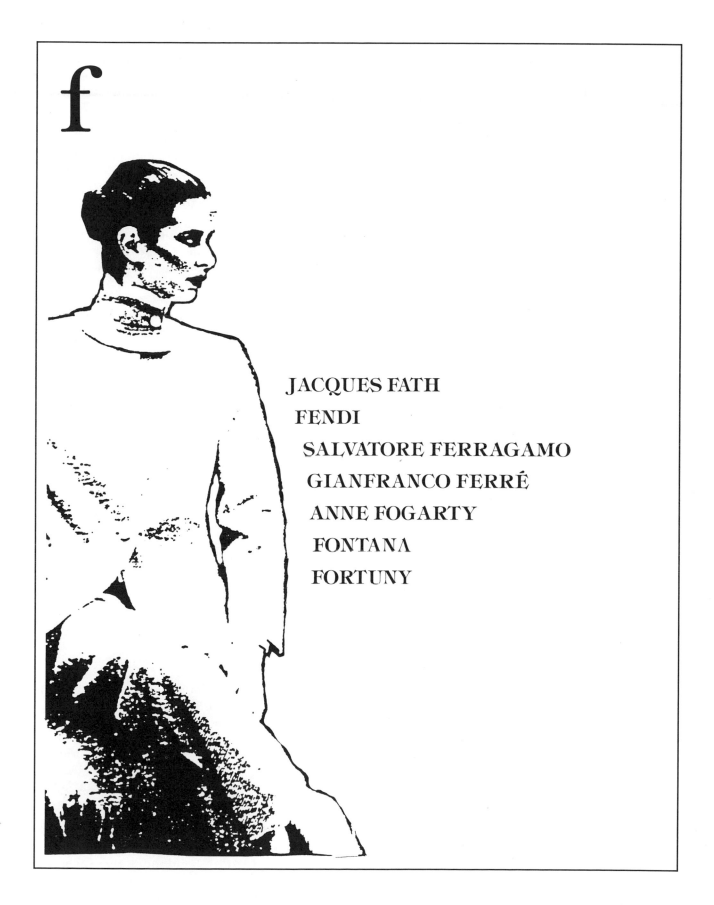

f

JACQUES FATH

FENDI

SALVATORE FERRAGAMO

GIANFRANCO FERRÉ

ANNE FOGARTY

FONTANA

FORTUNY

FATH, JACQUES

BORN: Lafitte (near Paris), France,
12 September 1912.

DIED: Paris, France,
14 November 1954.

AWARDS:
1949—Neiman-Marcus Award

1947

Son of an Alsatian businessman, grandson of a painter, and great-grandson of a dressmaker, Fath attended both business school and drama school, acted briefly in films. He early showed his design talent in costumes for the theater and films, opened his first couture house in 1937 with a small collection of twenty models.

He went into the Army in 1940, was captured, and on his release reopened his house which he managed to keep open during the war. After Liberation, he became enormously successful, eventually expanded his salon from the single wartime workroom with one fitter to an establishment with six hundred employees.

In 1948 he signed with a United States manufacturer to produce two collections a year, one of the first French couturiers to venture into ready-to-wear. Other such agreements followed. The Fath name also went into perfume, scarves, stockings, millinery.

Fath's clothes were flattering, feminine, and sexy without slipping into vulgarity. They followed the lines of the body with hourglass shapes and swathed hips, often had full pleated skirts, plunging necklines. He did not sew or sketch but draped material while his assistants made sketches.

Handsome and personable, Fath had a flair for publicity and showmanship and became one of the most popular designers of his time. He loved parties and with his wife, actress Geneviève de Bruyère, gave elaborate entertainments at their Corbeville chateau. He was also an excellent businessman. After his death of leukemia at the age of forty-two, his wife continued the business for a few years, closed it in 1957.

FENDI

Specializing in furs, handbags, luggage, and sportswear, Fendi is a family business founded in 1918 by Adele Fendi. After her husband's death in 1954, Signora Fendi called on her five daughters for help, Paola, Anna, Franca, Carla, and Alda, at that time aged 14 to 24. The sisters have worked as a team to build and expand the Fendi empire, continuing to explore new areas. Their daughters, in turn, have also come into the firm. Adele Fendi died 19 March 1978, at the age of 81.

In 1962 the Fendis hired KARL LAGERFELD to design their furs and backed him with a dazzling array of new, unusual, or neglected pelts and the most inventive techniques. Their mother made coats out of squirrel and made them fashion-

Fendi Family (from left): Maria Silvia, her son, Federica, and Alda

able, the Fendis today still use squirrel, as well as badger, Persian lamb, fox, and sundry unpedigreed furs, often several in one garment. They are noted for innovations, such as furs woven in strips, coats left unlined for lightness or lined in silk. And the furs are always fun.

Fendi styles have glamour but their success appears based on an understanding of what women need and want. The Fendi double F initials designed by Lagerfeld have become an international status symbol.

1978

Lagerfeld for Fendi, 1987

FERRAGAMO, SALVATORE

BORN: Bonito (near Naples), Italy, June 1898.

DIED: Fiumetto, Italy, 7 August 1960.

AWARDS:
1947—Neiman-Marcus Award

Ferragamo began working as a shoemaker in Bonito when he was thirteen, emigrated to the United States in 1923. He studied mass shoemaking techniques then opened a shop in Hollywood, designing shoes and making them by hand for such film stars as Dolores Del Rio, Pola Negri, Gloria Swanson. He also maintained a successful business in ready-made shoes.

He returned to Italy and in 1936 opened a business in Florence. By the time of his death in 1960 he had ten factories in Italy and Great Britain. Since then, the business has been carried on by his daughters Fiamma and Giovanna, and his son Ferruccio. In additon to shoes, the Ferragamo name appears on handbags, scarves, and luxury ready-to-wear, sold in free-standing boutiques in Europe and the United States, and in boutiques in major United States specialty stores.

Early Ferragamo designs are fantasies of shape, color, and fabric. He is said to have originated the wedge heel and the platform sole, also the Lucite heel. In recent years, while still elegant, the emphasis has been on ladylike, conservative styling and comfortable fit.

FERRÉ, GIANFRANCO

BORN: Legnano, Italy, c. 1945.

Ferré originally intended to be an architect, studied in Milan and qualified in 1967. After a period working for a furniture maker and time off for travel, he began designing jewelry, by 1970 had made a name for himself as an accessories designer. He sold his shoes, scarves, and handbags to other designers, including LAGERFELD, designed striped T-shirts for Fiorucci which made him famous in Italy. As a freelancer he began designing sportswear and raincoats in 1972, by 1974 was showing under his own name.

Ferré's day clothes are exceptional, with a strong sculptural beauty marked by intricate pleating, tucks, and top stitching on a complexly structured base. Yet they are fluid, clean-lined, and comfortable. A fine tailor and leading exponent of architectural design, Ferré is now accepted as one of Europe's top ready-to-wear designers.

Ferré and model, 1981

FOGARTY, ANNE

BORN: Pittsburgh, Pennsylvania,
2 February 1919.

DIED: New York City, 15 January 1981.

AWARDS:
1951—Coty American Fashion Critics'
Special Award (dresses)
1952—Neiman-Marcus Award
1955—International Silk Award
1957—Cotton Fashion Award

After study at Carnegie Tech, Fogarty moved to New York where she worked as a model and stylist. Between 1948 and 1957 she designed junior-size dresses for Youth Guild and Margot, Inc., next spent five years at Saks Fifth Avenue. She established Anne Fogarty Inc. in 1962, closed it twelve years later. At the time of her death she had completed a collection of spring-summer dresses and sportswear for a Seventh Avenue firm.

Fogarty is best known for her "paper doll" silhouette, for crinoline petticoats under full-skirted shirtdresses with tiny waists, for the *camise*, a chemise gathered onto a high yoke, and for lounging coveralls. In the early 1970s she showed a peasant look with ruffled shirts and hot pants under long quilted skirts. She also designed lingerie, jewelry, shoes, hats, coats, and suits.

In 1940 she married Tom Fogarty. Later divorced, they had two children. She married twice again: Richard Kollmar, who died in 1971, and Wade O'Hara, from whom she was divorced.

FONTANA

FOUNDED: Parma, Italy, 1907

Originally a small dressmaking establishment founded in Parma by Amabile Fontana, the business was taken over by her daughters, Micol and Zoe as designers, Giovanna in charge of sales. In 1936 they moved to Rome and after World War II made a name for themselves in the emerging Italian haute couture as *Sorelle Fontana*, or *Fontana Sisters*. They were particularly admired for their evening gowns, both in Europe and North and South America. Their designs were marked by asymmetric lines and interesting necklines, and were noteworthy for delicate handwork.

Fontana created Ava Gardner's costumes for *The Barefoot Contessa* and Margaret Truman's wedding gown, also clothes for Jacqueline Kennedy. The house was at its peak in the 1950s, when it contributed largely to Italian fashion. Fontana boutiques still exist in Italy and Geneva.

FORTUNY

BORN: Granada, Spain, 1871.

DIED: Venice, Italy, 1949.

Fortuny's father was a famous painter who died when his son was only three years old. After art studies—painting, drawing, and sculpture—Fortuny became interested in chemistry and dyes. At the turn of the 20th century he moved to Venice, where he experimented with every aspect of design, from dyeing and printing silks by methods and in patterns of his own invention, to shaping clothing to his own esthetic standards.

His silk tea gowns in rich and subtle colors have been widely collected, both by museums and by women who are, of necessity, both rich and slender. The most famous design is the *Delphos* gown, which first appeared in 1907 and which he patented. This is a simple column of many narrow, irregular, vertical pleats permanently set in the silk by a secret process. It is slipped over the head and tied at the waist by thin silk cords, clinging to the figure and spilling over the feet. It may have sleeves or be sleeveless. There is also a two-piece version called *Peplos*, with a hip-length overblouse or longer, unpleated tunic. The dresses are both beautiful and amazingly practical. For storage, each is simply twisted into a rope and coiled into a figure eight, then slipped into its own small box. Status symbols at the time they were made, the dresses have become so once again, bringing such high prices at auction they're almost too costly to wear. He also designed tunics, capes, scarves and kimono-shaped wraps to be worn over the *Delphos*.

Fortuny invented a process for printing color and metals on fabrics to achieve an effect of brocade or tapestry. Velvets were dyed in many layers and sometimes printed with metallics, gold or silver. Fortuny fabrics are still used in interior design, still manufactured in Venice.

Painter, photographer, set and lighting designer, inventor, Fortuny has again in recent years been recognized for his originality and wide-ranging creativity. An exhibition of more than 100 examples of his work opened in Lyons, France, in May 1980. From there it travelled to New York's Fashion Institute of Technology and on to the Art Institute of Chicago. Included were dresses, robes, textiles, and clocks.

Mariano Fortuny, 1910–1950s. The Metropolitan Museum of Art, The Costume Institute. *Left:* Gift of Irving Drought Harris, in memory of Claire McCardell Harris, 1958. *Center:* Gift of Phyllis Hume Spalding, 1976. Right: Gift of The Estate of Agnes Miles Carpenter, 1958.

Mainbocher, 1949. Photograph by Louise Dahl-Wolfe. Fashion Institute of Technology, New York.

Above: **Chanel, c. 1927.** The Metropolitan Museum of Art, Purchase, The New York Historical Society by exchange, 1984, and Purchase, Irene Lewisohn Bequest, Catharine Breyer Von Bomel Foundation Fund and Hoechst Fibers Industries and Chauncey Stillman Gifts, 1984.

Top Left: **Madeleine Vionnet, 1947.** Photograph by Louise Dahl-Wolfe. Fashion Institute of Technology, New York.

Left: **Elsa Schiaparelli, 1937.** Philadelphia Museum of Art. Given by Elsa Schiaparelli.

Above: Missoni, 1974.

Above right: Karl Lagerfeld, 1986. *Women's Wear Daily.*

Right: Emanuel Ungaro, 1986. *Women's Wear Daily.*

Valentino, 1980. *Women's Wear Daily.*

Giorgio Armani, 1988. *Women's Wear Daily.*

Above: Adrian, 1944. The Metropolitan Museum of Art, Gift of Joseph S. Simms, 1979.

Right: Geoffrey Beene, 1982. *Women's Wear Daily.*

Charles James, 1948. Photograph by Louise Dahl-Wolfe. Fashion
Institute of Technology, New York.

GALANOS, JAMES

BORN: Philadelphia, Pennsylvania,
20 September 1925.

AWARDS:
  1954—Neiman-Marcus Award
  Coty American Fashion Critics' Award:
    1954—"Winnie"
    1956—Return Award
    1959—Hall of Fame
  1958—Cotton Fashion Award (for high
    fashion use of cotton)
  1984—Council of Fashion Designers
    of America (CFDA), Lifetime
    Achievement Award

James Galanos

Widely considered the greatest, most independent designer working in America today and the equal of the great European couturiers, this son of Greek immigrants left Philadelphia for New York and Traphagen School of Fashion, after only a few months at Traphagen began selling sketches to manufacturers. He worked for HATTIE CARNEGIE in 1944, went to Paris where he worked with ROBERT PIGUET, 1947-1948. He returned to New York and designed for Davidow, moved to Los Angeles and worked for Jean Louis on film costumes. In 1951 he started his own business with $200 and two assistants, gave his first New York showing in 1952 in a private apartment.

Galanos produces ready-to-wear that has become a symbol of luxury, both for its extraordinary quality and for stratospheric prices comparable to those of the couture. He believes a garment should be as luxurious inside as out and still insists on lining his clothes. Intricate construction,

1963

1962

EXHIBITION:
1976—"Galanos—25 Years"—Special
fashion show and exhibition at the
Fashion Institute of Technology, New
York, celebrating his twenty-fifth
year in business

flawless workmanship, and magnificent imported fabrics are his hallmarks, as well as detailing rarely found in ready-to-wear. Impeccably precise matching of plaids and the delicate cross pleating of his legendary chiffons are just two examples. An exacting perfectionist, he designs the complete look for his showings: hats, shoes, hosiery, accessories, hair, makeup.

Long admired by connoisseurs of fashion, Galanos achieved wider recognition as one of Nancy Reagan's favorite designers. She chose a white satin Galanos gown for the first Inaugural Ball in 1981, a slim, jeweled dress with bolero top for the second in 1985.

Because he likes the climate and relaxed living style, he lives and works in Los Angeles, where he has assembled a workroom of near-miraculous proficiency and skill, still housed in the same studio in which he started his business.

1987

1987

GALITZINE, PRINCESS IRENE

BORN: Tiflis, Russia, c. 1916.

Raised in Rome after her family fled the Russian Revolution, Galitzine studied art and design in Rome, worked three years for the FONTANA sisters. She opened an import business in Rome in 1948, first showed her own designs in 1949. She closed her business in 1968, continuing to design for various companies—cosmetics, furs, household linens—revived her couture house in 1970 and showed sporadically for several years.

Galitzine made her name in the 1960s with silk *palazzo pajamas*, an instant sensation as a sophisticated evening look. Cut with wide legs from fluid silks, they were often fringed with beads, sometimes had attached necklaces. She was also known for at-home togas, evening suits, tunic-top dresses, evening gowns with bare backs or open sides.

GAULTIER, JEAN-PAUL

BORN: Paris, France, 1952.

Jean-Paul Gaultier

Interested in fashion from an early age, Gaultier was at fourteen presenting minicollections of clothes to his mother and grandmother, and at fifteen had invented a coat with bookbag closures, an idea he was to use in a later collection. When he was seventeen, he sent some design sketches to CARDIN, for whom he worked as a design assistant for two years. Other stints followed at Esterel and PATOU, after which he turned to freelancing in 1976.

Once on his own, Gaultier rejected the attitudes of his couture training, reflecting much more the spirit of London street dressing. He has become the bad boy of Parisian fashion, using his considerable dressmaking and tailoring skills to produce irreverent send-ups of the fashion establishment. His juxtapositions of fabrics and shapes are unexpected and often witty, such as gray lace layered over voluminous gray wool knits, over-scaled coats over tiny vests cropped above the waist.

His considerable commercial success is backed by an Italian firm for Europe and America, another backer in Japan.

1985

GERNREICH, RUDI

BORN: Vienna, Austria, 8 August 1922.

DIED: Los Angeles, California,
21 April 1985.

AWARDS:
Coty American Fashion Critics' Award:
1960—Special Award (innovative
body clothes)
1963—"Winnie"
1966—Return Award
1967—Hall of Fame
1975—Crystal Ball Award, Knitted
Textile Association
1985—Council of Fashion Designers
of America (CFDA), Special Tribute

Probably the most original and prophetic American designer of the 1950s and 1960s, Gernreich was the only child of a hosiery manufacturer who died when his son was eight years old. First exposed to fashion in his aunt's couture salon, Gernreich made sketches there and learned about fabrics and dressmaking. In 1938 he left Austria with his mother and settled in Los Angeles. He attended Los Angeles City College and Art Center School, in 1942 joined the Lester Horton Modern Dance Theater as dancer and costume designer. He became a U.S. citizen in 1943.

After five years with Horton, Gernreich decided he was not sufficiently talented as a dancer and left the company. For the next few years he sold fabrics, designing a series of dresses to demonstrate them. These aroused so much interest that in 1951 he formed a partnership with William Bass, a young Los Angeles garment manufacturer, and began developing his personal view of fashion. He established his own firm in 1959, and in addition, designed a collection for Harmon Knitwear, a Wisconsin manufacturer.

Gernreich specialized in dramatic sport clothes of stark cut, enriched by bold graphic patterns and striking color combinations. Always interested in liberating the body, he introduced a knit maillot without an inner bra in 1954, the era of constructed bathing suits. He favored halter necklines and cut-back shoulders to allow free movement, designed

Rudi Gernreich and model, 1968

the soft *no-bra bra* in skin-toned nylon net, *Swiss cheese* swimsuits with multiple cutouts, see-through blouses, knee-highs patterned to match tunic tops and tights. His favorite shifts kept getting shorter until they were little more than tunics, which he showed over tights in bright colors or strong patterns.

Gernreich's innovations often caused a commotion, the see-through blouse, for example, and the topless bathing suit he showed in 1964. He was never interested in looking back, disdaining revivals of past eras. In 1968, at the height of his career, he announced he was taking a sabbatical from fashion. He never again worked at it full time, although he did return in 1971 with predictions for a future of bald heads, bare bosoms with pasties, unisex caftans. He also did some free-lance design in the fields of furniture, ballet costumes, professional dance and exercise clothes.

Quiet and cultivated in his tastes, Gernreich lived in the Hollywood Hills in a house furnished with modern classics by Charles Eames and Mies van der Rohe.

GIGLI, ROMEO

BORN: 1950.

1987

Gigli's father and grandfather were antiquarian book-sellers and he grew up in an aura of antiquity in considerable contrast to the simplicity and modernity of his clothing designs. Trained as an architect, he began designing in 1979, gave his first show in March 1982.

His approach to clothes is low key and minus frills and has been compared to that of the Japanese—the pieces meaning little on the hanger but taking shape on the body. Using rich and luxurious fabrics in sun-dried colors, he achieves a kind of throwaway chic and could be considered one of the minimalists. Although his collections cover day into evening, he specializes in soft sportswear, gentle and unassertive, out of the mainstream of Italian fashion. The total effect is quiet and poetic.

GIRBAUD, MARITHÉ & FRANÇOIS

BORN:
Marithé—Lyons, France, 1942.
François—Mazamet, France, 1945.

Champions of relaxed sportswear, the Girbauds established their business in 1965, are best known in the United States for their jeans and fatigue pants of soft, stonewashed denim. The clothes, for men and women, seem totally unconstructed but are more complex than they appear, and entirely functional. Jackets are often double, with one layer that buttons on for warmth; sweaters may be wool on the outside, cotton inside. The same thinking goes into their clothes for children.

GIVENCHY, HUBERT DE

BORN: Beauvais, France,
20 February 1927.

Givenchy studied at the École des Beaux Arts in Paris, at age seventeen went to work in the couture at LELONG, later at PIGUET and FATH. He spent four years at SCHIAPARELLI, where he designed for the boutique. In February 1952 he opened his own house near BALENCIAGA, whom he admired greatly and by whom he was much influenced.

His youthful separates brought early recognition, especially the *Bettina* blouse, a peasant shape named for the famous French model who worked with him when he first opened. When Balenciaga closed his house, Givenchy took

1964

Givenchy and models, 1979

over many of the workroom people, assuming as well much of the older designer's reputation for super-refined couture. His clothes are noted for masterly cut, exceptional workmanship, and beautiful fabrics. Those for day remain within a framework of quiet elegance, the late-day and evening segments of the collection are more exuberantly glamorous. He has an extensive and conservative clientele.

In addition to his couture house, one of the few truly profitable ones, Givenchy's interests include his Nouvelle Boutique ready-to-wear distributed worldwide, perfumes for women, men's toiletries. Licensing commitments extend from sportswear and shirts for men and women to small leathers, hosiery, furs, eyeglasses, home furnishings.

1964

1979

1982

GRÈS, ALIX

BORN: Paris, France, c. 1910.

Mme. Grès

Madame Grès wanted to be a sculptor, but the combination of family disapproval and lack of money turned her to dressmaking. She apprenticed at the House of Premet and in the early 1930s under the name Alix Barton, was making and selling toiles, the muslin patterns of the couture. Before World War II, she had a salon, Alix, which closed in 1942. After the war she reopened using her married name, Grès.

Madame Grès is widely considered one of the most talented, imaginative, and independent designers of the couture, ranked by many with VIONNET, although very different. Her background as a sculptor shows in her mastery of draping, especially in the evening dresses of chiffon and the fine silk jersey called *Alix* after her use of it. She molds the fabric to the figure, often baring some portion of the midriff. Other recurring themes are evening gowns in two colors, jersey day dresses with cowl necklines, deep-cut or dolman sleeves, kimono-shaped coats, asymmetric draping.

Small, serious, intensely private, Grès is shy of publicity, details of her life are scarce. It is known she married Serge Grès, a painter and sculptor, has one daughter.

Professionally, she goes her own way, was the last of the couture designers to undertake ready-to-wear. Perhaps symbolically, her perfume is named *Cabochard*, which means obstinate.

She has served as president of the Chambre Syndicale de la Haute Couture.

1975

GUIBOURGÉ, PHILIPPE

BORN: Paris, France, 1931.

DIED: Paris, France, 7 March 1986.

Guibourgé studied at the École des Beaux Arts Decoratifs in Paris, met JACQUES FATH during Army service and went to work for him after discharge. He stayed three years with Fath, training in all departments, assisted with couture as well as ready-to-wear. In 1960 Guibourgé went to CHRISTIAN DIOR. For twelve years at Dior as assistant to MARC BOHAN, he was responsible variously for the English ready-to-wear, fashion accessories for the boutiques, Miss Dior ready-to-wear. He also collaborated on the couture. He was director of CHANEL ready-to-wear from 1975 to 1982, a post taken over by KARL LAGERFELD in 1983. Guibourgé worked briefly for LANVIN and after Lagerfeld left, for Chloë. At the time of his death, he was planning a line of his own.

h

BILL HAIRE

HALSTON

KATHARINE HAMNETT

CATHY HARDWICK

HOLLY HARP

NORMAN HARTNELL

DANIEL HECHTER

SYLVIA HEISEL

CAROLINA HERRERA

CAROL HORN

HAIRE, BILL

BORN: New York City.

1984

After attending the High School of Industrial Art (now High School of Art and Design), Haire went on scholarship to the Fashion Institute of Technology, graduated in 1955. In 1956 he married Hazel Keleher, a classmate, taught evenings at F.I.T. He traveled extensively in Europe, returned to the United States in 1959 to design evening wear for Victoria Royal. After fourteen years, he moved to Henry Friedricks & Co. as co-designer with his wife, which allowed him to do a complete range of clothes. When his wife left Friedricks to free-lance, he continued under the Bill Haire for Friedricks Sport label.

An accomplished professional, Haire respects the sophistication and design intelligence of his customer, endeavors to anticipate the direction she is taking in order to meet her changing needs. He prefers natural fibers, tailors choice fabrics to simple, classic lines for a blend of style and practicality, avoiding faddishness.

HALSTON

BORN: Des Moines, Iowa,
   23 April 1932.

AWARDS:
   Coty American Fashion Critics' Award:
      1962, 1969—Special Award
         (millinery)
      1971—"Winnie"
      1972—Return Award
      1974—Hall of Fame

Halston grew up in Evansville, Indiana, attended Indiana University and the Chicago Art Institute. While still in school he designed hats and sold them. He moved to New York in 1957, worked for LILLY DACHÉ, and in 1959 joined Bergdorf Goodman. There he gained a name and a fashionable clientele. His fashion influence was immediate: he originated the scarf hat, designed the pillbox hat Jacqueline Kennedy wore for her husband's inaugural. In the late 1960s he started designing ready-to-wear.

In 1968 Halston opened his own firm for private clients and immediately established himself with a pure, ungimmicky, all-American look. His clothes were elegant and well made, with the casual appeal of sportswear. His formula of luxurious fabrics in extremely simple, classic shapes made him one of the top status designers of the 1970s. He has been quoted as saying, "I calmed fashion down."

Among his successes are the long cashmere dress with a sweater tied over the shoulders, wrap skirts and turtlenecks, evening caftans, long, slinky, haltered jerseys. He pioneered in the use of Ultrasuede®. Halston has worked closely with ELSA PERETTI, showing her accessories and jewelry with his clothes. She also designed the containers for his immensely successful fragrance.

Halston expanded into knitwear and accessories in 1970, ready-to-wear in 1972. In 1973 he sold the business to Norton Simon, which was acquired by Esmark, Inc. a decade later. In 1983 he signed with J. C. Penney for a cheaper line, prompting a number of his accounts to drop his regular line. In late 1984 he attempted to regain ownership of his made-to-order business and high-priced ready-to-wear line, but was unable to do so and went out of business.

1973

Halston and models, 1982

HAMNETT, KATHARINE

BORN: Gravesend, Kent, England, 1948.

Both a feminist and a supporter of the peace movement, Hamnett often carries her political concerns into her work. Her oversize T-shirts printed with statements such as "Worldwide Nuclear Ban Now" and "Stop Acid Rain," were inspired by the women's anti-nuclear protests in England.

She was born into a diplomatic family, educated at Cheltenham Ladies College, studied art in Stockholm before enrolling at St. Martin's School of Art in London to study fashion. She worked as a free-lance designer while still in school, after graduation in 1970 opened a sportswear firm, Tuttabanken, with a school friend. After its demise, she designed for a number of firms in England, France, Italy, and Hong Kong before establishing Katharine Hamnett Ltd. in 1979.

Her clothes are relaxed and easygoing, often based on work clothes. Men's wear, with the same feeling as her women's clothes, appeared in 1982. Hamnett has shown in Paris and Milan and has been widely copied, especially in Italy.

HARDWICK, CATHY

BORN: Seoul, Korea, 30 December 1933.

1987

After music studies in Korea and Japan, Hardwick came to the United States and at the age of twenty-one opened a boutique in San Francisco. Although she had no design training, she designed much of the merchandise for the shop, and began to free-lance for Alvin Duskin and another firm. She moved to New York in the late 1960s. In New York she did work for a number of ready-to-wear manufacturers and for Warner's Lingerie, opened her own design studio in 1972, established Cathy Hardwick & Friends, a manufacturing firm. She has designed home furnishings collections as well as ready-to-wear, since 1980 has licensed her designs to various manufacturers.

Hardwick is known for clean-cut, fluid, sensuous clothes, advanced fashion at a price. She wants her clothes to be comfortable and useful as well as fashionable. She has also sold them in England and Japan.

HARP, HOLLY

BORN: Buffalo, New York,
24 October 1939.

1987

The daughter of a machinery designer, Harp dropped out of Radcliffe in her sophomore year and went to Acapulco where she designed sandals and clothes to go with them. She returned to school at North Texas State University to study art and fashion design, moved to Los Angeles. In 1968, with a loan from her father, she opened a boutique on Sunset Strip. Henri Bendel gave her a boutique in 1972, she started her wholesale line in 1973. Her clothes are now sold in fine specialty stores around the United States. Other design commitments have included Simplicity Patterns and Fieldcrest bed linens.

Holly Harp's early designs were costumy, off-beat evening clothes, popular with entertainment figures and rock stars. She soon switched from feathers and fringe to subtler, sophisticated cuts, often on the bias, usually two-piece and in one size. These were elegantly engineered in matte jersey or chiffon, frequently decorated with hand-painted or air-brushed designs.

Her clothes are always wearable and essentially very simple. They are also imaginative, unconventional, and expensive, making her customer a free-thinking woman with money. Harp's design philosophy leans to risk-taking: "Whenever I'm trying to make an aesthetic decision, I always go in the direction of taking chances."

Holly Harp

HARTNELL, NORMAN

BORN: London, England, 12 June 1901.

DIED: Windsor, England, 8 June 1979.

AWARDS:
1947 — Neiman-Marcus Award

Educated at Cambridge University, where he designed costumes and performed in undergraduate plays, Hartnell was expected to become an architect but instead turned to dress design. After working briefly for a court designer and selling sketches to Lucile, he opened a business with his sister in 1923. At the time, a French name or reputation was indispensable to success in London so in 1927 he took his collection to Paris. In 1930 he again showed in Paris, resulting in many orders, particularly from

American and Canadian buyers. The Hartnell couture house became the largest in London. He was dressmaker by appointment to H.M. the Queen, whose coronation gown he designed, and to H.M. the Queen Mother.

Hartnell is most identified with his elaborate evening gowns, lavishly embroidered and sprinkled with sequins, particularly the bouffant gowns designed for H.M. the Queen Mother and for Queen Elizabeth II. He also made well-tailored suits and coats in British and French woolens and tweeds. By the 1970s he was making clothes in leather, designing furs and men's fashions.

He was knighted in 1977.

HECHTER, DANIEL

BORN: Paris, France, 1938.

In business for himself since 1962, Hechter started his career designing for Pierre D'Alby. On his own, his first designs were for women, followed in 1965 by children, with men's sportswear appearing in 1970. He has also designed active sportswear including tennis and ski clothes. He distributes and licenses around the world.

The clothes embody sportswear ease, function, and dash. Wearable and affordable, they are comfortable fashion for young, active people who are both career oriented and imaginative. Hechter strives for a sense of reality, continuity of line and color from season to season so that one collection adds to and is compatible with the one before.

HEISEL, SYLVIA

BORN: 22 June 1962.

After graduation from high school in Wallingford, Connecticut, Heisel went to Barnard College in New York City for one and a half years, left in December 1981. During 1981 and 1982 she designed and sold costume jewelry, and with the money started making clothes. Her first break came in 1982 when a Bendel's buyer admired the coat she was wearing and offered to buy it if she would make more. The coats sold and in 1983 she established her own company, Postmodern Productions, Inc., with herself as designer and president, using the Sylvia Heisel label.

Heisel specializes in designer dresses and dressy sportswear, has attracted attention with her soft, feminine dresses and special bias cuts. Her aim is elegant, minimal dressing, dressy clothes with sportswear fit and attitude for the sophisticated woman. She has also designed men's wear and film costumes.

Like other young designers who have made a go of it, she recognizes that it takes more than ideas to succeed. "Fashion is not art, it's a business ... You have to learn business to get anywhere."

HERRERA, CAROLINA

BORN: Caracas, Venezuela,
8 January 1939.

Herrera came to fashion with a background of couture clothes and private dressmakers. She grew up in Caracas and was educated there at El Carmen School. Going into the dress business seemed a natural step as she had worked closely with her Caracas couturiers, often designing her clothes herself. She established her firm in April 1981 with the backing of a South American publisher, quickly made a name and developed a following.

Best known for her designer ready-to-wear, elegant clothes with a couture feeling and feminine details, she also makes clothes to order for private clients, many of whom are her friends. In 1983 she signed a licensing agreement with the Japanese manufacturer Itokin, in October 1984 presented her first fur collection for Revillon. A lower-priced line of ready-to-wear called CH was introduced in 1986. Jacqueline Onassis, Estée Lauder, and Nancy Reagan have all worn her designs; she made Caroline Kennedy's wedding dress.

Herrera recognizes BALENCIAGA as her greatest influence. His example can be seen in her emphasis on a clear, dramatic line and her insistence that women can be feminine, chic, elegant, and at the same time comfortable.

Carolina Herrera and model, 1987

HORN, CAROL

BORN: New York, 12 June 1936.

AWARDS:
  1975—Coty American Fashion Critics'
    "Winnie"

Horn studied fine arts at Boston and Columbia Universities, began her career working as a fashion coordinator in retailing. She designed junior sportswear for Bryant 9, was sole designer for Benson & Partners for four years, then designer-director of the Carol Horn division of Malcolm Starr International. In 1983, after a number of years with licensees, she opened her own company, Carol Horn Sportswear, to which Carol Horn Knitwear has been added.

Her trademarks are easy, uncontrived shapes in muted tones, preferably using natural fibers. The clothes are contemporary in feeling, comfortable and seasonless, at a moderate price.

j

BETTY JACKSON

MARC JACOBS

CHARLES JAMES

BETSEY JOHNSON

ANDREA JOVINE

ALEXANDER JULIAN

JACKSON, BETTY

BORN: Bacup, Lancashire, England, 1949.

After a three-year fashion course at Birmingham College of Art, Jackson worked in London as a free-lance illustrator for two years, joined WENDY DAGWORTHY in 1973 as an assistant designer. In 1975 she moved to Quorum, stayed four years then spent two years at still another firm. In 1981 she opened under her own name.

Jackson is well known for her imaginative use of prints. Her clothes are young, classic in feeling, but updated with a fresh sense of scale. They have sold well in America and Italy. Her first men's wear appeared for fall 1986.

JACOBS, MARC

BORN: New York City, 1964.

AWARDS:
    1987—Council of Fashion Designers of America (CFDA) "Perry"

Jacobs was designing sweaters while still a student. He began his fashion career as a stock boy at one of New York's Charivari stores and continued to work there while attending Parsons School of Design. He was hailed as a "hot talent" on his graduation, and went to work for Ruben Thomas, Inc. under the *Sketchbook* label. He was building a reputation as an original designer of young fashion when his firm went out of business in October 1985. He reopened for fall 1986 with a new backer and a hardheaded and realistic approach to the fashion business. His clothes are lighthearted and individualistic, "fun and young."

1987

JAMES, CHARLES

BORN: Sandhurst, England,
   18 July 1906.

DIED: New York City,
   23 September 1978.

AWARDS:
   Coty American Fashion Critics' Award:
      1950 — "Winnie"
      1954 — Special Award (innovative cut)
      1953 — Neiman-Marcus Award

1961

Stormy and unpredictable, fiercely independent, James is considered by many students of fashion to be a genius, perhaps *the* greatest designer, ranking with BALENCIAGA.

He was educated in England and America. His father was a colonel in the British Army, his mother an American from a prominent Chicago family. After a brief stay at the University of Bordeaux, he moved to Chicago where he began making hats. He moved to New York in 1928, went on to London, where he produced a small dress collection which he brought back to New York. He then travelled back and forth between the two cities before moving to Paris around 1934 to open his own couture business.

In Paris, James formed close friendships with many legendary couture figures, including PAUL POIRET and CHRISTIAN DIOR, whose obituary he wrote for *The New York Post*. His exceptional ability was recognized and acknowledged by his design peers. He admired SCHIAPARELLI in her unadorned period. MADAME GRÈS was his favorite designer because as he did, she thinks in terms of shape and sculptural movement.

He returned to New York around 1939 and established his custom house, Charles James, Inc. He worked exclusively for Elizabeth Arden until 1945, continued to operate in New York, and sometimes London, until 1958, when he retired from couture to devote himself to painting and sculpture.

During the 1960s James conducted seminars and lectured at the Rhode Island School of Design and Pratt Institute. He

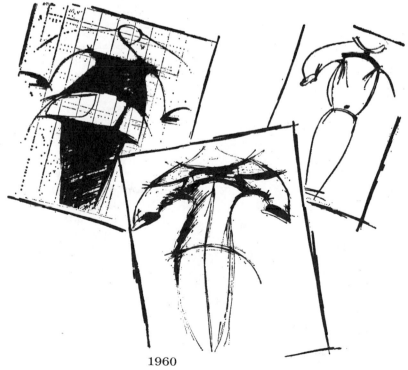

1960

designed a mass-produced line for E. J. Korvette in 1962, invented new techniques for dress patterns, created a dress form, jewelry designs, and even furniture. In the 1970s he occupied himself with preparing his archives, working with the illustrator Antonio, who made drawings of all his work to be kept as a permanent record.

James was a daring innovator, a sculptor with cloth. Each design began with a certain "shape," and hours were spent on the exact placement of a seam. Bold and imaginative, his designs depend on intricate cut and precise seaming rather than on trim. He was noted for his handling of heavy silks and fine cloths, for his batwing, oval cape coat, for bouffant ball gowns, for dolman wraps and asymmetrical shapes. In 1937, when his short white satin evening coat filled with eiderdown appeared on the cover of *Harper's Bazaar*, Dali called it "the first soft sculpture."

Since he considered his designs works of art, it is only appropriate that they are in the costume collections of many museums, including the Brooklyn Museum and the Smithsonian Institution, and also at the Fashion Institute of Technology. His ideas are still influential today.

JOHNSON, BETSEY

BORN: Wethersfield, Connecticut, 1942.

AWARDS:
1971—Coty American Fashion Critics' "Winnie"

Betsey Johnson

Johnson attended Pratt Institute for one year, went to Syracuse University, graduating cum laude, a member of Phi Beta Kappa. In her senior year she was guest editor at *Mademoiselle* magazine where sweaters she made for editors were seen by the owner of the Paraphernalia boutiques, who gave her a job designing. These collections, original and irreverent, established her at age twenty-two as a leader of the youth-oriented, anti-Seventh Avenue design movement of the 1960s.

In 1969, Johnson and two friends started the boutique *Betsey, Bunky and Nini*. She has designed for Alley Cat, Michael Milea, Butterick Patterns. In July 1978, she formed Betsey Johnson, Inc. to manufacture sportswear, bodywear, and dresses. She now operates three Betsey Johnson retail stores in New York City: in SoHo, on the Upper East Side, and on Columbus Avenue.

Johnson is unique. Imaginative and uninhibited, she designs for spirited nonconformists like herself. Typical ideas over the years include: the *Basic Betsey*, a clinging T-shirt dress in mini, midi or maxi lengths; a clear vinyl slip-dress complete with a kit of paste-on stars, fishes, and numbers; the *noise* dress with loose grommets at the hem. She designs her own fabrics and knits, has worked in cotton-and-spandex knits, rayon challis, heavyweight spandex in vibrant colors. She makes body-conscious clothes in a range that includes everything from bathing suits to bodysuits, tight pants to dance dresses.

KITS:

JOHNS BETSY FISH KIT

or:
STARS ☆
DOTS ○
TRIANGLES △
LETTERS Ⓐ
NUMBERS ③
LINES

1966

HE LOVES ME NOT!

1987

1987

JOVINE, ANDREA

BORN: Closter, New Jersey,
8 August 1955.

Following high school, Jovine studied in Switzerland for a year then attended the Fashion Institute of Technology in New York City where she won an ILGWU "Next Great Designer" award. After graduation in 1977 she worked for Bill Kaiserman at Rafael for three years, free-lanced for a year before going into business for herself. From 1981 to 1983 she designed belts and handbags for Omega, in 1983, with Victor Coopersmith, formed Andrea Jovine, Inc. for better sportswear, with a first collection of knits.

Jovine's aim is to make modern, uncomplicated, sophisticated clothing for the busy woman who needs "clothes that are interesting and versatile without being overdesigned and impractical." She picks up the nuances of the latest happenings and translates them into her own idiom, feels clothing should be easy to wear, easy to care for, and affordable. Essentially contemporary sportswear, her clothes give designer looks at reasonable prices.

JULIAN, ALEXANDER

BORN: Chapel Hill, North Carolina,
1948.

AWARDS:
Coty American Fashion Critics' Award:
1977—Men's Wear Award
1979—Men's Wear Return Award
1981—Men's Apparel
1983—Special Award Citation
1984—Special Award (men's wear)
1980, 1985—Cutty Sark Outstanding Designer Award
1981—Men's Woolknit Design Award
1981—Council of Fashion Designers of America, (CFDA) Designer of the Year

Primarily known for men's wear, Julian also designs for women and boys. He grew up in Chapel Hill where his father was a retailer, designed his first shirt when he was twelve. At the age of eighteen he was managing his father's store and at twenty-one had his own shop. In 1975, he moved to New York.

A frustrated artist, Julian is an inspired colorist, and appropriately, a number of his lines are named COLOURS. He has studied weaving and designs his own unusual and intricate fabrics, which can contain as many as sixteen colors, even designing the yarns that go into them if necessary to get the desired effect. These are produced in Scotland and Italy. Because they are expensive, he uses his fabrics to interpret traditional themes that do not quickly go out of date, leavening tradition with a lively dose of imagination and wit.

Julian has a highly successful business, licensing to manufacturers here and abroad. He keeps control over all his divisions, which produce clothes for men, women, and children, hosiery, home furnishings and decorative fabrics, small leather goods, pocket accessories.

Julian has a highly successful business, licensing to manufacturers here and abroad. He keeps control over all his divisions, which produce clothes for men, women, and children, hosiery, home furnishings and decorative fabrics, small leather goods, pocket accessories.

k

ROBIN KAHN

NORMA KAMALI

DONNA KARAN

HERBERT KASPER

REI KAWAKUBO

PATRICK KELLY

KENZO

EMMANUELLE KHANH

BARRY KIESELSTEIN-CORD

ALEXIS KIRK

ANNE KLEIN

CALVIN KLEIN

ROLAND KLEIN

DON KLINE

KOOS VAN DEN AKKER

MICHAEL KORS

REGINA KRAVITZ

KAHN, ROBIN

BORN: London, England,
12 January 1947.

AWARDS:
1984 — Coty American Fashion Critics'
Menswear Special Award (belt and
buckle designs)

Kahn arrived in the United States at the age of five. He graduated from the High School of Art and Design and Parsons School of Design, studied at Haystack Mountain School of Crafts, and took special training with goldsmiths. He has designed accessories for KENNETH J. LANE, OSCAR DE LA RENTA, and PIERRE CARDIN, as well as one-of-a-kind pieces for Bloomingdale's. Robin Kahn, Inc. was established in April 1978.

Kahn describes himself as a "constructionist," forming his designs directly from the metal. He has made his name working in three non-precious metals: brass, copper, and bronze. He has also employed ivory, ebony, turquoise, lapis, and such diverse materials as leather cording and taffeta. His jewelry, which has been described as futuristic Art Deco, is strong, bold, clean, elegant, and essentially classic in feeling.

KAMALI, NORMA

BORN: New York City, 27 June 1945.

AWARDS:
Coty American Fashion Critics' Award:
1981 — "Winnie"
1982 — Return Award
1983 — Hall of Fame
1982, 1985 — Council of Fashion
Designers of America (CFDA)
1984 — Fashion Institute of Design &
Merchandising (Los Angeles) FIDM
Award
1986 — The Fashion Group "Night of
the Stars" Award

Norma Kamali

Of Basque and Lebanese descent, Kamali grew up on the Upper East Side, where her father owned a candy store. Her mother made most of her daughter's clothes, as well as costumes for neighborhood plays, dollhouse furniture, paper flowers, "anything and everything." Kamali studied fashion illustration at the Fashion Institute of Technology, graduating in 1964. Unable to find work in her field, she took an office job with an airline, using the travel opportunities to spend weekends in London.

In 1968 she married Eddie Kamali, an Iranian student, and in 1969 they opened a tiny basement shop in which they sold European imports, largely from England, and Norma's own designs in the same funky spirit. In 1974 they moved to a larger, second floor space on Madison Avenue, and Kamali moved away from funk, started doing suits, lace dresses, delicate things. Divorced in 1977, she left the boutique she had started with her husband and in March 1978, established OMO (which stands for On My Own) Norma Kamali, a retail boutique and wholesale firm. In 1983 she bought a 99-year lease for a building across the street and moved her thriving business into a multilevel, multiangled environment finished in concrete. Here, with video monitors showing film productions of her collection, she can display everything she does, from accessories to couture.

Kamali was first recognized for adventurous, body-conscious clothes, definitely not for the timid. These were collected by such members of the fashion avant-garde as Donna Summer, Diana Ross, Barbra Streisand. A wider following developed for her swimsuits, cut daringly hip-high. In 1978, her draped and shirred "parachute" jumpsuits, using parachute fabric and drawstrings, were included in the "Vanity Fair" show at the Costume Institute of the Metropolitan Museum of Art. Giant removable shoulder pads have become her signature. From 1981 to 1986 she designed a highly successful, moderate-priced collection for the Jones Apparel Group using down-to-earth fabrics, notably cotton sweatshirting. It was discontinued following a labor dispute. She has also done children's clothes and lingerie.

1976

1982

1984

1987

KARAN, DONNA

BORN: Forest Hills, New York,
4 October 1948.

AWARDS:
Coty American Fashion Critics' Award:
1977—"Winnie" (with Louis
Dell'Olio)
1982—Hall of Fame (with Louis
Dell'Olio)
1984—Special Award (women's
wear) (with Louis Dell'Olio)
1985, 1986—Council of Fashion
Designers of America (CFDA)
1986—The Fashion Group "Night of
the Stars" Award

The daughter of a fashion model and a haberdasher, Karan was steeped in fashion from childhood. She attended Parsons School of Design, after her second year took a summer job with ANNE KLEIN, and never returned to school. She was fired by Klein after nine months, went to work for another sportswear house, returned to Klein in 1968. She was made associate designer in 1971. When Anne Klein became ill, Karan became head designer and asked LOUIS DELL'OLIO, a school friend, to join her as co-designer. In 1984, Karan was given her own firm by Takihyo Corporation of Japan, Anne Klein's parent company.

While it is impossible to separate her designs at Anne Klein from Dell'Olio's, their hallmark has always been wearability—classic sportswear looks with a stylish edge—terrific blazers, well-cut pants, strong coats, sarong skirts, easy dresses. And an element of tough chic.

Donna Karan and models, 1987

Karan's first collection under her own label established her immediately as a new fashion star. It was limited in size, based on a bodysuit over which went long or short skirts, blouses, pants, to make a complete, integrated wardrobe. These were combined with well-tailored coats and bold accessories, everything made of luxurious materials. As the clothes followed the body closely without excess detail or overt sexiness, the effect was both spare and sensuous. Her idea was to design only clothes and accessories she would wear herself—the best of everything for a woman who, like her, is a mother, a traveller, perhaps a business owner, someone who doesn't have time to shop. They are definitely in the status category.

In May 1987 she was awarded a Bachelor of Fine Arts degree by Parsons.

1986

1987

KASPER, HERBERT

BORN: New York City,
12 December 1926.

AWARDS:
Coty American Fashion Critics' Award:
1955—"Winnie"
1970—Return Award
1976—Hall of Fame

Kasper was majoring in English at New York University when World War II intervened. While serving in the army, he designed costumes for army shows and after the war attended Parsons School of Design. He spent two years in Paris, where he worked for FATH and ROCHAS and at *Elle* magazine. On his return to the U.S. he designed hats for John-Frederics and costumes for Broadway revues.

From 1953, Kasper worked for several Seventh Avenue firms, joined Leslie Fay in 1963. In 1967, Kasper for Joan Leslie Inc., a division of Leslie Fay, was established, then Kasper for JL Sport Ltd. and Kasper for Weatherscope. He resigned as vice president and designer in March 1985 to open his own company.

Noted for his well-tailored, sophisticated sportswear and dresses, Kasper is cognizant of current trends and interprets them for a specific American woman who does not like extremes but for whom dressing with style is an important part of life. Other design projects have included furs, handbags, bed linens.

KAWAKUBO, REI

BORN: Tokyo, Japan, 1942.

AWARDS:
1983—Mainichi Newspaper Fashion Award
1986—The Fashion Group "Night of the Stars" Award

Rei Kawakubo

The most avant of the Tokyo avant garde, Kawakubo was a Literature major at Keio University in Tokyo, graduated in 1965. She came to fashion design after working in the advertising department of a textile firm for two years and as a free-lance stylist for three years. She founded Comme des Garçons for women's clothes in 1973, since then has added men's wear and knits. She is president and designer of everything, shows her collections in Tokyo and Paris.

Originally, Kawakubo designed almost exclusively in tones of gray and black, has since softened the severity of her view with subtle touches of color. She plays with asymmetrical shapes, drapes and wraps the body with cottons, canvas, linens that are torn and slashed. In her early Paris showings, she emphasized the violence of her designs by making up her models with an extreme pallor and painted bruises and cuts.

She has been highly successful in the United States with in-store boutiques and her own free-standing shops. These are so minimalist that often, nothing at all is on display. In spring 1987, the Fashion Institute of Technology included her clothes in an exhibition entitled, "Three Women: Kawakubo, Vionnet, McCardell."

KELLY, PATRICK

BORN: Vicksburg, Mississippi, c. 1950.

1987

KENZO

BORN: Kyoto, Japan, 28 February 1940.

An American who made his name in Europe, Kelly is the son of a seamstress, grew up in Vicksburg and Atlanta, arrived in Paris in 1979 after a stopover in New York. He has never looked back. In Paris, his first job was making stage costumes, which he produced in a tiny hotel room on a domestic Singer. His first signature ready-to-wear collection was for fall 1985.

Kelly designs with a light, happy touch in an affordable price range. His specialty is sexy, clingy dresses in knits or stretchy fabrics, the tops often covered with buttons or with tiny black dolls. Models were the first to discover him and his designs are so popular with them that they have been known to work his shows in return for nothing more than some of the clothes. In September 1986 he signed with Benetton, the Italian sportswear manufacturer and retailer, to do a special collection of fifty pieces to be incorporated in the regular line. He has sold to Bergdorf Goodman in New York and to shops in France and Italy.

The son of hotelkeepers, Kenzo won top prizes in art school, began in fashion in Tokyo designing patterns for a magazine. He arrived in Paris in 1964, one of the first of his compatriots to make the move, and found work with a style bureau. He sold sketches to Feraud, free-lanced several collections, including Rodier.

In 1970 he opened his own boutique, decorated every inch with jungle patterns, and named it *Jungle Jap*. The clothes were an immediate success with models and other young fashion individualists. Money was scarce for his first ready-to-wear collection so although designed for fall-winter, it was made entirely of cotton, much of it quilted. He showed it on photographic mannequins rather than regular runway models, to the sound of rock music. These were innovations and like many other Kenzo ideas, were the beginning of a trend. Immediately successful with American stores, Kenzo designs are now widely distributed in the United States. A Kenzo-Paris boutique opened in New York on Madison Avenue in 1983, in 1984 Kenzo agreed to produce *Album by Kenzo* for the Limited Stores.

Kenzo is known for his spirited combinations of textures and patterns. His clothes are young, always wearable, and have been widely copied. He is a prolific originator of fresh ideas.

Kenzo

1978

1981

KHANH, EMMANUELLE

BORN: Plain, France,
7 September 1937.

Khanh started designing in 1959 with a job at Cacharel. Although she began her fashion career as a mannequin for BALENCIAGA and GIVENCHY, she rebelled against the couture in her own work and is credited with starting the young fashion movement in France. She was a revolutionary who is quoted as saying, "This is the century of sex. I want to make the sexiest clothes."

She first became known for the *Droop*, a very slim, soft, close-to-the-body dress which contrasted sharply with the structured couture clothes of the time. Her clothes had a lanky 1930s feeling with such signature details as dogs' ear collars, droopy lapels on long, fitted jackets, dangling cuff-link fastenings, half-moon moneybag pockets. Altogether, her work reflected an individual approach symbolic of the 1960s. Khanh survived the sixties and has continued to produce soft and imaginative fashions.

She is married to Vietnamese engineer and furniture designer, Nyuen Manh (Quasar) Khanh, also prominent in avant-garde fashion circles of the 1960s.

KIESELSTEIN-CORD, BARRY

BORN: New York City,
6 November 1943.

AWARDS:
1967 — Art Directors Club of New York
1969 — Illustrators Society of New York
1979, 1981, 1984 — Coty American
   Fashion Critics' Award
1981 — Council of Fashion Designers
   of America (CFDA)

Kieselstein-Cord comes from a family of designers and architects, including his mother, father, and both grandfathers. He studied at Parsons School of Design, New York University, the American Craft League. He has worked as an advertising agency art director-producer of commercial films, made an educational film on the platinum industry, put in a stint as creative director for a helicopter support and maintenance company.

Courtesy of Barry Kieselstein-Cord

His first jewelry collection was introduced at Georg Jensen around 1972. By the end of the decade his designs were sold around the United States and exported abroad. In 1984, he introduced a collection of personal and home accessories in precious metals and rare woods.

Working mainly in gold and platinum, Kieselstein-Cord starts with a sketch, moving from there directly into metal or wax, depending on whether the design will be reproduced by hand or from a mold. Each piece is finished by hand. He aims at timeless design not tied to fashion. His jewelry, widely featured in the press, has been praised for elegance, beauty, and superb craftsmanship. Pieces such as the Winchester buckle and palm cuffs are collected by fashion designers and celebrities everywhere

He has served as vice president of the Council of Fashion Designers of America.

KIRK, ALEXIS

BORN: Los Angeles, California,
29 December 1938.

AWARDS:
1970 — Coty American Fashion Critics' Joint Special Award (costume jewelry)
Numerous U.S. and European awards for accessories and jewelry.

Alexis Kirk traces his artistic roots back to ancestors who were armorers at the time of the Crusades. More recently, a grandfather was a jeweler with Lalique in Paris and his father an artist with Walt Disney Studios. Kirk attended Cambridge College, studied jewelry design at the Rhode Island School of Design and the Boston Museum School of Fine Arts. He studied and taught architecture at the University of Tennessee, became interested in fashion while doing textile research at Eastman Kodak. He studied at Harvard under famed architect, Walter Gropius, a continuing influence on his work.

In 1961 he opened a workshop in Newport, Rhode Island, to develop jewelry and clothing designs, then opened three boutiques. He moved to New York and worked for Design Research, El Greco Fashions, Hattie Carnegie Inc., established his own costume jewelry company in 1969, winning special notice for his work in pewter.

Kirk works toward the ideal of pure line and form, has applied himself to projects ranging from accessories and furnishings to bodywear. He has designed costumes, sets, and special effects for films, designed and constructed his own home in the Hamptons, produced and directed a short film for the Smithsonian Institution on the history of design. He designed the official Bicentennial eagle in pewter; his work is in the permanent collections of the Museum of the City of New York and the Metropolitan Museum of Art.

KLEIN, ANNE

BORN: Brooklyn, New York,
3 August 1923.

DIED: New York City, 19 March 1974.

AWARDS:
Coty American Fashion Critics' Award:
1955—"Winnie"
1969—Return Award
1971—Hall of Fame
1959, 1969—Neiman-Marcus Award

Anne Klein got her first job on Seventh Avenue at the age of fifteen as a sketcher, the next year joined Varden Petites. In 1948, she and her first husband, Ben Klein, formed Junior Sophisticates. She designed for Mallory Leathers in 1965, operated Anne Klein Studio on West 57th. In 1968, with Sanford Smith and her second husband, Chip Rubenstein, she formed Anne Klein & Co., now wholly owned by Takihyo Corporation of Japan. Since her death, the firm has continued, first with DONNA KARAN and LOUIS DELL'OLIO as co-designers, then when Karan established her own label, with Dell'Olio alone.

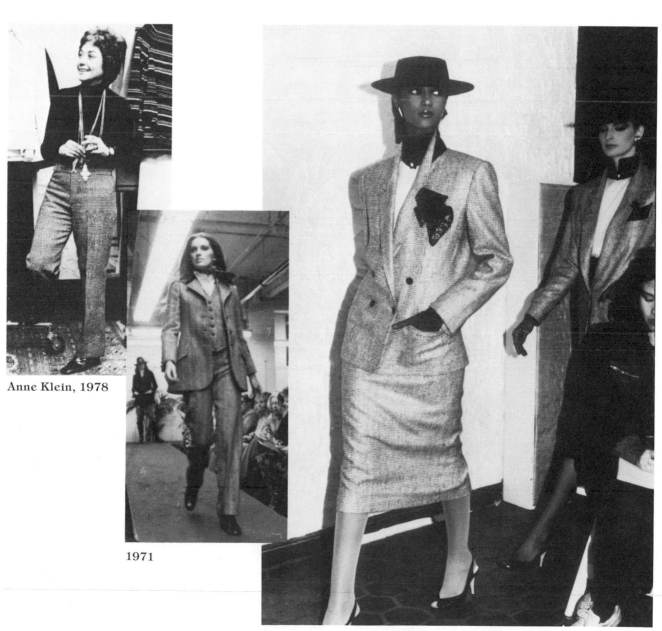

Anne Klein, 1978

1971

Karan and Dell'Olio for Anne Klein, 1983

Early in her career, Klein became known for her pioneering work in taking junior-size clothes out of little-girl cuteness and into adult sophistication. At Junior Sophisticates there was the skimmer dress with its own jacket, long, pleated plaid skirts with blazers, gray flannel used with white satin. At Anne Klein & Co. the emphasis was on investment sportswear, an interrelated wardrobe of blazers, skirts, pants, sweaters, with slinky, hooded jersey dresses for evening.

Klein was also a pioneer in recognizing the value of sportswear as a way of dressing uniquely suited to the American woman's way of life. In 1973, she was among the designers invited to show at the Grand Divertissement at Versailles.

KLEIN, CALVIN

BORN: New York City,
19 November 1942.

AWARDS:
Coty American Fashion Critics' Award:
1973 — "Winnie"
1974 — Return Award
1975 — Hall of Fame
1975 — Special Award (fur design for
Alixandre)
1979 — Special Award (contribution
to international status of
American fashion)
1981 — Women's Apparel
1981, 1983 — Council of Fashion
Designers of America (CFDA)

Klein attended the High School of Industrial Art (now High School of Art and Design), graduated from the Fashion Institute of Technology in 1962. He spent five years at three large firms as apprentice and designer, first won recognition for his coats.

In 1968, with long-time friend Barry Schwartz, he formed Calvin Klein Ltd., which has developed into a design empire. Besides women's ready-to-wear and sportswear, and men's wear, it has included everything from blue jeans to furs to women's underthings modeled on traditional men's undershirts and briefs, and from bed linens to cosmetics, skin care, fragrances, and pantyhose. He has promoted his products with provocative, sexy, often controversial advertising, notably the jeans and *Obsession*, the second of his two women's fragrances.

Considered the foremost exponent of spare, intrinsically American style, Klein presents a full wardrobe, day into evening. He has said, "It's important not to confuse simplicity with uninteresting," executes his simplified, refined, sportswear-based shapes in luxurious natural fibers such as cashmere, linen, silk, as well as leather and suede. His color preferences are for earth tones and neutrals. His hallmark is a lean, supple elegance, an offhand, understated luxury.

Calvin Klein and models, 1985

1979

1984

1983

KLEIN, ROLAND

BORN: Rouen, France, 1938.

A Frenchman who moved to London in 1965 to learn English, then decided to stay, Klein studied at L'École de la Chambre Syndicale from 1955 to 1957. From 1960 to 1962 he worked in the tailoring department at CHRISTIAN DIOR where he learned cut. From Dior he went to PATOU as assistant to KARL LAGERFELD, whom he considers his greatest influence.

In London he worked at Marcel Fenz, where in 1973, he became managing director with his own label. He opened his own ready-to-wear business in 1979. Klein's clothes demonstrate his sound training. They are well cut, simple, elegant, and extremely well made.

KLINE, DON

BORN: Vandergrift, Pennsylvania.

AWARDS:
  1973—Coty American Fashion Critics'
    Special Award (hats)

A 1969 graduate of New York's Fashion Institute of Technology, Kline worked several years for the milliner, Emme. After a six-month stint designing sportswear, he took a collection of his hats around to fashion magazines and stores, sold enough to open a showroom. His design projects have included furs and ready-to-wear; he at one time had his own boutique on Madison Avenue.

Kline is frequently given credit for inspiring a revival of interest in hats. His early successes included draped turbans, small tilted felts in the manner of the 1930s and 1940s, an urbane version of the stitched tweed sportsman's hat. For several years he designed hats to complement the collections of other designers, now does them only to complete the look of his own ready-to-wear. His collection has grown to include dresses and sportswear, evening clothes and outerwear.

KOOS VAN DEN AKKER

BORN: Holland, c. 1932.

AWARDS:
  1983—Print Council of America's
    "Tommy" Award for his unique use
    of prints.

Koos started making dresses when just eleven years old. He entered the Netherlands Royal Academy of Art at fifteen, quit school in 1950 to work at design. He worked in department stores in The Hague and in Paris, completed a two-year fashion program at L'École Guerre Lavigne in Paris in seven months. After an apprenticeship at CHRISTIAN DIOR, he returned to The Hague and spent six years there selling custom-made dresses in his own boutique.

In August 1968, with a portable sewing machine and very little money, he came to New York and set up his "office" by the fountain at Lincoln Center, taking commissions from passers-by. One customer introduced him to Eve Stillman, who gave him a job designing lingerie. Eventually, he opened his own boutique, at the same time wholesaling to other shops and to Henri Bendel. He moved to Madison Avenue in 1975, opened a shop in Beverly Hills and a boutique for

Koos van den Akker

men. In 1983 he inaugurated Hot House, a moderately-priced wholesale line.

Koos designs everything from lingerie to furs to day and evening clothes to sheets to home furnishings. His women's clothes are distinguished by simple shapes in beautiful fabrics enriched with his signature "collages," insertions of colorful prints and lace.

His clothes are considered collectors' items and have been on display in the Museum of Contemporary Crafts, New York. Customers have included Cher, Madeleine Kahn, Elizabeth Taylor, Gloria Vanderbilt.

1987

1976

KORS, MICHAEL

BORN: Long Island, New York,
9 August 1959.

Michael Kors and model, 1987

Kors attended the Fashion Institute of Technology for one semester in 1977, worked for three years as designer, buyer, and display director for a New York boutique before starting his own business in 1981. His first collection of sixteen pieces, entirely in brown and black, sold to eight accounts. In five years, the list has grown to over seventy-five specialty stores. In 1985 he began an association with the Scottish firm of Lyle & Scott, to design cashmere knits.

Kors designs individual pieces then combines them into outfits. His aim is a flexible, versatile way of dressing by which a woman can put together pieces in different ways to achieve anything from the most casual to the most dressy effect. The clothes belong in the designer sportswear category, dresses and separates in luxurious fibers and fabrics, clean and understated in cut and line. They are meant for a sophisticated, modern, affluent woman who dresses to please herself.

KRAVITZ, REGINA

BORN: New York City, 24 March 1949.

Kravitz grew up in New Jersey, graduated from New York University with a B.A. in English, took her Masters in costume design. Theater was another college interest. In 1971 she became partner-designer in Pineapple, a men's wear company, in 1975 began designing young men's sportswear, sweaters, and rainwear for Peters Sportswear under her own Reggie label. In 1978, she established Regina Kravitz, Inc. to meet her own need for a professional wardrobe, and the needs of women like her.

Early on she began designing a certain kind of dressy clothes she calls "night sportswear." These special items grew into a collection of late-day to late-night fashions. The jumpsuit has become a keynote of her collections, which now cover every time of day. Practical, comfortable, feminine, and affordable, the clothes have a modern, sexy feeling, relaxed but elegant, span the range from office to evening. They are designed for the young, contemporary executive woman.

1

CHRISTIAN LACROIX
KARL LAGERFELD
KENNETH JAY LANE
JEANNE LANVIN
MARYLL LANVIN
GUY LAROCHE
ANDRÉ LAUG
RALPH LAUREN
RON LEAL
LUCIEN LELONG
TINA LESER

LACROIX, CHRISTIAN

BORN: France, 1951.

Christian Lacroix and model, 1987

Lacroix is given credit by some critics for revitalizing the Paris couture with his irreverent wit and sense of humor, and for returning an element of adventure to fashion. A native of Provence in the South of France, he grew up surrounded by women, developing an early interest in fashion and accessories. After studies in Art History and classic Greek and Latin at Montpellier University, he went to Paris in 1972 to attend L'École du Louvre. A stint as a museum curator followed, then in 1978 Lacroix turned to fashion, first as a design assistant at Hermès then for two years at Guy Paulin. He went to Japan for a year as an assistant to a Japanese designer, returned to Paris and joined JEAN PATOU in 1982 as chief designer of haute couture.

At Patou he produced collection after idea-filled collection of theatrical, witty clothes and fantastic accessories. Imaginative and elegant, not all were wearable by any but the most daring, but many would appeal to an adventurous woman with flair and confidence in her own style.

After five years with Patou, Lacroix announced in January 1987 that he was leaving to establish his own couture house backed by Financière Agache, the French conglomerate that owns Dior. His new arrangement includes ready-to-wear.

1987

LAGERFELD, KARL

BORN: Hamburg, Germany,
10 September 1939.

AWARDS:
1980 — Neiman-Marcus Award for Distinguished Service in the field of fashion
1982 — Council of Fashion Designers of America (CFDA)

The son of a Swedish father and German mother, Lagerfeld arrived in Paris in 1953, at fourteen already determined to become a clothes designer. In 1954, after winning an award for the best coat submitted in the same International Wool Secretariat design competition in which Saint Laurent won an award for the best dress, he was working for BALMAIN. Three and a half years later he went to work for PATOU.

He left Patou, tried to go back to school, was at loose ends for two years, and began free lancing. In 1963 he went to work for the upscale ready-to-wear house, Chloë, as one of a team of four designers. The team of four became two, Lagerfeld and the Italian Graziella Fontana. They continued to jointly design the collection until 1972 when Lagerfeld became sole designer.

Commencing in 1982 he designed for Chanel while continuing with Chloë, left Chloë in 1984 for Chanel and to inaugurate his first collection under his own label. In spring 1985 he introduced a sportswear collection designed specifically for the United States. He has also designed gloves, shoes for Mario Valentino and Charles Jourdan, sweaters for Ballantyne. He does both furs and sportswear for FENDI. He

Karl Lagerfeld

1980   1987

has a number of successful fragrances for women and men.

Lagerfeld is a prolific, unpredictable, original designer, highly professional and a master of his craft. At his best he mixes inventiveness and wearability, spicing the blend with a dash of wit. He likes to remove clothes from their usual contexts, at various times has showed crepe de Chine dresses with tennis shoes, used elaborate embroidery on cotton instead of the usual silk, made dresses that could be worn upside down. He is credited with bringing Chanel into the 1980s while retaining its distinctive character.

LANE, KENNETH JAY

BORN: Detroit, Michigan, 22 April 1932.

AWARDS:
1966—Coty American Fashion Critics' Special Award (jewelry)
1968—Neiman-Marcus Award

Lane attended the University of Michigan for two years, graduated from the Rhode Island School of Design in 1954. He worked on the promotion art staff at *Vogue* and there met French shoe designer Roger Vivier. Through him, Lane became an assistant designer for Delman Shoes, then associate designer of Christian Dior Shoes, spending part of each year in Paris working with Vivier.

In 1963, still designing shoes, Lane made a few pieces of jewelry which were photographed by the fashion magazines and bought by a few stores. Working nights and weekends, he continued to design jewelry, using his initials K.J.L., by June 1964 was able to make jewelry design a full-time career. Kenneth Jay Lane, Inc. became part of Kenton Corporation in 1969, was repurchased by Lane in 1972. In addition to jewelry, he designs special accessories for the home.

Like a designer of precious jewels, Lane first makes his designs in wax or by carving or twisting metal. "I want to make real jewelry with not-real materials." He sees plastic as the modern medium, lightweight, available in every color, perfect for simulating real gems. He likes to see his jewelry intermixed with the real gems worn by his international roster of celebrity customers.

LANVIN, JEANNE

BORN: Brittany, France, 1867.

DIED: Paris, France, 6 July 1946.

AWARDS:
French Legion of Honor

The eldest of a journalist's ten children, Lanvin was apprenticed to a dressmaker at the age of thirteen, became a milliner when she was twenty-three. The dresses she designed for her young daughter, Marie-Blanche, were admired and bought by her hat customers for their children and this business in children's clothes evolved into the couture house of Lanvin, Faubourg St. Honoré.

1931

Lanvin's designs were noted for a youthful quality, often reflecting the influence of the costumes of her native Brittany. She collected costume books, daguerreotypes, historical plates, and drew inspiration from them, notably for the *robes de style* for which she was famous, and for her wedding gowns. She took plain fabrics and decorated them in her own workrooms, maintaining a department for machine embroidery under the direction of her brother. The house also produced women's sport clothes and furs, children's wear, and lingerie. In 1926 she opened a men's wear boutique, the first in the couture, directed by her nephew, Maurice Lanvin.

She was famous for her use of quilting and stitching, for her embroideries, for the discreet use of sequins. She introduced the chemise during World War I, fantasy evening gowns in metallic embroideries were a signature. She was one of the first couturiers to establish a perfume business, among her most notable fragrances being *Arpege* and *My Sin*.

Mme. Lanvin was an accomplished businesswoman and was elected President of the Haute Couture committee of the Paris International Exhibition in 1937. She represented France and the couture at the 1939 New York World's Fair.

After her death the House of Lanvin continued under the direction of her daughter, the Comtesse de Polignac. It is now owned by Bernard Lanvin and his designer wife, Maryll, who first took over design direction of ready-to-wear, and after the retirement of JULES-FRANÇOIS CRAHAY, of the couture collection. The couture was designed by Antonio del Castillo from 1950 to 1963, and from 1963 until 1984, by Crahay.

Jeanne Lanvin

LANVIN, MARYLL

BORN: France.

Maryll Lanvin studied at the École des Arts Décoratifs and the École de la Chambre Syndicale de la Haute Couture. She was a student of JULES-FRANÇOIS CRAHAY, for twenty years designer of the Lanvin couture collections. In 1980 she took over design of the Lanvin ready-to-wear collections, and when Crahay retired in 1984, assumed direction of the haute couture.

LAROCHE, GUY

BORN: La Rochelle (near Bordeaux), France, c. 1923.

1987

Laroche arrived in Paris at age twenty-five with no previous interest in clothes and no immediate goals. Through a cousin working at JEAN PATOU, he toured several couture houses and fell in love with the business. He got a job as assistant to JEAN DESSÈS, stayed with him five years, free-lanced in New York from 1950 to 1955, returned to Paris and opened a couture establishment in his apartment. His first collection was for fall 1957. In 1961, he expanded and moved to the Avenue Montaigne, where the house is still located.

In the beginning influenced by BALENCIAGA, Laroche soon developed a younger, livelier, less formal look. "It was very, very conservative when I started. I gave it color...youth, suppleness and informality." His evening pants were worn by the most fashionable women in Paris.

Laroche had his greatest fame during the early 1960s. Today he maintains his couture atelier but has also expanded successfully into highly profitable ready-to-wear and licensing ventures covering everything from intimate apparel, furs, luggage, sportswear, rainwear, dresses, and blouses, to sunglasses, accessories and, of course, fragrances.

LAUG, ANDRÉ

BORN: Alsace, France, 1932.

DIED: December, 1984.

Laug worked briefly for NINA RICCI and ANDRÉ COURRÈGES before moving to Italy. He designed for ANTONELLI for five years, in 1968 opened a couture house in Rome. He also produced ready-to-wear which he showed in Milan.

He was noted for translating young ideas into chic, wearable clothes for a conservative international clientele. Both the couture and deluxe ready-to-wear are refined in cut and attitude, beautifully made. The house continues in business through the efforts of a devoted staff.

LAUREN, RALPH

BORN: New York City,
14 October 1939.

AWARDS:
Coty American Fashion Critics' Award:
1970—Men's Wear Award
1973—Return Men's Wear Award
1974—"Winnie"
1976—Return Award
1976—Hall of Fame (men's wear)
1977—Hall of Fame (women's wear)
1981—Men's Apparel
1984—Special Award
(women's wear)
1981, 1986—Council of Fashion
Designers of America (CFDA)

The son of an artist, Lauren took night courses in business while working days as a stock boy at Alexander's. After college he sold at Brooks Brothers, was variously, an assistant buyer at Allied Stores, a glove company salesman, the New York representative for a Boston necktie manufacturer. He started designing neckties and in 1967 persuaded a men's wear firm to handle them, establishing the Polo neckwear division. The ties were unique, exceptionally wide and made by hand of opulent silks. They quickly attracted attention to the designer and brought Lauren a contract to design the Polo line of men's clothing for Norman Hilton, with whom in 1968, he established Polo as a separate company producing a total wardrobe for men.

In 1971 Lauren introduced finely tailored shirts for women and the next year a total ready-to-wear collection: sophisticated separates in such fabrics as English flannels, Harris tweeds, silk, cashmere, camel hair. Polo boys' wear followed, then Western Wear, then Ralph Lauren for Girls. There is a less expensive men's line called Chaps, Polo University Club for the college student and young businessman, and a rugged outdoor collection called Roughwear. His licensing for both men and women has expanded worldwide

1982

Ralph Lauren and models, 1987

to include men's robes, swimwear, and furnishings, small leathers, furs, and scarves. Other involvements are fragrances, cosmetics and skin care, luggage, and 1983, a total home environment: sheets, towels, blankets, tableware, accessories.

In addition, Lauren has done film work, designing for the leading men in *The Great Gatsby* in 1973, and in 1977, for Woody Allen and Diane Keaton in *Annie Hall*.

Lauren chose the name *Polo* as a symbol of men who wear expensive, classic clothes and wear them with style. He extends the same blend of classic silhouettes, superb fabrics, and fine workmanship to his women's apparel. For both women and men, the attitude is well bred and confident, with an offhand luxury. Lauren has projected his romantic view of the American dream in his advertising, which features a large cast of models in upper crust situations: at the beach, on safari, watching polo matches. Definitely investment caliber, the clothes are known for excellent quality and high prices.

1978

1987

LEAL, RON

BORN: Hanford, California,
23 April 1944.

After study at the University of California at Santa Barbara, Leal attended the American Academy of Dramatic Arts for two years, worked in Italy from 1972 to 1973 for Walter Albini. He had his own business from 1975 to 1977 then went to work for Betty Hanson & Co., where he stayed two years. He again opened his own business in 1979, returned to Betty Hanson in 1985.

For Hanson, Leal designs sophisticated sportswear and evening separates, entirely current but rooted firmly in tradition, with all that means in style and quality. The clothes appeal to the self-assured woman who adapts fashion to her own needs rather than following fads.

LELONG, LUCIEN

BORN: Paris, France, 11 October 1889.

DIED: Anglet (near Biarritz), France,
10 May 1958.

Lucien Lelong, 1938

Lelong made his first designs at the age of fourteen for his father, who was a successful dressmaker. At first trained for a business career he decided on a career in couture but in 1914 was called into the army two days before the presentation of his first collection. He was wounded in World War I, invalided out after a year in the hospital, received the Croix de Guerre.

In 1918 he entered his father's business and took control soon after. By 1926, the year he established *Parfums Lelong,* the house was flourishing, continuing to do so up until the Second World War. He was one of the first to have a ready-to-wear line, *Éditions,* established in 1934, in 1937 was elected president of the Chambre Syndicale de la Couture. He held the post for ten years, including the occupation period when the Germans wanted to move the entire French dressmaking industry to Berlin and Vienna. Lelong managed to frustrate the plan and guided the couture safely through the war years. He reopened his own house in 1941, with DIOR and BALMAIN as designers. A serious illness in 1947 caused him to close his couture house, he continued to direct his perfume business.

Lelong was considered a director of designers rather than a creator. PIERRE BALMAIN, CHRISTIAN DIOR, and GIVENCHY all worked for him, and Dior particularly praised him as a good friend and a generous employer. From 1919 to 1948, his house produced distinguished collections of beautiful, ladylike clothes for a conservative clientele. Lelong believed strongly in honest workmanship and good needlework and it was his credo that a Lelong creation would hold together until its fabrics wore out.

He was an accomplished painter, sculptor, composer, and sportsman.

LESER, TINA

BORN: Philadelphia, Pennsylvania,
12 December 1910.

DIED: Sands Point, Long Island,
24 January 1986.

AWARD:
    1945—Neiman-Marcus
      Award
    1945—Coty American
      Fashion Critics'
      "Winnie"

1945

Leser studied art in Philadelphia and Paris, in 1935 opened a shop in Honolulu to sell her fashion designs. She returned to New York in 1942 following the outbreak of World War II, and began to make the glamorous sportswear which became her trademark. For ten years she designed for a sportswear manufacturer, in 1952 formed her own company, Tina Leser Inc. She retired in 1964, returned to fashion in 1966, quit for good in 1982.

One of the group of innovative sportswear designers that included CLAIRE MCCARDELL and TOM BRIGANCE, Leser always was distinguished by her romanticism and her use of exotic fabrics from the Orient and Hawaii, which she often enriched with embroidery and metallic threads. She used hand-painted prints, designed harem pajamas and toreador pants long before other designers who were later credited with them. She is also given credit for making the first dress from cashmere.

She was married first to Curtin Leser, from whom she was divorced, then to James J. Howley, who survived her. They had one daughter.

m

BOB MACKIE

MAINBOCHER

MARIUCCIA MANDELLI

MARY JANE MARCASIANO

MITSUHIRO MATSUDA

VERA MAXWELL

CLAIRE McCARDELL

JESSICA McCLINTOCK

MARY McFADDEN

ROSITA & OTTAVIO MISSONI

ISSEY MIYAKE

CAPTAIN EDWARD MOLYNEUX

CLAUDE MONTANA

HANAE MORI

FRANCO MOSCHINO

REBECCA MOSES

THIERRY MUGLER

JEAN MUIR

MACKIE, BOB

BORN: Los Angeles, California,
24 March 1940.

Bob Mackie

Mackie grew up in Los Angeles, studied art and theater design. While still in art school he worked as sketcher for designers Jean Louis and Edith Head, and for Ray Aghayan, whose partner he became. The spectacular costume designs he and Aghayan have designed for nightclub performers and for stars of TV and movies have established the two in the top rank of their field. Among the celebrities they have dressed are Marlene Dietrich, Carol Burnett, Mitzi Gaynor, Barbra Streisand, Raquel Welch, Carol Channing, and notably, Cher.

In addition to costumes, Mackie has been successful in ready-to-wear, not surprisingly with emphasis on glamorous evening clothes. He has designed bathing suits and loungewear, in 1969 opened a boutique on Melrose Avenue in Los Angeles.

1987

MAINBOCHER

BORN: Chicago, Illinois,
24 October 1891.

DIED: Munich, Germany,
26 December 1976.

Encouraged by his mother, Mainbocher studied art at the Chicago Academy of Fine Arts, and in New York, Paris, and Munich, was taken to *Vogue's* 1914 "Fashion Fête," by a manufacturer for whom he was sketching. He went to Paris in 1917 with an American ambulance unit and stayed on after the war to study singing, his first love. To support himself he worked as a fashion illustrator for *Harper's Bazaar* and *Vogue*. By 1922 he had given up the idea of becoming a singer and was a full-time fashion journalist. He first was Paris editor for *Vogue*, then editor of French *Vogue* before resigning to open his own salon in Paris in 1929.

It is said that in his first year in business he introduced the strapless evening gown and also persuaded French textile manufacturers to again set up double looms and weave wide widths not produced since before World War I. With his many influential contacts and sure fashion sense he made an immediate success, the first American to do so in Paris. The Duchess of Windsor, whose wedding dress he made, and Lady Mendl were among his clients.

Mainbocher left Paris on the outbreak of World War II and in 1939 opened a couture house in New York. He became the designer with most snob appeal for the rich and conservative, retaining his preeminence until he closed his doors in 1971.

Noted for a nearly infallible sense of fashion, Mainbocher created high-priced clothes of quiet good taste, simplicity, and understatement. He was greatly influenced by the work of VIONNET and used the bias cut with great mastery. Elegant evening clothes were his forte, from long ball gowns of lace or transparent fabrics to short evening dresses and beaded evening sweaters with jeweled buttons. He made dinner suits of tweed, combining them with blouses of delicate fabrics. Pastel gingham was a signature, accessorized with pearl chokers, short white kid gloves, plain pumps. He also designed uniforms for the American Red Cross, the WAVES, SPARS, and Girl Scouts.

Known as a skillful editor of others' work as well as a creator, Mainbocher has been ranked with MOLYNEUX, SCHIAPARELLI, LELONG. His design philosophy has been widely quoted: "The responsibility and challenge...is to consider the design and the woman at the same time. Women should look beautiful, rather than just trendful."

Mainbocher 1931

MANDELLI, MARIUCCIA

BORN: Near Milan, Italy, c. 1933.

Mariuccia
Mandelli

The child of a grain merchant, Mandelli's intention from the age of eight was to be a designer. To please her mother she taught school briefly, then opened her own business with only two workers. Contrary to couture tradition, her clothes were unconstructed and met considerable resistance from the establishment. Her first show in 1967 won a press award and then her business blossomed. She persuaded her husband, Aldo Pinto, to become her business partner and supervise her knitwear company, Kriziamaglia, which took off in the early 1970s. Further success led to the inevitable licenses, boutiques, and highly successful fragrances.

Mandelli is a witty, fertile designer, each collection bursting with ideas, veering between extremes of classicism and craziness. Perhaps most famous for her animal sweaters, a different bird or beast for each collection, she introduced Hot Pants in the 1960s, and is also known for fantastic evening designs such as tiered cellophane fan dresses that looked like the Chrysler Building.

An accomplished businesswoman with a sure grasp of company affairs, she is a hard worker, produces ten collections a year, including children's wear. She has devoted her considerable energy to various causes of the Milan design community and is considered responsible for moving the ready-to-wear showings from Florence to Milan.

1986

MARCASIANO, MARY JANE

BORN: New Jersey, 23 September 1955.

AWARDS:
  1981 — Cartier "Stargazer" Award
  1983 — Wool Knit Award
  1984 — Dupont Award (most promising designer)
  1984 — Cutty Sark Award (most promising men's wear designer)

A 1978 graduate of the Parsons School of Design, Marcasiano designed her first collection in 1979, has been working since then under her own label. She added men's wear in 1982, began licensing in 1985 with a shoe collection, fine and semi-precious jewelry, and furs for Ben Kahn.

Her clothes — sportswear, dresses, outerwear — belong in that desirable category that combines elegance with comfort and ease. She sees her customer as a woman without age limits, a traveller active in business who appreciates subtle, luxurious clothes that enhance her individuality.

MATSUDA, MITSUHIRO

BORN: Tokyo, Japan, 1934.

Matsuda graduated from Waseda University, studied at Tokyo's famous Bunka College of Fashion, where KENZO and Junko Koshino were classmates. After graduation in 1962, Matusuda worked as a ready-to-wear designer, in 1965 travelled with Kenzo to Paris, stayed six months, returned to Japan via the United States.

In 1967 he founded his own company, named "Nicole" after a model he admired in *Elle* magazine. It initially did poorly, took off when he began to make custom T-shirts. Today, Nicole, Ltd. produces ready-to-wear for women and men, a full range of accessories, and a small housewares program.

Matsuda's work shows a bold, off-beat sense of proportion. He sticks largely to black and tones of gray, balances layers and levels with complete mastery of scale and texture. His clothes are reminiscent of YAMAMOTO and KAWAKUBO, but lighter, slimmer, less severe, more wearable. They are well-tailored, with an edge of wit, walk a fine line between East and West.

MAXWELL, VERA

BORN: New York City, 22 April 1903.

AWARDS:
  1951—Coty American Fashion Critics'
    Special Award (coats and suits)
  1955—Neiman-Marcus Award

1970

The child of Viennese parents, Maxwell's education came from her family and through travel and reading. She studied ballet, modeled in a wholesale house where she learned clothing construction and sketching, designed and made clothes for herself and other models. On a visit to London she admired the ease of men's clothes and was inspired to study tailoring. On her return to the United States she worked with sportswear and coat houses, established Vera Maxwell Originals in 1947.

Maxwell was one of a small group of craftsmen-designers of the 1930s and 1940s, true originals such as CASHIN and McCARDELL who worked independently of Europe, and one of an even smaller group of women who successfully ran their own businesses. Her specialties, simple, timeless clothes, go-together separates in fine Scottish tweeds, wool jersey, raw silk, Indian embroideries, Ultrasuede®.

Among her numerous innovations were the weekend wardrobe of 1935, war workers' clothes designed under the fabric-restricting rules of wartime regulation L85, print dresses with coats lined in matching print, and the "speed dress" with stretch-nylon top, full skirt of polyester knit, print stole—no zippers, no buttons, no hooks.

She was honored in 1970 with a retrospective show at the Smithsonian Institution in Washington, D.C. In 1978, a party and show were given at the Museum of the City of New York to celebrate her 75th birthday and 50th year as a designer. She continued to work until early in 1985, when she abruptly closed her business.

Early in 1986, at age eighty-three, she went back to work with a fall collection of sportswear, dresses, and coats for the Peter Lynne Division of Gulf Enterprises.

Vera Maxwell

MCCARDELL, CLAIRE

BORN: Frederick, Maryland,
24 May 1905.

DIED: New York City, 23 March 1958.

AWARDS:
Coty American Fashion Critics' Award:
1944 — "Winnie"
1958 — Hall of Fame (posthumous)
1948 — Neiman-Marcus Award
1950 — National Women's Press Club
1956 — Parsons Medal for
Distinguished Achievement

Claire McCardell, 1944

As the daughter of a banker and state senator, McCardell grew up in comfortable circumstances. She first showed her interest in clothes as a child with paper dolls, and as a teen-ager she designed her own clothes. After attending Hood College for Women in Maryland, she studied fashion illustration at Parsons School of Design and for a year in Paris. After returning to New York, she painted lampshades for B. Altman & Co., and modeled briefly.

In 1929 she joined Robert Turk, Inc. as a model and assistant designer, and in 1931 went along with him when he moved to Townley Frocks, Inc. She took over as designer after his death and stayed with Townley until 1938, then worked for HATTIE CARNEGIE for two years. In 1940 she returned to Townley, first as designer, then as designer-partner, remaining until her death.

McCardell is credited with originating the American Look, forerunner of today's easy, travel-oriented clothes. She had complete understanding of the needs of the American woman with her full schedule of work and play, and designed specifically for her. Her philosophy was simple — clothes should be clean-lined, functional, comfortable, and appropriate to the occasion. They should fit well, flow naturally

string-tied
Empire line

the Popover

with the body and, of course, be attractive to look at. Buttons had to button, sashes were required to be long enough, not only to tie, but to wrap around and around.

She picked up details from men's clothing and work clothes, such as large pockets, blue-jeans topstitching, trouser pleats, rivets, gripper fastenings. Favorite fabrics were sturdy cotton denim, ticking, gingham, and wool jersey. She used colored zippers in an ornamental way, was partial to spaghetti ties and surprise color juxtapositions. The result was sophisticated, wearable clothes, often with witty touches.

Among her many innovations were the diaper bathing suit, the monastic dress—waistless, bias-cut, dartless—harem pajamas, the Popover, the kitchen dinner dress, ballet slippers worn with day clothes. She also designed sunglasses, infants' and children's wear, children's shoes, and costume jewelry. Her designs were totally contemporary, and the proof of her genius is that they would look contemporary today.

Stanley Marcus described her as "...the master of the line, never the slave of the sequin. She is one of the few creative designers this country has ever produced."

Evening dress and coat, 1950s
(The Brooklyn Museum, Gift of Sally Kirkland)

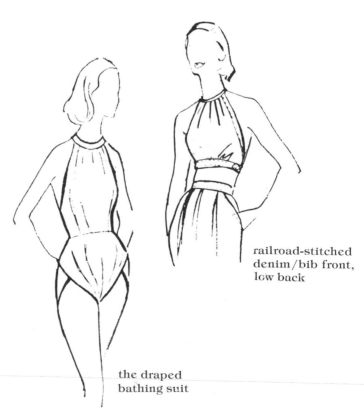

railroad-stitched
denim/bib front,
low back

the draped
bathing suit

MCCLINTOCK, JESSICA

Based in San Francisco, McClintock has carved a niche in the market with her highly personal blend of prettiness and old-fashioned allure. Gunne Sax, a staple of junior departments with its formula of lace and country charm, was established in 1970. Ten years later the contemporary Jessica McClintock collection appeared, romantic fantasies with Victorian and Edwardian overtones. There is also the moderately priced Scott McClintock line and the children's clothes, largely adapted from Gunne Sax. In 1980 McClintock opened her own San Francisco shop featuring better-priced designs, accessories, and her own cosmetics. In March 1985 she presented her first sleepwear collection.

MCFADDEN, MARY

BORN: New York City, c. 1936.

AWARDS:
Coty American Fashion Critics' Award:
1976—"Winnie"
1978—Return Award
1979—Hall of Fame
1979—Neiman-Marcus Award

Mary McFadden

Until she was ten, McFadden lived on a cotton plantation near Memphis, Tennessee, where her father was a cotton broker, after his death, returned North with her mother. She attended Foxcroft School in Virginia, Traphagen School of Fashion in New York, École Lubec in Paris, studied sociology at Columbia University and the New School for Social Research.

From 1962 to 1964, McFadden was director of public relations for Christian Dior-New York. She married a De-Beers executive and moved to Africa in 1964, became editor of *Vogue* South Africa, and when it closed continued to contribute to both French and American *Vogue*. She also wrote weekly columns on social and political life for *The Rand Daily Mail*. In 1968 McFadden remarried and moved to Rhodesia, where she founded *Vokutu*, a sculpture workshop for native artists.

In 1970 McFadden returned to New York with her daughter Justine, went to work for *Vogue* as Special Projects Editor. Using unusual Chinese and African silks she had collected on her travels, she designed three tunics which were shown in the magazine as a new direction and bought by Henri Bendel, New York. The silks were hand painted using various methods of resist techniques, colorings were oriental in feeling, with a characteristic use of calligraphy and negative spacing, all hallmarks of her future style.

Mary McFadden, Inc. was established in 1976. In addition to the very high-priced luxury collection, McFadden's projects have included lingerie and at-home wear, Simplicity Patterns, scarves, eyewear, furs, shoes, bed and bath designs, and upholstery fabrics.

Unique fabrics have always been a preoccupation and

prints have become a "full-time hobby," earning her a special Tommy award from the American Printed Fabrics Council. Exotic colorings, extensive use of fine pleating and quilting, ropes wrapping the figure—these are recurring themes. Her poetic evening designs are best known but all her work shares the same original viewpoint, refined and sophisticated.

She is a past president of the Council of Fashion Designers of America.

1987

1976

MISSONI, ROSITA & OTTAVIO

AWARDS:
  1973—Neiman-Marcus Award

Tai & Rosita Missoni

The Missonis met in 1948 in London, where Ottavio (Tai) was competing with the Italian Olympic track team and Rosita was studying languages. He was a manufacturer of sweatsuits, some of which were part of the official Olympics uniform, she also worked for her parents in their small manufacturing company. They married in 1953, and the same year went into business with four knitting machines.

Their first designs appeared anonymously in department stores or under the names of other designers. Looking for more adventurous styling, they hired Paris designers, first EMMANUELLE KHANH and later Christiane Bailly. After a few seasons Rosita took over design of the clothes, while Ottavio created the knits.

At a time when knits were considered basics, Ottavio's startling geometric and abstract patterns created a furor, as did the first Missoni showing in Florence in 1967. Rosita had the models remove their bras so they would not show through the thin knits. The stage lighting caused the clothes to look transparent, resulting in a scandal in the Italian press. The Missonis were not invited back to Florence and decided to show in Milan, which was also nearer home.

The collections are a joint effort. Ottavio creates the distinctive patterns and stitches and works out the color-

1983

ings. He and Rosita then work together on the line. She does not sketch but with an assistant, drapes directly on the model. Shapes are kept simple to set off the knit designs, each collection is built around a few classics: pants, skirts, long cardigan jackets, sweaters, capes, dresses. Production is limited and the clothes are expensive.

In addition to the women's styles, there are a limited number of designs for men and children. The patterns have been licensed for bed and bath linens and there is a line of interior decorating textiles.

The three Missoni children are all in the family business: Vittorio is in charge of administration; Luca helps his father in the creation of new patterns; Angela handles public relations.

In April 1978, to celebrate the 25th anniversary of their business and their marriage, the Missonis gave a party to show their fall line, first at an art gallery in Milan and again at the Whitney Museum in New York. Live mannequins in new styles posed next to dummies displaying designs from previous years, arranged without regard to chronological order. Except for miniskirts and hot pants it was nearly impossible to date the designs, an effective demonstration of their timeless character.

1978

1987

MIYAKE, ISSEY

BORN: Hiroshima, Japan,
   22 April 1938.

AWARDS:
   1976, 1984—Mainichi Newspaper
      Fashion Award
   1983—Council of America Fashion
      Designers (CFDA)
   1984—Neiman-Marcus Award

A 1964 graduate of Tama Art University in Tokyo, Miyake moved to Paris in 1965 to study at La Chambre Syndicale de la Couture Parisienne. From 1966 to 1968 he worked as assistant designer at GUY LAROCHE and GIVENCHY, spent 1969 in New York with GEOFFREY BEENE.

In 1970 he formed Miyake Design Studio and Issey Miyake International in Tokyo, showed in Paris for the first time in 1973, established a company in Europe in 1979, in the United States in 1982. Licenses range from home furnishings and hosiery to bicycles and luggage.

One of the earliest Japanese to make the move to Europe, Miyake shows regularly at the Paris prêt-à-porter collections. He designs a full range of sportswear, but sportswear at a far remove from the conventional. The 1968 Paris student revolution shook up his thinking, led him to question traditional views of fashion as applied to the modern woman. At that time he began to use wrapping and layering, combining Japanese attitudes toward clothes with exotic fabrics of his own design. He has developed steadily, going his own way as a designer, and has exerted a considerable influence on younger iconoclasts.

His design credo is, "the shape of the clothing should be determined by the shape of the body of the wearer, and clothing should enhance, not restrict, freedom of the body." He is known for beautiful fabrics, brilliant use of textures, and mastery of proportion.

Issey Miyake

1984

MOLYNEUX, CAPTAIN EDWARD

BORN: Hampstead, England,
5 September 1891.

DIED: Monte Carlo, 23 March 1974.

Capt. Molyneux, 1938

1931

Molyneux was of French descent and Anglo-Irish birth. In 1911 he won a competition sponsored by the London couturière, Lucile, and was engaged to sketch for her. When she opened branches in New York and Chicago, he went with her to the United States, remaining until the outbreak of World War I. He joined the British army in 1914, earned the rank of captain and was wounded three times, resulting in the loss of one eye. He was twice awarded the Military Cross for bravery.

In 1919 he opened his own couture house in Paris, eventually adding branches in Monte Carlo, Cannes, and London. His distinguished clientele included Princess Marina, whose wedding dress he made when she married the Duke of Kent, the Duchess of Windsor, such stage and film personalities as Lynn Fontanne, Gertrude Lawrence, and Merle Oberon.

Molyneux showed an excellent head for business. He enjoyed a flamboyant social life, opened two successful nightclubs, and was a personal friend of many of his clients. He assembled a fine collection of 18th century and Impressionist paintings.

At the outbreak of World War II he escaped from France by fishing boat from Bordeaux. During the war he worked out of his London house, turning over profits to national defense. He established international canteens in London and was one of the original members of the Incorporated Society of London Fashion Designers.

In 1946 he returned to Paris and reopened his couture house, adding furs, lingerie, millinery, perfumes. Because of ill health and threatened blindness in his remaining eye, he closed his London house in 1949 and turned over the Paris operation to Jacques Griffe in 1950. He retired to Montego Bay, Jamaica, West Indies, devoting himself to painting and travel.

Persuaded by the financial interests behind his perfumes to reopen in Paris as Studio Molyneux, he brought his first ready-to-wear collection to the United States in 1965. The project was not a success. Molyneux's elegant, ladylike designs were totally out of step with the youth-obsessed 1960s. He soon gave up the design reins to his nephew, John Tullis, and retired again, this time to Biot, near Antibes.

Molyneux is remembered for fluid, elegant clothes with a pure, uncluttered line, well-bred and timeless. Printed silk suits with pleated skirts, softly tailored navy blue suits, coats and capes with accents of bright Gauguin pink and bois de rose. He used zippers in 1937 to mold the figure, was partial to handkerchief point skirts and ostrich trims.

Art lover, war hero, bon vivant, sportsman, Molyneux gave generously of his personal resources — money, time, and energy. He worked with the British Government during World War II and later financed dressmaking schools for French workers.

MONTANA, CLAUDE

BORN: Paris, France, 1949.

Claude Montana

Montana began designing in 1971 on a trip to London. To make money, he concocted papier-mâché jewelry encrusted with rhinestones, which were featured in fashion magazines and earned him enough money to stay on for a year. On his return to Paris, he spent a year doing little then went to work for MacDouglas, a French leather firm.

Beyond the biker's leathers which made his name, Montana has developed into one of the more interesting of the French designers, with an exacting eye for proportion, cut, and detail. He is a perfectionist, with the finesse of a true couturier and a leaning toward operatic fantasy. His clothes feature strong silhouettes and a well-defined sense of drama.

Montana has also designed knitwear for the Spanish firm Ferrer y Sentis, collections for various Italian companies, including Complice. His clothes are sold in fine stores in the United States as well as Italy, Germany, England. Under license, they are made and distributed in Japan.

1987

1983

MORI, HANAE

BORN: Tokyo, Japan, 8 January 1926.

AWARDS:
   1973 — Neiman-Marcus Award

A graduate of Tokyo Christian Women's College with a degree in Japanese literature, Mori went back to school after her marriage to learn sewing, sketching, designing. She opened a small boutique in the Shinjuku section of Tokyo where her clothes attracted the attention of the burgeoning Japanese movie industry. In 1955, after designing costumes for innumerable films, she opened her first shop on the Ginza, Tokyo's famous shopping street, went on to develop a multi-million dollar international business. Her husband, Ken Mori, formerly in the Japanese textile industry, helps manage the company. Akira, the older of her two sons, manages the New York business from their townhouse showroom on East 79th Street.

Hanae Mori brought her couture collection to Paris in January 1977 and continues to show there each season. Her ready-to-wear is sold at fine stores throughout the world, while her boutiques in many countries sell her accessories, sportswear, and innerwear. Her fabric designs are licensed for bed and bath linens, she designed skiwear for the Sapporo Winter Olympic Games in 1972. In June 1978 she opened a building in Tokyo which houses boutiques, the couture operation, and her business offices.

While the most international in design approach of her compatriots, Mori makes extensive use of her Japanese background in her fabrics, woven, printed, and dyed especially for her. She has utilized the vivid colors and bold linear patterns of Hiroshige prints, while butterflies and flowers, the Japanese symbols of femininity, show up frequently in her prints. She is best known for her cocktail and evening dresses, carefully executed in Eastern-flavored patterns and with Western fit.

1975

MOSCHINO, FRANCO

BORN: c. 1950.

Moschino, a former art student, began his fashion career around 1971 as a sketcher for GIORGIO ARMANI, with whom he worked on collections for Beged'Or and Genny. Beginning in 1977 he designed for Cadette, launched his own line in 1983. Since then he has become known, if not universally admired, for his send-ups of conventional fashion thinking. He has sent pairs of models out on the runway in the same outfit, one wearing it as it would appear in a serious fashion presentation, the other as it might be worn on the street. He has also distributed fresh tomatoes to the audience so they could let fly at any styles they disliked. He believes that people should take fashion and wear it with their own particular style. His motto is, *De gustibus non est disputandum*—Who's to say what is good taste?

MOSES, REBECCA

Moses graduated from the Fashion Institute of Technology in 1977 in the same class as ANDREA JOVINE, received the ILGWU Designer of the Year award. For three years she designed coats and suits for Gallant International decided the times called for sportswear and went into business for herself, starting with a huge, 200-piece collection. Her company closed in June 1982 and in August of the same year Moses went into business with Victor Coopersmith, her first offering a small, tightly-edited group of mixable sports separates. "You learn fast that fashion is not just pretty clothes. It's a business and if you don't understand it you go out of business, fast." She left Coopersmith in October 1986, reopened doing business as R.M. Pearlman, her married name. Her new line, The Moses Collection, appeared in March 1988 and included everything from sportswear to suits and blouses to evening coats and accessories.

The Moses target customer is the career woman who wants good, classic clothes that are comfortable and feminine without being sexy or overpowering. Her marketing strategy is to make it easier for this woman to buy, presenting the choice and showing her how to put it all together.

MUGLER, THIERRY

BORN: Strasbourg, France, 1946.

The son of a doctor, Mugler started making his own clothes while in his teens. He was part of a Strasbourg ballet company, dressed windows in a Paris boutique, moved to London in 1968. Ater two years he moved on to Amsterdam, then back to Paris. His first collection appeared in 1971 under the label Café de Paris, by 1973 he was making clothes under his own name.

Inventive and individual, Mugler came into prominence in the late 1970s with high-priced separates and dresses with a broad-shouldered, defined-waistline silhouette. His tendency toward histrionic presentations often tends to obscure what he is trying to say but he cuts a sexy, saucy suit as well or better than anybody, and his collections are known for a sunny freshness and gaiety.

As shown on the runway, his clothes are apt to appear aggressive and tough. Close up, they prove to be simple, well-cut, body-fitted, not overly detailed; the ready-to-wear is more accessible than the couture. They have sold well in the United States.

Thierry Mugler

1982

1979

MUIR, JEAN

BORN: London, England, c. 1933.

AWARDS:
  1967, 1968, 1974, 1976— Maison
    Blanche "Rex" Award, New Orleans
  1973—Fellow of the Royal Society of
    Arts
  1973—Neiman-Marcus Award
  1983—Commander of British Empire

Jean Muir

Of Scottish descent, Muir began her career in 1950 in the stockroom at Liberty, then sold lingerie and became a sketcher. She joined Jaeger in 1956 and soon became responsible for designing the major dress and knitwear collections. Starting in 1961, she designed under her own label for Jane and Jane, established Jean Muir, Inc. in 1966, and opened the Jean Muir Shop at Henri Bendel, New York, the same year.

Muir is one of the breed of anti-couture, anti-establishment designers who came on the scene in the late 1950s and early 1960s. While others have disappeared, she has not only survived but flourished, her clothes treasured by women looking for a low-profile way of dressing and quality of a very high order. She has created a signature look in gentle, pretty clothes of the luxury investment category, flattering, elegant, refined. She is especially admired for her leathers, which she treats like jersey, and for her jerseys, tailored shapes that are completely soft and feminine.

Muir believes in technical training as the only serious foundation for a designer, with more emphasis on craft, less on art. She encourages and works with English art students, is known as hard working and demanding. She is married to Harry Leuckert, formerly an actor and now her business manager.

1975

1984

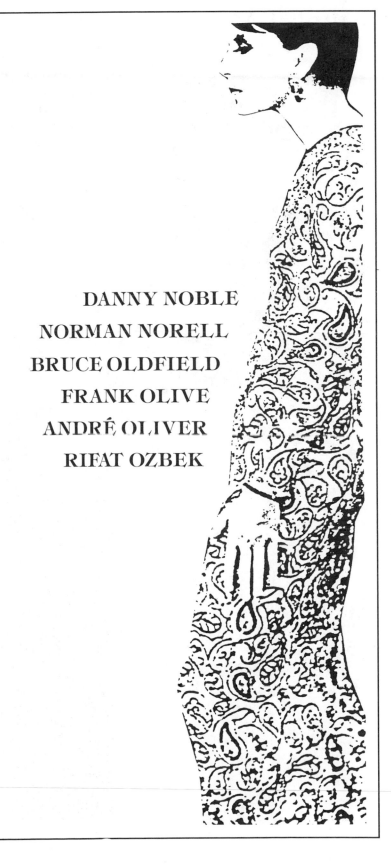

n/o

DANNY NOBLE
NORMAN NORELL
BRUCE OLDFIELD
FRANK OLIVE
ANDRÉ OLIVER
RIFAT OZBEK

NOBLE, DANNY

BORN: Canada, 1951.

Danny & Annette Noble

Raised in London, where his family moved when he was three, Danny Noble attended fashion college there, worked as assistant to Bill Gibb. After leaving Gibb, he designed for a chain of London boutiques, then established his own label. He met his wife, Annette, a designer and patternmaker, when he went to her to have patterns made for his designs. In 1980 he came to the United States to work for a Philadelphia manufacturer. Annette followed and after two years they decided to go on their own.

Danny is the designer, Annette cuts the patterns and edits the collection. They specialize in contemporary sportswear, clean-cut, sophisticated classics with a fresh, young point of view. They have a New York showroom but live and maintain a design studio in Philadelphia.

1987

NORELL, NORMAN

BORN: Noblesville, Indiana, 1900.

DIED: New York City, 25 October 1972.

AWARDS:
Norell's career was distinguished by a number of "firsts":
   Coty American Fashion Critics' Award
      1943—First "Winnie"
      1951—First Return Award
      1958—First to be elected to Hall of Fame
   11 June 1962—First designer to receive Honorary Degree of Doctor of Fine Arts, conferred upon him by Pratt Institute, Brooklyn, in recognition of his influence on American design and taste, and for his valuable counseling and guidance to students of design.
1942—Neiman-Marcus Award
1956—Parsons Medal for Distinguished Achievement
1972—City of New York Bronze Medallion

As a young child, Norell moved to Indianapolis, where his father opened a haberdashery. From early boyhood, his ambition was to be an artist and in 1919 he moved to New York to study painting at Parsons School of Design. He switched to costume design and in 1921 graduated from Pratt Institute. His first costume assignment was for *The Sainted Devil*, a Rudolph Valentino picture. He did Gloria Swanson's costumes for *Zaza*, then joined the staff of the Brooks Costume Company.

In 1924, in a move from costume to dress design, he went to work for dress manufacturer Charles Armour, remaining until 1928 when he joined HATTIE CARNEGIE. He stayed with Carnegie until 1940, not only absorbing her knowledge and sense of fashion, but travelling with her to Europe where he was exposed to the best design of the day. In 1941 he teamed with manufacturer Anthony Traina to form Traina-Norell. The association lasted nineteen years, at which time Norell left to become president of his own firm, Norman Norell, Inc. The first collection was presented in June 1960.

From his very first collection under the Traina-Norell label, the designer established himself as a major talent, quickly becoming known for a lithe, cleanly-proportioned silhouette, an audacious use of rich fabrics, for faultless

Norman Norell and models, 1960

workmanship, precise tailoring, and purity of line. Over the years he maintained his leadership, setting numerous trends that have become part of the fashion vocabulary and are taken for granted today. He was first to show long evening skirts topped with sweaters, initiated cloth coats lined with fur for day and evening, spangled them with sequins, revived the chemise, introduced the smoking robe, perfected jumpers and pantsuits. His long, shimmering, sequined dresses were so simple they never went out of date, worn as long as their owners could fit into them and treasured even longer. *Norell* perfume, made in America, was a major success and is still available.

He was founder and president of the Council of Fashion Designers of America. On 15 October 1972, the eve of his retrospective show at the Metropolitan Museum of Art, Norell suffered a stroke. He died ten days later. His company continued for a brief period with GUSTAVE TASSELL as designer.

Norell and Hattie Carnegie could be said to be the parents of American high fashion, setting standards of taste, knowledge, and talent, opening the way for the creators of today.

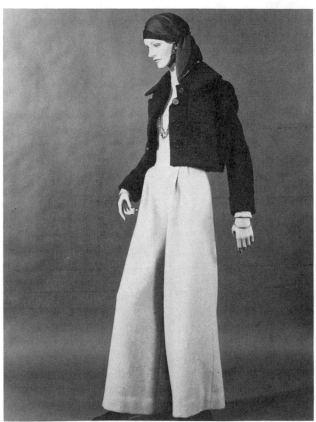

Norell, 1972 (The Brooklyn Museum, Gift of Gustave Tassell)

Norell, c. 1965 (The Brooklyn Museum, Gift of Norman Norell, Inc.)

OLDFIELD, BRUCE

BORN: London, England, 1950.

Trained as a teacher, Oldfield taught English and art before turning to fashion. He attended Ravensbourne College of Art from 1968 to 1971, St. Martin's School of Art from 1972 to 1973. He free-lanced in London, designed a line for Henri Bendel, New York, sold sketches to other designers, showed his first collection under his own name in 1975.

Oldfield opened his own London retail shop in 1984 as the only outlet for his ready-to-wear, previously sold in the United States to such stores as Saks Fifth Avenue, Bergdorf Goodman, Bendel's. He has a considerable custom business and is especially recognized for his evening wear, worn by British royalty and aristocracy as well as by entertainment personalities.

OLIVE, FRANK

BORN: Milwaukee, Wisconsin, 1929.

Olive studied art and fashion in Milwaukee and Chicago before going to California to try costume design. He worked in San Francisco for a dance company, came to New York in the early 1950s hoping to design for the stage. His sketches were seen by NORELL, who persuaded Olive to try hats. He apprenticed with Chanda, sold fabrics, worked in the Tatiana custom hat department at Saks Fifth Avenue and then for Emme.

His first boutique was in Greenwich Village on MacDougal Street, where he designed hats and clothes. He still does boutique items such as gloves and fur shrugs in addition to three major hat collections: mass market Counterfits, moderately priced Frank's Girl, and Frank Olive, the designer label. In addition, he has a Private Collection for women who want something different.

Even through the 1960s when hat makers "had everything going against them," Olive worked with Seventh Avenue designers on hats for their collections, and also had fashionable customers who considered a hat a necessary part of their total appearance. The majority of his customers are young, care about their appearance, and put themselves together with a great sense of style.

1978

OLIVER, ANDRÉ

BORN: Toulouse, France, 1932.

Oliver studied at the École des Beaux Arts in Paris, in 1952 went to work for PIERRE CARDIN in the capacity of men's wear designer. In time he took over design duties for both the men's and women's ready-to-wear collections, in the women's field showing special affinity for evening wear.

In July 1987 Oliver was named artistic director of the Cardin couture house with total artistic control, sharing design responsibilities of the collection with Cardin. In their long association, Cardin has acknowledged Oliver's design contribution with a generosity rare in the fashion world.

OZBEK, RIFAT

BORN: Turkey, 1954.

Ozbek arrived in England in 1970, studied architecture for two years at the University of Liverpool, then switched to fashion, studying at St. Martin's School of Art. After graduation in 1977, he worked in Italy for Walter Albini and an Italian manufacturer before returning to London and a stint designing for Monsoon, a made-in-India line. He presented his first collection under his own label in October 1984, showing out of his apartment. A second collection was also shown at home, but by his third, he had a stylish new studio off Bond Street, his business backed by a Geneva-based oil company.

While he feels the influence of London street fashion, Ozbek translates it with refinement and understatement. He has also been inspired by the way African natives mix traditional and Western elements in their dress, and by the Italian and French movies he saw when growing up. Whatever the inspiration, his clothes are sophisticated and controlled, with none of the rough-edged wackiness associated with much of London fashion.

Ozbek admires the fashion greats: Balenciaga for cut, Schiaparelli for her sense of humor, Chanel for timelessness, Yves Saint Laurent for classicism.

p

PAQUIN

MOLLIE PARNIS

EMERIC PARTOS

JEAN PATOU

SYLVIA PEDLAR

ELSA PERETTI

DIANE PERNET

BERNARD PERRIS

ROBERT PIGUET

GÉRARD PIPART

PAUL POIRET

THEA PORTER

PRÉMONVILLE ET DEWAVRIN

EMILIO PUCCI

PAQUIN
(French couture house)

1941

Founded in 1891 by M. and Mme. Isidore Paquin, the house of Paquin became synonymous with elegance during the first decade of the 20th century. Mme. Paquin, who trained at Maison Rouff, was one of the couture's great artists. Her husband, a banker and businessman, provided the initial backing for his wife's business.

The Paquin reputation for beautiful designs was enhanced by the decor of the establishment and the lavishness of its showings, as well as by the Paquins' extensive social life. Management of the house and its relations with its employees were excellent, some workers remaining for more than forty years. Department heads were women. The Paquin standards were so high that there was always a demand from other couture houses for any employees deciding to leave.

Mme. Paquin was the first woman to achieve importance in haute couture and was president of the fashion section of the 1900 Paris Exposition. Hers was the first couture house to open foreign branches—in London, Madrid, Buenos Aires. She was the first to take mannequins to the opera and the races, as many as ten in the same costume. She claimed not to make any two dresses exactly alike, individualizing each model to the woman for whom it was made. Customers included queens of Belgium, Portugal, and Spain, as well as the actresses and courtesans of the era.

She was a gifted colorist, a talent especially evident in her glamorous and romantic evening dresses. Other specialties were fur-trimmed tailored suits and coats, furs (the house was credited with being the first to make fur garments that were soft and supple), lingerie, blue serge suits with gold braid and buttons. Accessories were made in-house, the first perfume appeared in 1939.

Mme. Paquin sold out to an English firm and retired in 1920. She died in 1936. The house closed in July 1956.

PARNIS, MOLLIE
BORN: Brooklyn, New York, 1905.

After leaving high school, Parnis went to work in a blouse showroom and was soon designing. In 1933, she and her husband Leon Livingston, a textile designer, opened a ready-to-wear firm, Parnis-Livingston. From there she went on to become one of the most successful businesswomen on Seventh Avenue, heading a firm which grew into a multi-million dollar enterprise, Mollie Parnis Inc.

The Parnis designer division produced flattering, feminine dresses and ensembles for the well-to-do woman over thirty, emphasizing becomingness in beautiful fabrics, a conservative interpretation of current trends. The boutique collection was for many years designed by Morty Sussman until his death in 1979, following the same principles but with a moderate price tag. The Mollie Parnis Studio collection aimed at a younger woman, was begun in 1979.

At the end of October, 1984, after more than half a century in business, Parnis announced she was dissolving her firm to become a "very part-time" consultant at Chevette Lingerie, owned by her nephew, Neal Hochman. Quickly becoming bored, she went back to work full time and produced her first loungewear collection for Chevette, Mollie Parnis At Home, for fall 1985.

A formidable organizer, Parnis routinely managed to administer her business, plan and edit collections with her design staff, supervise selling, advertising, and promotion, and follow through on her civic interests, all in a day that began at 10 A.M. and seldom went beyond 5 P.M. She is also a noted hostess.

Parnis is well known as a philanthropist. She has contributed scholarships to fashion schools and both New York and Jerusalem have honored her for her outstanding contributions to the two cities. She was a founder of the Council of Fashion Designers of America and served on the Board of Directors.

PARTOS, EMERIC "IMRE"

BORN: Budapest, Hungary, 18 March 1905.

DIED: New York City, 2 December 1975.

AWARDS:
1957—Coty American Fashion Critics' Special Award (furs)

1975

Partos studied art in Budapest and Paris, jewelry design in Switzerland. He served in the French army during World War II and in the underground movement, where he met Alex Maguy, a couturier who also designed for the theater. After the war he joined Maguy, designing coats and also ballet costumes.

In 1947 he went to work for his friend CHRISTIAN DIOR, whom he considered the greatest living designer. He stayed with Dior three years creating coats and suits, was wooed away in 1950 by Maximilian, New York. He designed furs for Maximilian for five years before moving to Bergdorf Goodman to head their fur department, remaining there until his death twenty years later.

At Bergdorf's, Partos was given a free hand with the most expensive pelts available. He showed a sense of fantasy and fun with intarsia furs such as a white mink jacket inlaid with colored mink flowers. He dyed mink in stripes or worked it in beige-and-white box shapes, designed coats that could be shortened or lengthened by zipping sections off or on, innovated with silk or cotton raincoats as slipcovers for mink coats. In addition, he was noted for subtle, beautifully-cut classics in fine minks, sables, broadtail.

Partos was one of the first to treat furs as ready-to-wear, always designed clothes to coordinate with his furs. He was a prolific source of ideas, noted for his theatrics but also as a master of construction and detail. He was a favorite with conservative customers as well as with personalities such as Barbra Streisand.

PATOU, JEAN

BORN: Normandy, France, 1887.

DIED: Paris, France, March 1936.

Of French Basque origin, Patou opened a small house called *Parry*, just in time for World War I to cause cancellation of his first major showing, scheduled for August 1914. He served in the army four years as a captain of Zouaves. Reopened as a couturier under his own name in 1919.

From the start, Patou's clothes were a success with private clients. They had simplicity and elegance and looked as if they were intended to be worn by real women, not just by mannequins. He was an excellent showman and in 1925, to attract the lucrative business of American store buyers, brought six American models to Paris, using them alongside his French mannequins. He instituted gala champagne evening openings, had a cocktail bar in his shop, chose exquisite bottles for his perfumes, which included *Moment Supreme* and *Joy*, promoted as the world's most expensive perfume.

Patou and models, 1924

He is given credit for being the first in 1929 to return the waistline to its normal position and lengthen skirts, which he dropped dramatically to the ankle. He was among the first couturiers to have colors and fabrics produced especially for him.

Patou was tall and handsome, gracious in manner, fond of the worlds of sport and fashion. He admired American business methods, introducing daily staff meetings, a profit-sharing plan for executives, a bonus system for mannequins. He was a director of designers as well as a creator.

After his death, the house remained open under the direction of his brother-in-law, Raymond Barbas, with a series of resident designers including: MARC BOHAN, 1953 to 1956; KARL LAGERFELD, 1960 to 1963; Michel Goma, 1963 to 1973; ANGELO TARLAZZI, 1973 to 1976; Roy Gonzalez, 1977 to 1982; and from 1982 to 1987, CHRISTIAN LACROIX.

1929

PEDLAR, SYLVIA

BORN: New York City, 1901.

DIED: New York City, 26 February 1972.

AWARDS:
Coty American Fashion Critics' Award:
1951—Special Award (lingerie)
1964—Return Special Award
(lingerie)
1960—Neiman-Marcus Award

Pedlar intended to become a fashion illustrator, studied at Cooper Union and the Art Students League. Instead, she became a designer and in 1929 founded her own firm, Iris Lingerie.

She was a gifted designer working in a difficult field where the temptation for vulgarity is strong. She specialized in soft, pure shapes that a woman of any age could wear and to her, comfort was the most important consideration. Her talent was recognized internationally and European designers such as DIOR, GIVENCHY, and EMILIO PUCCI would visit Iris to buy Pedlar models.

Among her more famous creations were sleep togas, the bed-and-breakfast look, the bedside nightdress for the woman who sleeps nude and wants a little something decorative to wake up to. Iris Lingerie was known for exquisite fabrics and laces and perfectionist workmanship, as well as for the originality and beauty of the designs.

Pedlar closed her firm after forty-one years because "the fun has gone out of our work now." She was married to William A. Pedlar, whom she survived by one year.

PERETTI, ELSA

BORN: Florence, Italy, 1 May 1940.

AWARDS:
1971—Coty American Fashion Critics'
Special Award (jewelry)
1978—Award for outstanding
contribution to the cultured pearl
industry of America and Japan
1986—The Fashion Group "Night of
the Stars" Award

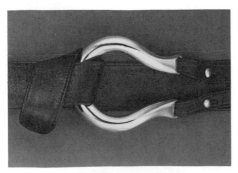

Steling silver horseshoe buckle
with leather belt

The daugher of a well-to-do Roman family, Peretti earned a diploma in interior design and worked for a Milanese architect. In 1961 she went to Switzerland, then moved on to London and started modeling. She was seen by models' agent Wilhelmina, who suggested that Peretti come to New York. She worked for a handful of top houses including HALSTON and OSCAR DE LA RENTA.

In 1969 Peretti designed a few pieces of silver jewelry which Halston and GIORGIO SANT'ANGELO showed with their collections. These witty objects—a heart-shaped buckle, pendants in the form of small vases, a silver urn pendant that holds a fresh flower—were soon joined by a silver horseshoe-shaped buckle on a long leather belt and other designs in horn, ebony, and ivory. She also designed the containers for Halston's fragrance and cosmetics lines.

In 1974, she began working with Tiffany & Co., the first time in twenty-five years the company had carried silver jewelry. Among her much-copied designs are a small, open, slightly lopsided heart pendant that slides on a chain, and diamonds-by-the-yard, diamonds spaced out on a fine gold chain. Her perfume, a costly scent in a refillable rock crystal bottle, is carried by Tiffany and she has designed desk and table accessories for the firm.

Peretti is influenced in her work by a love of nature and inspired by Japanese designs. She works in Spain and New York, has travelled to the Orient to study semiprecious stones. Prototypes for the silver and ivory designs are made by artisans in Barcelona, the crystal pieces are produced in Germany.

PERNET, DIANE

Pernet started out as a photographer and documentary filmmaker, switched over to fashion around 1978. She enrolled in fashion school but never got her degree, believing that school cannot teach you to design. Her designs are regal, controlled, and subtle, in luxurious fabrics from France, Italy, and Japan, perfectly constructed and meticulously finished. She calls them "new fashion couture...a little more relaxed than real couture clothes." Pernet began as a "downtown New York" designer, has since moved into a showroom uptown. She also designs a more expensive line for the Japanese market.

PERRIS, BERNARD

BORN: Millau, France, 1944.

1987

An early starter in fashion, Perris as a child drew dresses on a blackboard in the window of his mother's shop in the south of France. In 1959 he went to Paris where he attended the Cours Bazot fashion school. He assisted MARC BOHAN at Dior and GUY LAROCHE, designed debutante and wedding dresses, opened his own ready-to-wear firm, Bernard Perris Nouvelle Couture, in 1969. A Bernard Perris shop opened on New York's Madison Avenue in 1986; his name has been licensed in Japan.

Crammed with ideas and loaded with fashion details, the Perris clothes are highly charged. The designer is couture oriented but with a younger attitude. In his sense of structure and volume he feels himself close to CLAUDE MONTANA.

PIGUET, ROBERT

BORN: Yverdon, Switzerland, 1901.

DIED: Lausanne, Switzerland,
22 February 1953.

CAMELIA BLANCHE

ROBE CREPE NOIR

1947

The son of a Swiss banker who expected him to follow his profession, Piguet instead went to Paris in 1918 to study design. He trained with conservative Redfern and brilliant POIRET, then opened his own house on the rue du Cirque.

In 1933 he moved his salon to the Rond Point where he designed little himself, largely relying on the work of free-lance designers. A number of designers, including DIOR and GIVENCHY, worked for him at the outset of their careers. JAMES GALANOS spent three months there working without salary. Dior said, "Robert Piguet taught me the virtues of simplicity... how to suppress."

Piguet's clothes appealed to a younger customer: perfectly-cut tailored suits with vests, black-and-white dresses of refined simplicity, afternoon dresses, fur-trimmed coats especially styled for petite women. He had a flair for dramatic effects used to advantage in his extensive work for the theater. In the United States his influence was greater on manufacturers than on custom design.

An aristocratic, solitary man, Piguet was super-sensitive and changeable, with a love of intrigue. Elegant and charming, he was a connoisseur of painting, literature, and music. He suffered from ill health throughout his life, retiring to seclusion after each showing to recuperate from the strain of his profession. He closed his house in 1951.

PIPART, GÉRARD

BORN: Paris, France, 1933.

Pipart started in fashion at the age of sixteen selling sketches to PIERRE BALMAIN, for whom he worked briefly, and to JACQUES FATH, with whom he stayed six months. He sketched for GIVENCHY, went with MARC BOHAN during the short time he had his own house.

After completing his two-year army service he free-lanced in ready-to-wear and in 1963, produced an unsuccessful couture collection. He returned to ready-to-wear with great success for firms on the Côte d'Azur, others in Italy and London. In 1963 he succeeded JULES-FRANÇOIS CRAHAY as chief designer at NINA RICCI, where he has remained ever since, responsible for both the couture and boutique collections.

Pipart has never learned to cut or sew. He works from detailed sketches and makes corrections directly on the toiles. Preferring simplicity, he avoids showiness and fussy details, detests gimmicks. Known for young, spirited elegant clothes a very Parisian sophistication, he has been compared to JACQUES FATH, whom he considers "the most wonderful personality I ever knew or saw." Among other designers, he greatly admires Givenchy and Balenciaga.

POIRET, PAUL

BORN: Paris, France, 20 April 1879.

DIED: Paris, France, 28 April 1944.

As a youth, Poiret was apprenticed to an umbrella maker, taught himself costume sketching at home. He sold his first sketches to Mme. Cheruit at Raudnitz Soeurs, joined Jacques Doucet in 1896, spent four years working for WORTH before opening his own house in 1904.

Fascinated by the theater and the arts, Poiret designed costumes for actresses such as Réjane and Sarah Bernhardt, his friends included Diaghilev, Léon Bakst, Raoul Dufy, ERTÉ, Iribe. He established a crafts school where Dufy for a while designed textiles, was the first couturier to present a perfume. In 1912 he was first to travel to other countries to present his collection, taking along twelve mannequins. In 1914, along with WORTH, PAQUIN, Cheruit, CALLOT SOEURS, he founded the Protective Association of French Dressmakers, and became its first president. He was shrewd and egotistical, spent fortunes on fêtes, pageants, and costume balls, and on decorating his homes.

Unable to adjust his style to changes brought about by World War I, Poiret went out of business in 1924. Bankrupt and penniless, he was divorced by his wife in 1929. Four years later he was offered a job designing ready-to-wear but his attitude toward money was so irresponsible that the venture failed. He scratched out a living taking bit parts in

1913

1923

movies, wrote his autobiography, moved to the south of France. He spent the war years in poverty, died of Parkinson's disease in a charity hospital.

Considered by many to be one of the greatest originators of feminine fashion, Poiret was extravagantly talented, with a penchant for the bizarre and dramatic. While his forte was costume, the modern silhouette was to a great extent his invention. He freed women from corsets and petticoats and introduced the first modern, straight-line dress. Yet he also invented the harem and hobble skirts, so narrow at the hem that walking was almost impossible. His minaret skirt, inspired by and named after a play he costumed, spread worldwide.

Influenced by the Ballets Russe, he designed a Russian tunic coat, straight in line and belted, made from sumptuous materials. His taste for orientalism showed up in little turbans and tall aigrettes with which he adorned his models, and he scandalized society in 1911 by taking mannequins to the Auteuil races dressed in *jupes culottes*, also called Turkish trousers.

Poiret's extraordinary imagination and achievements flowered in the brilliant epoch of Diaghilev and Bakst. It influenced the taste of two decades.

Poiret and models, 1925

PORTER, THEA

BORN: Damascus, Syria, 1927.

Porter grew up in Damascus; lived in Lebanon and Turkey, returned to London in 1963 and opened an interior decorating shop in the Soho district. As atmosphere she imported a number of caftans of the kind worn by Middle Eastern brides and these became so popular with her customers that she began to reproduce them. From there she went to fantasy evening dresses and pajamas in unusual materials.

Her work has been strongly influenced by ethnic themes from the Middle and Far East and by past periods in Western history, ranging from the Renaissance and Gothic eras through Victorian times and into the 1940s. She has continued to develop her favorite themes—dressy djellabahs, beading, sequins, hand embroidery—in couture and deluxe evening ready-to-wear, popular with entertainment personalities and well-off private customers looking for something different.

In 1976 she opened a couture boutique in Paris and moved her entire operation there.

PRÉMONVILLE ET DEWAVRIN

BORN: de Prémonville—France, 1950.
Dewavrin—France, 1958.

De Prémonville and Dewavrin met on the ski slopes, went into business together in 1983 with $5,000 of their own money. She is a veteran of the French fashion industry who has free-lanced for years but had never gone on her own. He studied business in school but was without fashion experience other than summer work in London men's boutiques. The partners originally divided their duties—she the designer, he in charge of the business—but eventually, Dewavrin began to share in the designing, eventually producing his own collection, separate but part of the same company and shown in the same showroom.

De Prémonville first drew attention with young, flirty peplum suits in crisp, refined fabrics. Subsequent collections included dresses for day and evening, and knits. The designers work exclusively with French fabrics and manufacturers and have acquired a following among better retailers in the United States. The clothes blend a youthful spirit of innovation with conservative French chic, fastidious cut, and fine tailoring.

Even with the growing success of their firm, de Premonville continues to free lance, her commitments including children's clothes for Fiorucci.

PUCCI, EMILIO

BORN: Naples, Italy, 1914.

AWARDS:
    1954—Neiman-Marcus Award

Emilio Pucci

Descended from Italian and Russian nobility, Pucci was educated in Italy and the United States. He was a member of his country's Olympic Ski Team in 1934, and officer of the Italian Air Force during World War II.

Pucci first gained notice as a designer of classic, well-cut sportswear, notably ski clothes. But it was his simple chemises of thin silk jersey that in the 1960s made him a favorite of the international jet set. The brilliant signature prints in designs inspired by heraldic banners were widely copied.

His design projects have included accessories, sportswear, intimate apparel, fragrances for women and men, porcelain, bath linens, rugs, airline uniforms.

1965

q/r

MARY QUANT

PACO RABANNE

MARY ANN RESTIVO

ZANDRA RHODES

NINA RICCI

MARCEL ROCHAS

CAROLYNE ROEHM

SONIA RYKIEL

QUANT, MARY

BORN: Blackheath, Kent, England,
11 February 1934.

AWARDS:
O.B.E. (Order of the British Empire)

EXHIBITION:
"Mary Quant's London," London
Museum, 1973-74

Mary Quant, 1978

Quant studied at Goldsmith's College of Art in London where she met Alexander Plunket Greene. With a partner, the two opened a small retail boutique called *Bazaar* in London's Chelsea district. They were married two years later in 1957.

At first, they sold clothes from outside designers, but soon became frustrated by the difficulty of getting the kind of clothes they wanted from manufacturers. Mary Quant then began to make her own designs, spirited and unconventional, instant hits with the young, probably because they were totally unlike anything their mothers would, or could, wear.

She began on a small scale, but her fame grew, along with that of "swinging London" and by 1963 she had opened a second *Bazaar* and was exporting to the United States. With her husband as business partner she had become a full-scale designer and manufacturer, with a less expensive *Ginger Group*. She designed for J. C. Penney in the United States and for Puritan's Youthquake promotion. A highly successful cosmetics line was established in 1966 and sold worldwide. In the 1970s, while no longer a fashion innovator, she added to her business with licenses for jewelry, carpets, household linens, men's ties, and eyeglasses.

Quant was a leading figure in the youth revolution of the 1950s and 1960s. She is given credit for starting the Chelsea or Mod Look of the mid 1950s and the miniskirts of the late 1960s. She used denim, colored flannel, and vinyl in clothes that only the young could wear, and showed them with colored tights. For her innovative showings with models dancing down the runway, she used photographic mannequins rather than regular runway models. Whatever her final stature as a designer, she was a pivotal figure in a fashion upheaval which reflected major social changes taking place around the world.

RABANNE, PACO

BORN: San Sebastian, Spain, 1934.

Rabanne's mother was head seamstress at BALENCIAGA in San Sebastian when the family fled to France in 1939 to escape the Spanish Civil War. Growing up in Paris, Rabanne studied architecture at the École Supérieure des Beaux Arts, began designing handbags, shoes, and plastic accessories.

In 1966 he attracted attention with dresses of plastic discs linked with metal chains, accessorizing them with plastic jewelry and sun goggles in primary colors. He continued the linked-disc theme in coats of fur patches and dresses of leather patches, and also used buttons and strips of aluminum laced with wire. In 1970 he was one of the first to use fake suede for dresses. He likes to put unlikely materials together, has designed coats of knit and fur, dresses made of ribbons, feathers or tassels, linked for suppleness. While hardly wearable in the conventional sense, his experiments have had considerable influence on other designers. He has two successful fragrances, *Calandre* for women, *Paco* for men.

RESTIVO, MARY ANN

After college, Restivo went on to the Fashion Institute of Technology, where in 1961 she received an Associates Degree in fashion design. She has worked as designer for Something Special and Sports Sophisticates, and for Genre where she was given her own label. From 1974 to 1980 she was head designer for the women's blouse division of Christian Dior, established her own firm, Mary Ann Restivo, Inc., in 1980.

A classicist, Restivo translates traditional sportswear into a modern idiom for contemporary living. She specializes in wearable clothes in beautiful fabrics, clothes with special appeal for the executive career woman who is her ideal customer.

RHODES, ZANDRA
BORN: Chatham, England, 1942.

Rhodes's father was a truck driver, her mother head fitter at WORTH in Paris before her marriage, afterward a senior lecturer at Medway College of Art. Rhodes graduated from the Royal College of Art in 1966, began her career as a textile designer, then set up her own print works.

By 1969 she was producing imaginative clothing designs, working largely in very soft fabrics—chiffon, tulle, silk—often hand-screened in her own prints. These included Art Deco motifs, lipsticks, squiggles, teddy bears, teardrops, big splashy patterns.

A complete original, Rhodes has always made news, alter-

Zandra Rhodes

1978

nately criticized and applauded. She has finished edges with pinking shears, made glamorized Punk designs with torn holes or edges fastened with jeweled safety pins, sleeves held on by pins or chains. Her champagne bubble dresses drawn in at the knee with elastic were acclaimed, flounced hems finished with uneven scallops and adorned with pearls or pompoms or braid have become a signature. The clothes are beautiful and romantic, a fantasy of dressing that's entirely distinctive and personal.

Her personal appearance is as imaginative as her clothing: her hair may be dyed in a rainbow of colors—magenta and bright green, for example—her makeup tends to such effects as eyebrows drawn in one continuous arc. Unlike many of her contemporaries from 1960s "swinging London" who have faded from the scene, she has continued to thrive and to take risks.

Rhodes has been involved in other design projects—sportswear, sleepwear, textiles, sheets, rugs. She pays frequent visits to the United States where her clothes are sold in stores as diverse as Bloomingdale's and Martha.

RICCI, NINA

BORN: Turin, Italy, 1883.

DIED: Paris, France, 29 November 1970.

Interested in clothes from childhood, Ricci made hats and dresses for her dolls, at twelve moved to Paris with her family. At the age of thirteen she was apprenticed to a couturier, at eighteen was the head of an atelier, and at twenty-one a premier stylist. In 1932, encouraged by her jeweler husband, Louis, she opened her own house.

Ricci was a skilled technician who usually designed directly from the cloth onto the mannequin. The house specialized in graceful clothes for elegant women who preferred to be in fashion rather than ahead of it. She was also known for trousseaux. She was one of the first in the couture to show lower priced models in a boutique. Typical of her attention to elegance and detail is the Ricci perfume, *L'Air du Temps*, presented in a Lalique flacon with a frosted glass bird on the stopper.

Since 1945, the house has been managed by her son, Robert. In 1951, JULES FRANÇOIS CRAHAY became Mme. Ricci's collaborator on the collections, took over complete design responsibility in 1959. He was succeeded in 1963 by GERARD PIPART.

ROCHAS, MARCEL

BORN: Paris, France, 1902.

DIED: Paris, France, 14 March 1955.

waist cincher, 1945

Rochas opened his couture house in 1924 in the Faubourg Saint-Honoré, moved to the avenue Matignon in 1931. According to legend, his reputation was made by the scandal which ensued when eight women wore identical dresses from his house to the same party.

Known for young, daring designs, Rochas used as many as ten colors in combination, was lavish with lace, ribbon, tulle. He had an abundance of fantastic, original ideas, showed a broad-shouldered military look before SCHIAPARELLI, an hourglass silhouette several years before the New Look, invented a waist-cincher. His perfume, *Femme*, was packaged in black lace and became a classic. He maintained a boutique for separates and acccessories, also designed for films.

ROEHM, CAROLYNE

BORN: Kirksville, Missouri, c. 1952.

A graduate of Washington University in St. Louis, Missouri, Roehm started work as a stylist for the Kellwood Co., eventually went as an assistant to OSCAR DE LA RENTA. In 1985, deciding that she didn't want to become "the world's oldest assistant," she went into business for herself with the backing of her financier husband.

Her first collection was mostly suits and dressy dresses, pretty and ladylike, sleek for day, glamorous for night. Her success was immediate, with special acclaim for the evening clothes. She designs especially for the woman in her thirties with a heavy social schedule, brings a young, feminine look to "benefit" dressing.

RYKIEL, SONIA

BORN: Paris, France, 1930.

AWARDS:
   1986 — The Fashion Group "Night of the Stars" Award

Sonia Rykiel

Rykiel began in fashion by making her own maternity dresses, continued to design after her child was born, first for friends, then for her husband's firm, Laura. The first Sonia Rykiel boutique opened in 1968 in the Paris department store Galeries Lafayette, followed by her own boutique on the Left Bank.

She has made her name with sweaters and sweater looks, in apparently endless variations, usually cut seductively close to the body, softened with detail near the face. Her mannequins are, of necessity, the thinnest in Paris. When her daughter became pregnant, Rykiel put pregnant-looking mannequins in oversize sweaters, added a new line of children's wear when her granddaughter reached an age to appreciate them.

Rykiel presents a dramatic appearance: a mane of red hair, pale complexion, almost invariably dressed in black. Her Paris apartment is also in black, brightened by colored neon lights and a menagerie of friendly stuffed animals.

1984

Dior, 1949. The Metropolitan Museum of Art, Gift of Mrs. Bryan C. Foy, 1953.

Above: Left: Norman Norell, **1954.** *Center:* Adrian, **1943.** *Right:* Claire McCardell, **1937.** The Metropolitan Museum of Art. *Left:* Gift of Mr. and Mrs. Richard V. Hare, 1976. *Center:* Gift of Gilbert Adrian, 1945. *Right:* Gift of Claire McCardell, 1949.

Left: Paul Poiret, c. **1922–23.** The Metropolitan Museum of Art, Gift of Mrs. Muriel Draper, 1943.

Claire McCardell, c. 1944. Photograph by Louise Dahl-Wolfe. Fashion Institute of Technology, New York.

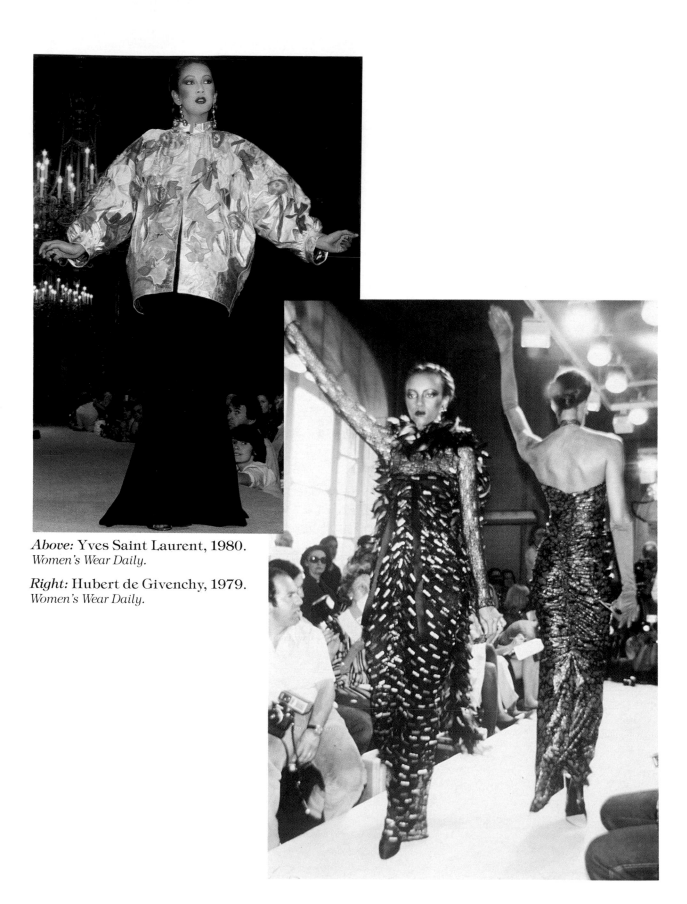

Above: Yves Saint Laurent, 1980.
Women's Wear Daily.

Right: Hubert de Givenchy, 1979.
Women's Wear Daily.

Balenciaga, c. 1959. The Metropolitan Museum of Art. Gift of Louise Rorimer Dushkin, 1980.

Above: Perry Ellis, 1982. *Women's Wear Daily.*

Top Left: Donna Karan, 1986. *Women's Wear Daily.*

Left: Ralph Lauren, 1987. *Women's Wear Daily.*

Above: Oscar de la Renta, 1985. *Women's Wear Daily.*

Top Right: Bill Blass, 1987. *Women's Wear Daily.*

Right: Calvin Klein, 1986. *Women's Wear Daily.*

Norman Norell, c. 1950. Photograph by Louise Dahl-Wolfe.
Fashion Institute of Technology, New York.

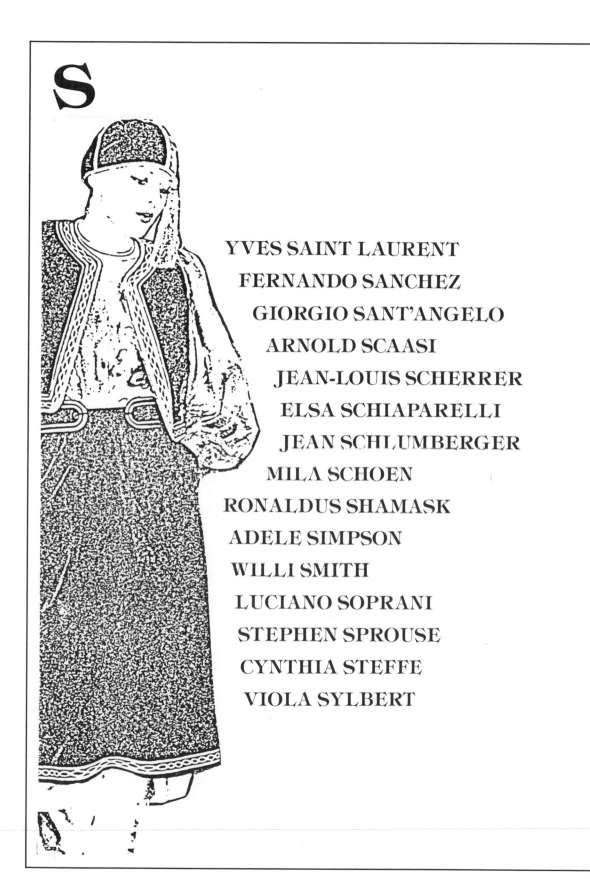

S

YVES SAINT LAURENT

FERNANDO SANCHEZ

GIORGIO SANT'ANGELO

ARNOLD SCAASI

JEAN-LOUIS SCHERRER

ELSA SCHIAPARELLI

JEAN SCHLUMBERGER

MILA SCHOEN

RONALDUS SHAMASK

ADELE SIMPSON

WILLI SMITH

LUCIANO SOPRANI

STEPHEN SPROUSE

CYNTHIA STEFFE

VIOLA SYLBERT

SAINT LAURENT, YVES

BORN: Oran, Algeria, 1 August 1936.

AWARDS:
  1958—Neiman-Marcus Award
  1981—Council of Fashion Designers
     of America (CFDA)

S on of a well-off family of Alsatian descent, Saint Laurent left Oran for Paris to study art. When he was seventeen his sketch won first prize in a fashion contest sponsored by the International Wool Secretariat, at nineteen he was introduced to CHRISTIAN DIOR, who hired him immediately. In 1957, on Dior's death, he was chosen to succeed him as head designer of the house, a post he held until called up for military service in 1960. In the army, he became ill and was discharged after three months.

Saint Laurent opened his own couture house in January 1962. He began his Rive Gauche prêt-à-porter in 1966, in 1974 established his men's wear. Since then his name and YSL initials have been licensed for everything from sweaters to bed and bath linens, from eyeglasses to scarves to children's clothes. His fragrances include *Y*, *Rive Gauche*, *Opium*, and *Paris*.

Within twenty years Saint Laurent established himself as the undisputed king of fashion. Alternately taking inspiration from the street and exerting influence on it, he is enormously sensitive to shifts in social attitudes. Above all,

See-through blouse, 1968

Yves Saint Laurent and model, 1987

Trapeze, 1965

he remains devoted to the ideal of haute couture and the art of dressing women sensibly, yet with a sense of poetry. Over the years he has become more involved with style, less with fashion, which by definition is transient.

More than any other designer, Saint Laurent has understood the life of the modern woman. The day clothes, in beautiful fabrics, are simple, wearable, with a slightly masculine quality, while the evening clothes are unabashedly luxurious and sensuous, enriched with fantasy and drama.

In December 1983, the Costume Institute of the Metropolitan Museum of Art mounted a retrospective of twenty-five years of his work, the first time a living designer has been so honored. In it could be seen many of the highlights of his career, from the 1958 "Trapeze" of his first Dior collection, to such classics as the pea coat and the "smoking", and the fantasy of the rich peasants. It was possible to track his increasing mastery and polish, and the blending of vision and rigorous dedication that have led to his preeminence.

Fisherman's Shirt, 1962

Mondrian Dress, 1965   Russian Fantasy, 1976   Longuette, 1970

Saint Laurent has an excellent commercial instinct for what will sell and has been widely copied. He leaves the business side of his ventures to his partner, Pierre Bergé, who has described him as "born with a nervous breakdown." He is never able to be complacent, no matter how successful, but is always driven by the fear that next time he will be out of inspiration, that his gifts will fail him.

Evening Tuxedo, 1978

1979

1987

SANCHEZ, FERNANDO

BORN: Spain, 1930s.

AWARDS:
Coty American Fashion Critics' Award:
1974, 1977, 1981—Special Award (lingerie)
1975—Special Award (fur design for Revillon)
1981—Council of Fashion Designers of America (CFDA)

His mother was Belgian and his father Spanish but Sanchez received his design education in France, making him a complete international. He studied at the École Chambre Syndicale de la Couture in Paris and was a prize winner in the same International Wool Secretariat competition in which SAINT LAURENT won an award. Both went on to the house of CHRISTIAN DIOR, where Sanchez designed lingerie, accessories, and sweaters for the Dior European boutiques.

He first came to New York to do the Dior American lingerie line and for several years commuted between Paris and New York. At the same time he began designing furs for Revillon, working for them for twelve years and becoming known for such unconventional treatments as his hide-out mink coats. He stopped doing furs after he opened his own lingerie company in 1973, re-signed with Revillon in 1984 to produce a collection for the United States.

Sanchez's first successes for his own firm were glamorous lace-trimmed silk gowns, to which he added camisole tops, boxer shorts, bikini pants. He went on to develop lingerie on the separates principle, mixing colors, lengths and fabrics to make a modern look. He calls his designs "home clothes," although many styles can also be worn on the beach or for dancing. This may have been his inspiration for the ready-to-wear he added in the early 1980s. His lingerie is seductive, luxurious, trend-setting, and expensive. He has been given credit for reviving interest in extravagant underthings. In December 1984, he signed with Vanity Fair for a moderately priced line of sleep and loungewear.

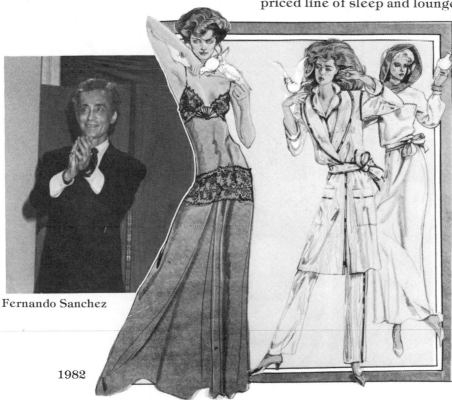

Fernando Sanchez

1982

SANT'ANGELO, GIORGIO

BORN: Florence, Italy, 5 May 1936.

AWARDS:
   Coty American Fashion Critics' Award:
     1968—Special Award (fantasy
       accessories and ethnic fashions)
     1970—"Winnie"
     1987—Council of Fashion Designers
       of America (CFDA) (contribution to
       evolution of stretch clothing)

Sant'Angelo spent much of his childhood in Argentina and Brazil where his family owned property. He trained as an architect and industrial designer before going to France to study art. He studied with Picasso, came to the United States in 1962 and worked with Walt Disney.

After moving to New York in 1963, he free-lanced as a textile designer and stylist, and served as design consultant on various environmental projects. This brought him into contact with E. I. du Pont de Nemours resulting in commissions for experiments with Lucite as a material for the home and for fashion accessories. The accessories were a sensation and received extensive and favorable press coverage.

Sant'Angelo Ready-to-Wear was founded in 1966, di Sant'Angelo, Inc. in 1968. For women he designs ready-to-wear and separates under the Giorgio Sant'Angelo label. His extensive licensing has included swimwear and active sportswear, furs, tailored suits, outerwear, men's outerwear, neckties and men's wear, environmental fragrances, sheets and domestics, furniture, rugs and carpets.

Sant'Angelo's first success was with accessories. His first collection of gypsy dresses and modern patchwork clothes was extremely influential, he went on to break more barriers with ethnic clothes, particularly a collection dedicated to the American Indian. He remains very much an individualist, interested in new uses for materials such as stretch fabrics incorporating spandex. His designs are for those who like their clothes a bit out of the ordinary and he maintains a couture operation for a roster of celebrity customers. He has also done costume design for films.

Giorgio Sant'Angelo

1984

1977

SCAASI, ARNOLD

BORN: Montreal, Canada, 8 May 1931.

AWARDS:
1958 — Coty American Fashion Critics'
"Winnie"
1959 — Neiman-Marcus Award
1987 — Council of Fashion Designers
(CFDA) (extravagant evening dress
designs)

The son of a furrier, Scaasi left Canada after finishing high school to live with an aunt in Melbourne, Australia. She dressed at CHANEL and SCHIAPARELLI, and influenced him with her disciplined approach to dress and living. He began art studies in Australia, returned to Montreal to study couture. There he designed clothes for private clients, saved enough money to go to Paris to complete his fashion studies at the Chambre Syndicale. After traveling in Europe for a year, he went to PAQUIN in Paris as an apprentice.

Arriving in New York in 1955, Scaasi worked as sketcher for CHARLES JAMES, designed coats and suits for a Seventh Avenue manufacturer, and in 1957, on a shoestring, opened his own wholesale business. In 1960 he bought and renovated a Manhattan town house for his ready-to-wear presentations, discontinued ready-to-wear and switched to couture in 1963. Another twenty years elapsed before he returned to ready-to-wear with Arnold Scaasi Boutique, a small collection of cocktail and evening dresses for fall 1984.

One of the last of the true custom designers in the United States, Scaasi is known for spectacular evening wear in luxurious fabrics, often trimmed with furs or feathers. He has also designed costume jewelry, furs, men's ties, and sweaters.

Arnold Scaasi and model, 1985

1987

SCHERRER, JEAN-LOUIS

BORN: Paris, France, 1936.

Scherrer trained as a dancer, but turned to fashion when he injured his back at the age of twenty. The sketches he made during his recuperation were shown to DIOR and he became Dior's assistant at the same time as SAINT LAURENT. It was at Dior that he learned the intricacies of cutting and draping that are the basis of his craft.

On Dior's death and the choice of Saint Laurent as his successor, Scherrer left the house and found a backer to set him up in his own business. Since then he has had considerable success in both couture and ready-to-wear, with elegant clothes in the more elaborate couture tradition.

1987

SCHIAPARELLI, ELSA

BORN: Rome, Italy, 10 September 1890.

DIED: Paris, France, 13 November 1973.

AWARDS:
1940 — Neiman-Marcus Award

The daughter of a professor of Oriental languages, Schiaparelli traveled to Tunisia as a child, later studied philosophy, wrote poetry and articles on music. She married and moved to the United States, where she lived until the end of World War I. Her involvement in fashion came about by accident when her husband left her in 1920. She returned to Paris with her daughter, Marisa, to support, and without money.

In Paris, a sweater she designed for herself and had knitted by a member of the Paris Armenian colony caught the attention of a buyer. An order resulted and she was on

The Talleyrand suit, 1945

Elsa Schiaparelli

Evening dress, late 1930s

her way. By 1929 she had established *Pour le Sport* on the rue de la Paix, by 1930 was doing an estimated 120 million francs worth of business a year from twenty-six workrooms employing two thousand people. In 1935 she opened a boutique on the Place Vendôme for sport clothes, later added dresses and evening clothes.

Like Chanel, Schiaparelli was more than a dressmaker, actually part of the brilliant artistic life of Paris in the 1920s and 1930s. She had close friendships with artists such as JEAN SCHLUMBERGER, who also designed jewelry for her, Dali, Cocteau, Van Dongen, and Man Ray. Highly creative and unconventional, she shocked the couture establishment by using rough "working class" materials and innovative accessories.

She was a genius at publicity, commissioned a fabric patterned with her press clippings then used the material in scarves, blouses, and beachwear. She pioneered in the use of synthetic fabrics, showed little "doll hats" shaped like a lamb chop or a pink-heeled shoe, gloves that extended to the shoulders and turned into puffed sleeves. Her signature color was the brilliant pink she called "shocking," the name she also gave to her famous fragrance in its dressmaker dummy bottle.

Schiaparelli changed the shape of the figure with broad, padded shoulders inspired by the London Guardsman's uniform. She fastened clothing with colored zippers, jeweler-designed buttons, padlocks, clips, dog leashes. She showed witty lapel ornaments in the shape of hands, teaspoons, hearts, or angels, amusing novelties such as glowing phosphorescent brooches and handbags that lit up or played tunes when opened. She was spectacularly successful with avant-garde sweaters worked with tattoo or skeleton motifs.

Following the fall of France, she came to the United States, returned to Paris after liberation and reopened her house in 1945. While she continued in business until 1954, she never regained her prewar position. She continued as a consultant to companies licensed to produce hosiery, perfume, and scarves in her name, lived out her retirement in Tunisia and Paris.

Schiaparelli's irreverence and energy sometimes resulted in vulgarity but she produced clothes of great elegance and extreme chic. Perhaps her major contribution was her vitality and sense of mischief, a reminder not to take it all too seriously.

SCHLUMBERGER, JEAN

BORN: Mulhouse, Alsace-Lorraine,
    24 June 1907.

DIED: Paris, France, 29 August 1987.

AWARDS:
    1958—Coty American Fashion Critics'
        Special Award (the first ever given for
        jewelry)
    1977—Made Chevalier of the National
        Order of Merit of France

Platinum and 18K-gold pavé diamond
bird stands on top of a citrine rock

Schlumberger's father was an Alsatian textile magnate and the son was sent to America in his teens to work in a New Jersey silk factory. On his return to France, he abandoned textiles and took a job with an art publishing firm, becoming part of the inventive Paris world of fashion, art, and society.

His first jewelry designs were clips made from china flowers found in the Paris flea market. These pieces attracted the attention of ELSA SCHIAPARELLI, who admired their originality and commissioned him to design costume jewelry. He progressed to gold and precious stones, and developed an influential international clientele, which included the Duchess of Windsor and Millicent Rogers.

Schlumberger went into the army at the advent of World War II, was evacuated from Dunkirk, and eventually came to the United States. He designed clothes for Chez Ninon, opened an office on Fifth Avenue, joined the Free French and served in the Near East. He returned to New York in 1946 and opened a salon on East 63rd Street, in 1956 joined Tiffany & Co. where he had his own salon on the mezzanine, reached by a private elevator.

Schlumberger has been equated with Fabergé and Cellini. His virtuosity, imagination, and skill brought forth exuberant fantasies: a sunflower of gold, emeralds, and diamonds with a 100 karat sapphire heart, planted in a clay pot set in a gold cachepot; snowpea clips of malachite and gold; moss-covered shells dripping with diamond dew. He revived the custom of mixing semiprecious stones with diamonds and such Renaissance techniques as enamelwork. He used enamel and stones as if they were paint. His work was the subject of a lecture at the Metropolitan Museum of Art and a loan exhibition of jewelry and objects at the Wildenstein Gallery, New York.

SCHOEN, MILA (OR SCHÖN)

BORN: Trau, Dalmatia, Yugoslavia.

Although based in Milan, Schoen shows her couture and deluxe ready-to-wear in Rome. Her parents went to Trieste, Italy, from Yugoslavia to escape the Communists, Schoen moved on to Milan where she led a privileged life until a change in financial circumstances forced her to earn a living. She first opened a small workroom to copy Paris models, in 1965 successfully showed her own designs in Florence.

She became well known during the 1960s for beautifully cut suits and coats in double-faced fabrics and for exquisitely beaded evening dresses. She has moved with the times toward a softer, more fluid look, but has always upheld the highest standards of design and workmanship.

In recent years she has added men's wear, swimsuits, and sunglasses to her design projects.

SHAMASK, RONALDUS

BORN: Amsterdam, Holland, 1946.

AWARDS:
  1981—Coty
    American
    Fashion Critics'
    "Winnie"

1987

One of a small group of designers with a strong architectural bias, Shamask is essentially self-taught. At fourteen he moved with his family to Melbourne, Australia, worked in the display department of a large department store, in 1967 left for London where he found work as a fashion illustrator and began to paint. His next move was to Buffalo, New York, where, for three years, he designed sets and costumes for ballet, theater, and opera. He left Buffalo in 1971 for New York City, obtained commissions from private clients to design interiors and also clothing.

Shamask next undertook a twenty-piece collection in muslin, which placed emphasis on cut and proportion. The clothes were cut from patterns which were actually life-sized blueprints. He later showed the collection to a new friend, Murray Moss, and in 1978 the two formed a partnership, *Moss*, a pristine, all-white shop and "laboratory" on Madison Avenue, which opened in 1979 to an audience of friends, family, and press. The presentation consisted of the original muslin collection now executed in three weights of linen. Immediate critical success was followed by commercial success, acceptance by leading stores, growth of a wholesale operation, and a move to Seventh Avenue.

The clothes, which combine strong architectural shapes with beautiful fabrics, are cut with the utmost precision and are exquisitely made. They have been praised for their purity of design and exceptional workmanship.

In 1986, starting with two coats, he branched out into men's fashion and by spring 1988 was turning out a full line of men's wear. These, made in Italy of European fabrics, were individual pieces intended to be chosen separately and put together in matched or unmatched outfits. The Council of Fashion Designers of America recognized his contribution to men's fashion in January 1988 when they named him men's wear designer of the year.

SIMPSON, ADELE

BORN: New York City, 8 December 1903.

AWARDS:
  1946—Neiman-Marcus Award
  1947—Coty American Fashion Critics'
    "Winnie"
  1953—First National Cotton Award

EXHIBITION:
  1978—"1001 Treasures of Design,"
    items collected by Adele and Wesley
    Simpson, Fashion Institute of
    Technology.

The youngest of five daughters of an immigrant tailor, Simpson started designing at seventeen while attending Pratt Institute at night. By the age of twenty-one she was earning the then staggering sum of $30,000 annually and travelling regularly to Paris for her firm. She worked for a number of companies before establishing her own company in 1940.

Simpson has always seen her purpose as dressing women, not just selling dresses. Her clothes are pretty, feminine, and wearable, can be coordinated into complete wardrobes. They are known for excellent design and impeccable quality, have always been intended for women of discerning taste, conservative but not old fashioned. As Donald Hopson took over the designing of the collection, a younger, more fluid look developed.

SMITH, WILLI

BORN: Philadelphia, Pennsylvania, 19 February 1948.

DIED: New York City, 17 April 1987.

AWARDS:
  1983—Coty American Fashion Critics' Award

One of the black designers who came to the fore in the late 1960s, Smith was slender and young-looking, gentle in manner, hard working. His innovative, spirited clothes—described as classics with a sense of humor—were fun to wear as well as functional, brought fashion verve to the moderate price range. Collections were consistent in feeling from one year to another so that new pieces mixed comfortably with those from previous years. Preferring natural fibers for their comfort and utility, he designed his own textiles and went to India several times a year to supervise production of the collections.

Willi Smith

1987

1978

Smith, the son of an ironworker and a housewife, grew up in a household where clothes were very important. He originally intended to be a painter and studied fashion illustration at the Philadelphia Museum College of Art. In 1965, aged 17, he arrived in New York with two scholarships to Parsons School of Design. He got a summer job with ARNOLD SCAASI, spent two years at Parsons, during which he free-lanced as a sketcher. Following school, he worked for several manufacturers, including Bobbie Brooks, Talbott, and Digits. After several failed attempts to set up his own business, WilliWear Ltd. was established in 1976 with Laurie Mallet as president, Smith as designer and vice president. WilliWear Men was introduced in 1978 "to bridge the gap between jeans and suits."

Smith also designed for Butterick Patterns, did lingerie and loungewear, textiles for Bedford Stuyvesant Design Works, furniture for Knoll International. He was a sponsor of the Brooklyn Academy of Music's "Next Wave" festival and designed one of the 1984 dance presentations.

The WilliWear company continued with a team of designers working under Mallet's supervision.

SOPRANI, LUCIANO

BORN: Reggiolo, Italy, 1946.

Luciano Soprani and model, 1987

Soprani was born into a farming family, studied agriculture and farmed for a year and a half before breaking away in 1967 to become a designer. His first job was with Max Mara, an Italian ready-to-wear firm, where he stayed for eight years, plus another two years free-lance. He free-lanced for a number of firms until 1981 when he signed his first contract with Basile to design their women's line. After a year, he added responsibility for the men's wear. He has also designed for Gucci. His first collection under his own name appeared 1981.

Essentially, Soprani works with strong shapes, enlivened by interesting details. His clothes are original and lively, among the best Italy has to offer.

SPROUSE,
STEPHEN

BORN: Indiana, 1954.

1983

At the time considered the archetypal "downtown" designer (as opposed to Seventh Avenue), Sprouse burst triumphantly on the New York design scene in 1983, disappeared from view just as dramatically only five seasons later.

His first collection of chemises and separates was reminiscent of the 1960s, except that they were printed or painted in graffiti-like designs or sequined and colored in a Day Glo spectrum. He was particularly admired for the perfection of his coats. Although he stayed in business so briefly, his fashion influence was extensive, particularly the hot, wild colors.

In June 1987, Sprouse resurfaced with a new backer and three collections: the low-priced S label; mid-priced Post-Punk Dress for Success; high-priced Stephen Sprouse. These were to be sold, together with Sprouse-designed accessories and Sprouse-approved records, tapes, and compact discs, from his own store in New York's SoHo district. The clothes, which showed their lineal connection to his original ideas, demonstrated that he had not lost his dynamism and drive.

STEFFE, CYNTHIA

BORN: Molville, Iowa, 30 June 1957.

Steffe grew up in Molville, Iowa, came to New York to study at Parsons School of Design from 1978 to 1982. She won many awards during her four-year stay: the Claire McCardell Scholarship her sophomore year, an award for the most original children's wear design and the Willi Smith Silver Thimble award during her junior year, and both the Donna Karan Gold Thimble and 1982 Designer of the Year awards in her senior year. In 1982, while still in school, she started working as a design assistant at Anne Klein & Co., left there in October 1983 to design for Spitalnick under the label Cynthia Steffe for Spitalnick & Co.

Essentially her clothes are luxury sportswear, combining ease, comfort, and sophistication, with emphasis on unusual and original fabrics. Her goal is true style, timeless and with a distinctly American viewpoint, for a knowledgeable professional woman who needs clothes of elegance and style for both her public and private lives.

SYLBERT, VIOLA

BORN: New York City.

AWARDS:
    1975—Coty American Fashion Critics'
      Special Award (fur design)

The daughter of a dress manufacturer, Sylbert earned her B.A. and M.Sc. in retailing at New York University. Her first love was writing, her second theatrical costume design, but to earn a living she became a fashion coordinator at Ohrbach's, gradually worked into designing.

Recognizing early that "I'm not a 9-to-5 person," she began to free-lance, enjoying the stimulation of working with different people on different kinds of projects. She established a routine of sketching and research at home, travels to Europe and Hong Kong.

Sylbert's first successes were in leathers, sportswear, and sweaters. In 1970, at the suggestion of Geraldine Stutz of Henri Bendel, she began designing furs, easy and casual in feeling with a unique fit and unusual colorings. She is fascinated with textures and the visual variations of different materials. Besides furs she is best known for outerwear and knitwear. She has designed "trend collections" of jersey dresses and men's sweaters for the Wool Bureau, also loungewear, children's clothes, accessories.

1970

TAMOTSU

ANGELO TARLAZZI

GUSTAVE TASSELL

CHANTAL THOMASS

BILL TICE

MONIKA TILLEY

PAULINE TRIGÈRE

PATRICIA UNDERWOOD

EMANUEL UNGARO

TAMOTSU

BORN: Tokyo, Japan, 29 July 1945.

Tamotsu studied textiles and fashion and costume design at the Kuwazawa Design School. Following school, a job with one of Japan's largest textile producers exposed him to color, texture, and fashion, and further stimulated his interest in clothing design.

Visiting the United States in the early 1970s, he decided to stay. He studied patternmaking and apparel at the Fashion Institute of Technology, supporting himself with odd jobs in the workrooms of designers and costume makers. In his spare time he made clothes for friends. His career took off when jumpsuits and dresses he designed for a New York boutique became hot items.

In his early clothes, sophisticated color and fabric choices and away-from-the-body cuts revealed Tamotsu's Japanese heritage and training in textiles. He has since developed a more Western look while retaining his interest in fabrics. Design projects have included sportswear, dresses, outerwear, and Vogue Patterns, and he has developed a thriving business in larger sizes. His chosen customer is "the woman who goes to work."

TARLAZZI, ANGELO

BORN: Ascoli Piceno, Italy, 1942.

1987

While he now works and presents his ready-to-wear in Paris, Tarlazzi received his fashion initiation and education in Italy. At nineteen he went to work at Carosa in Rome, stayed five years and became chief designer, left for Paris in 1966 and a job with PATOU. After three years at Patou he went to New York, could not find work and returned to Europe. He then free-lanced for Carosa, went back to Patou from 1972 until 1977, the year he established his own business. He has also free-lanced for Basile and BIAGIOTTI.

Tarlazzi's clothes are a blend of Italian fantasy and French chic. His knits, described as "suave and sexy," are produced in Italy, the remainder of his collection is French-made.

TASSELL, GUSTAVE

BORN: Philadelphia, Pennsylvania,
4 February 1926.

AWARDS:
1959—International Silk Association
1961—Coty American Fashion Critics'
"Winnie"

Tassell studied painting at the Pennsylvania Academy of Fine Arts, after army service, did window displays for HATTIE CARNEGIE. At Carnegie he was exposed to the designs of NORELL, which inspired him to become a dress designer. He had his own small couture business in Philadelphia, then returned to Carnegie as a designer. He left in 1952 to spend two years in Paris, supported himself there by selling sketches to visiting Americans, including GALANOS. He returned to the United States and in 1956, aided by Galanos, opened his own ready-to-wear business in Los Angeles. After Norell's death in 1972, Tassell took over as designer, remaining until the firm closed four years later. He then reopened his own business.

Tassell was a friend of Norell, sharing with him a sure sense of proportion, an insistence on simplicity of line and refined detail. He is known for clothes of near-couture sophistication and perfect finish.

THOMASS, CHANTAL

BORN: Paris, France, 1947.

Thomass began designing without formal training:—in her teens it was clothes for herself to be made up by her mother, later she made dresses from silk scarves painted by an art student boyfriend. In 1967 she sold these to DOROTHÉE BIS and to a shop in Saint Tropez, where they were bought by Brigitte Bardot. The same year she married Bruce Thomass and together they started a firm called Ter et Bantine, making "very junior," rather eccentric clothes. The firm, Chantal Thomass, was established in 1976 for a more expensive line, pretty and feminine, with a young up-to-the-minute spirit.

TICE, BILL

BORN: Indiana, 1946.

AWARDS:
  1974—Coty American Fashion Critics
    Special Award (lingerie)

Tice majored in fashion design at the University of Cincinnati. He arrived in New York in the mid-1960s, designed for a number of ready-to-wear firms before becoming designer for Royal Robes in 1968. He worked for Sayour in 1974, moved to Swirl in 1975, remaining there until 1984. In May 1987, he signed a licensing agreement for robes and loungewear under his label, while continuing to design an all-stretch bodywear collection and a lingerie collection under other licenses.

Known as a perfectionist who truly loves loungewear, Tice has always done a great many personal appearances "to keep me realistic about fashion." Many key at-home ideas originated with him, such as the jersey float, the quilted gypsy look, closely-pleated caftans. At Swirl he produced widely-imitated fleece robes, innovative and salable loungewear from sundresses to printed sarongs to quilted silk coats and narrow pants. He has also designed domestic linens.

1976

TILLEY, MONIKA

BORN: Vienna, Austria, 25 July 1934.

AWARDS:
  1975 — Coty American Fashion Critics
    Special Award (swimsuits)
  1976 — Print Council of America's
    Tommy Award (twice in one year,
    once for beach clothes and
    sportswear, once for loungewear and
    lingerie "for her original designs and
    use of prints")

The child of a diplomatic family, Tilley grew up in Austria and England, took her M.A. degree in 1956 from the Academy of Applied Arts, Vienna. She came to the United States in 1957, worked briefly as an assistant to JOHN WEITZ, then as a free-lance designer of ski wear and children's clothes. She was head designer for White Stag then moved to design positions at Cole of California, the Anne Klein Studio, Mallory Leathers, and in 1968, Elon of California. In 1970 she incorporated as Monika Tilley Limited, continuing her association with Elon; in 1984 began designing for the Christie Brinkley division of Russ Togs, Inc. Design projects have included swim and beachwear, children's swim things, at-home fashions, intimate apparel.

Tilley has always been involved in sports so that her sportswear designs, while fashionable and often seductive, are thoroughly functional. She has used bias cuts, cotton madras shirred with elastic, a technique of angling the weave of a fabric so it shapes the body. Her reputation as a top swimwear designer, which she explains as a matter of longevity ("I've stuck to swimwear longer than anyone else has"), is based on fit. She is very product-oriented and, insists on strict production control, works hard at promoting new lines with trunk shows and personal appearances.

1973

TRIGÈRE, PAULINE

BORN: Paris, France, 4 November 1912.

AWARDS:
  1950—Neiman-Marcus Award
  Coty American Fashion Critics' Award:
    1949—"Winnie"
    1951—Return Award
    1959—Hall of Fame
  1972—Silver Medal of the City of Paris
  1982—Medaille de Vermeil of the City
    of Paris

The daughter of a dressmaker and a tailor who came to Paris from Russia in 1905, Trigère learned to cut and fit in her father's shop, where she made her first muslins. She worked with her father until his death in 1932, arrived in New York in 1937 en route to Chile with her family, and decided to stay. She found work with Ben Gershel & Co. and as assistant to TRAVIS BANTON at HATTIE CARNEGIE. In 1942, with a collection of eleven styles, she opened her own business.

Trigère cuts and drapes directly from the bolt—coats, capes, suits, and dresses of near-couture quality in luxurious fabrics, unusual tweeds and prints. The deceptive simplicity of the clothes is based on artistic, intricate cut, especially flattering to the mature figure. The Trigère name has appeared on scarves, jewelry, furs, men's ties, sunglasses, bedroom fashions, paperworks, servingware, and a fragrance.

She takes care of the designing for her firm while her elder son, Jean-Pierre Radley, is president of Trigère Inc. and takes care of the business end.

Pauline Trigère   1985   1962

1964

UNDERWOOD, PATRICIA

BORN: Maidenhead, England, 1948.

Convent educated, Underwood worked in Paris as an *au pair* and at Buckingham Palace as a secretary before moving to New York in 1968. She studied at the Fashion Institute of Technology then, with a friend, went into business making hats. Her strength is in elegantly updating classic, simple shapes from the past, such as boaters, milkmaids' hats, nuns' coifs. Her designs have been bought by leading stores and featured in fashion magazines. They have frequently been chosen by leading ready-to-wear designers to complement their collections.

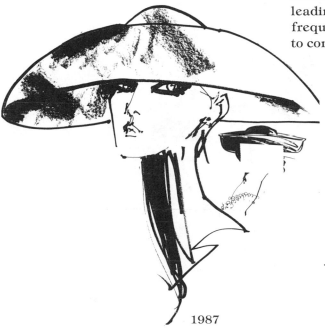

1987

UNGARO, EMANUEL

BORN: Aix-en Provence, France, 13 February 1933.

AWARDS:
1969—Neiman-Marcus Award

Ungaro's parents were Italian immigrants, his father a tailor. He gained his initial training from working with his father, from whom he learned to cut, sew, and fit men's clothes. At twenty-two, he left Provence for Paris and a job in a small tailoring firm. In 1958 he went to work for BALENCIAGA, stayed until 1963, then spent two seasons with COURRÈGES, opened his own business in 1965.

His first collections were reminiscent of Courrèges—tailored coats and suits with diagonal seaming, little girl A-line dresses, blazers with shorts. The clothes were widely copied in the youth market. Many of his special fabrics and prints were designed by Sonja Knapp, a Swiss graphic artist who still designs most of his fabrics and is his business partner.

In the 1970s he turned to softer fabrics and more flowing lines, mingling several different prints in a single outfit and piling on layers. His designs became increasingly seductive, evolving into a body-conscious, sensuous look, strategically draped and shirred, a look which was immediately copied. His excellent tailoring remained in evidence in creations

Ungaro

such as a men's wear striped jacket tossed over a slinky flowered evening dress, or daytime suits with soft trousers cut on the bias.

He has added ready-to-wear, Ungaro boutiques in Europe and the United States, a perfume, *Diva*. Other design projects include furs and men's wear, sheets, wallcoverings, curtains, knitwear.

1987

1981

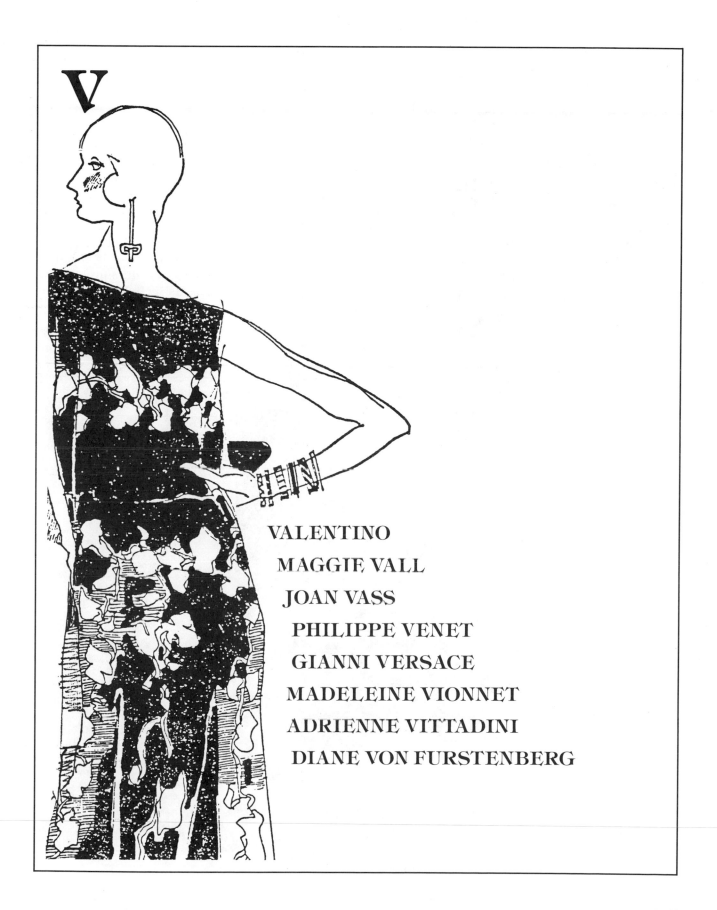

VALENTINO

MAGGIE VALL

JOAN VASS

PHILIPPE VENET

GIANNI VERSACE

MADELEINE VIONNET

ADRIENNE VITTADINI

DIANE VON FURSTENBERG

VALENTINO

BORN: Voghera, Italy, c. 1932.

AWARDS:
1967 — Neiman-Marcus Award

Valentino

Valentino studied French and fashion in Milan before leaving for Paris at age seventeen to study at the Chambre Syndicale de la Couture. In 1950 he went to work for JEAN DESSÈS, stayed five years, then worked as design assistant at GUY LAROCHE until 1958.

He returned to Rome, opened his own couture house in 1959 in a tiny atelier in the Via Condotti, within a few years was successful enough to move to his present headquarters. His first major recognition came in 1962 when he showed for the first time in Florence. In October 1975 he began showing his ready-to-wear collections in Paris and has continued to do so, one of the few foreigners to show there successfully. His couture showings are still held in Rome.

His first boutique for ready-to-wear opened in Milan in 1969, followed by one in Rome and then others around the world, including Japan. Other interests include men's wear,

1984   1987

Valentino Piu for gifts and interiors, bed linens, drapery fabrics, etc.

Valentino's clothes are noted for refined simplicity and elegance—well-cut coats and suits, sophisticated sportswear, entrance-making evening dresses—always feminine and flattering. They are worn by an international roster of fashionable women.

In October 1978 he introduced his signature fragrance in France in the grand manner, sponsoring a ballet performance in Paris, after-theater parties at Maxim's and the Palace. In July 1984, he celebrated his 25th year in business and 50th couture collection with an enormous outdoor fashion show in Rome's Piazza d'Espagna.

VALL, MAGGIE

BORN: Germany.

Maggie Vall began designing hats and headgear in 1974, at a time when hats were practically an extinct fashion species. Her education and background were in fine arts, including study at both the Pennsylvania Academy of Fine Arts and the Art Students League in New York, and exhibitions of her work in galleries in this country and Italy. Her first job, during summer vacation, was in the millinery department at Wanamaker's in Philadelphia. Her first hat was the result of a challenge from her husband to do something with her talent that would make more money than painting brought in. She made it of blue-and-white Dutch wax batik and when she took it to Henri Bendel, they bought it.

Vall says she learned her craft on the job. She believes in soft, unconstructed forms, emphasizes shape, color, line, and fabric, often using two or more fabrics in one hat. She keeps her company small and special so that she can do the kind of individual and original work she enjoys, such as sponge printing and air brushing color directly to the hats. Her customer is the active, aware urban woman with a strong personal style and the confidence to express it.

VASS, JOAN

BORN: New York City, 19 May 1925.

AWARDS:
  1978-"Extraordinary Women in
    Fashion," Smithsonian Institution,
    Washington, D.C.
  1979—Coty American Fashion Critics'
    Special Award (crafted knit fashions)

1987

Vass made her reputation with crochets and handmade or handloomed knits, and imaginative, functional clothes in simplified shapes and subtle colorings, usually in her preferred natural fibers. She is recognized by retailers and the press as a highly creative, original designer. From the beginning, her aim has been to make modern clothes for modern women and men.

A graduate of the University of Wisconsin, majoring in philosophy, she did graduate work in aesthetics, was a curator at the Museum of Modern Art, an editor at Harry N. Abrams, publisher of art books. With no formal fashion training, she got into designing in the early 1970s when two of her concerns intersected.

First, she was bothered by the plight of women with salable skills but no way to sell them—specifically, women who either could not work away from home or did not want the confinement of offices or factories. Second, she was convinced there was a market for handmade articles of good quality.

Vass, who had always knitted and crocheted, found a number of older women with superior craft skills and in 1973 began designing things for them to knit and crochet, selling the articles privately. The new enterprise took so much time that she wanted to give it up but was dissuaded by her workers. Then came her first large order from Henri Bendel, other stores followed, and she was in business. Her firm was incorporated in 1977. In addition to Joan Vass New York, better-priced clothes for men and women, there is the moderately-priced Joan Vass USA line. A London boutique opened in March 1985.

VENET, PHILIPPE

BORN: Lyons, France, 22 May 1929.

Venet began in fashion at fourteen when he was apprenticed to the best couturier in Lyons. He stayed there six years then moved on to Paris. At twenty-two, while working at SCHIAPARELLI, he met GIVENCHY, for whom he went to work as master tailor in 1953, remained there until 1962 when he left to open his own house.

Venet is a superb tailor, especially noted for his coats. His clothes are beautifully cut, have great elegance and ease. In addition to couture, he has designed costumes for the Rio de Janeiro Carnival, done sumptuous furs for Maximilian, produced a ready-to-wear line and men's wear, and opened a boutique.

VERSACE, GIANNI

BORN: Calabria, Italy, 1946.

Gianni Versace and model, 1987

Versace's mother was a dressmaker so he was surrounded by fashion from an early age. He studied architecture but became more and more involved in his mother's couture business until, in the late 1960s, he was acting as buyer for their atelier.

After finishing his architectural studies, he moved to Milan where he expanded his interest in fashion and textile design and began working as designer for several prêt-à-porter lines, including Genny and Callaghan. In 1979 he showed for the first time under his own name, a collection of men's wear.

Since then Versace has become one of Europe's most popular designers, with a vivid and far-ranging imagination. He offers women many options, always sensuous and sexy whether slender, controlled silhouettes or wide cuts. One of his trademarks is the slithery evening dress of chain mail, so soft and pliable it is sewn by machine, worn from California to the Riviera.

There are Gianni Versace boutiques around the world for men's and women's clothing, Versace accessories, knits, leathers, furs, and fragrances for men and women. He has also designed ballet costumes for La Scala and for Béjart's *Ballet of the 20th Century*.

1985

1986

VIONNET, MADELEINE

BORN: Aubervilliers, France, 1876.

DIED: Paris, France, 2 March 1975.

AWARDS:
  1929—Chevalier Légion d'Honneur

Madeleine Vionnet and mannequin

One of the towering figures of 20th century couture, Vionnet was the daughter of a gendarme. She began her apprenticeship when she was twelve, at sixteen was working with a successful dressmaker called Vincent. By the age of nineteen she had married, had a child who died, and was divorced. At twenty she went to London, stayed five years, working in a tailor's workroom and for CALLOT SOEURS.

She returned to Callot Soeurs in Paris, working closely with one of the sisters, Mme. Gerber, for whom she made toiles and whom she considered even greater than POIRET. She left Callot Soeurs in 1907 to work for Doucet. In 1912 she opened her own house, which closed during World War I. She reopened in 1918 on the avenue Montaigne, closed finally in 1940.

Even while working for others, Vionnet had advanced

Beaded and embroidered dresses

ideas not always acceptable to conservative clients. She eliminated high, boned collars from dresses and blouses, claimed to have eliminated corsets before Poiret. One of the couture's greatest technicians, she invented the modern use of the bias cut, producing dresses so supple they could, without the aid of placket openings, be slipped on over the head to fall back into shape on the body, eliminating the need for fastenings of any kind. For even more suppleness, seams were often stitched with fagotting.

She did not sketch, instead, draped, cut, and pinned directly on the figure. For this purpose she used a small-scaled wooden mannequin with articulated joints. Designs were later translated into full-size toiles, then into the final material. Most probably she chose this method for convenience. It is doubtful she could have achieved her effects as economically or with as little physical effort by any other means.

1912

1913

1918-19

Vionnet still influences us. Her bias technique, her cowl and halter necklines, her use of pleating, are part of the designer's vocabulary today. She introduced crepe de Chine, previously confined to linings, as a fabric suitable for fashion; transformed Greek and medieval inspirations into completely modern clothes, graceful and sensuous; made considerable use of handkerchief hems.

Many designers trained with her. Her assistant for years was Marcelle Chaumont, who later opened her own house. Others included Mad Maltezos of the house of Mad Carpentier, and Jacques Griffe.

Herself a person of complete integrity, Vionnet was the implacable enemy of copyists and style pirates. Her motto was, "To copy is to steal."

1920

1931

1931

1936

1939

VITTADINI, ADRIENNE

BORN: Hungary.

AWARDS:
1984 — Coty Fashion Critics' Award

Vittadini left Hungary with her family in 1956, grew up in Philadelphia. She always wanted to be a fashion designer, but studied art at the Moore College of Art in Philadelphia. In 1965 she won a fellowship to study in Paris with Louis Feraud.

Returning to the United States, she went to work as a designer for Sport Tempo, then for the Rosanna division of Warnaco. On a sabbatical in Europe in the early 1970s, she met and married Gianluigi Vittadini, a Milanese business-man. She retired briefly, soon went back to work part time for Warnaco, then for Kimberly Knits. In January 1979, she established her own business.

Vittadini finds knits more of a challenge than wovens because the designer must begin by creating the fabric itself. Since she starts with the yarns, she also mixes her own dyes to obtain subtle and distinctive colorings, the closest thing, she says, to painting. She also likes the practi-cality of knitted clothes, the way they travel, their ease of care, and the seductive way they cling to the body. She has developed a sophisticated style, now produces women's ready-to-wear, petites, active sportswear, and dresses, and designs a swimsuit collection for Cole of California.

Adrienne Vittadini and model, 1987

VON FURSTENBERG, DIANE

BORN: Brussels, Belgium, c. 1946.

Educated in Spain, England, and Switzerland, Von Furstenberg took a degree in economics from the University of Geneva, moved to the United States in 1969. She saw a need for moderately-priced dresses that were both comfortable and fashionable and decided to try designing. Her first patterns were cut on her dining table, shipped to a friend in Italy to be made up. In 1971, she packed her first samples in a suitcase, started showing them to store buyers, and her business took off.

She gained her first recognition for lightweight jersey dresses, usually in prints, especially the wrapdress with surplice top and long sleeves. This is the dress Von Furstenberg says taught her three essential F's in designing for women. "It's flattering, feminine and, above all, functional."

Von Furstenberg left the moderate-price dress market in 1977, reentered it in February 1985 with a collection of day and evening styles centered on the wrapdress that is her trademark.

She has a successful makeup and treatment line of cosemetics, a fragrance, *Tatiana*, named after her daughter. Licenses have included stationery, costume jewelry, loungewear, furs, handbags and small leathers, designs for Vogue Patterns, raincoats, scarves, shoes, sunglasses, table linens, wallcoverings.

W

ILIE WACS

CHESTER WEINBERG

JOHN WEITZ

VIVIENNE WESTWOOD

HARRIET WINTER

CHARLES FREDERICK WORTH

WACS, ILIE

BORN: Vienna, Austria,
11 December 1927.

1963

1987

Wacs's father was one of Vienna's leading men's custom tailors until 1938 when the Germans invaded Austria. The family escaped to Shanghai, where in 1941, the Japanese occupied the city and forced all refugees into a ghetto. The elder Wacs supported the family by stripping old suits and reversing them to make new garments. His son helped him in the work, learning the art of tailoring literally from the inside out.

After the 1945 liberation he went to Paris with a scholarship to study art at the École des Beaux Arts, turned to fashion and worked in the Paris couture. He was brought to New York by Philip Mangone, a leading American tailor, worked for Mangone and others, had his own couture house. In 1964 he joined Originala, a top-ranking coat and suit maker, where he was head designer until 1972, then designed under his own label for a conglomerate, acquired ownership of Ilie Wacs Inc. in 1975.

Wacs is known for excellent tailoring in fine fabrics, works in the better price range. He believes that contemporary clothes should be uncomplicated and free of gimmicks, and that good fit is synonymous with good fashion.

WEINBERG, CHESTER

BORN: New York City,
    23 September 1930.

DIED: New York City, 24 April 1985.

AWARDS:
    1970—Coty American Fashion Critics'
        "Winnie"
    1972—Maison Blanche "Rex" Award,
        New Orleans

Weinberg graduated in 1951 from Parsons School of Design, went on to earn a B.S. degree in art education from New York University, studying at night while working as a sketcher during the day. He began teaching at Parsons in 1954, continued to do so until the year before his death.

After graduation, he worked for a number of better dress houses before opening his own business in 1966. From 1977 till 1981 his company was a division of Jones Apparel Group, and when it closed he went to work for Calvin Klein Jeans as design director.

Weinberg built his reputation on simple, elegant designs, sophisticated and classic, never exaggerated or overpowering. They were always marked by beautiful fabrics, which were his passion. "Fabrics set the whole mood of my collection. I cannot design a dress until I know what the fabric will be."

WEITZ, JOHN

BORN: Berlin, Germany, 25 May 1923.

AWARDS:
    1974—Coty American Fashion Critics'
        Special Men's Wear Award

John Weitz

Educated in England, Weitz apprenticed at MOLYNEUX in Paris, arrived in the United States shortly before Pearl Harbor, served in U.S. Army Intelligence. After the war he showed his designs—women's sportswear based on men's clothes—to Dorothy Shaver, President of Lord & Taylor, who helped him get started in business. He began licensing in 1954, began his men's wear business in 1964.

Weitz is considered a pioneer of practical, modern clothes for sports and informal living. He introduced women's sports clothes with a men's wear look in the 1950s, showed pants for town wear, a strapless dress over bra and shorts. In the 1960s he presented "ready-to-wear couture", where the design could be chosen from sketches and swatches, and for men, his Contour Clothes inspired by jeans, cowboy jackets, fatigue coveralls. He was one of the first U.S. designers to show both men's and women's wear, one of the first to license his work worldwide.

He has designed accessories such as watches, scarves, jewelry. Was a licensed racing driver and designed a two-seater aluminum sports car, the X600. His portrait photographs have been shown at the Museum of the City of New York.

WESTWOOD, VIVIENNE

BORN: Tintwhistle, England, 1941.

Westwood belongs to the anti-fashion branch of design exemplified by Comme des Garçons. Her torn, rough-edged clothes show a fierce rejection of polite standards of dress. They are often inspired by London street life, with wild swings in influences—from the leather and rubber fetishism, Punk Rock, S & M of the 1970s, to the "new romanticism" and "pirate" looks of the early 1980s.

She came into fashion around 1970 through her association with Malcolm McLaren of The Sex Pistols. At the time she was earning her living as a teacher, having left Harrow Art School after only one term. Despite poor finances, she has regularly shown in Paris, and her anarchic view of dressing has had a considerable influence on other designers, both in England and around the world.

1987

WINTER, HARRIET

The daughter of an actors' agent, Winter began in fashion without formal design training, reworking old clothes which her husband Lewis collected and which they then resold. Winter went on to make her own designs as Mrs. H. Winter of Yesterday's News, at first reminiscent of the 1930s and 1940s, gradually evolving into a thoroughly modern, completely personal style.

She feels that as fashion changes, the changes should be expressed by modern means and new constructions. For example, when shoulders broaden she prefers to accomplish it by cut or draping rather than by shoulder pads.

Her collection includes day clothes and evening separates of the sports-evening genre—easy, contemporary, individual—for the woman who doesn't want to look exactly like everyone else.

1978

WORTH, CHARLES FREDERICK

BORN: Bourne, Lincolnshire, England, 13 October 1825.

DIED: Paris, France, 10 March 1895.

The founder of the house that became the world's longest-running fashion dynasty started work at age eleven, worked for a number of London drapers before leaving for Paris in 1845. He took a job with a dealer in fabrics, shawls, and mantles, persuaded the firm to open a department of made-up dress models, which he designed. He was the first to present designs on live mannequins, used his young French wife as a model.

In 1858 he opened his own couture house on the rue de la Paix, which closed from 1870 to 1871 during the Franco-Prussian War. In 1874, Maison Worth was established, a fashion leader for eighty years.

Worth was court dressmaker to Empress Eugénie of France and to Empress Elizabeth of Austria. He dressed the ladies of European courts and society women of Europe and America. A virtual fashion dictator, he required his customers, except for Eugénie and her court, to come to him instead of attending them in their homes as had been the custom. He was an excellent businessman, was the first couturier to sell models to be copied in England and America, was also widely copied by others. He enjoyed his success and lived in the grand manner.

Worth designs were known for their opulence and lavish use of fabrics, elaborate ornamentation with frills, ribbons,

Worth, c. 1864

One of Worth's sketches

lace. He promoted the use of French-made textiles, is held responsible for the collapsible steel frame for crinolines and then for abolishing crinolines in 1867. Whether he actually invented it or not, he certainly exploited the crinoline to the utmost, as it reached its most extravagant dimensions during the Second Empire and disappeared when the Empire collapsed. Worth is said to have invented the princess-style dress, court mantles hung from the shoulders, the ancestor of the tailor-made suit. He was influenced by the paintings of Van Dyck, Gainsborough, and Velasquez.

After his death, the House of Worth continued under the leadership of his sons, Jean Philippe and Gaston, then of his grandson, Jean Charles, and finally of his great-grandsons, Roger and Maurice. When Roger retired in 1952, Maurice took over and in 1954 sold the house to PAQUIN. A London wholesale house continued under the name until the 1970s. Parfums Worth was established in 1900, continues today with *Je Reviens* the best known fragrance.

y/z

YOHJI YAMAMOTO

YUKI

ZORAN

YAMAMOTO, YOHJI

BORN: Yokohama, Japan, c. 1943.

A graduate of Keio University, Yamamoto studied fashion at Tokyo's Bunka College of Fashion under Chie Koike, who had attended the Chambre Syndicale School in Paris with SAINT LAURENT. From 1966 to 1968 he studied all aspects of the clothing industry, by 1972 had his own company. He showed his first collection in Tokyo in 1976. In 1981 he established himself in France with a boutique in Paris. Since then he has shown at the Paris prêt-à-porter collections.

Yamamoto likes surprise details: an unexpected pocket, a long, flowing shawl that began life as a lapel, a new placement of buttons. Oversize clothes are his signature, and a playful diversity of textures, asymmetrical hems and collars, holes and torn edges.

YUKI

BORN: Miyazaki-ken, Japan, c. 1940.

Yuki's primary training was as a textile engineer. He worked in Tokyo as an animator, moved to London, then to Chicago where he studied architecture and interior design at the Chicago Art Institute. Returning to London in 1964, he studied at the London College of Fashion until 1966, became a design assistant to a London dressmaker for two years. After that he worked for HARTNELL, and in 1969, went to Paris and a job with CARDIN. He free-lanced in Europe and America, presented his first collection under his own name in 1972.

Yuki works in both couture and ready-to-wear, making refined, elegant clothes with the flowing, sculptural quality of MADAME GRÈS. He has also designed for theater and television, has a successful licensing program.

In 1978, his work was honored by a retrospective showing at the Victoria and Albert Museum.

ZORAN

BORN: Belgrade, Yugoslavia, 1947.

Zoran

One of the fashion minimalists, Zoran studied architecture in Belgrade, moved to New York in 1971. His first fashion recognition came in 1977, when his designs were bought by Henri Bendel.

The early collections were based on squares and rectangles in silk crepe de Chine, cashmere, and other luxurious fabrics. They have evolved from there, always in pure shapes, always in the most expensive, most luxurious fabrics. It is a relaxed look, sophisticated and utterly simple, a perfection of understatement by a master of proportion and balance.

Zoran works in a limited color range, usually black, gray, white, ivory, and red. He prefers not to use buttons and zippers, as far as possible avoids any extraneous detail. Since his customers lead a highly mobile life, he has produced a jet-pack collection of ten pieces that fit into a small bag so that a woman can look casual and glamorous wherever her travels take her.

At a less costly level, Zoran has produced daytime clothes in cotton knit, although evenings are still devoted to satin, velvet, cashmere. Inevitably, they are for women of sophisticated tastes and well-filled pocketbooks.

1983

names
to
know

SIR CECIL BEATON

EDNA WOOLMAN CHASE

JESSICA DAVES

ERTÉ

VIRGINIA POPE

CARMEL SNOW

DIANA VREELAND

BEATON, CECIL

(English photographer, artist, costume and set designer)

BORN: London, England,
14 January 1904.

DIED: Broad Chalke, Wiltshire, England.
18 January 1980.

AWARDS:
Antoinette Perry Award:
1955—*Quadrille*
1957—*My Fair Lady*
1970—*Coco*
1956—Neiman-Marcus Award
1957—C.B.E.
Motion Picture Academy Award:
1958—*Gigi*
1965—*My Fair Lady* (sets and
costumes)
1960—French Legion of Honor

Beaton was educated at Harrow and Cambridge University. In 1928 began a long association with *Vogue* magazine, his first contributions being spidery sketches, caricatures of well-known London actresses, and drawings of clothes worn at society parties. Photographs appeared later. In her memoirs, EDNA WOOLMAN CHASE of *Vogue* described him at their first meeting: "...tall, slender, swaying like a reed, blond, and very young..." He gave an impression that was "an odd combination of airiness and assurance." And later, "What I like best is his debunking attitude toward life and his ability for hard work."*

In photography he did both fashion and portraiture, became the favored photographer of the British royal family. During World War II, he photographed for the Ministry of Information, travelling widely to North Africa, Burma, and China.

Beginning in 1935, Beaton designed scenery and costumes for ballet, opera, and many theatrical productions in both London and New York. Among his credits: *Lady Windermere's Fan, Quadrille, The Grass Harp, The School for Scandal* (Comédie Française). He did the costumes for the New York, London, and film productions of *My Fair Lady*, costumes for the films *Gigi* and *The Doctor's Dilemma*. He also designed hotel lobbies and clubs.

Prolific writer and diarist, Beaton published many books, illustrated them and those of others with drawings and photographs. He was knighted by Queen Elizabeth II in 1972. In 1975 he suffered a stroke which left him partially paralyzed, but he learned to paint and take photographs with his left hand. From 1977 until his death, he lived in semi-retirement at his house in Wiltshire.

CHASE, EDNA WOOLMAN

(Fashion editor)

BORN: Asbury Park, New Jersey, 1877.

DIED: 1957.

AWARDS:
1935—French Legion of Honor
1940—Neiman-Marcus Award

The child of divorced parents, Edna was raised by her Quaker grandparents, whose principles and plain style of dress were to prove a lasting influence. In 1895 when she was eighteen she went to work in the Circulation Department at *Vogue*, then just two years old. Salary, $10 a week. She was to spend fifty-six years at *Vogue*, thirty-seven of them as editor.

She fell in love with the magazine immediately. As she was enthusiastic, hard-working, and willing to take on any and all chores, she acquired more and more responsibility. By 1911 she was the equivalent of managing editor. Her name first appeared on the masthead as editor in February 1914. British and French *Vogue* were born in 1916 and 1920; Mrs. Chase was editor-in-chief of all three editions.

*Edna Woolman Chase and Ilka Chase, *Always in Vogue* (New York, 1966), pp. 212-213.

Edna Woolman Chase.
Photograph by John Rawlings.

During her tenure *Vogue* survived two world wars, a depression, tremendous social changes. With Condé Nast, who acquired the magazine in 1909, she helped shape it according to her own strong sense of propriety and high standards of professionalism. She suffered the second-rate badly, respected talent and hard work, wrote directly to the point.

She is credited with originating the modern fashion show in 1914 when *Vogue* produced a benefit "Fashion Fête," sponsored by prominent society women. During World War I she also began to feature American designers in *Vogue*'s pages.

Her advice to those thinking of a career in fashion is still worth considering. Requirements for success were taste, sound judgment...and experience, the training and knowledge gained from actually working in a business, which she valued above course-taking.

Taste, business ability, and a capacity for hard work brought her to the top of her profession and kept her there for an amazing time span. She retired as editor-in-chief in 1952 and became chairman of the editorial board.

She was married to and divorced from Francis Dane Chase and had one child, the writer and actress Ilka Chase. A second marriage in 1921 to Richard Newton ended with his death in 1950.

DAVES, JESSICA
(Fashion editor)

BORN: Cartersville, Georgia,
   20 February 1898.

DIED: New York City, 1974.

Daves arrived in New York in 1921, worked in the advertising departments of various New York stores, including Saks Fifth Avenue, where she wrote fashion copy and learned fashion merchandising. In 1933 she went to *Vogue* magazine as fashion merchandising editor. Her ability was spotted by EDNA WOOLMAN CHASE, then editor-in-chief, and in 1936 she was made managing editor, rose to editor in 1946. In 1952, upon Mrs. Chase's retirement, she became editor-in-chief of American *Vogue*. She was a director of Condé Nast Publications from 1946 until she retired in 1963, served as editorial consultant for a year then worked on specialized books until November 1966.

An accomplished writer and editor, she could fix a piece of ailing copy in minutes. She is remembered for clearheadedness and sound judgment—of all the great fashion editors she was probably the most astute at business.

The years of her editorship coincided with a phenomenal growth of the American ready-to-wear industry. She recognized its increasing importance and broadened the magazine's coverage of domestic ready-to-wear, including more moderately priced clothes. Under her direction *Vogue* assumed a more serious tone and ran more articles of intellectual interest than before.

Short and plump, Miss Daves dressed well but her figure precluded real style. Her manner was warm, her voice retained charming overtones of her southern origin. In her later years she became rather regal with something of a queen mother effect. She was married to Robert A. Parker, a writer, who died in 1970. They had no children.

ERTÉ
(ROMAIN DE TIRTOFF)

(Fashion artist and designer)

BORN: St. Petersburg, Russia, 10 November 1892.

The son of an admiral in the Russian Imperial Navy, Erté studied painting in Russia, went to Paris in 1912 to study at L'Académie Julian. He got a job sketching for PAUL POIRET, went on to design for opera and theater, did costumes for such luminaries as singer Mary Garden. He took his name from the French pronunciation of his initials R.T. (air-tay).

Beginning in 1914 and into the 1930s, he produced illustrations and covers for various magazines, including *Harper's Bazaar*, designed for the Folies Bergère, came to the United States in the 1920s to work for Ziegfeld and other impresarios. He tried Hollywood briefly in 1925, creating beautiful and esoteric costumes for several films, including *The Mystic*, *Ben Hur*, and King Vidor's *La Bohème*. Impatient with financial restrictions, he returned to Paris after eight months.

In 1967, to celebrate his 80th birthday, Erté selected over a hundred of his designs for clothes, jewelry, and accessories, to be shown in London and at the Grosvenor Gallery in New York. The exhibition contained some of the most elegant and individual designs of the Art Deco period. The New York exhibition was bought in its entirety by the Metropolitan Museum of Art.

POPE, VIRGINIA

(Fashion editor)

BORN: Chicago, Illinois, 29 June 1885.

DIED: New York City, 16 January 1978.

Virginia Pope is credited with practically inventing fashion reportage. She was a late starter in journalism, but once started had a long run.

Following her father's death, the five-year-old Virginia was taken to Europe by her mother, touring the continent for the next fifteen years. She became fluent in French, German, and Italian, and familiar with the best of European art and music. They returned to Chicago in 1905.

After serving in the Red Cross during World War I, she tried various careers in Chicago and New York, including social work, theater, book translations, writing. Her first published pieces were obtained through her facility with languages and ran in *The New York Times*, which she joined in 1925 as a member of the Sunday staff. Eight years later she became fashion editor, a position she held and developed for twenty-two years. Following retirement from *The Times* in 1955, Miss Pope joined the staff of *Parade* magazine as fashion editor. Her name remained on the masthead until her death.

In addition, she held the Edwin Goodman chair established by Bergdorf Goodman at the Fashion Institute of Technology, where she gave a course on "Fashion in Contemporary Living." She could frequently be seen on Seventh Avenue, escorting her students to fashion shows, going behind the scenes to see how a business worked. And since she believed that exposure to culture was essential to a designer's development, she regularly took students to performances of the Metropolitan Opera.

Miss Pope took American fashion seriously at a time when only style changes originating in Paris were thought worth reporting. She considered the people who made clothes newsworthy, encouraged the American fashion industry in its early years, setting taste standards for young designers.

At *The Times* she originated the "Fashions of The Times" fashion show in 1942 as a showcase for American designers, staging it each fall for the next nine years. In 1952 this was transformed into a twice-yearly fashion supplement of the same name, still published.

While her personal style of dressing was conservative, she could look at clothes objectively and understood innovation. Referring to her appearance and her well-deserved "grande dame" reputation, a fellow editor once said, "she could play the Queen of England without a rehearsal." She never married.

SNOW, CARMEL

BORN: Dublin, Ireland, 1888.

DIED: New York City, 9 May 1961.

Carmel Snow, 1958

Raised in the fashion business, Mrs. Snow grew up in New York City. Her mother, who came to the United States to promote Irish industries at the 1893 Chicago World's Fair, owned a dressmaking business, Fox & Co. The firm was one of the exhibitors at *Vogue*'s first "Fashion Fête" in 1914, and made the dress worn on that occasion by *Vogue*'s editor, EDNA WOOLMAN CHASE. A friendship developed and in 1921 Mrs. Chase offered Carmel a job in the magazine's fashion department.

In 1929 Mrs. Snow was made editor of American *Vogue*. Then in 1932, sending shock waves through the fashion world, she went as fashion editor to *Harper's Bazaar*, *Vogue*'s great rival. Condé Nast, *Vogue*'s publisher, never spoke to her again. She remained with *Bazaar* as fashion editor, then editor, until 1957, when she became chairman of the editorial board. Her successor was Nancy White, her niece and godchild.

Mrs. Snow was a woman of wit and intelligence, of strong views expressed frankly and with passion. CHRISTIAN DIOR spoke of her "marvelous feeling for what is fashion today and what will be fashion tomorrow." Like a high priestess of fashion she espoused each change as it appeared. She recognized BALENCIAGA's genius well before the majority of the fashion press and promoted him indefatigably. She was a loyal and powerful champion of the talented, demanding their best and receiving their finest efforts. After World War II, she took a leading role in helping the French and Italian textile and fashion industries get back on their feet.

A major fashion presence and forceful personality, Mrs. Snow was tiny and chic, dressed in clothes from the Paris couture. Legends about her abound: Christian Dior delayed openings until she arrived; even when she dozed off at showings her eyes would snap open when a winner appeared; she is said to have had total ocular recall.

She married George Palen Snow in 1926, had three children. She and her husband bought a place in County Mayo in 1957, later sold it when the climate proved unhealthy. She never completely lost her Irish accent nor her attachment to the country of her birth. She worked there and in New York on her memoirs, written in collaboration with Mary Louise Aswell, for eleven years fiction editor at *Bazaar*. Even after she no longer had official connections, and despite precarious health, she continued to go to Paris twice yearly for the collections.

VREELAND, DIANA

BORN: Paris, France, 1906.

Diana Vreeland and Bill Blass, 1979

The daughter of an English father and an American mother who brought their two daughters to America at the outbreak of World War I, Vreeland was exposed from early childhood to the world of fashion, and to extraordinary people and events. Her parents entertained such celebrities as Diaghilev, Nijinsky, Ida Rubinstein, Vernon and Irene Castle, and she remembers being sent to London in 1911 for the coronation of George V. She was married in 1924 to Thomas Reed Vreeland, lived in Albany, New York, until 1928, moved to London. They returned to New York City in 1937.

Her fashion career began in 1937 when CARMEL SNOW asked her to work for *Harper's Bazaar*. Her column "Why Don't You" quickly became a byword for such suggestions as, "Why don't you . . . rinse your blond child's hair in dead champagne to keep it gold as they do in France . . . ?" After six months she became fashion editor, working closely with Mrs. Snow and art director Alexey Brodovitch to make *Bazaar* the exciting, influential publication it was. She left the magazine in 1962, went to *Vogue* the following year as associate editor and was soon made editor in chief, a post she held until 1971. Since 1971 she has been a consulting editor at *Vogue* and a consultant to the Costume Institute of the Metropolitan Museum of Art.

At the museum, she has mounted a series of outstanding exhibitions, among them, "Balenciaga," "American Women of Style," "The Glory of Russian Costume," "Man and the Horse." Opening nights are a major social event, with tickets both expensive and in great demand.

Mrs. Vreeland, who felt like an ugly duckling as a child, has created herself as an elegant, completely individual woman with a strong personal style: short, jet black hair, heavily rouged cheeks, bright red lips. She dresses in simple "uniforms" for day and small dinners—sweaters and skirts or sweaters and pants—appearing for big evenings in dramatic gowns from favorite designers—SAINT LAURENT, GRÈS, GIVENCHY. Her conversational and writing style is as original as her appearance, dramatic, exaggerated, and quite inimitable. At *Vogue* the Vreeland memos were cherished and passed around among the magazine's staffers.

As an editor, she not only reported fashion but promoted it vigorously, showing something she believed in repeatedly until it took hold. For nearly five decades she has been a powerful influence on the American fashion consciousness, with perhaps her greatest achievement, her ability to understand the era of the 1960s with all its upheavals.

BIBLIOGRAPHY

Not all the listed books have contributed to this edition of *Who's Who in Fashion*. This bibliography is compiled to help the reader in the study of fashion.

The Age of Worth. New York: Brooklyn Museum of Arts & Sciences, 1982.

Amies, Hardy. *Just So Far.* St. James Place, London: Collins, 1984.

————. *ABC of Men's Fashion.* London: Newnes, 1964.

————. *Still Here.* London: Weidenfeld and Nicolson, 1984.

Baillen, C. *Chanel Solitaire.* Translated by Barbara Bray. New York: Quadrangle-The NY Times Book Co., 1974.

Ballard, Bettina. *In My Fashion.* New York: David McKay Co., Inc., 1960.

Balmain, Pierre. *My Years and Seasons* (autobiography). Translated by E. Lanchbery and G. Young. London: Cassell & Co. Ltd., 1964. New York: Doubleday & Company, Inc., 1965.

Beaton, Cecil. *The Glass of Fashion.* New York: Doubleday & Company, Inc., 1954.

————. *Fair Lady.* New York: Holt, Rinehart & Winston, 1964.

————. *The Years Between Diaries 1939–1944.* New York: Holt, Rinehart & Winston, 1965.

————. *Cecil Beaton: Memoirs of the 40s.* New York: McGraw-Hill Book Co., 1977.

————. *The Book of Beauty.* London: Duckworth, 1930.

————. *Cecil Beaton's New York.* London: Batsford, 1938.

————. *Persona Grata* (with Kenneth Tynan). London: Wingate, 1953.

————. *The Glass of Fashion.* London: Weidenfeld & Nicolson, 1954.

————. *Cecil Beaton's Diaries—1922–1929, The Wandering Years* (1961); *1939–1944, The Years Between* (1965); *1944–1948, The Happy Years* (1972); *1948–1955, The Strenuous Years* (1973). London: Weidenfeld & Nicolson.

————. *The Gainsborough Girls,* a play. 1951.

Bender, Marylin. *Beautiful People.* New York: Coward, McCann & Geoghegan, Inc., 1967.

Blum, Stella. *Designs by Erté. Fashion Drawings & Illustrations from Harper's Bazaar.* New York: 1976.

Boucher, François with Yvonne Deslandres. *20,000 Years of Fashion: The History of Costume and Personal Adornment,* Expanded Edition. New York: Harry N. Abrams, 1987.

Brady, James. *Super Chic.* Boston: Little, Brown & Co., 1974.

Brogden, J. *Fashion Design.* London: Studio Vista, 1971.

Byers, Margaretta, *Designing Women.* New York: Simon & Schuster, 1938.

Calasibetta, Charlotte Mankey, *Fairchild's Dictionary of Fashion,* 2nd edition. New York: Fairchild Publications, 1988.

Carter, Ernestine. *Magic Names of Fashion.* New Jersey: Prentice-Hall, Inc., 1980.

Charles-Roux, Edmonde. *Chanel: her life, her world, and the woman behind the legend she herself created.* France: Editions Grosset & Faquelle, 1974. Distributed by Random House, New York.

Chase, Edna Woolman and Ilka Chase. *Always in Vogue.* New York: Doubleday & Company, Inc., 1954.

Chierichetti, David. *Hollywood Costume Design.* New York: Crown Publishers, Inc., 1976.

Coleman, Elizabeth Ann. *The Genius of Charles James.* Published for the exhibition at the Brooklyn Museum. New York: Holt, Rinehart and Winston, 1982.

Creed, Charles. *Made to Measure.* London: Jarrolds, 1961.

Daché, Lilly. *Talking through My Hats.* Edited by Dorothy Roe Lewis. New York: Coward-McCann, Inc., 1946.

————. *Lilly Dache's Glamor Book.* 1957.

Davenport, Millia. *The Book of Costume.* New York: Crown Publishers, Inc., 1948.

Daves, Jessica. *Ready-Made Miracle.* New York: G.P. Putnam's Sons, 1967.

Daves, Jessica, Alexander Liberman, Bryan Holmes and Katherine Tweed. *The World in Vogue.* Compiled by The Viking Press and *Vogue* Magazine, 1963.

de Marly, Diana. *Worth, Father of Haute Couture.* London, 1980.

De Osma, Guillermo. *Mariano Fortuny: His Life and Work.* New York: Rizzoli International Publications, Inc., 1980.

Deslandres, Yves. *Poiret.* New York: Rizzoli International Publications, Inc., 1987.

Diamonstein, Barbaralee. *Fashion: The Inside Story.* New York: Rizzoli International Publications, Inc., 1985.

Dior, Christian. *Talking about Fashion.* Translated by Eugenia Sheppard. New York: G.P. Putnam's Sons, 1954.

————. *Christian Dior and I.* Translated by Antonia Fraser. New York: E.P. Dutton & Company, Inc., 1957.

————. *Dior by Dior.* Translated by Antonia Fraser. London: Weidenfeld & Nicolson, 1957. Harmondsworth, England: Penguin Books, 1968.

Dixon, H. Vernon. *The Rag Pickers.* New York: David McKay Co., Inc., 1966.

Emanuel, Elizabeth and David. *Style for All Seasons.* 1983.

Erté. *Erté Fashions.* New York: St. Martin's Press, 1972.

_____. *Erté—Things I Remember* (autobiography). London: Peter Owen Limited, 1975.

Etherington-Smith, Meredith. *Patou.* New York: St. Martin's/Marek, 1983.

Ewing, Elizabeth. *History of 20th Century Fashion.* New York: Charles Scribner's Sons, 1974.

Fairchild, John. *The Fashionable Savages.* New York: Doubleday & Company, Inc., 1965.

Ferragamo, Salvatore. *Shoemaker of Dreams* (autobiography). England: George G. Harrap & Co. Ltd., 1972.

Fogarty, Anne. *Wife-Dressing.* New York: Julian Messner Inc., 1959.

Fraser, Kennedy. *The Fashionable Mind.* Boston, Mass: David R. Godine, 1985.

Galante, Pierre. *Mademoiselle Chanel.* Chicago, 1973.

Garland, Madge. *Fashion.* London: Penguin Books, 1962.

_____. *The Changing Form of Fashion:* London: J.M. Dent & Sons, 1970.

Giroud, François. *Dior.* New York: Rizzoli International Publications, 1987.

Glynn, Prudence. *In Fashion: Dress in the Twentieth Century.* New York: Oxford University Press, 1978.

Gold, Annalee, *75 Years of Fashion.* New York: Fairchild Publications, 1975.

_____. *One World of Fashion,* 4th edition. New York: Fairchild Publications, 1986.

Gorsline, Douglas Warner. *What People Wore: A Visual History of Dress from Ancient Times to 20th Century America.* New York: Viking Press, 1952.

Haedrich, Marcel. *Coco Chanel, Her Life, Her Secrets.* Boston: Little, Brown & Co., 1971.

Hartnell, Norman. *Silver and Gold* (autobiography). London: Evans Brothers, 1955.

_____. *Royal Courts of Fashion.* London: Cassell & Co. Ltd., 1971.

Hawes, Elizabeth. *Fashion Is Spinach.* New York: Random House, 1938.

Horst. *Salute to the Thirties.* New York: Viking Press, 1971.

Howell, Georgina. *In Vogue: Six Decades of Fashion.* London: Allen Lane, 1975.

Karan, Donna. *An American Woman Observed.* 1987.

Kawakubo, Rei. *Comme des Garçons.* Japan: Chikuma Shobo, 1987.

Keenan, Brigid. *Dior in Vogue.* New York: Harmony Books, 1981.

Kybalova, Ludmila, Olga Herbenova and Milena Lamorova. *The Pictorial Encyclopedia of Fashion,* 2nd ed. Translated by Claudia Rosoux. England: Hamlyn Publishers, 1968. New York: Crown Publishers, Inc., 1969.

Lagerfeld, Karl. *Lagerfeld's Sketchbook: Karl Lagerfeld's Illustrated Fashion Journal of Anna Piaggi.* London: Weidenfeld & Nicolson, 1986.

Lambert, Eleanor. *World of Fashion: People, Places and Resources.* New York: R.R. Bowker Company, 1976.

Langlade, Emile. *Rose Bertin: The Creator of Fashion at the Court of Marie-Antoinette.* Adapted from the French by Dr. Angelo S. Rappoport. New York: Charles Scribner's Sons, 1913.

Latour, Anny. *Kings of Fashion.* Translated by Mervyn Saville. London: Weidenfeld & Nicolson, 1958.

_____. *Paris Fashion.* London: Michael Joseph, 1972.

Laver, James. *Taste and Fashion.* London: George G. Harrap & Co. Ltd., 1937.

_____. *A Concise History of Costume.* London: Thames and Hudson, 1969.

Lavine, W. Robert. *In a Glamorous Fashion.* New York: Charles Scribner's Sons, 1980.

Leese, Elizabeth. *Costume Design in the Movies.* New York: Frederick Ungar Publishing Co., 1977.

Levin, Phyllis Lee. *The Wheels of Fashion.* New York: Doubleday & Company, Inc., 1965.

Leymarie, Jean. *Chanel.* New York: Rizzoli International Publications, 1987.

Lynam, Ruth, editor. *Couture.* New York: Doubleday & Company, Inc., 1972.

Madsen, Axel. *Living for Design: Yves Saint Laurent Story.* New York, 1979.

Marcus, Stanley. *Minding the Store.* Boston: Little, Brown & Co., 1974.

McCardell, Claire. *What Shall I Wear?.* New York: Simon & Schuster, 1956.

McDowell, Colin. *McDowell's Directory of Twentieth Century Fashion.* New Jersey: Prentice-Hall, Inc., 1985.

Milbank, Caroline Rennolds. *Couture, The Great Designers.* New York: Stewart, Tabori & Chang, Inc., 1985.

Milinaire, Caterine and Carol Troy. *Cheap Chic.* New York: Harmony Books, 1975.

Miyake, Issey. *Issey Miyake East Meets West.* Tokyo: Shogaku Kan Publishing Co. Ltd., 1978.

_____. *Issey Miyake Bodyworks.* Tokyo: Shogaku Kan Publishing Co. Ltd., 1983.

Morris, Bernadine. *The Fashion Makers: An Inside Look at America's Leading Designers.* New York: Random House, 1978.

O'Hara, Georgina. *The Encyclopaedia of Fashion.* New York: Harry N. Abrams, Inc., 1986.

Payne, Blanche. *History of Costume: From the Ancient Egyptians to the Twentieth Century.* New York: Harper & Row, 1965.

Perkins, Alice K. *Paris Couturiers & Milliners.* New York: Fairchild Publications, 1949.

Picken, Mary Brooks. *The Fashion Dictionary.* New York: Funk & Wagnalls, 1957.

Picken, Mary Brooks and Dora Loues Miller. *Dressmakers of France: The Who, How and Why of French Couture.* New York: Harper & Brothers Publishers, 1956.

Poiret, Paul. *En Habillant l'Epoque.* Paris: Grasset, 1930.

_____. *King of Fashion* (autobiography). Translated by Stephen Haden Guest. Philadelphia: J.B. Lippincott Company, 1931.

_____. *Revenez-Y.* Paris: Gallemard, 1932.

_____. *Art et Finance.* Paris: Lutetia, 1934.

Quant, Mary. *Quant by Quant.* London: Cassell & Co. Ltd., 1966.

_____. *Colour by Quant.*

Rhodes, Zandra and Anne Knight. *The Art of Zandra Rhodes.* Boston, Mass.: Houghton Mifflin Company, 1985.

Riley, Robert, Dale McConathy, Sally Kirkland, Bernadine Morris, and Eleni Sakes Epstein. *American Fashion: The Life and Lines of Adrian, Mainbocher, McCardell, Norell & Trigère.* Edited by Sarah Tomerlin Lee. New York: Quadrangle/The NY Times Book Co., 1975.

Rochas, Marcel. *Twenty-Five Years of Parisian Elegance, 1925–1950.* Paris: Pierre Tisne, 1951.

Ross, Josephine. *Beaton in Vogue.* New York: Clarkson N. Potter Inc., 1986.

Rykiel, Sonia. *And I Would Like Her Naked,* 1979.

Saint Laurent, Yves. *Yves Saint Laurent.* New York: Metropolitan Museum of Art, 1983.

Salomon, Rosalie Kolodny. *Fashion Design for Moderns.* New York: Fairchild Publications, 1976.

Saunders, Edith. *The Age of Worth: Couturier to the Empress Eugénie.* Indiana: Indiana University Press, 1955.

Schiaparelli, Elsa. *Shocking Life.* New York: E.P. Dutton & Co., Inc., 1954.

_____. *Elsa Schiaparelli: Empress of Paris Fashion.* New York: Rizzoli International Publications, Inc., 1986.

Snow, Carmel and Mary Louise Aswell. *The World of Carmel Snow.* New York: McGraw-Hill Book Co., 1962.

Spencer, Charles. *Erté.* New York: Clarkson N. Potter, Inc., 1970.

Tice, Bill (with Sheila Weller). *Enticements: How to Look Fabulous in Lingerie.* New York: The MacMillan Company, 1985.

Tolstoy, Mary Koutouzov. *Charlemagne to Dior: The Story of French Fashion.* New York: Michael Slains, 1967.

Vecchio, Walter and Robert Riley. *The Fashion Makers: A Photographic Record.* New York: Crown Publishers, Inc., 1968.

Von Fürstenberg, Diane. *Book of Beauty.* New York: Simon & Schuster, Inc., 1976.

"W": The Designing Life. Staff of W, edited by Lois Perschetz. New York: Clarkson N. Potter, Inc., 1987.

Weitz, John. *Man in Charge.* New York: The Macmillan Company, 1974.

_____. *Sports Clothes for Your Sports Car.* New York: Arco Publishing Co., Inc.; 1958.

White, Palmer. *Poiret.* New York: Clarkson N. Potter, Inc., 1973.

Williams, Beryl Epstein. *Fashion Is Our Business.* Philadelphia: J.B. Lippincott Co., 1945.

_____. *Young Faces in Fashion.* Philadelphia: J.B. Lippincott Co., 1957.

Wilcox, R. Turner. *The Mode in Costume.* New York: Charles Scribner's Sons, 1958.

The World of Balenciaga. New York: Metropolitan Museum of New York, 1973.

Worth, Jean Philippe. *A Century of Fashion.* Translated by Ruth Scott Miller. Boston: Little, Brown & Co., 1928.

Yarwood, Doreen. *The Encyclopaedia of World Costume.* London: Anchor Press, 1978.

INDEX